Praise for the novels of Johanna Edwards

How to Be Cool

"A hilarious tale . . . [Edwards] romps through the faults and foibles of the human condition with prose that is at once snappy, saucy, and sophisticated." —*The Tennessean*

"This should come with a 'beach read' alert. I mean that as a compliment." —*The Tampa Tribune*

"Smart and funny." —*Romantic Times*

Your Big Break

"More than just hilarious—it will ring true with anyone who's been on either side of a breakup." —*Detroit Free Press*

"Ably plotted and brimming with escapist fun."
—*Publishers Weekly*

The Next Big Thing

"A fresh, funny treat."
—*New York Times* bestselling author Jennifer Weiner

"Engaging . . . Edwards is good where it counts."
—*The Boston Globe*

"In this saucy sendup, a feisty young Memphis publicist . . . drops the pounds, but learns that fame has a cost . . . and that being skinny isn't always pretty." —*US Weekly*

continued . . .

More praise for the novels of Johanna Edwards

"A lighthearted, well-plotted debut with a surprise romantic ending and over-the-top charm." —*USA Today*

"In just her second novel, Johanna Edwards makes the most of this can't-miss [idea]. Four stars." —*Detroit Free Press*

"Required reading." —*New York Post*

"Deliciously dishy." —Jennifer Coburn, author of *Tales from the Crib*

"Fresh and funny." —*Booklist*

"Tell-all honesty, pitch-perfect sass, and a generous and tender heart . . . highly addictive." —Jennifer Paddock, author of *Point Clear*

"Fabulous fun." —Jennifer O'Connell, author of *Insider Dating*

Titles by Johanna Edwards

THE NEXT BIG THING
YOUR BIG BREAK
HOW TO BE COOL

How to Be Cool

Johanna Edwards

BERKLEY BOOKS, NEW YORK

THE BERKLEY PUBLISHING GROUP
Published by the Penguin Group
Penguin Group (USA) Inc.
375 Hudson Street, New York, New York 10014, USA
Penguin Group (Canada), 90 Eglinton Avenue East, Suite 700, Toronto, Ontario M4P 2Y3, Canada
(a division of Pearson Penguin Canada Inc.)
Penguin Books Ltd., 80 Strand, London WC2R 0RL, England
Penguin Group Ireland, 25 St. Stephen's Green, Dublin 2, Ireland (a division of Penguin Books Ltd.)
Penguin Group (Australia), 250 Camberwell Road, Camberwell, Victoria 3124, Australia
(a division of Pearson Australia Group Pty. Ltd.)
Penguin Books India Pvt. Ltd., 11 Community Centre, Panchsheel Park, New Delhi—110 017, India
Penguin Group (NZ), 67 Apollo Drive, Rosedale, North Shore 0632, New Zealand
(a division of Pearson New Zealand Ltd.)
Penguin Books (South Africa) (Pty.) Ltd., 24 Sturdee Avenue, Rosebank, Johannesburg 2196,
South Africa

Penguin Books Ltd., Registered Offices: 80 Strand, London WC2R 0RL, England

Cover design by Judith Lagerman.
Cover photograph by Wendi Schneider.

PRINTING HISTORY
Berkley hardcover edition / June 2007
Berkley trade paperback edition / June 2008

Berkley trade paperback ISBN: 978-0-425-22142-6

The Library of Congress has cataloged the Berkley hardcover edition of this book as follows:

Edwards, Johanna.
How to be cool / Johanna Edwards. — 1st ed.
p. cm.
ISBN 978-0-425-21384-1 (hardcover)
1. Overweight women—Fiction. 2. Weight loss—Fiction. 3. Body image—Fiction. 4. Rejection (Psychology)—Fiction. 5. Psychological fiction. I. Title.

PS3605.D886H69 2007
813'.6—dc22 2007000398

PRINTED IN THE UNITED STATES OF AMERICA

10 9 8 7 6 5 4 3 2 1

For my mom,
Paula Edwards

Acknowledgments

Thank you to Jenny Bent, agent extraordinaire. Jenny took a chance on me four years ago, when I was just a struggling writer from Memphis. Her enthusiasm and support (and occasional tough love) have meant the world to me. Simply put, none of this would be possible without her.

Thanks a million times over to my editor, Kara Cesare. Kara is the kind of editor every writer dreams about working with. She is *always* there when I need her, be it evenings, weekends, or holidays. Kara's friendship, humor, grace, patience, and guidance have helped me so much during the past year. I feel extremely lucky to have her on my team.

Thank you to Leslie Gelbman, my wonderful publisher. Leslie has given my books a very happy home at Berkley, and I am so grateful for all the hard work she has done on my behalf.

Thanks to everyone at Berkley, especially Michele Langley and Lindsay Nouis. Thanks also to Jenny's assistant, Victoria Horn.

Thank you to my father, Les Edwards, and my younger sister, Selena. Not to sound cheesy, but you guys are the best.

I am lucky to have a great support system of friends and family. I could *not* have done this without them! Thanks so much to Candy Justice, Rachel Worthington, James Abbott,

Chris Carwile, Hugo Reynolds, Susanne Enos, Teresa Johnson, Anastasia Nix, Velda Nix, Paul Turner, Alan Turner, Sallie Turner, Eva Edwards, Leslie Edwards, Helen Turner, Leo Edwards, Bert Edwards, Tommy Edwards, Laura Turner, Waymon Turner, Valerie Gildart, Emily Trenholm, Erin Hiller, Virginia Feltus, Dr. James Patterson, Jay Eubanks, Christy Paganoni, Dr. Cynthia Hopson, Kate Simone, Matt Presson, Stephen Usery, Cheryl Hudson, Paul Simone, Runi Afsharpour Perkins, Christie Bangloy, Alan Klein, Debra Hall, Alicia Funkhouser, Melissa Stroud, Demonica Santangilo, Nikki Hatchel, Maralou Billig, Lynn Kloker, Debby Mirda, Donna Pineau, Paula Rogers, and Tiffany Werne. And a thank-you to William Clanton, a wonderful friend and tireless supporter of my work, who died shortly before this book was published.

Along the way, I've received encouragement and support from so many wonderful writers. I am thankful to Karin Gillespie and Jennifer Paddock, both of whom inspire me. And a huge, huge thank-you to the irreplaceable Jennifer Weiner. I have been a fan of her work since the moment I picked up *Good in Bed* six years ago. I am in awe of not only her incredible talent, but also her kindess and generosity. Jennifer took the time to read my first novel, *The Next Big Thing*, when I was a complete unknown. Her endorsement of my writing has opened so many doors for me, and was one of the reasons why my first novel was a success. I will always be grateful to her.

And finally, thank you to all of my readers and to everyone who has taken the time to stop by my website, come to my book signings, or send me an e-mail. It is so humbling to hear from all of you, and I save and cherish every letter I receive. You guys are the reason I am able to live out my dream of being a full-time writer. I owe everything to you.

How to Be Cool

Prologue

My name is Kylie Chase, and I used to be fat.

I also used to be a nerd, but we'll get to that in a minute.

Now, when I say I was fat, I don't mean I needed to lose five pounds so I could look hot in a bikini. It was actually more like *seventy*-five pounds. And I needed to lose it so I could see my feet again, so my thighs wouldn't squish together when I walked, so I could buy my clothes from the "skinny stores" instead of the plus-size rack—you know, all those things you take for granted.

Because I'm here to tell you: being fat sucks.

I'm not trying to be mean or make anyone feel bad about themselves.

I have nothing against fat girls (that would be awfully hypocritical if I did). I just didn't want to *be* one. I had been there, done that, for roughly ten years. I knew what being fat was like inside and out, backward and forward. I wanted to lose weight so I could find out how the other half lived.

Plus, I thought life would be *immeasurably* better if I looked a little bit less like me, and a lot more like Charlize Theron.

Don't get me wrong. I believe that you can be beautiful at any size. My best friend, Ruby Gallagher, is proof of that.

Ruby is a plus-size model and she's one of the most gorgeous girls I've ever met. The thing about Ruby is, she makes her size work for her. She knows how to stand, how to walk, how to hold her body so her curves look sexy and appealing, instead of lumpy and misplaced, the way mine always did. At the risk of sounding cheesy, I'd say Ruby loves herself and it shows.

When I was fat I was just one big ball of self-hate.

Which is why, at age twenty-two, I decided to take the plunge, to stop talking about losing weight and finally *do it.*

I had some damn good motivation.

I wanted to slim down in my early twenties, while I was still young enough for it to matter. My "good years" were slipping away at an alarming pace. I was terrified I'd wake up tomorrow and be fifty, with my dream of being young and hot gone forever. I wanted to get thin before I was too old to wear cute, skimpy clothes. Too old to go skinny-dipping. Too old to pick up guys in bars (bars that I would also be dancing on top of, *Coyote Ugly*–style, because that's the kind of stuff you do when you're skinny, right?).

But most of all, I wanted to find out what life was like for the girls with the perfect bodies. Of course, now that I'm thin I don't have a perfect body. That's the thing they don't tell you about losing weight—the stretch marks, the loose skin, the cellulite patches that won't go away no matter how many times you slather them with $200 skin-smoothing lotion.

But I'm getting ahead of myself. First, let me tell you how I lost the weight. Then we can discuss what happened after.

As you might have guessed, shedding seventy-five pounds doesn't happen overnight. It's not the kind of thing that can be accomplished by a quick-fix diet. In my former life—you know, before I got thin—I used to laugh at all the weight-loss headlines splashed across the covers of glossy magazines. I needed those articles more than anybody, yet none of them applied to me:

Have rock-hard abs in time for summer!
The Your-Butt-Will-Knock-'Em-Dead Diet!
The miracle plan that will slim you down in 10 days or less!
Six weeks to thinner thighs!

Every month I browsed through the magazine racks, waiting to see a cover story that was actually geared toward people like me, people with *real* weight problems:

Go from size 20 to size 2!
The Your-Butt-Will-Fit-in-an-Airplane-Seat Diet!
The miracle plan for people who need to lose more than 10 pounds!
Six weeks till you can see your feet again!

During the ten years I was fat, not a day went by that I didn't fantasize about losing weight (or, more specifically, I fantasized about the way my life would be once the scale registered a number below one hundred fifty).

Yet, despite my preoccupation with slimming down, year after year I stayed fat.

When you're overweight, it often feels like the world is made up of two parallel universes: the world of the skinny and the world of the fat. Everyone in the Fat World has the same goal—to break free and unleash the thin version of themselves that's waiting underneath.

But no matter how hard I tried, I couldn't reach the Promised Land. I knew it was out there waiting for me. If only I could find my way. . . .

T. S. Eliot may have measured out his days with coffee spoons, but for a long time my days were measured out with forks and plates and bowls. And with McDonald's wrappers and pizza boxes and "Grab Bag" packets of Lays potato chips.

It was almost like falling on and off the wagon. I was either on a diet or I wasn't. I was eating nothing, or I was eating everything in sight. If it was a "good day," then I was counting all of it—the calories in a piece of gum, the carbs in a glass of orange juice, the handful of sunflower seeds I'd grabbed from the break room at work. If it was a "bad day," then I was counting nothing. On bad days, there was no balance, no order, no rules. I could have a slice of lemon meringue pie for breakfast, or a plate of garlic bread for dinner, or two desserts, or five cappuccinos. It didn't matter.

There was no middle ground for me. I was either on or I was off. And I was off, it seemed, most of the time.

So how did I finally break the cycle and reinvent myself as a thin girl?

The chain of events that led to my weight loss was disappointingly simple. Disappointing, because I had wasted an awful lot of time trying to figure out what was actually staring me right in the face. It's difficult to explain, but I'll try.

There was a (somewhat evil) guy involved—but you probably already guessed there would be. Although, despite what you might suspect, he wasn't the biggest part. (Noel Klinowski—remember his name. We're coming back to him later.)

The biggest part was me (and, no, that's not a pun). The biggest part took place inside my brain.

It was a few days before graduation and I was sitting in my dorm room at UCLA, alone and depressed and searching for a job that I feared would never materialize. I had stepped on the scale that morning, for the first time in more than a year. I'd been avoiding it because I knew the number was going to be bad. But I couldn't have predicted *how* bad. Let's just say it started with a two and ended with a five. I'll leave the middle digit up to your imagination.

So there I was, scrolling through Monster.com, bemoaning the fact that I was single and broke and fat. And that in a matter of days I would be just another unemployed college graduate, all degreed up with no place to go.

Then it happened.

I had what I guess you would call an epiphany.

This was it.

This was the life I had been dealt. I wasn't going to wake up tomorrow and suddenly find my world reversed. I wasn't going to miraculously grow a superfast metabolism or teleport into Jessica Alba's body. Carrot sticks weren't going to start tasting good; chocolate wasn't going to start tasting bad. And I wasn't going to get thin. It just wasn't going to happen for me. This was how I was going to spend *my entire life*: always wishing I could lose weight, but never actually losing it.

And if I didn't wake up right this instant, then one day my life would be over and I'd realize that I had spent all of it, every blasted year, as a fat girl. If I was ever going to do something about it, I had to do it now. It couldn't be next summer, or next Monday, or next January first.

It had to be today.

Because I am a person of extremes, it only made sense that my diet had to be extreme, too.

So I made a deal with myself. I would work out six days a week, and I would eat "the things I was supposed to" and avoid the things I knew had made me fat.

I had the entire rest of my life to indulge in what I wanted, but for now I would abstain. Certain foods—macaroni and cheese, mashed potatoes, brownies—I didn't trust myself around. So they were out. Period. Not so much as a morsel of these forbidden treats would pass my lips until I reached old age.

It was as simple as that. I would suffer for the next decade or two, avoiding all the foods I loved. And then I could eat how I wanted again. Once it all clicked, losing weight was amazingly simple—and my life was simply amazing.

Now here I am, Not Thirty years old (that's code for twenty-nine), with a terrific career and a size eight (size ten on a bad day) physique.

I have everything I've ever wanted—bodywise, at least—and no one can take that away from me. I've succeeded in leaving my fat life far, far behind.

At least I *think* I have. . . .

1

Cool Rule #1:

You are exactly who you think you are.

"I expected her to be prettier."

"The alumni newsletter said she'd lost a few pounds. And I guess her body's *slightly* improved, but she's still got a face like a—"

"Mack truck. Wide load, of course!"

They're talking about me.

Hayley Hill and Joanie Brixton. I'd know their voices anywhere, even if I hadn't spied them browsing through the designer collections five minutes ago. They sound exactly the same as they did a decade ago. Nasal, high-pitched, and obnoxious.

"Did you see that picture of her in *Us Weekly*? The one where she's standing next to Jennifer Aniston at some premiere or another?"

"Yeah, you told me about it," Hayley snorts. "I bet she paid off the editor to get that."

"Paid off? Try *sucked* off."

They dissolve into laughter while I stand there, red-faced and shaking. *What the hell are they doing here?* Of all the department stores in all the world, they choose to come to *this* Saks Fifth Avenue on *this* day?

I suck in my stomach, even though I'm standing out of view.

I can't believe they're still friends. Sure, Hayley and Joanie were inseparable all four years of high school. But those relationships are supposed to be fickle, passing. God knows I didn't keep in close touch with any of my high school pals. But it's like Joanie and Hayley haven't missed a beat. They might as well be back in the cafeteria, sipping Diet Cokes and examining their French manicures while they ruffle through the latest issue of *Vogue.*

I try to focus, to get into the zone. *Deep breath in, hold it . . . two . . . three . . . four . . . exhale.* This is what I tell my clients to do. Not the breathing part. I mean, I'm not a yogi. But I try to help them slow their inner dialogue down, rearrange their self-talk so they feel stronger, better, less intimidated.

This doesn't bother me. I might have been a loser once, but I'm not now. . . . I've got nearly seventeen hundred numbers stored in my PDA. I've been in People *magazine, the* New York Times. *I've taken business trips to Europe (okay, trip, singular). I've ridden in dozens—no, hundreds!—of limousines. I've eaten at the Ivy. I never sit home on Friday or Saturday nights. I've dated just the right number of guys—not too few, not too many. I've slept with the right number, too. I'm not a slut, not a prude. Everything is balanced, everything is right. My life is full, rich, and exciting.*

"Hey, remember in the ninth grade when we put that poster of *Moby-Dick* on Kylie's locker?"

Bitches.

I peek through the slats of the dressing room door, spying on them as they shop. I only caught a fleeting glimpse earlier. As soon as I saw Joanie and Hayley I took off. Now, cloaked by the safety of the dressing room, I strain to get a better look. Once I do, I regret it.

Damn.

The twelve years since high school have been incredibly kind to them. It's ridiculous. Same gorgeous hair and skin. Same flawless couldn't-gain-weight-if-they-tried figures. Where is their postpregnancy fat, their crow's-feet, their premature wrinkles? These two girls made my teenage years a living hell and, petty though it may be, I'd love to see them knocked down a peg or two.

Karma truly is a bitch—because it never seems to work the way you want it to.

And some people, like Joanie and Hayley, appear to be Karma-proof. (That is, if Karma even exists. The fact that someone like Paris Hilton is so rich, successful, and beautiful kind of makes you wonder.)

"Of course I remember. Kylie Chase was such a fucking whale."

"*Was?* Try *is.* She's more like a baby whale now, I guess. But she's still super fat. . . ."

"My favorite prank was when we Photoshopped her face on Notorious B.I.G.'s body and hung the picture up in the band room."

I'm having dinner tonight with a journalist who's writing a profile about me, yes, that's right, ME! We're going to China Grill, where I will order a $50 steak and a $30 starter and a $14 side dish (but no lobster mashed potatoes—carb city!). And we'll have pricey cocktails with our meal and I won't pay a dime; all of this will be on the magazine's expense account, and when was the last time Joanie or Hayley could say that?

"Do you think I should get the Dolce & Gabbana print?"

Hayley asks. "It's seventeen hundred, which I guess is a bit much just for dinner."

"Like Rick would even care! You charged eighteen hundred dollars in shoes last month and he barely noticed."

"True. But he just spent a fortune on our trip to Kitzbühel, remember." She huffs. "Why that idiot won't go skiing in Aspen like a normal person is beyond me."

"Too true. And if you're going to fly halfway around the world, Rick could at least have the decency to pick St. Moritz," Joanie chimes in. "Who skis in Austria when they could just as easily go to Switzerland? It would be like James taking me to Belgium instead of France. If I'm getting on a plane for eight hours, I'd better land somewhere fucking *spectacular*—otherwise it's not worth the jet lag."

So this is what their lives are now. They have rich husbands (boyfriends?) who bankroll lavish shopping sprees and vacations in Europe.

I take another deep breath. Why am I freaking out over this? I've always thought being skinny would make me invincible.

Bulletproof.

As if once I crossed the barrier from fat to thin, no one would be able to touch me. I'd be perfectly gorgeous, perfectly happy, and well, just plain perfect. A thin body is the ultimate suit of armor; it protects you from depression and heartache and all the assorted ills of the world. At least, that's what they always tell you when you're fat.

But as I cower in the dressing room, struggling to get the size eight Roberto Cavalli dress over my hips (not gonna happen) while listening to Joanie and Hayley, I feel weak, insecure, and pathetic. In other words, I feel sixteen again. (And twelve. And twenty. And pretty much every age up until my twenty-fourth birthday—you know, the year I officially became a thin person.)

"Did you see what Kylie was wearing?" Hayley squeals. "She looks like a garbage collector!"

Hayley and Joanie aren't supposed to see me now. I'm supposed to run into them some fateful night when I'm looking exceptionally good—decked out in an insanely sexy designer gown with my hair perfectly coiffed and my nails manicured and my teeth freshly bleached. Instead, here I am in a pair of ratty Gap jeans and an ill-fitting lime-green sweater that makes me look pale as a ghost. My hair is in desperate need of a cut, and my bangs are hanging haphazardly past my eyes. Good God, I'd broken one of my own rules: *Never go out in public looking like a wreck. Do, and you're guaranteed to run into at least five people you know.* Oh, sure, messy hair and slouchy clothes can be hot. But it has to look like you've done it on purpose. There's a way to pull off casual chic, and it usually involves a Juicy Couture tracksuit and a carefully tousled ponytail.

"Her outfit today is better than that urine-colored dress she had on in *Us Weekly*," Joanie says.

Mustard. The color was mustard.

"And all that makeup!" Joanie continues. "She looked like a drag queen!"

"I can't believe Kylie can afford to shop here," Hayley mutters.

"She probably shoplifts. I wouldn't put it past her."

I press my body against the back wall of the changing room and struggle to ignore them because, really, what else can I do? I'm not going out there to confront them looking like this.

Even when I was fat things were still pretty exciting. My

father's a gourmet chef, my mother's a former model. Okay, so her modeling work was largely confined to Playboy. *And, uh, "artistic nudes." But that's still way more glamorous than anything you two can come up with.*

"What does she do for a living, anyway? I know the alumni newsletter said, but I seriously didn't pay attention."

"She gives *cool lessons.* Whatever the hell that is."

"Please! As if Kylie Chase knows even one iota about what's cool," Joanie snickers.

"She used to be an image consultant, I think. She helped, like, celebrity clients make themselves over after scandals. But she got fired, so she had no choice but to open some weird little business."

Fired! I want to scream that I wasn't fired, that I'm still at the same company I've been with for almost five years. I've just changed gears—I've stopped working with "celeb clients" ("celeb" is being kind of generous—I helped one soap opera actress and assisted on a case with a TV star) and started helping average joes improve their social lives and images. But, of course, I stay quiet.

I stare at myself in the dressing room mirror, and I relax a little. Despite Hayley and Joanie's rantings, I don't actually look *that* bad. Sure, my clothes and hair are a bit disheveled, but that doesn't change the fact that I'm seventy-five pounds lighter than I was the last time they saw me. That's got to count for something. I study my face, which is fuller than it should be. Losing weight had only a minimal effect on my cheeks and jawline. If you catch me from the neck up, I still look a little chubby.

I occupy myself by sorting through the gowns in my dressing room, which makes me feel better. There are few things that Michael Kors, Marc Jacobs, or Zac Posen can't cure. Still, I'm relieved when I hear Joanie's and Hayley's voices fade away as they head back out into the store.

But my relief doesn't last long. Something far worse is happening. The dresses—the piles and piles of gorgeous, showstopping designer dresses that I've carefully selected to try on—aren't fitting. Ever the careful shopper (you never know how things are cut), I asked the salesgirl to bring me outfits in two different sizes. After the Roberto Cavalli no-go, I pick up a silk velvet-trimmed James Coviello dress in size ten and attempt to pull it down over my hips. No dice.

What the hell is happening? I am supposed to be an eight. Ten on a bad day.

But at the moment I seem destined for twelves.

I hear a knock on the dressing room door. "Would you like me to fetch anything for you?" the salesgirl asks in a clipped British accent. "Another size or style, perhaps?"

I crack open the door. "As a matter of fact, this Roberto Cavalli is absolutely stunning, but I don't know if," I lower my voice to a whisper, "I don't know if a size eight is quite right for me. Would you mind bringing it in a, uh, a size twelve?"

She wrinkles her nose. "That particular gown doesn't come larger than an eight, I'm afraid."

I feel my face grow hot. "Oh, okay. Thanks."

"I believe Michael Kors has a few selections available in larger sizes," the salesgirl continues. "And I can also recommend Salon Z."

I gulp. "Salon Z," I repeat, horrified.

"Yes, that's our department for sizes fourteen to twenty-four," she explains, even though it's unnecessary. I know all about the plus-size section of Saks. I've been there, done that, and vowed to never, ever go back. If I'm going to spend this much money on a dress, it had damn well better be the size I want.

Still, the salesgirl's suggestion stuns me.

Do I really look that big? Have I really gained so much weight that I need to be shopping alongside the twenty-fours? Full disclosure: I've recently put on a few pounds. This is February, after all. It's like I tell my clients. This is the recovery period. The holidays are always rough, and with all the catered parties, fireside cocktails, and family gatherings, I usually suffer some regain. (Even though I stick to a strict low-carb, no-dessert menu, the alcohol alone usually gets me. Couple that with a disrupted workout schedule, and you'll see why I tend to gain at least ten pounds every November–December.) It's rarely anything major, but this year I've had more trouble getting back on track than usual. For some reason, the weight hasn't chipped back off the way it used to—the perils of being Not Thirty, I guess. My metabolism's getting slower as I age. Even so, I'm not Salon Z big. Am I?

I am so above this. I do not care what anybody thinks.

"Salon Z is a wonderful . . ."

Okay, yes I do. I really, really do.

I glance down at my watch. "Oh my gosh, four o'clock!" I announce with faux surprise. "I didn't realize it had gotten so late." It's the oldest, lamest excuse in the book, but I can't help it. I have to get out of there.

"If you'd like—"

"Thanks so much for your help," I say, cutting her off. "But I just realized I'm late for a mani/pedi."

And then, brushing past her, I hurry out of Saks as fast as my tennis-shoed feet can carry me.

* * *

As soon as I'm outside, I call my best friend, Ruby, and beg her to meet me for drinks. She's busy packing—she's leaving for a job assignment in Southeast Asia in a few days—but she says she's got time for a quick glass of wine at one of our favorite bars.

"*A* glass," she laughs. "One. Otherwise I'll be completely dehydrated by the time I get to Thailand."

"How long is the flight?"

"I'm not sure. Twenty-three hours, I think. I'm stopping over in Japan, but I don't know how long the layover is." She sighs. "But you know how much I hate flying. Twenty-three hours will feel like ten years."

"It won't be so bad," I tell her, shivering in the frigid Chicago air. "At least you're going somewhere warm."

"That's true." She pauses. "You're not okay, are you? Something happened today, right?"

Ruby has an uncanny knack for this. She's ridiculously perceptive, almost to the point of being scary. And when she suspects something, she usually cuts right to the chase. It's one of the things I've always loved about her.

"Kind of." I really wish Hayley and Joanie hadn't affected me so much. I'm not that bothered by what they said—I'm bothered that I couldn't brush it off. I feel like a baby, overreacting to nothing. "I'm a little bummed out. . . ."

"You sound it. Well, hold tight, honey. I'll be there in half an hour," she says, and we click off. The bar we're meeting at is just under a mile away, so I decide to hoof it. It's subzero outside and the ground is slick with snow, but I don't care. It's one of the changes I made to lose weight, and I've kept it up ever since. Walk instead of drive, always take the stairs, park farther away. All that cheesy advice you hear—it does actually work. Just so long as you do it 90, 95 percent of the time.

Today the cold air feels good, sobering. I need to burn off energy, to clear my head.

A few months ago, an incident like the Saks run-in wouldn't have left me rattled at all. I don't know for sure if I'd have confronted Hayley and Joanie . . . but I definitely wouldn't have panicked and cowered in the dressing room while they shopped. And I wouldn't have run out of the store without at least buying the awesome Marc Jacobs bag I saw on sale. Thinking about how I acted makes me feel ashamed, defeated. Like I let them get the best of me.

With each passing day, I feel myself sliding backward toward what I like to call Vintage Kylie. (It has a nicer ring than Fat Kylie.) The weird part is, I haven't regained the weight I've lost. I've kept it off for almost six years. But in my head, I'm starting to feel like the insecure, quivering mess I was before I started this whole "personal makeover."

I don't know when the slide in my confidence started—it's hard to put my finger on it exactly; there was no one defining event. It was almost as if I looked up one day and noticed my confidence was drifting. I've given it a lot of thought, and here's what I think happened. When you accomplish a tremendously important goal (for me, losing seventy-five pounds), you get a sudden jolt. Almost like a B-12 shot of self-esteem. Your old demons slip into the background and the new you takes over. But that wears off. Oh, it takes awhile. Years, maybe. But eventually you stop being so impressed with yourself and what you've done.

And even though the weight is gone, new things come along all the time to shake my self-esteem. (I'm very good, maybe all people are, at finding new reasons to doubt myself.)

From a professional standpoint, this is really bad.

I hate to sound all self-help preachy, but confidence is 99 percent of the game. Not only do confidence (and we're not talking about arrogance; that's a whole 'nother ball game) and coolness go hand in hand, but if you have a bad self-image, you'll be your own undoing at every turn.

It's the first thing I tell my clients: *you are exactly who you think you are.* Envision yourself a loser, and you'll become one. The only way to get to the top of the pack is to believe—and I mean firmly, *truly* believe in your gut—that you belong there. The second you think someone is better than you, they are.

But lately I haven't been able to follow my own rules.

Ever since my Not Thirtieth (twenty-ninth) birthday last April, I've been on this downturn. I know in the scheme of things this is silly and I'm probably overreacting. I know that thirty isn't ancient, that thirty is the new twenty. (Actually, I made that up. But since they're always saying "forty is the new thirty," then doesn't it make sense to bump thirty down a decade as well?)

But I have to be honest: I'm absolutely terrified of my upcoming birthday.

I can't stop thinking that this is it; this is where the pendulum swings. Oh, I've fooled around for a while; I've taken things lightly. But I'm too old for that now. The stuff you can get away with in your twenties—the fuckups, the self-delusions, the decisions you put off making. It all grows increasingly pathetic as you near the big 3-0. In two months and twenty-five days I'll be forced to shed any lingering immaturities.

I kick my shoe against a chunk of ice, sending pieces scattering down the sidewalk. I love the snow, have since I was little. It's one of the reasons I moved back to Chicago after graduating college. (UCLA . . . wow, what was I thinking? A fat girl in Southern California. Yeah, it wasn't fun.)

I exhale loudly, watching my breath make small circles of condensation. Sometimes I wish I could be a kid again, before I got fat and then thin. Before weight was even an issue and when I hadn't yet learned how to hate myself.

Before I just decided that this is what my life was, and I stopped trying to make it more. I guess that's the other thing that bugs me.

With each passing year you let go of different dreams. When you're five, you realize you'll never be a superhero, so you stop trying to fly. At twelve, you accept that even though your bedroom is wallpapered with posters of him, you'll never get to make out with Brad Pitt (or, in my case, Corey Haim). At sixteen you forget about buying that ice-blue BMW convertible and start saving for a secondhand non-air-conditioned Honda. At eighteen you pack up and head off to your "safe school," visions of an Ivy League education long gone. At twenty you kiss your dream of becoming the most popular girl on campus good-bye and settle for the small notoriety that comes from writing for the school paper. At twenty-eight you realize that you're never going to have Eva Longoria's body—and even if you did, you still wouldn't have her bank account or her sexy Latina charm—and so you start eating dessert (well, I didn't) and you toss out your self-bronzer.

And on and on it goes, until, slowly but surely, you come to the realization that you're never going to marry a doctor, backpack through Europe, win the Nobel Peace Prize, record a chart-topping album, or vacation in the Mediterranean on a private yacht—not to mention a million other more realistic, though still unattainable, dreams. They're not coming true. Not in this lifetime. So you give them up.

There's nothing sad or defeatist about it—it's just part of getting older.

My cell phone rings in my pocket. I pull out my Razr and check the Caller ID screen. It's my dad. I don't feel like talking to him now. My dad and I are, in some ways, two peas in a pod. My mother has always joked that if one of us isn't on the verge of a nervous breakdown, the other is. (This joke lost its humor many years ago. If it ever had any.) There's some truth to that, although I've done a stellar job of keeping my insecurities in check for most of my twenties.

I'm sure it's nothing too important. I hit the button to send Dad's call to voice mail and stuff my Razr back in my pants.

At a certain point you also have to accept that the best years of your life are probably over. Oh, sure, you could meet your soul mate at fifty, hit the Powerball jackpot at sixty-five. Those kinds of flukes can and do happen. But for the majority of us, once we peak, we peak. No matter how unhappy you are with your body at thirty, you're going to be a hell of a lot unhappier with it when you're sixty. No matter how shitty you think your social life is now, wait until you're seventy and you're falling asleep at eight o'clock and your vision is too bad to drive at night.

It's horribly depressing if you actually stop and think about it. So I don't.

I move briskly down the street, rushing toward the bar. I can't wait to see my best friend. Hopefully she can help me erase the nightmare that was today.

You're probably wondering why I care so much, why I let Joanie and Hayley get to me, why I let their fat comments bog me down.

The thing about losing weight is, you never *really* lose it. I don't mean physically, although that part's hard, too. Everybody knows most people who shed pounds gain them back, and then some. No, I'm talking about the mental part. Even if you're one of the lucky ones who manages to hang on to her slimmer waistline, deep down inside you'll always feel like "the fat girl."

2

Cool Rule #2:

There's nothing cooler than self-confidence.

I think it was Confucius, or Shakespeare, or maybe even Donald Trump on *The Apprentice* who said, "Choose a job you love, and you will never have to work a day in your life."

That's definitely true. How to Be Cool is so much fun that it rarely feels like work.

My job probably sounds insane to you. *How is this a career?* you might ask. But I fill a void.

Everybody wants to be cool.

Sure they do. Oh, they may not admit it at first—they may hold out, pretending to be "above all that," professing not to care about mainstream society.

But if you dig a little deeper, it's easy to see. Even your hippest hipsters, your least conforming nonconformists, are out to impress *somebody.* Everybody needs friends. Everybody needs to fit in somewhere.

The ironic thing is, How to Be Cool started out as a joke.

"If only there were a way to bottle this up," Ruby had said one night over caipirinhas at a trendy downtown bar. "Package what you did and sell it to the masses. I bet you'd make a million bucks."

As it turned out, she was right. About me bottling up my idea and selling it to the masses. Not about the million bucks part. Although I have done surprisingly well for myself.

I was working at Sloane Image Consultants at the time, doing low-level PR grunt work and trying to get ahead. And then Ruby suggested pitching the idea of How to Be Cool to my bosses.

At first I didn't get what she was saying.

"Yeah, but there are tons of diet books out there already . . ." I twirled my drink, sloshing the liquid around in the glass. I was feeling nervous, exposed. I had just shown Ruby a few of my "before" pictures, back from the days when I was geek personified. We'd been friends for three years, and before that night, I'd never told Ruby the truth about my past. And I'd certainly never shown her any photos. I guarded those things with my life.

"I'm not talking about a diet book." Her eyes lit up. "What you did is so much more than that."

"Maybe."

She wouldn't let up. "Do you know how many people are wandering around, feeling lost, bored, and lonely? Do you know how many people wish they could throw away their old life and start over as somebody else? You figured out how to do that." She waved my "before" picture in the air, marveling at my miraculous transformation. "You figured out how to go from D-list to A-list. From dork to diva." She giggled at the thought. "You should give cool lessons."

So that's exactly what I did. To most people, it probably seemed crazy. But I had just shed seventy-five pounds following my epiphany. I felt on top of the world, capable of anything. And I had reinvented myself, wholly, completely. I'd morphed from a shy, awkward nerd to a savvy, confident trendsetter. It only seemed fair to share the wealth. I met with my boss, Kevin, a week later and he loved the idea. Business was booming at the time, and they were looking for a way to expand.

And so How to Be Cool was born.

As a bona fide "cool instructor," I now spend my days transforming the socially inept from geek to chic. In eight weeks or less, I can help you become a stylish dresser, plan a stellar date, master the art of small talk, fit in at parties, or generally reinvent your social life.

Sounds great, right?

There's only one problem. None of it is true. Despite my carefully crafted public image, and despite my ability to tease the cool out of even the biggest nerd, I am nothing more than a giant fraud. I am, if you want to get technical, the least cool person on the planet. Consider the evidence:

1. Movie sex scenes make me blush. (And sweat. And bite my nails.)

2. Most nights when I can't sleep I watch reruns of ridiculously uncool shows like *Becker* and *Diagnosis Murder.*

3. I am nostalgic to a stupid degree.

4. I have no idea what wine goes with what food.

5. I sometimes design, and sew, fake tags into my clothing, so people will think I'm a size six. (I usually do this before a big date, if I anticipate my clothes will be coming off at some point in the evening.)

6. I have bizarre taste in men. My type is pale and pasty. Guys with glasses who are slightly less than perfect looking. I'd rather sleep with Rivers Cuomo than Brad Pitt. I prefer short and scrawny over tall and beefy. Maybe it's the non-threatening thing. This could explain a lot, including why I once dated a gay guy. (Please don't make me talk about that now.)

7. I have absolutely no sense of rhythm, but I'm always the first one on the dance floor.

8. I watch *Entourage*, and instead of lusting after Adrian Grenier, the way I'm supposed to, I want Ari Gold. Which I guess goes against the nonthreatening thing, but whatever.

9. I often pretend I am at places that I'm not. This is possibly a bit psychotic, but when I'm riding on the El, I love to imagine I'm on the Metro in Paris, cruising along to meet my French lover. Or when I'm trudging through the snow outside my apartment, I imagine I'm actually in a village in Switzerland.

10. I often pretend I am people that I'm not. Again, maybe this is a bit psychotic. But whenever life gets to be too much, I bring in a little fantasy. Like if I'm stuck in a downpour without my umbrella, instead of thinking about how drenched I am, I imagine I'm Rachel McAdams in *The Notebook* and I'm having a rain-soaked kiss with Ryan Gosling. Or if I'm strolling down the streets of Chicago, I pretend I'm Carrie Bradshaw, as old-school as it might be, because I really did love the way she walked. Sometimes I'm Marilyn Monroe, Audrey Hepburn, Jayne Mansfield. But mostly, pathetic though it may be, I like to imagine I'm Alicia Silverstone in the Aerosmith videos. Because during my senior year of high school, she was the ultimate It Girl.

11. I walk around with a soundtrack in my head. Wherever I go, whatever I do, there are songs in my mind—and they kinda set the tone for my day. Sometimes it's *Gimme Shelter* by the Rolling Stones and sometimes it's the Christina Aguilera version of *Lady Marmalade*. Sometimes I hear Nick Lachey.

12. If it weren't for my job, I probably wouldn't own a single designer outfit. Most of what I know about fashion is a sham. I keep index cards in my purse, to help me remember

the difference between Jimmy Choo and Christian Louboutin. I love clothes, don't get me wrong. I've just never understood why I should pay $800 for a shirt when I could buy one at the Gap for $35.

13. I like *Star Wars* so much that I once went to a convention.

My clients are well aware that in my former life I was something of a dork—it's a big selling point.

But they don't know the full story. They don't know the extent of my chubbiness. They think I shed a small amount of weight—twenty pounds or so. And they have no idea that I haven't kicked my geeky ways. They don't know that inside, I'm a big, blubbery ball of insecurity.

It's not that I'm trying to take advantage of people. Believe it or not, I'm only trying to help. I know from personal experience what it's like to go through life feeling like a loser. I know what it means to be alienated, ignored by society at large.

And in all fairness, I've spent a lot of time squashing that side of my personality so that I'm about 90 percent cool Kylie, 10 percent dork.

* * *

Ruby's already there by the time I reach the bar.

"Oh, God, I'm sorry," I apologize, when I see her. I know her schedule's really tight today; I feel awful for making her wait. I switch my cell phone to silent—something I always do when hanging out with Ruby.

"Honey, please," she says, standing to hug me. "I've been here three seconds. I just got a table."

A waiter comes over and she orders a bottle of Caymus Conundrum. "I know you like red," she explains. "But gotta watch the teeth." She taps her pristine white smile, the result of

$15,000 worth of veneers. "Is that okay? We can always get a second bottle if you want."

"White sounds great," I tell her, sitting down across from her. "I thought we were just having a glass, though."

"Glass, bottle." She waves her hand dismissively. "You know me, no willpower."

That's not exactly true. Sure, Ruby eats what she wants, more so than most other girls—definitely more than any model I've ever met. But she's incredibly disciplined about pretty much everything. She works out more than I do—no small feat considering I hit the gym six days a week. And Ruby doesn't know the meaning of the word *procrastination.* Whenever she has an idea, she follows through with it almost immediately.

The waiter arrives with our wine, as well as a small dish of wrinkly Greek olives. He sets everything out on the table, pours our glasses, and then leaves.

"So tell me, what happened today?" Ruby prompts, sipping her wine.

"I ran into these two girls. Correction—these two *bitches* from high school."

"Oh, no," Ruby groans. "Don't tell me. You're going to bust out the list, aren't you?"

"I am *not.*"

"Come on. Out with it. I know these girls are at least *on* the list, are they not?" She's referring to the List of People Kylie Chase Is Going to Get Revenge On Now That She Is Thin and Successful. (C'mon, it's not that weird. Lots of people make these kinds of lists. I actually wrote mine down in a notebook. So what?)

"Yes." I blush.

She buries her face in her hands.

"All right, all right. It's pathetic. I'll admit that." I sigh. "But if you'd gone to Coverland High, you'd understand."

"Ah, so they're from the infamous Coverland Days."

I am always talking about Coverland High. Mostly how much I hated going there.

"You know, I don't think I've ever met any of your friends from that era," she muses.

"I don't keep in touch with anyone from back then," I remind her. "It's better that way."

"Maybe." Ruby pops a pitted olive into her mouth, chews, swallows, and then says, "But as your best friend and de facto shrink, I've gotta tell you, Kylie. This obsession with all the people who've wronged you . . . it's not healthy."

I clear my throat. "I know."

"You can't dwell on how bad the past was. You can't dwell on getting bullied or whatever. Yes, these people hurt your feelings or screwed you over at one time or another. But you have to let it go." Ruby takes another drink. "You don't think I've been through some crap before? If I spent all my time worrying about the ways I've been wronged . . . I probably wouldn't be able to accomplish much in the meantime. I'd be obsessed." She shoots me a concerned look.

"I get it, okay," I say. "And I will let it go. Just as soon as I have my, you know, revenge."

"Which consists of?"

"Nothing bad. Showing them up, mostly. Letting them see what they've missed out on." I need to organize a gala event and invite a bunch of people from my high school. We didn't have a ten-year reunion—due to some gross mismanagement by the organizing committee—and it really bugs me that I never got the chance to show everyone how much I've changed.

"So you want to tell me the backstory about the two 'bitches' you ran into today?" Ruby asks.

I recount my history with Joanie and Hayley. It's your boring high school stuff. They called me names, picked on me, laughed in my face. I finish up with the scene at Saks.

"That sucks." Ruby tilts her head back and downs her glass of wine. "They're obviously jealous of your success. Look how quickly they brought up the *Us Weekly* thing. They've been following your career, to know something like that." She smiles. "And since they can't compete with you fair and square, their only option is to try to discredit what you've accomplished, make it seem less important."

She's right. I know she is. "I just wish it didn't bother me so much."

We talk about Hayley and Joanie for a few more minutes, and then Ruby changes the subject. "You have a dinner date tonight at China Grill, don't you?"

"Nah, it's not a date. Bob Somebody from *Metro Guy* magazine is interviewing me for a feature." I cringe. This is bad. I need to reread Bob's bio, at least learn his last name. I hate going into press events unprepared—even though I'm the one who's being interviewed.

"Should be fun," she says.

I start thinking about what I'm going to order because, sad though it may be, my mind still focuses on food way more than it should. I'm fantasizing about the lobster mashed potatoes that I won't be having, when the talk turns to Ruby's modeling trip.

"I can't believe they wanted me," she says, sounding surprised. "They usually only do the toothpick girls in Asia. It's the worst fucking market for a plus girl."

"And what's the best?"

She laughs. "There isn't one. The work's hard to come by, no matter what continent you're on. But it's certainly easier in the U.S. and Western Europe. I just hope I don't get to Thailand only to find out the magazine changed its mind."

"That won't happen."

"It could. Remember New Mexico?"

"Oh, yeah. God, I forgot all about that. Assholes," I say, wrinkling my brow. Last summer Ruby flew out to Santa Fe for a catalog assignment, only to be turned away at the photo shoot. Once the clients saw Ruby in person they threw a fit, calling her "bloated" and "geriatric" and claiming that her portfolio misled them. I would have been horrified, but Ruby said it was par for the course. At twenty-five, she's pushing the modeling age limit. Her goal has always been to work until the assignments dry up. Which, luckily, hasn't happened yet.

I probably don't tell her this enough, but I really admire Ruby. I could never live like that—flying by the seat of my pants, just waiting to see where the ride takes me. She's got more moxie than anyone I've ever met. All the stuff I teach my clients—she really embodies it. She does her thing and doesn't lose sleep worrying about her detractors.

"You're going to have a great time," I say, feeling excited for her.

"Thanks!"

We continue talking about work—hers and mine—while we finish up the Caymus Conundrum. Before long, the bottle's empty and she's paying the bill.

I try to put some money down, but she stops me.

"No way. This one's on me."

We hug good-bye and then go our separate ways. As soon as she's out of sight I feel sad. I know we just hung out, but I miss Ruby. It seems like I don't get to see her very often anymore. Our schedules always conflict, plus she travels a lot. . . . Sure, I have other friends, but none compare to her. It's snowing again and the sun has set, causing the windchill to drop several degrees. Shivering, I catch a cab back to my apartment. I need to shower, change, and gussy up before heading to China Grill. It sucks because I just bought a new car recently, and my permanent tags haven't yet come in, and the temp ones expired a week ago. It's a pain in the ass having to rely on public transportation to get everywhere. I have to plan ahead and allow myself more time than I usually wind up needing.

I turn my cell phone ringer back on and listen to my voice mails while the cab inches along in traffic. It's mostly standard stuff: a hang-up call from my father, a message from an acquaintance asking if I want to go bar hopping this weekend, and three calls from Dennis Moop, one of my neediest clients. I'm about to return Dennis's call when I hear a frantic message from my assistant, Courtney.

"Kylie, I know it's your day off, but call me back AS SOON AS YOU GET THIS! I've got big, big news for you!" Courtney can be a little melodramatic, but this truly sounds urgent. I dial my office. She picks up right away.

"Oh, my God, I'm so glad you called back. I didn't know if you were planning to stop by for a minute or not."

"Nah, I'm taking an actual day off." I laugh. "Well, except for the interview tonight at China Grill."

"Funny you should mention your interview. I have the most exciting news ever. It's canceled!"

This is exciting? "The magazine killed the piece?" I ask, confused as to why she's so happy. That's terrible news. *Metro Guy* has a huge circulation and they were planning to run a giant feature on How to Be Cool. My boss has been on cloud nine about it for days.

"No, they didn't kill it. But the journalist, Bob Sellenbach, is no longer writing it—they've reassigned it. You're now going to be interviewed by . . ." she pauses for effect, "TY BENEDICT!"

I nearly drop the phone.

"You know who he is, right?"

"Of course I know who he is," I say hotly. It'd be pretty lame for me—someone who professes to know the ins and outs of what's hot—to be unaware of Ty Benedict. The guy's a permanent fixture on the party circuit, a bona fide Page Six boy. His picture crops up in magazines more often than his byline does. "Considering he's one of the most famous writers in America, how could I not?" I try to remember the nickname the press has for him. The Playboy Journalist? I scratch my head. This doesn't sound right . . . I can't remember exactly. "But Ty Benedict doesn't write for *Metro Guy*. He's at *Cosmo*."

"Not anymore!" Courtney says, clearly pleased to be in the know. "His assistant told me he just accepted a position at *Metro Guy* three days ago. He was looking to get out of the New York party scene and jumped at the chance to move to Chicago, to settle into a more normal life. Apparently you're one of his first stories. She said . . . Ty . . . asked . . . *for you* . . . specifically!" Courtney draws it out.

Whoa. I try to digest this. "Ty Benedict has heard of me?" It slips out before I can stop myself.

"That's what his assistant said! Did you know Ty made *People*'s list of the 50 Most Beautiful People in the world last year?" She's practically screaming. "Though if you ask me, they should have crowned him the Sexiest Man Alive. He's filming a movie too, did you know that?"

I did not. "Yes, uh-huh." I'm suddenly nervous. And I never get nervous for interviews.

"So, anyway, Ty needs a few days to prepare, go over Bob's notes. He's supposed to call you tonight to reschedule."

Ty Benedict is going to call me. Tonight. Good freaking God.

"I wonder if you'll get to meet Kirsten," Courtney muses.

"Who?"

"Kirsten Dunst. Isn't he dating her?"

"I think he did . . . at one point. I'm not sure." I feel very flustered. I can't explain why. I've met celebrities before; I've even worked with a few, for God's sake. This shouldn't be a big deal. Ty Benedict is just another famous face. It's not like we're going to hit it off and become best friends or anything.

"No, wait. I think I read the other day that he's seeing somebody else now. Paris Hilton, maybe?" Courtney says.

Ugh. Please, not Paris Hilton. I will lose all respect for you, Ty Benedict.

Courtney catches me up to speed with what's been happening in the office and then we say good-bye. "Tell Ty I said hello!" she says, giddily. "Maybe you'll meet and fall in love and—"

"Calm down," I say, stopping her before she gets carried away. "It's just business, remember? He's interviewing me. I'll probably talk to him on the phone a few times, meet with him in person once or twice. And then we'll go our separate ways." But inside I feel giddy, too.

As the cab bumps along I stare at my cell phone, thinking, *The next time this rings it could be Ty Benedict.* Thinking, *I can't believe how lucky I am!*

Having no clue what's about to happen at all.

3

Cool Rule #3:

Always play the part of the one who cares the least.

Growing up, I used to think my father was a rock star.

I don't mean that I idolized my dad and put him on this godlike pedestal. Quite the opposite, in fact. I used to think my father was too dorky and plain (and uncool) for someone like my mother. I kept expecting to have this Liv Tyler–esque moment where I'd suddenly discover that my parents' relationship was a well-constructed sham, and that my real dad was actually Steven Tyler. Or Mick Jagger. Or Bruce Springsteen.

I'm not sure if my mother ever slept with any of those guys, but it's definitely possible. As a model and rock 'n' roll hanger-on in the '70s, my mom spent her days trailing bands around the country, camping out in dressing rooms, and cruising along on tour buses.

And doing lots of stuff that I don't need to spell out for you.

In other words, she was a groupie. But she hates the G word. She prefers being called a former model-slash-actress-slash-friend-of-the-band. As if there's anyone on earth who can't read between the lines of *that*.

You know, it's funny. Most girls fear they'll turn out like

their mothers. My biggest fear has always been that I'd turn out nothing like her.

And really, can you blame me? If you saw her, you'd understand. She bears more than a passing resemblance to Michelle Pfeiffer, complete with the lithe body, cornsilk hair, and glass-sharp cheekbones. The resemblance has faded a bit as she's gotten older. But back when I was in high school, when my mom was still in her thirties, she looked almost exactly like Michelle Pfeiffer.

I look nothing like Michelle Pfeiffer.

For a while I didn't get this. I was in denial, I guess. I liked showing Mom off, liked being anywhere that she was, as if her beauty would somehow rub off on me. I loved taking her to school for open house, parent-teacher day—any excuse to get her in front of my classmates. I thought they'd see us side by side, and I'd somehow become beautiful by association.

Which was stupid. Because that's not what happens, is it? Standing next to Uma Thurman doesn't make you look like Uma Thurman; it actually makes you look shorter and dumpier than you normally do.

Once the whole beauty-by-association myth was shattered, I found a new kind of denial. I hung all my hopes on the idea that I would eventually blossom into a younger version of my mother. I'd hit thirteen or sixteen or twenty-one, and the proverbial duckling-to-swan scenario would take place. I'd go from plain Jane to Michelle Pfeiffer look-alike. It had to happen, right? Girls always grew up to look like their mothers.

Except I didn't.

And because I didn't look like her, it made no sense to act like her. Which probably isn't such a bad thing. Back in the day my mother was pretty wild.

She flew to Paris on job assignments. Partied at Studio 54. She even posed topless in a 1974 issue of *Playboy*. Her pictorial is just a Google search away, as several of my ex-boyfriends have been all too happy to point out. Which is why I've quit telling people. When guys learn about my mother, they get the wrong idea about me. They think I'm some free-spirited party girl who wakes up most days not remembering whose bed she slept in the night before.

My mother and I are about as different as you can get. My God, she showed her breasts on the pages of a national magazine! Sure, she was nineteen years old at the time, but still . . .

All of this freaks me out to no end. Growing up as a zitty, self-conscious chubbette isn't fun for anybody. But when your mother is this great beauty, this sophisticated NUDE MODEL who hung around actors and rock stars, it's almost too much to handle.

As I jog up the four flights of stairs to my apartment, I can't stop thinking about the irony of it all. I inherited all of my father's goofy qualities—the weight problem (my dad has always had a bit of a pot belly), the shyness, the awkward anxiety around people. And virtually none of my mother's glamour and sophistication.

Maybe all these years I've had it backward. Maybe my mother is the stand-in. Maybe some day I'll discover that Lucia Lyle, sexy '70s style queen, didn't actually give birth to me. And that my real mom is nothing more than a fat, gawky suburban housewife who sells Mary Kay products and drools over Bo Brady on *Days of Our Lives*.

My mother is not the type to drool over anyone. Ever since I was very young she always cautioned me against letting a man get the upper hand.

"Relationships are dangerous. You should never take them

lightly," she loved to say. "The only way to protect yourself is to make sure you have more power. You accomplish this by making him think you care less than he does, convincing him that he needs you more than you need him. Whether it's true or not."

"Uh-huh," I'd say, eating my bowl of Froot Loops, not seeing how I could translate her advice into anything useful.

It disturbed me when she talked like this. I hated the way she was so fatalistic—assuming that all romances ended in disaster, unless, of course, you manipulated things so you had control. And I hated how hypocritical she was. Telling me not to enter into relationships lightly when she, herself, had engaged in many a one-night stand. But, mostly, I hated what it said about my father.

It confirmed my worst fears. That she didn't really love him, had only married him because—unlike David Bowie or Keith Richards or some other rock god—my dad was someone she could wrap around her pinky finger and control. (I'm exaggerating a little here—my mother's not quite so Machiavellian.)

But I did take her advice on one front. It's best, especially in a new relationship, to try to appear at least a little bit indifferent, at least a little disinterested. You never get the guy by playing easy to get.

Although that's precisely what I'm doing right now.

Despite all conventional wisdom, despite the fact that *I really do know better*, I sit around my apartment and wait for Ty Benedict to call.

This guarantees that my night will drag by at a snail's pace.

I eat an egg-white omelet, watch a TiVo'd rerun of *Grey's Anatomy*, organize my CD collection, return my backlog of e-mails, and do four hundred sit-ups. This takes about three hours, but it feels like two weeks have gone by.

Once I'm done with all that, I start sorting through my art supplies. This is always good for killing a few hours. Most people don't know this, but I have a giant collection of art stuff tucked away in the back of my bedroom closet. I was something of an art geek back in high school—I spent almost all of my spare time drawing. I'm not half bad at it, but the hobby died out a long time ago. It's something I've always meant to get back to, but like so many other things, it gets stuck on the back burner.

I lose track of time as I look through my old sketches and paintings, mulling over all the various projects I've worked on during the years. But my mind keeps drifting back to Ty Benedict.

I suppose it's a bit pathetic to care this much.

(I care too much about a lot of things: Hayley and Joanie, my weight, what other people think, my weight, my lackluster love life, my weight.)

I keep trying to pass the time, but my phone is silent.

By ten-thirty I lose hope. We've crossed that barrier. If he calls me now it will seem weird, too intimate for a work relationship. My mind goes through all the scenarios of what Ty Benedict might be doing right this minute, all the reasons he's not burning up my phone line.

I love picturing what other people are up to. This has been a favorite pastime of mine for as long as I can remember.

I tend to imagine other people's lives being packed with a never-ending series of thrilling adventures. I never think about them shopping for toilet paper, or raking leaves, or channel surfing in their pajamas. No, I picture them throwing wild parties, French kissing in the rain, making love so loudly the neighbors complain. This usually leaves me feeling sour, like there's this huge, exciting world right outside my door. Only I'm not a part of it.

I snap out of it by reminding myself just how boring and mundane most people's lives are.

But I can't do this with Ty Benedict.

The Playboy Pen Pusher. That's what they call him. I remembered it earlier, somewhere around my three-hundred-forty-seventh sit-up.

God, there's no way Ty is camped out at home watching TiVo'd reruns. The Playboy Pen Pusher. You don't earn that kind of nickname by being a homebody.

Ty is probably at a nightclub right this instant—someplace so hot no one outside the A-list has heard of it. I can see it all so clearly. He's flanked by Kirsten Dunst on one arm, Paris Hilton on the other. Then, for good measure, Jessica Simpson saunters up, tells Ty how cute he is, asks if he wants to find out if her breasts are real. In my mind, I watch as he buys all three girls drinks, dirty-dances up against them, makes out with them while the paparazzi feverishly document the whole thing for tomorrow's Page Six. Maybe he even flew to New York for the night so he could visit some of his old haunts.

I feel stupid for waiting around for him.

I climb into bed around eleven and flip off my bedside lamp. I toss and turn for a few minutes, struggling to fall asleep. I realize that in all my fervor over Ty Benedict I completely forgot to return the calls from my dad and Dennis Moop. Believe it or not, this makes me feel better. I've had a horribly dull night—no Page Six, no kissing in the rain—and I've still managed not to return messages. Sometimes you just get distracted for no good reason. Then again, Dennis and

Dad weren't exactly foremost in my thoughts this evening. In fact, they never crossed my mind at all.

Which is probably where I rate with Ty Benedict.

* * *

I don't remember falling asleep the night before, but I must have dropped off pretty quickly. I wake up to find there's a missed call on my cell phone from 11:41 p.m. Whoever it was didn't leave a message, and I don't recognize the number, which starts with 917. I hop online to check my e-mails, then quickly pull up Google and do an area code search. My pulse quickens as I realize that 917 is the prefix for New York cell phones.

Could it be? I know Ty just moved here from NYC. It's definitely possible he doesn't yet have a Chicago exchange. When I moved back from Los Angeles after college, I had a California cell number for the first three months.

The thought that Ty might have called makes me happy, but I don't dwell on it for long.

Instead, I spend my morning at the gym, putting in thirty minutes on the elliptical and thirty on the treadmill. I do a quick circuit of weights and then shower, dress, and hit the market near my apartment.

My fridge is almost empty and, as any recovering foodie can tell you, this is not a good thing. If I let myself get too hungry, I'm likely to binge. So I stock up on staples: almonds, bananas, green apples, tuna fish, turkey bacon, eggs, protein bars, celery sticks. I don't eat a lot of bread—my diet is pretty low-carb for the most part—but I am allowed an occasional piece of wheat. (Just so long as it's whole grain and made with 100 percent stone-ground flour.) I pay for my purchases, run back to my apartment, and drop off my stuff. Then it's time to head to work.

I have a new-client consultation first thing in the morning and I have to book it if I want to make it to the Loop by nine-thirty a.m. I make a mental note to have Courtney call the DMV today and harass them about my missing plates. This public transportation business is really starting to suck. I study the client's case file while I ride the El.

Today should be interesting.

I'm being paid to turn a nineteen-year-old genius into a slacker. It's his parents' idea. They've hired me to help him goof off, to teach him the fine art of laziness.

"Less overachiever, more couch potato," is the way his mom describes it when I walk through their front door thirty minutes later.

It might sound like an odd request, but you have to understand—Austin Dunbar is not your typical teenager. He comprehends complex chemical equations, but he hasn't heard of Matthew McConaughey. He can solve a Rubik's Cube in less than thirty seconds, but he's never played a game of spin the bottle.

"Have a seat," Mrs. Dunbar says, steering me toward the couch. Mr. Dunbar hands me a bottled water.

"We're so grateful you could make it on such short notice."

"It's no problem," I say, turning the bottled water over in my hands, peeling the label off with my fingertips. I'm acutely aware of my cell phone, nestled in my Dior clutch. I've switched it to silent—like I always do when I'm working—but I can't shake the feeling that any minute now Ty Benedict is going to call. Or, call back, as the case may be? "So tell me about your concerns."

"Our concerns?" Mrs. Dunbar wrinkles her brow. "There are so many." She turns to her husband. "You want to start?"

He nods. "It's simple. Austin should be enjoying video games, watching football, partying with his friends."

"He never goes out," his mother adds. "Rarely ever leaves his room."

"We bought him an iPod for Christmas but he didn't put a single song on it—only computer files."

"He's never had a girlfriend."

"I doubt he's even kissed anyone. And it's safe to say he's a virgin."

They shouldn't know this stuff. I'd be horrified if my parents talked about me this way.

"That's not normal, is it? Don't kids today have sex when they're, say, fourteen? What if Austin remains celibate his entire life? How can he grow up . . . get married . . . give us grandchildren . . . if he never even goes on his first date? Has his first kiss? It's going to be like that awful movie . . ."

"*The Forty-Year-Old Virgin*," Austin's dad finishes. "Of course, I can't blame girls for not liking him. He shuns mainstream life." Mr. Dunbar gestures toward the satellite receiver on their back porch. "Eight hundred sixty TV stations, yet the only channel he watches is Discovery Space."

"I'm sure with a little work he will—" I begin, but Austin's mom doesn't let me finish.

"He reads books on combinatorial mathematics in his spare time, for God's sake!" She throws up her hands in exasperation. "I don't even know what that is. Can't you get him interested in something normal? Something like, I don't know, *Dawson's Creek*?"

"You might want to go for something more current. That show's been off the air for quite a while now," I throw in.

"But you know what I mean," she says.

"I do."

I am their last resort. And, despite professing to want my help, they've yet to ask me any specifics—what I can do, how the program works. In fact, they haven't let me get a word in edgewise.

"Austin is already seeing two physicians and a psychologist and a nutritionist. And we're not getting the results we had hoped for," Mrs. Dunbar explains. "But when Austin's therapist told us about How to Be Cool . . . well, I have to admit at first I didn't take her seriously. Sign Austin up for *cool* lessons? I thought she was joking."

Austin's dad continues, "But then once we checked into it, once we read about your qualifications and your success rate, and about all the people you'd helped . . ."

"And once we saw that clip of you on the *Today* show . . ."

"*Good Morning America,*" I correct her. That appearance was ten months ago—and I spoke for maybe forty seconds. My boss, Kevin, did most of the talking. Yet nearly everyone I meet still remembers that appearance.

"Right," she continues. "Once we saw that, we knew this was it—this was the answer we'd been searching for. And when we ran the idea by Austin, he seemed completely open to it. That's a big step, because he's hated all the things—ashtanga yoga, church youth groups, competitive sports—we've suggested so far."

Austin is a nervous wreck. As in, just-spent-three-weeks-in-a-treatment-center-due-to-a-mental-breakdown. He finished high school early and got a full scholarship to MIT at age seventeen. He breezed through his first two years, pursuing an honors degree in advanced analytical physics. For nineteen years Austin's life has been made up of one success after another. But then last summer everything fell apart. Austin abruptly announced that he was dropping out of school and then locked himself in his room for the next six months. At first his parents thought it was just a phase, so they cut him some slack. But before long he had completely withdrawn from life. Now they aren't sure what to do.

I shift positions, struggling to get comfortable on the couch. It's freezing in the Dunbars' living room and, try as I might, I can't stop shivering.

"Are you cold?" Mrs. Dunbar asks.

Before I can answer, Mr. Dunbar cuts in. "No—she's cool. How to Be *Cool*, not How to Be *Cold*," he says, cracking up over his mortifyingly bad joke.

Oh, Jesus. I haven't even met Austin yet and I already feel sorry for him.

But despite all of this, I expect him to be an easy case. The ones with the obvious problems usually are. We can set some tangible goals for him: go back to school or figure out what else he wants to do; join a few social groups; learn more about pop culture.

"Come on, let's go see if the boy wonder is up and about," Mrs. Dunbar says, motioning for her husband to follow her up the stairs. "Be right back!" she calls over her shoulder.

I can't wait to meet Austin. This is my favorite part of the job—the initial consultation. I adore sitting down with clients, going over what they hope to get out of the lessons, and tailoring a program to suit them. Every case is unique, and I love that. I love the idea that I can actually help somebody change.

Over the past couple of years I've dealt with a really versatile roster of clients. Most of them are not the overt dorks that you'd expect. Oh, sure, I get some *Star Trek* nerds, some never-been-kissed thirty-somethings. But I also get a lot of seemingly well-adjusted, socially adept people who are shockingly dissatisfied with their lives and who, deep down inside, believe they don't measure up.

Coolness is a complicated issue. For starters, there are a million different kinds of cool: art house, trendy, retro, glamour, laid back, et cetera. The list goes on forever, hence the diversity of my clients. It seems like everybody's trying to fit into one scene or another, and most of them fear they're failing miserably at it. You'd be surprised how many people want to overhaul their image and become somebody new.

The thing you start to realize is that very few people in the world are truly content. If there's one thing that How to Be Cool has taught me, it's that. Oh, sure, lots of us are passably happy. But deep down most people are plagued by this nagging feeling that something's missing.

I've seen it a million times.

You're a size twenty and you want to be a twelve. You're a twelve but you're desperate to be an eight. You're an eight who won't be happy until she's a two.

You have a great apartment, but what you really long for is a house. You own a house, but you want two more bedrooms and an in-ground pool. You get the perfect house, but what you now need is a new job.

You're single and life can't really get going until you're married. You're married, but things suck because you don't have a baby. You have a baby and a hubby, but you're stifled and you want to be a crazy girl-about-town again.

And on and on it goes.

We're like the proverbial horse chasing a carrot around the racetrack, never, ever getting anywhere close to what we're trying to catch.

Maybe we set goals that we know we'll never reach. That way we get to keep our dream—our excuse for not living in the moment and being happy—intact. It sounds crazy, almost, but I'm starting to believe it's true.

But I'd better stop now. I'm getting a little too "thinky." That was the word my ex-boyfriend Noel Klinowski used to describe me. Noel always complained that I thought too much. Which was better than what he did, which was thinking too little. (Sorry, easy shot.)

"Okay, we have a small problem," Mrs. Dunbar says, coming back into the living room. "Austin won't see you."

"*Can't.* Not won't," Mr. Dunbar corrects. "He's got a terrible migraine. He needs to sleep. Is it okay if we reschedule?"

"You sure it's not a stalling tactic?" I ask.

"Oh, definitely not. He really does have a migraine."

"Maybe I could talk to him for just a few minutes," I press on. "It might be good to at least say hi."

"I don't know if that's a good idea."

We go back and forth for a minute. I figure Austin's just leading them on, agreeing to meet with me so they'll get off his back. I doubt he has any genuine interest in getting my help. But they don't see it that way. We reschedule for next week.

I'm disappointed—and skeptical. But what choice do I have? I agree to come back next Friday. That's eight days from now. Presumably Austin's migraine will be gone by then.

"I'm so sorry," Mrs. Dunbar says, showing me to the door.

"It's fine," I tell her, pulling my cell phone out of my purse and switching it back on. No new messages.

"I hate that you came all the way out here for nothing."

"Really, it's okay." I have a feeling it's going to be one of those days.

* * *

As soon as I get to the office, I realize I'm right. I also realize something else:

The state of Illinois hates me.

How else can you explain it? They have slapped my brand-new Toyota Prius with a license plate that reads:

BIG ONE

I try to be a good person. I buy a nice, ecologically friendly car so I can help the environment (and look good doing it—hybrid cars are very in right now), and what happens? The DMV curses me to a roadway of ridicule.

"I can*not* drive around Chicago like this," I complain, flopping back into my Herman Miller Aeron desk chair.

"It's not *that* bad." Courtney shrugs her shoulders. "At least your license plates finally came in. You won't have to keep taking the El."

" 'Big One,' " I mumble. I can picture it now. The honks, the stares, the obnoxious shouts as I cruise down the highway. They'll call me *whale, fatso, big mama*—all the names Hayley and Joanie dreamed up for me in high school come rushing back. I turn the license plates over in my hands, willing the letters to change into something less offensive. To think I was so excited about getting these stupid plates. I was sick of sloshing through the snow to the El train. I was dying to drive again. Well, at least I *had* been.

"Everyone will think it's about my body."

She bursts out laughing. "No they won't. Don't be silly."

Of course Courtney would react that way. She doesn't know the real me. She knows Kylie Chase, version 2.0. Cool Kylie. Thin Kylie. Courtney doesn't know Vintage Kylie.

Ah, fuck it. Let's stop pretending here.

Fat Kylie.

She doesn't know Fat Kylie.

Kylie who used to spend Friday and Saturday nights at home with a carton of mint chocolate chip ice cream, a game of online Scrabble, and a cheesy romance novel to keep her company.

"I cannot have those things on my car," I say firmly.

"I don't think you have much choice. Your temporary tags expired last week, so you'd better get these on the Prius."

I squeeze my eyes shut. "I guess so. It's going to be a nightmare, though. Mark my words."

She giggles. "You're too paranoid, Kylie. Here, I'll attach them for you." Courtney takes the license plates from me. "By the end of the day, you won't even remember they're there."

Maybe she's right. But I still can't shake the fear that driving around with BIG ONE on the back of my car will inevitably prompt random motorists to scream out "Hey, Big Girl!"—or worse—when I drive past. It's a cruel world we live in. There are lots of assholes just waiting to pounce at the first opportunity to insult someone. And in the past, that someone has often been me. It's not an easy thing to forget.

My boss, Kevin Malanik, pokes his head into my office.

"Just so you know, the national director is flying in from New York next week," he says, rubbing at the corner of his jaw, smoothing in his foundation. Kevin Malanik is the only straight man I know who wears makeup. And he's open about it, too.

"Base, concealer, and mascara," he told me once. "The three essentials every man should have. Along with a nose-hair trimmer. And an on-call manicurist."

That was nearly a year ago. Since then Kevin's added a brow pencil and—I'm almost certain—a lip plumper. Plus, he's tossed out his mascara in favor of having his eyelashes professionally dyed every month.

But, make no mistake, the man looks good. He's thirty-six, but could easily pass for twenty-three.

"We're going to be going over some things," Kevin continues. "I think you know what I mean."

I most certainly do. And it makes me nervous. Things have been a little shaky lately, businesswise. Image consulting is not a recession-proof field. Fortunately, though, How to Be Cool seems to be one of the bright spots. It's such a new, unique idea—and people have responded really well to it—that I've actually helped improve our overall business.

"I do," I say. "Thanks for the heads-up."

"That's great news about Ty Benedict," Kevin adds, before he leaves. "Keep me posted, Courtney."

"Will do," she says. As soon as Kevin's out of earshot, she adds, "Speaking of which, I'm dying to know . . . how did things go with Ty? Did you guys wind up chatting well into the night?" she asks, the license plate issue seemingly resolved.

"Nah. I fell asleep early and missed his call."

Her eyes bug out. "How in the world do you sleep through something like that?"

I shrug. "You've gotta remember, I've worked with celebrities before. You get used to it; it becomes routine." I'm pretty proud of that response. I'm even fooling myself a little bit.

"I don't think I could ever get used to being around celebrities." Courtney grins. "But I guess that's why you're a cool instructor, instead of me."

She's blatantly kissing my ass, but I pretend to be flattered. "Thanks."

"Oh! I read an update online about that screenplay Ty just sold to Paramount! Reese Witherspoon's rumored to be starring in it. Can you believe that?"

"It's pretty impressive," I say, trying my best to sound casual. But on the inside I'm screaming *REESE WITHERSPOON!! PARAMOUNT!!* I read the same rumors when I Googled Ty this morning.

"Anyway, I know it's a little early, but is it all right if I take my break now? Kevin's got me doing some filing for Josh later this afternoon."

Josh is the agency's fashion consultant. He's not the friendliest guy. He doesn't do small talk, believes smiling is a sign of weakness, and seems to spend more time working on his budding handbag design business than actually consulting with clients. (In case you were wondering, yes, Josh is gay.) If it weren't for the fact that we share an assistant—Courtney, natch—then Josh and I would probably never talk.

"After that, I have to reply to a stack of like two hundred e-mails." Josh doesn't believe in answering his own e-mails. Courtney answers all of them—even the ones that come in from his close friends and family. "I don't know if I'll get a lunch or not."

"Sure, go ahead."

"Thanks!" She smiles. "I usually bring some brownies but I left them at home this morning and I'm starved." She pats her smooth, flat stomach. "I'm trying to put on a few pounds so I have to make sure I eat, pretty much, all day. It's such a pain."

She makes a face. "Every time you turn around, there's some magazine article advertising the latest diet. It's so one-sided. They never, ever write anything about how to *gain* weight. It's annoying. I eat loads of food, but I can't put on five pounds to save my life. I'd kill to have a nice round butt."

Oh, God. She's one of *those* people. Forgive me for being bitter. But I find it hard to buy her "Woe is me, being thin is such a burden, it sucks that my metabolism forces me to have a body like Mischa Barton" routine. I try to see it from her point of view. Gaining weight, after all, might genuinely be hard for some people.

I drum my perfectly French-tipped nails against my desktop. "You have a valid point," I say diplomatically. "Magazines don't often talk about how to gain weight." I want to add that there is a reason for that—because gaining weight is ridiculously easy for 90 percent of the population—but I don't. Courtney has a fabulous body, and, the truth is, I'm insanely jealous. What I wouldn't give to trade metabolisms with a girl like her.

"I won't be gone long. I'm just going to pop out for a smoothie and some cookies. Want anything?"

I do, but I know better. You don't lose seventy-five pounds by indulging in postbreakfast pig-outs. "Nah, I'll just wait till lunch."

"Give me a buzz if you change your mind."

I return a few phone calls and, a short while later, Courtney resurfaces. True to her word, she's been gone less than twenty minutes. She has a Jamba Juice cup in one hand, a stack of papers in the other.

"I have something for you," Courtney says, strolling into my office. "With all the hoopla over your Big One license plates," she giggles, "I forgot to bring in the rest of your mail." She sets down three stacks on my desk. "Business, personal, and junk." She gestures toward the different piles. "This is like the fifth one of these you've gotten this month. I guess I *can* see why you're a little paranoid about the fat thing. It's almost like someone's setting you up for a joke," Courtney says, indicating a brightly colored item on the top of the junk mail stack before turning and heading out the door. I look down to what she's pointing at and cringe.

It's a coupon from Lane Bryant.

I swear to God, whoever does the mailings for Lane Bryant should work for the CIA. It's been almost six years since I've set foot in that store. I no longer have one of their credit cards; I don't subscribe to their mailing list or visit their website. Yet they continue to inundate me with coupons and catalogs. They've even tracked me down through three address changes.

I don't know why, but this bugs me. It's almost as if they're taunting me, reminding me of the fact that, yes, I might be skinny now, but, let's face it, Lane Bryant is only a few cupcakes and a canceled gym membership away.

I'm about to toss the coupon in the trash when something catches my eye. I do a double take. *It can't be.* Can it . . . ? I wonder, staring hard at the image. A curvy, olive-skinned girl smiles up at me. Decked out in a lavender Cacique bra and panty set, her thick, black hair hangs down past her shoulders. She looks confident, exotic, sexy. I can't suppress my smile. Yep, it's definitely her!

I pick up the phone and excitedly dial Ruby's number.

"You didn't tell me you were doing a Lane Bryant ad campaign! I got the coupon today in the mail. That's fucking awesome!" I shriek when Ruby answers on the second ring.

"Slow down, Kylie." She giggles. "I wanted it to be a surprise. I didn't think the coupons would be out so soon. I was going to show you the photos when I got back from Thailand. Wow, I think you're even more jazzed than Davey. And, let me tell you, he was pretty thrilled when I showed him the test shots."

Davey is Ruby's on-again, off-again boyfriend. "And why shouldn't he be? You look gorgeous! Simply gorgeous." Despite my love-hate relationship with Lane Bryant, I'm suitably impressed. "You're gonna be famous."

"I seriously doubt that."

"Stop being so modest." I twirl the phone cord around my fingers. "This is a huge, huge deal. Aren't you excited about becoming a celebrity?"

"Oh, absolutely!" she enthuses. "But I think 'celebrity' is stretching it. I didn't become a household name after doing *Seventeen*, *Cosmo*, and French *Vogue.* I kind of doubt it's going to happen now."

"Don't sell yourself short. You're well on your way to being the next Emme or Kate Dillon."

"We'll see. I do have a few great shoots coming up. I just found out this morning that I'm going to Sardinia for an assignment for Italian *Vogue* in a few weeks."

"That's awesome." I lean back in my chair. "Sounds like you're conquering the world one *Vogue* at a time. Who knows, maybe you'll crop up in the U.S. version soon."

"I highly doubt that. Remember, 'Miss Anna don't like fat people,' " she says, mimicking the line Andre Leon Talley famously uttered on an episode of *Oprah.*

"You're not fat," I argue, shaking my head vehemently, even though I know she can't see me.

"I wear between a fourteen and a sixteen," she confides.

"Considering that a size six passes for obese at *Vogue*, I'd say my chances of gracing their cover are pretty low."

"Their loss. Anyway, I've got to run. I've got a ton of new clients at the moment."

"Yeah, I need to finish packing. . . ."

As we're about to hang up I remember the other thing I'd called to tell her. "Oh, my God, I almost forgot! You'll never *believe* what came in the mail today."

"You mean, besides the Lane Bryant coupon with yours truly on it?"

I giggle. "Yeah, besides that."

"Uh . . . I don't know. I'm terrible at guessing games."

"The new plates for my car finally arrived. And, are you ready for this? They say Big One."

"What do you mean, they say Big One?" She sounds confused.

"Instead of having just random letters and numbers, they spell out Big One!"

"They're not supposed to do that," she says quickly. "Illinois tags typically don't have vowels in order to avoid that kind of thing. You must have accidentally gotten personalized plates."

"But I didn't order any!" I exclaim.

"Well, *obviously.* Who in their right mind would order personalized license plates that say Big One?"

"I don't know, Ron Jeremy?"

"Big One." Ruby laughs. "Yeah, that's total porn star."

"Or frat boy," I offer.

"At least they don't say Big Ass."

"Ha! True."

"You know something?" she suggests. "You ought to call the DMV and make sure they sent you the right tags. Somewhere in this city a guy with a freakishly large cock is probably pissed off that he didn't get the personalized plates he paid good money for."

"Great point. I'll have Courtney check into it."

At the mention of her name, Courtney appears in the doorway. I wish Ruby a fabulous trip and then we get off the phone.

"Did you need anything?" Courtney asks, slurping noisily from her smoothie.

"Yeah, would you mind calling the DMV?" I explain about the license plates.

She snaps her fingers. "Duh! Why didn't I think of it before? This is just like that *Seinfeld* episode. You remember the one?"

I shake my head. "I don't watch much TV, remember." This isn't true at all. In truth, I watch way too much television, always have. But seeing how couch potato doesn't gibe with my cool façade, I often pretend otherwise.

Courtney launches into a description of the *Seinfeld* episode in question. "Kramer accidentally gets the wrong license plate. Only his reads Assman."

I grimace. "Okay, that's definitely worse than Big One."

"It turns out Kramer's license plate got switched with some guy who's a proctologist."

"Ah, I see."

"I can't believe I didn't think of it before. Only with a name like Big One, they've got to belong to . . ." Her voice trails off.

"A porn star?" I supply.

"Ick." She makes a face. "Whenever you get your real plates we'd better scrub those things down with disinfectant. No telling what kind of bodily fluids will be on them."

"Something to look forward to," I crack. "Hey, look!" I

say, changing the subject to something more pleasant. "You remember my friend Ruby Gallagher?"

Courtney nods. "The model?"

"Yep," I say proudly. "She's one of the new models for Lane Bryant." I pull out the coupon and show it to Courtney.

"Awesome."

"I think I'm going to frame it and hang it on the wall by my desk."

Courtney looks at me with alarm. "Really?"

"Why, you think that's a bad idea?"

"I don't know . . . it's just, no offense to your friend, but, well, this is a business that's known for being cool. Image is pretty important around here."

"Yeah, so what?" I say hotly.

"Kevin might have a problem with it. Fat girls," she scrunches up her face as if she's embarrassed of what she's about to say, "well, they're kind of the opposite of cool, aren't they?"

I know I should defend Ruby. I know I should blast Courtney for overstepping her boundaries. Instead, I reply, "I think it would be a fun way to support Ruby."

"Maybe." She looks unsure. "But if people walk in here and see half-naked fat girls hanging on the wall—well, they just might turn around and walk back out."

* * *

Against my better judgment, I drive home in the BIG ONE car. I decide to blare the stereo—the music will drown out any insults people might lob at me.

I flip around until I find a radio station that's playing '90s music. I love '90s music. I'm eternally nostalgic for anything that reminds me of high school, even though that was one of the crappiest periods of my life.

Still, I like feeling that age again.

I cruise along, happily listening to Pearl Jam, Counting Crows, REM. I change the station briefly when "Heart-Shaped Box" comes on, because Kurt Cobain killed himself during my senior year and I don't like remembering that.

He did it on April 5, 1994. I can recall the date for two reasons. One, it was exactly twenty days before my eighteenth birthday. And two, a freshman from my school named Sherri had the distinction of committing suicide on the same day as Kurt Cobain. She did it in the morning, slit her wrists in the bathroom after her parents left for work. She was dead hours before any of us knew about Kurt, but that didn't stop the faculty and most of the parents from panicking that Kurt Cobain had kicked off some sort of suicide domino effect. For the next month we were all forced to meet with counselors, and we had school assemblies where we watched cheesy videos about how suicide is a permanent solution to a temporary problem.

I understood that the faculty meant well, and part of me appreciated their effort. Even though I didn't know her—we'd never so much as spoken—Sherri's suicide depressed me. I understood firsthand just how hellish freshman year could be. Still, I couldn't stop wondering what pushed Sherri over the edge. A lot of people consider suicide—most people, maybe—at some time or another in their lives. But for the majority of us it's merely a fleeting thought, a casual "what if?" that we don't even come close to acting on. What causes somebody to take that plunge?

I'm starting to feel upset, but luckily "Heart-Shaped Box" is over and the Gin Blossoms start up, singing about "whispers at the bus stop." Instantly, I feel better. Even though "Found Out About You" was written about infidelity, the music is so upbeat that it's impossible for me to be depressed while listening to it.

I sing along, knowing all the words.

I wish I could go back, be a teenager again. Trouble is, I don't want to relive my teenage years the way they actually happened. I want to relive that fun, flawless *Beverly Hills, 90210* version of high school. Or, at the very least, I'd like to have Hayley Hill's and Joanie Brixton's teenage experiences.

Stylized. Fun-filled. Perfect.

Blind Melon's "No Rain" comes on and I crank the volume way up. I love this song. I love everything about it. The stupid, silly lyrics; the simple guitar tune; the chubby bee girl at the talent show. This song is so '90s, it hurts!

And then I remember. Blind Melon's lead singer is also dead. One-hit wonder and then he was gone, drug overdose, before he'd even reached the age of thirty.

I change the station.

4

Cool Rule #4:

Never pretend to be someone you're not.

As you may have already noticed, I spend a lot of time thinking about the past. This is not a very cool habit. It's not a healthy one, either.

However, there are certain occasions when it's perfectly acceptable to live in the past.

One of those occasions arrived on my desk this morning in the form of a postcard.

I'm grumpy when I come into the office, because a second day has passed with no call from Ty Benedict. And because my iPod battery went dead this morning, and I was forced to run for forty-five minutes with nothing but gym noise to propel me on. Gym noise, it turns out, is not a great motivator. I gave up early and hit the showers after only half my workout.

But as soon as I see the postcard, I instantly cheer up.

Attention Coverland High School Graduates:

Better late than never!

Your ten-year reunion is finally here!

Get ready to party like it's 1994!

March 24, 2006 @ 7 p.m.

Location TBA
Contact: Dr. Zack Naylor at (312) 555-4865
for more information

Please send a current bio and head shot to
Dr. Naylor at TopDocNaylor@yahoo.com.
Achievement awards will be given out.

"I can't believe they're actually doing it!" I say, shocked. I run into Courtney's office and wave the postcard in front of her. "Do you know what this means?"

She glances over it. "Yeah, whoever made this needs to go back to high school and learn how to do math. Or is that a misprint?" she asks, pointing at the date. "Shouldn't it say nineteen ninety-six instead of nineteen ninety-four?"

"That's not a misprint. It's been twelve years since I graduated high school," I reluctantly admit. "That's what the whole 'better late than never' thing means." I explain to her how my high school reunion should have been two years ago, but the organizing committee outsourced the planning to some shady events coordinator from Evanston. Long story short, the party planner wound up filing bankruptcy and pocketing the hefty sum they'd paid her. Rather than pull something together at the last minute, the organizing committee decided to postpone the reunion indefinitely. Their official claim was that we'd just had our five-year reunion, so letting a little more time pass might make things fun. But the truth was they'd dropped the ball and were scrambling to save face.

I remember being furious when it happened.

Ordinarily, something like this wouldn't have been a big deal. But I'd waited for my ten-year reunion with all the patience of a five-year-old kid on Christmas Eve. And can you really blame me? I'd done the impossible. I was living the dream. Here was my chance to set the record straight, to erase the image of Kylie Chase, loner fat girl and meganerd. I left high school a Lane Bryant–swathed ugly duckling, and I was coming back a Gucci-clad swan.

I remember sending the organizing committee a letter of complaint, urging them to go on with the reunion as planned. I got a semi-nasty e-mail back telling me I was the only one who seemed to have such a problem with this new arrangement. Most of my peers, it said, had taken part in the five-year get-together and did not mind waiting a bit longer to see each other again.

But I'd skipped our first reunion. I was fresh out of college, temping at an advertising agency in suburban Chicago and trying to lose weight. I didn't have anything great to show off—so I no-showed.

"So why didn't they just call it a twelve-year reunion?" Courtney asks.

"I don't know. I guess they're trying to stay in the spirit of things."

"Wow, you graduated in nineteen ninety-four." She arches an eyebrow. "That means you're . . . thirty, right?"

"This year," I admit. But for the moment I am Not Thirty.

"I didn't realize you were . . ." Her voice trails off. "It's just, Josh is only twenty-four. I thought you guys were the same age."

I take that as a compliment. At least I don't look ancient, even if I feel it.

"Of course, Kevin looks younger than both of you," Courtney says, then blushes. "I didn't mean . . . he just has that baby face."

"Uh-huh," I say. "He sure does."

"Excuse me, Kylie?" I look up to see Kevin standing in the doorway. Speak of the devil.

"Yes?"

"Did you take one of my Custo shirts?"

"What?"

He heaves a sigh. "Did. You. Take. One. Of. My. Custo. Shirts?" It takes a good minute for him to get this sentence out, he's so angry.

"No. . . ."

"You do know what I'm talking about?" He's exasperated.

"Not exactly."

"Custo is a *designer.* From *Barcelona.*"

"Oh, yes, I know that," I say quickly. Even though I don't.

"Well, then, would you mind telling me what the fuck you did with the shirt?"

This is heading somewhere bad. Kevin is always losing stuff—shoes, keys, jackets—and he's always accusing us of stealing them. He doesn't usually come right out and say *steal.* He says *borrow.* Or *throw out.* Or *misplace.* It is never his fault, always ours.

"I'm sorry, I don't—"

"Did you *misplace* my Custo shirt, Kylie? I had two of them. I just bought them yesterday and I left one sitting in my office and now it's gone."

"Are you talking about that baby-blue Sasquatch tee?" Courtney asks.

"It's long sleeve, Courtney, not a tee," he corrects. "But, yes, that's the one."

"I think I saw it draped over a chair in Josh's office."

"Josh!" he thunders, heading off to harass someone else.

Before I can say anything, my cell phone starts beeping, signaling a text message. I don't even have to look; I instinctively know who it is.

Charity St. James—one of my clients.

Charity sends me at least five text messages a day, usually with some random question or another. I don't know why she keeps me on retainer (I don't feel she's getting her money's worth—I spend most of my time answering inane questions that she could Google herself) other than the fact that she's rich.

I'm not being flip; the rich really aren't like you and me. If I've learned one thing from hanging around Charity, it's that. Most people dream of being rich so they can buy yachts or BMWs or luxury homes. But when you've got fancy stuff coming out of your ears—when you have so many material things that the thought of buying one more Fendi baguette bores you to tears—then you find other, more inventive ways to spend money.

For example, when Charity's Havanese began "acting out" last fall, she hired a dog whisperer to sort the pooch out. She has a personal psychic who advises her on everything from where to go on vacation to what earrings to buy (earrings, after all, are so close to the brain that they affect a person's thought processes—or so says the psychic). Charity's got four cell phones—work, play, and family, plus one "brush-off" number she gives out but never answers. (It goes straight to a voice-mail box, which she rarely checks. "This way I don't have to hurt anyone's feelings. If some freak asks for my number, I can give him that one and he'll never be the wiser," she told me once. "Or if I have an acquaintance who annoys me, but who I have to keep up with for political reasons, then I give them that line.")

It would be easy to dismiss Charity St. James as just another Paris Hilton wannabe. And on some level, that's true. Charity is a twenty-six-year-old Chicago socialite (and budding fashion designer) who dreams of becoming spectacularly famous.

Trouble is, nobody in the world has a clue who she is. Her whole family is pretty low-key, for a bunch of borderline billionaires. A few months back, Charity's father was featured on *Forbes* magazine's list of The Richest People You've Never Heard Of.

Still didn't help.

And despite her flawless looks, her A-list friends, and her constant appearance on the party circuit, Charity has yet to break into the mainstream. For the past eighteen months she's had a team of publicists working on upping her public profile, to little avail. Every now and again she manages to get her picture in one gossip column or another, but the interest is always fleeting. She's able to grab attention here and there, but she's hardly a household name. Which is why she's recently decided to shift focus. Now she wants to become the thinking man's Paris Hilton—a socialite/brainiac.

It was my idea, actually, dreamed up when she came to see me six weeks ago. "Spoiled rich girls have been done to death," I said. "Nobody's going to embrace a Paris Hilton clone. Most people are already sick of the original . . . why would they want one more?" I gently suggested she try a different approach, a sort of anti–Paris Hilton.

"So what am I supposed to do? Chop off all my hair? Buy some ugly-ass Tina Fey glasses? Clomp around in combat boots and Salvation Army junk?" Charity ran her fingers through her white-blond hair.

"You don't have to change your appearance. It's more about attitude."

"Good. Because my appearance is vital. Do you know how many people like me just because of my belly button?" She lifted her shirt up and flashed her tiny stomach, complete with a diamond navel-stud. "Do you know how many people like me because I weigh eighty-nine pounds?"

Eighty-nine pounds. Wow. That number seemed so alien, as unachievable as weighing, say, negative one hundred thirty. But it was certainly possible. Charity was five foot one, tops. And she was bone thin.

"Right. And you've got to make people like you for something else," I said. "Your hobbies. Opinions. Interests. Come out blazing like Paris, but then wow them with how complicated and smart you are."

She huffed. "But I'm not complicated. And as for being smart . . . I am, but not in the book sense."

"You mean street smarts?" I asked, suppressing a smile. It was hard to imagine someone who spent five years at a Connecticut boarding school being particularly streetwise.

"I see where you're going. . . ." She sighed. "You mean I should know about shit? Know about, say, the crisis in North Korea with that dictator guy. Or why America's two-party political system is outdated." Charity snapped her fingers. "Kim Jong-Il, right?"

She surprised me there. I hadn't expected her to know about things like that, but then again the girl had attended one of the finest prep schools in the country.

"Exactly! That's what I mean. Show people something new. A socialite party girl with an astronomical IQ."

"But how am I supposed to accomplish that?"

"Work on it. Take some classes at Yale. Read *everything.*

Learn about art, politics." I hoped she wouldn't take this as an insult. "Familiarize yourself with classic literature, so if someone quotes Edith Wharton you'll know what they're talking about."

She was writing this down.

"You really think that would work? You think being a bookworm will get me famous?"

I wasn't sure. "It's worth a shot." A part of me doubted that my advice would work. I wasn't sure she *could* accomplish what she was setting out to do.

"At this point, I'll try anything. But you have to understand something, Kylie." The snotty tone was back. "I do not merely want to be some smart rich girl. I want to be a *character*, a persona."

"You can still be crazy and over the top. Just alternate. Act like a tabloid"—I was going to say *whore*, but caught myself right in time— "fixture half the time. That will get you the attention. But once they're watching, play around with it. Stun them. And then maybe you'll be able to keep them interested this time."

"You know something," she mused. "Ever since I was five years old, you know who I've wanted to be?" Before I could answer, she said, "Barbie. I thought they could name a doll after me—Filthy Rich Barbie, or something like that." She laughed. "And you know what? Twenty years later I still want to be Barbie. Only now, instead of being Filthy Rich Barbie . . ."

"I guess you're more of a Bookworm Barbie."

"Bookworm Barbie," she said, smiling. "It has kind of a nice ring."

Ever since that meeting Charity has thrown herself, headfirst, into changing. And she keeps in constant contact, e-mailing and texting with a barrage of weird questions. Today she writes:

I'm on a lunch date with a sculpture major from UC. What am I supposed to think about Christo? You know, the artist who put the orange curtains in Central Park last year.

Christo. Custo. *Orange curtains?* It's all too much. And why is she asking me what she should think? Charity always does this. She always wants me to help her have the "correct" opinion on one subject or another. I want to write back and tell her that it doesn't matter, that whatever she thinks is fine, it really is. But I don't. Instead, I combine and recycle opinions I've read numerous places, including the *New York Times* and online art blogs. The ones I can remember, at least. And then I write back:

You thought the Gates installation was charming, if a bit overrated. But you've been anticipating it for decades, so that's to be expected. You are always interested in what Christo does. You find his entire body of work immensely fascinating.

Sometimes I wonder what kind of living this is, helping people assemble fake personas, helping them pretend to be someone they're not.

I push the thought out of my head and turn my attention back to my twelve-year reunion. As I glance over the postcard again, something catches my eye. *Achievement awards will be given . . . send bio and head shot.*

I freely admit that this is very immature, very twelve-year-old-girl of me.

But I have to win an award. *I just have to.*

And even if I don't . . . at least I've got a chance to finally impress Zack Naylor. Excuse me, *Dr.* Zack Naylor.

Every girl has a Zack Naylor. The guy you pine away for all during your teenage years. The one you persist in loving, despite the fact that he barely knows you're alive. When I was in high school, I liked Zack so much it was painful. It got to the point where I started to hope he'd do something boorish—beat someone up, pick his nose in public. Something, anything, unattractive. That way I could stop worshipping him and get on with my life.

And I thought I had.

But, here it is, twelve years since graduation, and my heart started fluttering when I saw his name and number on that postcard. I know it's pathetic, I know it's immature . . . and I know I'm probably in love with the Zack Naylor I've invented in my head. But for some strange, stupid reason, I still like him. (And, to tell you the truth, I have for a while now. Ever since I discovered the joys of Google Image last summer. I looked Zack Naylor up, found his profile—he's a dentist working in the city—and discovered that he was just as cute as he'd always been, if not cuter. Plus, no wedding ring. No mention of a wife in his bio. Which means he's fair game.)

And I'm grateful for the chance to make up lost ground, to save face. Because the way things ended between us was pretty horrifying. Allow me to explain.

Senior year, I bought Zack Naylor a Christmas gift. I don't know what motivated me to do this. It wasn't like Zack and I were close friends. We were barely friends at all. The only thing we shared was sixth-period world geography. He sat right in front of me, and since both our preceding classes were across the hall, we were always the first two people to arrive.

Zack would stroll in every day, smiling brightly as he plopped down at his desk. He'd pull his *Earth Through the Ages* textbook out of his monogrammed L.L. Bean backpack and then set to work arranging his paper and pen on the desk. Then, because I was the only other person in the room, he'd turn around and engage me in a two- or three-minute conversation about his weekend or his favorite TV show or his latest soccer game. Our conversation usually died off once Zack's other friends arrived. But I relished our brief talks before class started. They were often the highlight of my otherwise boring day. (I told you my high school years were kinda sad.)

I desperately longed for a way to make myself stand out to Zack, and the Christmas gift seemed like the perfect solution. I wasn't stupid; I didn't expect him to instantly fall in love with me just because I'd given him a present. But I wanted to leave my mark. That way, when we crossed paths at our high school reunion ten years (or twelve, as it would turn out) down the line, he would at least remember who I was.

I searched high and low before finally finding the perfect gift—a rare U2 bootleg called *Mango*, which featured techno remixes of some of the band's biggest hits.

Zack was a major U2 fanatic. He had an *Achtung, Baby!* bumper sticker on the back of his Jeep Wrangler (right next to the bright yellow sticker that said "Soccer players do it for 90 minutes"), and at least once a week he wore his faded *Zoo TV '92* T-shirt to school.

After overhearing Zack mention how much he wanted a copy of *Mango*, I'd gone to record store after record store looking for the thing. It took me nearly two months to track it down. This was before the days of Napster and iTunes and online music fan clubs, where you could find anything at the click of a mouse. I finally located a used copy of *Mango* at an indie record store downtown. It cost $34.99—which seemed ridiculously overpriced, considering the cover was scratched up. But the CD itself looked to be in good condition, so I went ahead and bought it.

I knew Zack would love the gift—I just didn't know how to give it to him without looking strange. I didn't want to set off any alarm bells; the last thing I needed was for Zack to figure out I had a massive crush on him. (This was actually my MO back in those days. If I liked a guy, I did everything in my power to hide it from him. I'm not sure what the logic was behind this. It certainly never resulted in my getting any dates . . . not that Zack would have asked me out anyway, but I digress.)

In the end I decided to do it the week before winter break. I had originally planned to give it to him on the last day, but decided against that. I wanted to allow enough time for Zack to buy me something in return, if he was so inclined.

"Hey, I've got something for you," I said, reaching into my backpack and pulling out a plastic shopping bag. "Merry Christmas."

He stared at me in surprise. "Oh. Uh . . . I didn't get you anything."

"That's okay." *There's still time. You can go out tonight and buy me a pair of earrings or a scarf. Even a card would do.*

Zack reached into the bag and pulled out the CD. I had decided not to wrap it. I didn't want to look like I'd tried too hard. I wanted Zack to think I'd picked it up on a whim. (But I left the price sticker on so he would know how much money to spend when he bought me a Christmas gift—I told you I was clueless.)

"*Mango*!" he exclaimed, looking totally shocked. "Awesome!" He turned around and gave me a high five.

"What's awesome?" Andy Lewiston, one of Zack's good friends, asked as he came into the classroom.

"Kylie got me this CD." He handed it over.

Andy examined the case and then let out a low whistle. "Thirty-four ninety-nine. That's quite a chunk of change. You must have a real thing for my boy Zachary, huh?"

I felt sick. "No!" I said a little too quickly. "Of course not."

Andy opened the CD case. His eyes bulged and he dissolved into a fit of uncontrollable laughter. "Damn, man, she's not very subtle, is she?" He passed the open CD back to Zack.

Zack glanced at it and didn't say anything. Instead his face grew pink. In all the time I'd known him I had never once seen Zack Naylor blush. But he looked really and truly embarrassed.

What the hell was inside that case? Had I accidentally slipped something embarrassing in there without realizing it? I had no idea what it could be. A stray pubic hair, perhaps? (Not that I'd had the CD anywhere near that region, but you never knew. This was long before I'd started going in for regular Brazilian waxes. Nowadays, I was as smooth and hairless as an eight ball.)

Andy must have sensed my confusion because he grabbed the *Mango* CD from Zack and thrust it in my face.

"Look!" he said, pointing to the picture on the cover of the actual CD itself. "That's . . . well, I don't have to tell *you* what it is. You're a girl." He burst out laughing again.

And suddenly it dawned on me. On the cover of the disc was a close-up picture of the inside of a mango. And if you've never seen a sliced-open mango, then you might not realize what it looks like.

A vagina. It looks *exactly* like a vagina.

I had given Zack Naylor a vagina CD.

A big, ripe, juicy vagina CD.

I might as well have handed him a naked snapshot of myself. It was *that* mortifying.

I wanted to throttle U2, the pervy bastards.

I had actually seen the picture a few days ago. A used CD, *Mango* hadn't come wrapped in cellophane, and I had taken the disc out in the store and examined it for scratches.

But I was so stupid, so naïve, that I had never put two and two together. Plus, it wasn't like I was super familiar with what the female anatomy looked like up close. True, I was a girl. But I was a virgin. I had never been to the gynecologist. I'd never paged through an issue of *Playboy.* And I certainly hadn't taken a mirror and held it between my legs to examine what was going on *down there.* I could hardly stand to look at my face in the mirror. I wasn't about to start exploring south of the border.

Of course, Zack and Andy were incredibly familiar with vaginas, and had probably spent countless hours in close proximity to them—looking, touching, licking, whatever.

And they assumed I had bought this CD as a cheeky way of alerting Zack that if he ever wanted to get up close and personal with my own private mango, he had an open invitation.

I got teased about it for the next couple of days. Then a sophomore got caught giving a blow job in the science lab, and my propositioning of Zack was old news. But Zack was never quite as friendly to me after that, and every once in a while, I'd hear one of the jocks shout out, "Hey, show me your mango!"

Ah, well. At least it was better than being called fat.

After that whole nightmare, Zack and I never really spoke again. Oh, God, I hope he doesn't remember it—that was a long time ago, and it's not like he's spent every moment since high school thinking about me.

But assuming that he does remember, this is my chance to erase the whole incident, cover it over with something new. Namely, my hot bio and even hotter picture.

You see, I am the queen of fat-free photography. They always say the camera adds ten pounds, but that isn't necessarily true. I know all the tricks to make the camera subtract, not add, weight. I know the perfect angle: camera positioned overhead, aiming down. The perfect pose: chin up, eyebrows arched, lips slightly parted into a pout. Trust me, it works. It can take several attempts to master this. But follow those instructions and you'll wind up looking coy and, most important, thin.

Whenever people see pictures of me, they always say, "You're so photogenic!"

I hate this. I worry they're implying that, under normal circumstances, I look ugly. After all, anyone can take a good picture. In person is another story.

I open up the jpegs on my computer and look through the various head shots of myself. It's tough to narrow it down, so I finally decide I'll send Zack two: one color, one black-and-white. With that matter settled, I open up my bio and get to work on revising it.

Kylie Chase knows what's hot and what's not. A bona fide "cool instructor," she spends her days transforming the socially inept from geek to chic. In eight weeks or less, she can help you become a savvy dresser, plan a stellar date, master the art of small talk, fit in at parties, or generally reinvent your social life.

Kylie got her start as a professional image consultant at Sloane Image Consultants, where she helped celebrity clientele cultivate the perfect public persona.

But after a few years of glitz and glamour, she decided to shift her focus. Now, instead of teaching celebrities how to be trendy and cool, she teaches everyday people. Her sessions on How to Be Cool have become one of Chicago's hottest offerings. Kylie has been featured in a variety of publications, including People, USA Today, *and the* Chicago Tribune.

When she's not making over the Windy City's residents, Kylie enjoys . . .

I stop reading. Wow, this is a big pile of crap. I never realized how boring, how stupid I sound.

It's a wonder I manage to get any clients at all—it's a wonder Kevin hasn't fired me and shut down How to Be Cool! There's no way Zack and the rest of the reunion committee are going to be impressed with that boring drivel.

If I want to get more attention, I have to be creative. I think for a minute. What I really need are some fun, unusual hobbies, like guerrilla gardening or water polo. Or even some dangerous ones like rock climbing or tow-in surfing. People are always more intriguing when they risk their life for sport.

I curse myself. Why hadn't I taken those cliff-diving classes last summer in Tenerife when I had the chance? At the time, I'd been preoccupied with getting off the island and into mainland Spain so I could visit the Salvador Dalí museum. Plus, the idea of willingly leaping off an eight-hundred-foot cliff scared the bejesus out of me. Now I could kick myself for passing up such a great opportunity.

The longer I think about it, the more depressed I get. What happened to all my big dreams? I was supposed to get skinny and then get a life. Yet I've become complacent, happy to sit on my butt and let the world pass me by. I've missed out on lots of fantastic, noteworthy things over the years. Instead of sitting here in boring Chicago, why wasn't I off teaching salsa dancing or digging for archaeological finds in Egypt or sledding down the sand dunes in Namibia?

Of course, I can always fib just a little bit. . . .

I've never been much of a liar. For one thing, I suck at it. And for another, I've never seen the point. If there's something you hate about your life, it's better to figure out a way to fix it than to waste a bunch of time trying to cover it up.

But now I'm tempted.

I pretty much cut myself off from the entire Coverland student body after graduation. It was easy to do—I had only one true friend in high school, Marjorie Malone, and she moved away when we were sixteen. (We had a bit of a falling out before then, so it wasn't a tragedy to see her go.) So it's not like anyone's been keeping tabs on me. I could alter a few things, invent a whole new life if I wanted, and no one would be the wiser.

I think it over. What harm would it cause? It's not like I'm friends with any of these people; it's not like I see them in my everyday life. Oh, sure, I have fluke run-ins now and again (like the Hayley/Joanie fiasco), but those are few and far between. Whatever lies I make up will only have to hold for one night.

And besides, it's not really a lie if you *intend* to make it true, is it?

I begin frantically typing, spicing up my bio until I sound like the coolest, most sophisticated person on the planet. I'm careful not to take it too far. Much as I want to pretend I've excavated ruins from an Egyptian tomb, I know that would be completely unbelievable. I feel slightly guilty for lying—but I reconcile it in my mind. All of the things I put down are hobbies that truly appeal to me. Things I plan on doing just as soon as time permits. As long as I intend to make the bio accurate *one day*, then it isn't so bad, right?

As soon as I'm finished, I hit Print and read over what I've written. My eyes light up as they scan the page. Wow! I've done a terrific job, if I do say so myself. I type a quick e-mail to Zack and upload the new-and-improved bio and two head shots. Then, before I can give it a second thought, I click Send.

I feel a twinge of guilt, but I push it away. I look over the bio again, and I feel a surge of pride.

It's amazing how interesting a person can become if you stretch the truth a little.

5

Cool Rule #5:

If you *do* pretend to be someone you're not,
make sure you have a backup plan—
a credible way to "fake it" in case you get caught.

When I get back from lunch later that day, Courtney is waiting for me by the door. "Your dad has called a bunch of times. He left a message, but his voice was pretty garbled on the machine. I think he said it was urgent, but I'm not sure. I did catch the part where he said something about how Mars has it in for you."

I groan. "Not *this* again."

"Uh-oh. Has this Mars person caused you trouble before?"

I sigh. "Mars is not a person. We're talking about *the* Mars—as in the planet Mars."

"Oh." She looks baffled. And rightfully so.

"My dad's something of an astrology freak," I explain. "Actually, *freak* is putting it mildly." My father is completely, totally addicted to astrology—every single morning I open my in-box to find a daily horoscope. He has a computer program that lets you calculate charts and predict futures, and he spends hours glued to the screen stressing out over planetary alignments. He lives and dies by what the stars say. Jupiter in retrograde? Bad day to plan a vacation. The sun in the second house? Time to buy a lotto ticket!

Astrology even affects his work. My dad is the head chef at Swank, a trendy fusion restaurant on the outskirts of Chicago. He's pretty highly regarded—he's published his own cookbook and been featured a couple of times on the Food Network. But despite all this success, I suspect his staff thinks of him as an eccentric kook—because, as those close to him know, Dad plans Swank's entire menu around the astrological forecast.

"Wait, let me guess . . . if the moon is in Pisces you serve a fish special, right?" I once joked. "And if it's in Capricorn, then you plan the evening around goat cheese!"

Dad shot me a horrified glance. "That's not how it works *at all*," he said sternly, obviously annoyed that none of his astrological guidance had rubbed off on me. Then he launched into a detailed explanation of how he charts the menu. "You see, the restaurant has a date of conception, a 'birthday,' if you will. In that way it's similar to a person. You know how you're a Taurus, Kylie, and how I'm a Gemini? Well, Swank is a Scorpio. And based on that 'birthday,' I can calculate a specific horoscope for Swank, which helps me discern . . ."

I tuned him out at that point. Try as I might, I will never understand how the position of Pluto alerts Dad to make chicken saltimbocca instead of veal.

"Whatever you do," I caution Courtney, "*don't* give him your birthday. If you do, he'll be calling you up three times a day to discuss your horoscope."

"It sounds kind of neat," she says. "My dad's a boring tax lawyer. I wish he'd get into something fun like astrology. Anyway, I'll let you get back to work," she says, heading back to the reception area. It's funny. As often as Courtney strolls into my office, I should almost move her desk in here.

I pick up the phone and dial Dad's cell.

"Hello?" My mother answers.

"Hi, Mom, I was trying to reach Dad. Did you guys accidentally swap phones again?"

"No," she says crisply. "Your father's getting fitted for a new Armani suit right now."

"He is?" I didn't realize my dad liked Armani.

"It took quite a bit of persuading—and I practically had to drag him here kicking and screaming," Mom admits. "You know how he doesn't like fancy stores and how much he worries about money. But he finally saw the light. Lately, he's been getting invited to a lot of important events, and he's got to have at least one appropriate suit to wear. If he wants to take the restaurant to the next level, he'll have to improve his image just a little bit."

I couldn't agree more. After all, isn't that what I just finished doing with my bio? "So have you found anything nice yet?"

"Oh, lots of things. The hard part is narrowing it down." Mom launches into a discussion about collars and cuffs, and different types of threadwork, and I get lost. My mother is something of a fashion hound. Back in the day—post-Playboy and pre-family—she worked for Louis Vuitton in New York. She was well on her way to launching her own line. Then she met my father at a food expo and they fell madly in love and moved to Chicago. Now my mom sells couture wedding gowns. She spends her days helping well-to-do brides choose between what she calls the Big Five—Carolina Herrera, Badgley Mischka, Reem Acra, Lazaro, and, of course, Vera Wang.

"Despite all the great choices these days, most brides still go with Vera," Mom often complains. "I try to explain to them the benefits of picking something a little less overdone, but they never listen." I get the feeling she's bored with her job and wants something with more variety.

I personally hope she'll give up the wedding business sooner rather than later. It's not that she pressures me to hurry up and settle down—she's very cool and modern in that way—but spending all day around wedding gowns has to make her wonder. Just when, exactly, will her only child finally take the plunge and walk down the aisle? Or at least get a boyfriend.

"So do you know what Dad called about?" I ask Mom. "He said it was something to do with Mars?"

"Oh, God, not *this* again." She lowers her voice. "Something on your chart alarmed him. He's been babbling about it all day. You know how he gets with these things." She sighs. She sighs a lot when she discusses my dad's astrology obsession.

"I'm afraid I do."

"Look, I tell you what. Your father's pretty distracted right now with the fitting. If you want my advice, avoid him for the rest of the day and hopefully he'll forget all about his latest astrological deduction. By this time tomorrow, it won't matter anyway. He'll have a different prediction to pester you about."

"True," I agree. "But why is he freaking out so much? I thought you'd gotten him under control."

Mom has been trying to rid Dad of his astrology addiction for years now. She's always viewed it as a silly little hobby, though recently Dad's gotten more attached to it. Personally, I worry that he might have a slight case of obsessive-compulsive disorder. Every time I see the Paxil commercial I can't help but marvel at how many of the symptoms my father has.

"Normally, he's not this bad. But apparently whatever he saw in your chart really flipped him out."

"Great," I say sarcastically. "Something to look forward to."

"Oh, by the way! I saw Ruby booked a gig with Lane Bryant."

I blink in surprise. "How do *you* know about that?"

My mother is a perfect stick figure. She's never set foot in Lane Bryant in her life—at least, not as far as I can tell. I know she sure didn't go there with me. When I was growing up, I did all of my clothes shopping alone. Mom would drop me off at the mall and then I'd slink around, digging through the slim pickings for big girls. Mom probably would have gone if I'd asked her, but I found it too humiliating. Who wants to have their ridiculously thin mother watching while they cram themselves into a size twenty?

"Did Lane Bryant send you a coupon or something?" I ask.

"No." Mom laughs. "I saw her on the news this morning when I was getting ready for work."

"Ruby was on the news?"

"Yep. Apparently, she's about to go on billboards all over the country. Although I don't know if that's for Lane Bryant or not. It's some kind of 'Women with Curves' campaign. I forget who it's for."

"Ruby's going to be on a billboard!" I shriek. I'm stunned. Why in the world didn't she tell me this before? This is a huge deal. I feel hurt, left out. And, truth be told, kind of jealous.

"Yes, they showed a shot of it on the news. She's up there with three other girls and she looks *fantastic.* Exotic, curvaceous, beautiful. You must be so proud to call her a friend," Mom muses. "She's really making a name for herself. What a great success story."

For some reason it annoys me to hear her say this. Since

when is being plus-sized so cool? Mom never acted that way when *I* was overweight.

"Thank you," I hear Mom mumble to someone in the background. "Kylie, honey, I'd better run. They've just brought over a fresh glass of champagne. Plus, your father's likely to be out here any minute, asking for my advice."

As soon as we hang up the phone I shoot Ruby an e-mail. I keep it short and sweet, because I know she probably won't have much free time while she's in Thailand.

> *Congrats on the billboard deal! Go you! My mom saw you on the news this morning and was very impressed. Call me when you get back in town.—Kylie.*

I still feel a little jealous, but as the day wears on it starts to drift away. Ultimately, as I keep reminding myself, I'm really happy for Ruby. I'm happy for her successes, and excited about what the future might hold.

But a nagging thought keeps creeping into my head.

If Ruby were a size two stunner gracing the cover of every major magazine in America, would I still feel this way? If the billboard she was on belonged to, say, Victoria's Secret, would I still be unequivocally, phenomenally thrilled for her? Or would I feel overcome with jealousy?

I can't help but wonder: is it easier for me to be happy for Ruby because she's plus-sized?

* * *

"Hey, Courtney," I call out into the reception area. "Will you call Ty Benedict's assistant at *Metro Guy* and see if you can set up an interview time?" I've grown tired of waiting for Ty to call. I'm ready to just book the interview and have this over with.

"I'll do it right away." A minute later she strolls into my office, clutching a piece of paper.

"Kylie, this is amaaaaaazing! I had no idea you used to play Texas Hold 'Em with Ben Affleck!"

"What?" I blink in surprise.

"I was just reading your bio."

"My bio?" Oh, shit! My bio. "How did you get that?" I demand.

"I found it sitting on top of the printer. Was I not supposed to read it?"

No. "It's fine." I wave my hand dismissively. "It's just, that's my personal bio. And it's still not finished. I really don't want anyone taking a look at it right now. So whatever you do, don't send it to any clients or media. Okay?"

"Sure, sure. I won't send it out." She smiles brightly. "Now, tell me about poker with Ben!"

"Oh, it was no big deal, a onetime thing." Ruby and I went to Vegas last summer on vacation. While we were there we got tickets to a celebrity poker tournament in which Ben Affleck happened to be playing. Even though I didn't actually get involved in the game, it was close enough.

Courtney quickly reads the rest of my bio, ticking off points. "Classically trained musician."

My French horn is gathering dust in a closet at my parents' house.

"Fluent in three languages!"

Does Pig Latin count?

"Well versed in fusion cooking."

My father is a master of fusion cuisine. I'm sure to have inherited some of his skills, right?

"Dove off eight-hundred-foot cliff while on vacation in Tenerife, Spain."

Did I really write that down?

"Anyway, like I said, this is a rough bio. It's not ready to go out yet." I take the paper from her hands and run it through the shredder. No sense taking any chances.

"Man, you've done some awesome stuff in your life!" Courtney says, eyeing me with newfound respect.

"Yeah, I guess so," I say, smiling back.

* * *

There are some definite advantages to lying. My trumped-up bio is an even bigger hit than I had imagined—maybe I should start using it all the time, not just to impress my high school classmates. (Uh . . . not exactly.)

Less than two hours after I sent it off, Zack Naylor e-mails me back.

Kylie Chase!
It's great to hear from you! What an interesting life you've had!! I'm afraid I'm a real dud in comparison. Can't wait to see you at the reunion! The committee hasn't made any firm decisions just yet, but I bet you'll be making a trip to the podium to collect one of those achievement awards!!!!
Zzzz

That whole Zzzz business is kind of annoying—and he went a little crazy with the exclamation points—but an e-mail from Zack Naylor is still an e-mail from Zack Naylor. I can't help but feel jazzed.

Today must be my lucky day, because a few hours later I get an out-of-the-blue e-mail from Ty Benedict.

What it says shocks me.

Kylie,
I'm really sorry I haven't gotten in touch with you. Moving is such a pain—I've spent every night for the last week unpacking. And it doesn't look like I've made any progress. I'm still knee-deep in boxes!

Anyway, I know it's last minute, but I'd love to get together tonight if you're free. I know a great little bar in the South Loop. It's casual and fun, yet quiet enough for us to have a real conversation. Let me know if you can make it.
Ty Benedict

I can't believe it! All this time the Playboy Pen Pusher hasn't been tearing up the club scene. He's been sitting at home, sorting through boxes.

And now he wants to get together. Tonight! With me! For drinks!

I'm dying to go, but there's just one problem. Today's Friday, and I don't want to appear like an uncool loser who doesn't have any plans. Part of me says, screw it. After all, Ty (a person who I think we've all established passes for cool) obviously doesn't have any plans for tonight. Is there really any shame in admitting that neither do I? Then again, I have a reputation to uphold. I've staked my career on the fact that I'm a "cool" person. I know from experience that journalists can be sneaky. Perhaps Ty isn't really interested in having a drink with me. Maybe this is just a clever ploy to trip me up. I can envision the article now:

It's Friday night and Kylie Chase, self-professed "Queen of Cool," sits alone in a crowded bar. This is how Kylie spends most of her weekend nights, despite the fact that she forces her clients to hit the town.

Yikes. It's a scary thought, and frighteningly close to the truth. I'm suspicious. Ty seems like a straight-up guy, but you never know. I've spent too many years building up my image—and this business—to have it come crashing down in a moment of weakness. I think it over for a few minutes, and then reply:

Ty—
Great to hear from you! Thanks for the invitation.
Unfortunately, I already have plans for tonight. I'm meeting friends for dinner around nine, but I could squeeze in a quick drink before then if you'd like. How does six o'clock sound? Let me know.
Kylie Chase

I figure this is a nice, neutral response. A few minutes later Ty writes back that six o'clock sounds great. He then lays out directions to the bar and gives me his cell number in case something comes up. I'm totally excited by his e-mail until I get to the end.

P.S. I can't wait to hear more about your adventures in the Australian outback.

Whoa. The Australian outback? I feel a wave of nausea washing over me.

"COURTNEY!" I scream.

She comes dashing in. "What's wrong?" she asks, catching my horrified expression.

"Remember the bio I printed out earlier? You didn't send that out to anybody, did you?"

She shakes her head. "No, I'm sending out your old one, just like you asked."

"Well then," I say, trying to keep my voice calm, "how did Ty Benedict get a copy of the new bio?"

Courtney looks confused. "He didn't. I e-mailed his assistant the old one. I swear."

I open Microsoft Word and frantically call up my bio. I open the file, and the first sentence causes me to catch my breath:

Kylie Chase likes to live life on the edge.

I gasp. "I must have accidentally saved over the original with the new one."

"That's okay, we've got a hard copy of the other. I'll pull it out of the filing cabinet."

"No, that's not the point." I massage my temple with my fingertips. "I didn't want anyone—much less Ty Benedict—to see that before it was finished."

Courtney smiles. "Why not? Kylie, it's great. It really is."

A great big bunch of lies.

"Yeah, but that focuses too much on my personal accomplishments . . . I want journalists to concentrate on How to Be Cool," I finish lamely.

"It'll be okay," she says. She returns a minute later with the hard copy of my original biography. "Want me to fax this over to *Metro Guy*?"

"No." That'd really confuse Ty if he suddenly got this dull rundown after receiving my thrill-a-minute life story.

"Can you do me a favor? Will you type my original bio back into the computer? Oh, and while you're at it, erase that other bio I've put on there."

"No problem." She looks confused, but she doesn't ask any questions.

Now I've gone and done it. I've completely screwed myself. There's nothing I can do about it now except hope that Ty has a great sense of humor. I'll have to come up with some bullshit story to explain the fake biography.

I decide to pass the time by looking over some of Ty's work. I used to read his columns in *Cosmo*, and I know he's done at least one or two freelance pieces for *Metro Guy*. I go to their website and type his name into the search box. The first thing that pops up is his bio:

> *Ty Benedict, 22, joins the staff of* Metro Guy *as managing editor. An Ivy League graduate, Ty interned at* The Howard Stern Show *before giving up his budding radio career to pursue journalism full time. During his short tenure at* Metro Guy, *he has written more than two dozen features and profiles as well as various opinion pieces. Ty has won numerous accolades for his work, including a prestigious Hearst Award. His screenplay,* The Bad Old Days, *was recently sold to Paramount as part of a six-figure, two-picture deal. A native of Nashville, Ty splits his time between the Windy City and his Tennessee homestead.*

Good God. Talk about impressive.

I think back to what I was doing at twenty-two. I was a mess. I was living in a crappy apartment and working as a waitress in a bookstore café. I can't fathom what it must feel like to have that kind of success at such a young age. Or any age, really.

The only thing that bugs me is the Howard Stern reference. Why on earth would someone who writes for *Metro Guy*—billed as the magazine for today's sensitive, enlightened man—want to work at *Howard Stern*? It's not that I dislike Howard Stern—in truth, I find some of his commentaries hilarious—but it seems like he's the polar opposite of everything *Metro Guy* stands for. In fact, I'm sure I heard the shock jock bashing *Metro Guy* on Sirius the other day, saying men who subscribe to that kind of thing are pussies.

Oh, well. I suppose it doesn't matter. I move on to Ty's articles. I pull up the first one, a commentary from last month's issue.

THE "I LOVE YOU" FREAK-OUT
Why your girlfriend won't say those three little words
by Ty Benedict

By now you know the scene. Girl and boy, happily coupled, are enjoying a romantic dinner for two. They're celebrating their one-month anniversary—or six, or ten, or twelve. Everything's going great. They sip wine, lovingly hold hands, trade sweet pecks, exchange presents.

And then it happens. In a moment of excitement, overwhelmed by emotion, the girl blurts out: "I love you."

Cue the sound of a record scratching as the scene

grinds to a screeching halt. The man's face goes white, then green, then white again. He doesn't return the phrase, but instead asks for the check and goes dashing out the door as soon as it's settled up.

And the girl knows she's blown it. This is it; their perfect relationship is ruined. She'll never hear from him again.

And so goes the "I Love You" Freak-Out, a scenario that has played out in numerous TV shows, movies, and books.

Only problem? It's a big fat lie.

The phrase "I love you" is not a relationship killer. Guys don't recoil in horror when we hear it uttered by our girlfriends. Quite the opposite—we melt. We feel overjoyed, aroused, warm in the glow of her affection. And we can't wait to say it back.

I have lived all over the world, from Nashville to New York to London. I've never once encountered a man so rugged, so afraid of commitment, that he hightailed it out of town when his girlfriend dropped the L-bomb. Any guy who's that freaked out by love needs to have his head examined. (And not the head that's between his legs.)

I have to laugh out loud at that one.

But while it makes for good comedic fodder, the "I Love You" Freak-Out is starting to take its toll.

According to Dr. Thomas G. Iverson, clinical psychologist and renowned relationship expert, women are more afraid to say "I love you" than ever before.

"They're worried about scaring the guy off and they don't want to appear vulnerable or clingy," Iverson says. "Movies and television frequently portray relationships in a false light, and this is no exception. The ironic part is, most men are completely comfortable with the phrase 'I love you.' They have no problem hearing it, and they have no problem saying it."

And while movies usually feature couples who have dated for months, even years, without professing their love, real-life lovers are rarely so gun-shy. "Believe it or not, most people say 'I love you' within the first six weeks of dating," Iverson reveals. "However, that's slowly starting to change as women are becoming more reserved emotionally. They're holding back more than ever before—while men are increasingly getting in touch with their emotional side. Women are terrified of the man's reaction, so they don't profess their feelings as openly as they once did."

You hear that, guys? Now, take my advice and show this article to your girlfriends. It may be just the nudge she's waiting for.

Well.

It's refreshing to see a guy who's so open about his feelings—although the article's a little cheesy. I scroll through the *Metro Guy* website, reading more of Ty's pieces. Some are humorous: "PMS: Pissy Man's Syndrome. Contrary to popular belief, we guys have our time of the month, too—here's what to do when it's yours." Others are heartfelt: "Cry, Baby! Why it's okay to release those pent-up tears." I'm slightly disturbed, though, when I run across a cover piece he's written titled "Multiple Orgasms and Me: One Man's

Journey into Uncharted Waters." I decide to save that one for later.

* * *

I pop out to pick up a few things for tonight—some breath mints, a fresh tube of lip gloss. I get back to find the office in disarray.

"Dennis Moop's been calling all afternoon," Courtney tells me. "He said it's 'a matter of life or death.' "

Uh-oh. "Do you know what it's about?"

"He wouldn't tell me. He said he wanted to speak with you directly. I tried your cell, but it went straight through to voice mail."

"It probably needs charging," I say, fishing my pink Razr out.

"Dennis said he would send you an e-mail explaining the situation."

Oh, brother. Knowing Dennis, there's no telling what's going on.

"Thanks, I'll check it now." I go into my office, boot up my computer, and wait for my Outlook in-box to load.

Dennis Moop took one of my seminars last summer and liked it so much that he signed up for it again in the fall. And then, just last week, he hired me as a personal, one-on-one consultant. I don't know what that says about me—either that I'm so good people keep coming back for more, or that I'm so bad you have to pay for the exact same thing multiple times before you improve.

Maybe it says that Dennis Moop is a special case who needs more attention than usual if he wants to overcome his geekiness. It's a definite possibility. I am constantly surprised by all the new strange and dorky things he comes up with.

Dennis is a twenty-seven-year-old geek who lives in his parents' basement. That, in and of itself, is not a big deal. Lots of my clients still live at home. Dennis also doesn't have a job. Again, not admirable, but not entirely unusual. The weird thing about Dennis is his hobby.

Dennis has a rock band.

I do not mean rock as in rock 'n' roll.

I mean rock—as in *actual* rocks.

All of their songs are about rocks. All of their music videos (taped on digital video equipment) feature rocks. It's a truly bizarre concept. It's kind of like how when you watch a Gorillaz video you see cartoon musicians. When you play a video of Dennis's band on YouTube, you see a table full of different hunks of rock—marble, granite, and God knows what else—swathed in bizarre outfits, dancing around in a fashion not dissimilar to the California Raisins. He accomplishes this with Final Cut digital editing software. It's a tedious, lengthy process, and a single video can take Dennis months to complete.

At first I thought it was the freakiest thing I'd ever heard of. But I must admit, it's grown on me.

The band is called Cummingtonite (pronounced exactly how you think) after Dennis's favorite rock. That's also the name of his most famous song (believe it or not, Dennis's faux band has a cult following on the Internet). I have a CD of the title song and, I have to admit, it's pretty damn funny. The chorus goes:

I'm cummingtonite,
You're cummingtonite,
Gonna please that body,
Gonna do it right.

Wanna ram your cave
With my big stalagmite.
You make me hard as granite,
Your pahoehoe tastes so nice.

Most of his songs are equally perverse, such as the classic tune "My Wood's Not Petrified When You're Around." Making matters worse, the name of Cummingtonite's self-produced CD is *Got a Boulder in My Pants.*

That's one thing I like about my job—I learn something new every day, whether I want to or not. Before I met Dennis, I had never realized there were rocks with nasty names like pahoehoe, petrified wood, and, of course, cummingtonite.

"You just know those dirty-minded scientists did that on purpose," I'd snickered when he told me about the band's name. "Who names a rock *cummingtonite*? A bunch of horn-dog scientists, that's who."

But Dennis got really offended. "No they didn't. Cummingtonite was discovered in Cummington, Massachusetts, and then they had to add *-ite* to the end because of its classification. And cummingtonite is actually a mineral, not a rock. Although that doesn't explain why the cracks in mineral rocks are called cleavage . . ."

Dennis has a geology degree from UMass Amherst, and his biggest passion in the world is his band. Because there's not a whole lot you can do with a bachelor's degree in geology, and because Dennis did not get into any of his graduate school choices, he spends all his days writing and recording stuff for Cummingtonite. Dennis sells Cummingtonite CDs and T-shirts on his website. And although he doesn't earn enough money to afford his own place, he's actually managing to pull in a decent amount of cash.

This morning, though, Dennis has a problem. His e-mail is short and frantic:

Ms. Chase,

For some inexplicable reason Dennis always calls me Ms. Chase even though we're only two years apart. For a guy with such raunchy taste in music, he has surprisingly good manners.

I think I have a girlfriend. I've been talking to someone named Jessica on eHarmony. We get along great online. But last night I said I loved her and now she wants to meet. HELP!!!!!!
Dennis Moop

Oh, no! I groan inwardly. Dennis is definitely not ready for this. In addition to being a "rock star," Dennis suffers from a severe case of social phobia, which causes him to have terrible dizzy spells whenever he's around girls—or people in general. In fact, it took nearly two months before he was able to act normal around me.

We have tons of work to do before he'll be equipped to face the dating world again. His last romantic outing was a disaster. He took a blind date to IHOP in the middle of the night and then got so nervous he fainted into his Rooty Tooty Fresh 'N Fruity breakfast. The fact that he suggested meeting at IHOP at three a.m.—and that he ordered something called Rooty Tooty Fresh 'N Fruity on a first date—speaks volumes.

Plus, call me crazy, but I can already tell this Jessica girl is not going to be Dennis's type.

Dennis is a geek personified. And Jessica? Well, Jessica is a "hot girl" name. Like Candice. Or Tiffany.

You can tell a lot about a person by his or her name. Have you ever met a nerd named Jake or Jack or Brad? A frumpy girl called Alexis or Simone? And, in the history of the world, has there ever been a dork named Zack? (I credit *Saved by the Bell* for part of this. Thanks to that show, Zack will forever be known as a "cute guy name." Zack Naylor is proof positive of that.)

And just as some names denote hotness, some names denote . . . notness. Like Stuart, Nigel, Winslow, Gilbert, and Eugene. Those poor boys never had a chance at coolness. And have you ever met a sexy, confident man named George? (Clooney being the rare exception—Costanza being the rule.)

I pick up the phone and call Dennis. He doesn't answer, so I leave a message: *"Hey, Dennis, it's Kylie Chase. I got your message. Don't do anything drastic. Let's talk. Call me at the office whenever you get this. I'll be here until three-thirty or so."*

"Hey, Kylie," Courtney says, as she strolls into my office. "Any luck catching Dennis?"

"Nah. I left a message, though. Patch him through if he calls back."

* * *

I have wisely chosen to leave the BIG ONE car in my office garage until the whole license plate issue gets sorted out. So I am, once again, at the mercy of the Chicago Transit Authority. I leave the office just after three-thirty, successfully bypassing the Friday afternoon traffic.

On the train ride back to my apartment I hear a melody in

my head of cheesy love songs—Barry White, Celine Dion, even "Let's Get It On" by Marvin Gaye. I mentally try to tune it out. No need to get carried away. . . .

If I want to look spectacular, I'll need plenty of time to prepare. I get dressed in my favorite navy Chanel pantsuit. It has a killer neckline, perfect for going braless. Unfortunately, weight loss has wreaked havoc on my breasts. Whereas they were once firm and round, losing weight has made them kind of deflated. They're droopier than they should be, and flatter, too. I'm forced to rely on a low-cut Miracle Bra (with a gel insert for extra lift). In the end, it's not quite the look I would have hoped for, but it's better than the alternative—old-lady breasts.

Once I finish applying a fresh coat of Sephora makeup (cheap, but good) and slip into my favorite (and only) Prada kitten heels, I head out the door. It's twenty minutes until I'm supposed to meet Ty. I have just enough time to catch a cab to the bar. If I've timed it right, I'll make it to the bar at exactly six. I grab my Prada clutch—a gift from Ruby, who's always getting fashion freebies—and head out the door. A message pops through from Charity St. James, but I ignore it. I don't want to keep Ty Benedict waiting.

6

Cool Rule #6:

Cool people do NOT sit home alone on Friday and Saturday nights. There is only one excuse for being home on the weekends: illness. So unless you're fighting a nasty case of mono, get out there and socialize!

Unfortunately, Ty Benedict doesn't seem to feel the same way about me.

I stand nervously by the bar, my eyes moving between the door and my watch. It's six twenty-eight and still no sign of Ty. I tried his cell phone, but it went straight to voice mail. I opted not to leave a message. I didn't want to sound desperate, like I was standing around eagerly awaiting his arrival. Even though I was. I figure I'll give him until six-forty and then call again, this time leaving a casual message. Something along the lines of, *"Hi Ty, Kylie Chase here. I was hoping to meet up with you tonight but no worries. I have to leave for my dinner date soon. But if you get this within the next ten minutes, we could probably squeeze in a quick aperitif."*

Maybe he's really ugly in person? Maybe the pictures in *Metro Guy* and on Page Six aren't truly representative of what he looks like.

Maybe he's forgotten?

I begin jockeying for a position at the bar. "Can I get a glass of white wine?" I ask the bartender. I've been holding off on getting a drink until Ty arrives. I don't want to look like a lush. But it's coming up on seven o'clock. I'd say it's a fair bet that he's not coming.

I'm bummed out, and even though I try to avoid having excessive amounts of alcohol (too many carbs), I figure I deserve a drink—or five. Once I have my wine I find a quiet table in the corner and plop down, feeling defeated. Sitting in a bar, alone, on a Friday night definitely doesn't fit in with my Rules of Cool. But at the moment I'm so depressed that I don't care.

Being stood up sucks. There's no other way to describe it. This hasn't happened to me in years, and I thought, perhaps foolishly, that this kind of thing didn't happen to thin people. In my mind, there's a great divide between the fat and the skinny. It's stupid, I know.

Few things are more depressing than sitting alone in a crowded room, so after one glass of wine I duck out of the bar and catch a cab home.

"Hey, wait up!" I hear a voice call out as I round the corner toward my apartment. "Is that you, Kyle?"

I whirl around. It's Genevieve, one of the pseudohippies from across the hall. Lately Genevieve has taken to calling me Kyle. I actually kind of like it. Boy nicknames are very in right now.

I offer a small wave. "Hi."

"What's shaking?"

"Not too much," I say, trying to strike the perfect balance between friendly and disinterested. It's not that I dislike her. But I'm self-conscious about being caught at home on a Friday night. Don't get me wrong. I spend lots of nights at home. But I'm usually more careful about hiding it.

Genevieve and her husband, Bill, moved in last summer and have been mildly amusing, mildly annoying ever since. They pride themselves on their lacto-vegan, all-organic lifestyle. I find that kind of cool. What's *not* cool is the way their apartment always reeks of incense (sometimes tinged with pot), which stinks up the entire floor. They also have this weird open relationship in which they're both free to sleep with other people.

Genevieve fixes her watery, glazed-over eyes on me. "Funny bumping into you, Kyle. You're usually way scarce during the weekends."

I blush. As I always tell my clients, there is only one acceptable excuse for being home on a weekend night. It's one of the first lessons I teach in class. "I'm not feeling well," I lie. "I think I'm coming down with a cold." I fake a tiny sniffle, for effect.

Genevieve pats me on the arm. "It's these February days. Chicago this time of year is murder on your immune system. Want to come over and partake in an herbal refresher?"

"If by herbal refresher you mean pot, then count me in!" I joke. Actually, a part of me is serious. I have never really been into that, but at the moment I could use the distraction. I want to forget about Ty Benedict and his stupid flirty e-mails and his six-figure screenplay deal and his Matt Damon–esque smile and his celebrity girlfriends. Which isn't easy to do.

"I was thinking of some echinacea tea, but if you're in the mood, I could make a few calls. . . ."

"Nah, I think I'd better pass," I tell her. "I'm gonna go climb into bed. Thanks, anyway."

A few minutes later I'm curled up on the couch in the fetal position when I hear my cell phone go off.

It's Ty! I think excitedly, running over and retrieving my cell from my purse.

My hopes are dashed when I see that it's not a call from Ty Benedict. Instead, it's a text message from Dennis Moop. The message is marked urgent, so I flip the phone open and start reading:

Ms. Chase,
I hope you don't mind this intrusion. I got your number from your assistant, Ms. Courtney Procter. Do you have a minute to help me with something?
Dennis Moop

Before I even have the chance to reply, my phone starts buzzing again. It's another text from Dennis. His message is so long that I have to keep scrolling and scrolling and scrolling to read all of it. Why can't he just call?

Ms. Chase,
Okay, here's the problem in case u r willing to help me.

There's a Star Wars *convention in town tonight and I was thinking of taking Jessica there. I know you said sci-fi stuff is bad for a first date, but maybe you're wrong? It would give me the chance to really impress Jessica. I'd be the best-looking guy in the room, what with all those Chewbacca and Jabba the Hutt clones walking around. And I wouldn't wear my Obi-Wan Kenobi uniform or bring my light saber. And I refilled my Xanax prescription this morning, so I won't have the fainting problem.*

Oh. God. No. He can't be serious. I dial Dennis's number. It rings and rings and he doesn't pick up. I try back and he doesn't answer. Fine, then. Texting it is! I'm in the process of replying to his text when yet another message comes through.

Never mind. It's decided. I'm going to ask Jessica to meet me there. I hope she says yes. I've decided to wear the costume. If she sees me as Obi-Wan maybe she'll think I look like Ewan McGregor. Ewan McGregor is popular with the ladies, is he not?

Oh, God. This is *bad.* Worse than I feared. I try calling again, but he still doesn't pick up. Finally, I text, *Answer your phone!*

It works.

"Hello," a tiny voice says. "Is this Ms. Chase?"

I recognize him right away.

"It's Kylie," I correct. "Kylie, not Ms. Chase."

He ignores this. "When my Caller ID showed your number I thought it was a mistake! I didn't think you'd buzz me back on a weekend. But you'll be so proud of me. I took your advice. For the first Friday night in three months, I'm not at home playing with my rocks!"

I bite my lip to keep from snorting. I wonder if Dennis realizes how bad that sounds. I figure anyone who writes lyrics about "pahoehoe tasting so nice" is probably well aware of the double meaning.

"I'm going out!"

"Yeah, I know. To the *Star Wars* convention? I didn't even realize you liked that series. I thought you were more of a Cartoon Network kind of guy."

"Cartoon Network is like my wife," he says. "But I'm cheating on her with the Federation tonight. *Star Wars* is my dirty little mistress." He dissolves into a fit of laughter.

Jeez. Why, oh, why does every nerd on the face of planet earth have to love science fiction? Or, more to the point, why do *I* have to love it? Why can't I like *Gilmore Girls* or *CSI: Miami* or something else totally normal? I curse myself for having such bad taste. As it is, the only "normal" show I genuinely love is *Grey's Anatomy.* Ruby got me into it at the end of the first season. And thank God for that. I'm happy that there's at least one trendy TV show I truly adore.

"So I assume this girl's into *Star Wars*, too, since she's agreed to meet you at the convention."

"I think everyone likes *Star Wars.*"

"Never assume that other people share your interests," I chastise him. "That's rule number nineteen!" No wonder he's hiring me for the third time.

"Uh-oh. Jessica said yes, but I didn't tell her where we were going. I'm going to let it be a surprise when she gets there. What if she gets mad when she shows up?" He sounds really nervous.

"All right, what time are you meeting there?"

"Eight-thirty. The convention stops at nine-thirty, so I thought that would be a good safety net. That way, if Jessica and I don't get along, we can end the date after an hour and there's no hard feelings. But if things do work out, we can always go have coffee somewhere. I was trying to follow rule number six."

At least he remembered something. "That's actually a really good plan. Except for the *Star Wars* part."

"I know," he moans. "What if she hates sci-fi? Why didn't I think to ask?" I can hear him banging something against the phone. I hope it's not his head.

"Hmm." It's almost seven forty-five. I think fast. "Okay, it's probably too late to cancel. So let's look at the bright side.

You like this girl, she likes you. Maybe you'll have a fantastic time together. But the costume . . . you can't go through with that. You need to meet her as yourself. Now, let's talk about your outfit."

"I have my outfit!"

"By outfit do you mean . . . is the Force with you?" I ask.

He quips, "The Force is with me."

Oh, fuck. "Okay, listen to me, Dennis. You have *got* to change into normal clothes." Of course, the clothes Dennis usually wears are far from normal. But I don't think this is the time to mention that. "That's one way you can guarantee the date will go smoother."

"I can't. I'm already on the El."

I groan inwardly. "You're on the El dressed as Obi-Wan Kenobi?"

"I am indeed. It's kinda cool. People keep looking at me and shouting lines from the movies."

"And you didn't happen to bring a change of clothes with you, by any chance?"

"No. I have a Darth Vader cape in my bag, if that helps."

"Not really." I take a deep breath, trying to think. "All right, I'm on my way now. I'll meet you there."

"It's at the convention center. If you take the El you have to transfer—"

"I know where it is," I cut him off. I don't mean to be rude, but time is of the essence. And, besides, I've been there before. To another *Star Wars* convention, in another lifetime. "What size are you?"

"What size?" he croaks. "You aren't talking about . . . I mean, well, a girl's never asked me *that* kind of question before. Except once in high school this cheerleader teased me about my shoe size, but that's a myth, isn't it?"

Oh, God. "I'm talking about *clothes*, Dennis. Not stalagmites," I say, putting it in a context I know he'll understand.

"Clothes?"

"Yes, clothes. You know, shirts, pants, et cetera." I balance the phone against my ear, pulling on my coat as I talk. "I need to know your clothing size."

"I thought it was impolite to ask a lady that kind of thing?"

I grimace. "Um, Dennis, I hate to break it to you, but you're not a lady."

Dennis laughs, a loud, almost maniacal bellow. It sounds out of place against his high-pitched voice. "I was making a little joke, Ms. Chase."

"I see." I steer him back on topic. "So about your clothes . . ." I quickly get his measurements and then dash out the door. "I'll meet you in front of the convention center in thirty minutes," I tell him as I thunder down the stairs. "And whatever you do, don't go inside and meet Jessica until *after* I get there."

The convention center is a good twenty-minute cab ride from my apartment. I make a pit stop at the Gap, where I purchase a pair of khakis and an XXL black wool sweater and then catch another cab. By the time I reach the convention center it's eight twenty-five. I dart out of the cab and make a beeline for the side entrance, which is where Dennis and I have agreed to meet.

"Ms. Chase!" I hear him scream as I approach. It's a good thing Dennis catches my attention. He blends in so well. I'd never have spotted him in the sea of *Star Wars* fanboys streaming in and out of the convention center. True to his word, Dennis is decked out in full Obi-Wan Kenobi garb. He even has a fake clip-on ponytail similar to the one Ewan McGregor wore in *The Phantom Menace*.

Dennis Moop does not look like how you're probably picturing him. Most people are expecting Screech or Urkel or some other classic nerd.

But Dennis is a bodybuilder. He spends a good three hours a day in the gym lifting weights. He's really short—no more than five foot four—and he probably weighs in the neighborhood of two hundred fifty pounds. Pure muscle, of course. I've seen this phenomenon before—short guys who are ridiculously ripped. Growing up, they were likely picked on for being "runts." And because they can't change their height, they compensate by buffing up.

"I brought Jessica a gift," he says, looking really pleased with himself. "On account of how you said it's always a good idea to give a girl something on a first date."

Uh-oh. I approach this delicately. "That depends."

"On what?"

"On the girl, the date, and the gift." It also depends on the guy, but I don't say that. A guy like Dennis probably needs a little coaching before he starts picking out presents. I hope he hasn't gotten her something really weird, like a Chia Pet.

"I don't understand."

"The biggest thing is to make sure the gift is date-appropriate. You wouldn't give a girl a big bouquet of flowers if your date is to play tennis, for example."

"Oh—oh, yes! This is *definitely* date-appropriate." Dennis reaches into his backpack and pulls out a large box. "Ta-da!" He starts jumping up and down and clapping his hands together. "Open it! Open it!"

I slowly ease the top off the box and pull out a Darth Vader costume.

"It's not really her size, but I think she'll like it."

I take a deep breath. Didn't we just go over this earlier? "How do you know she'll like it? You don't even know if she's into *Star Wars*," I point out.

"It's a gift. Everyone likes a gift."

"Would you like it if I gave you a Strawberry Shortcake doll?" I move out of the way to let a guy in a Han Solo costume pass by. "And just FYI, if the answer to that question is yes, I really don't want to know."

"I'd hate a Strawberry Shortcake doll. A cake I could live with, but a doll? Blech."

"See where I'm going with this?"

He shifts anxiously from one foot to the other. "Yeah. But I remembered something after I got off the phone with you. Jessica's seen all the *Star Wars* films. We discussed it once before. So she'll definitely like the Vader costume."

"Maybe . . . but there's a difference between an armchair fan and a fanboy. Keep that in mind." I hand him the bag of clothes.

He makes a face. "I hate the Gap. I've never even been in there."

"You've never been in the Gap? Then how do you know you hate it?"

Dennis shrugs. "It's one of those things."

"You should be more open-minded," I suggest.

"I bet you've never watched a video of a four-hour knee surgery like I have."

"Uh. . . ." I give him a strange look. "I don't believe so."

"And would you want to?" He fingers the Gap bag in his hands.

"No. Of course not."

"See. *You* should be more open-minded, too."

I laugh. "Fair enough. Now, hurry up and go get changed!" I'm starting to get antsy. A corn dog vendor is set up in front of the convention center, and I can smell the food aroma wafting toward us. It's taking every fiber of self-control not to go over and buy something. I'm extremely bummed out about Ty—although being here with Dennis is a pleasant enough distraction. Even so, my first instinct, whenever I'm feeling blue, is to eat. Despite losing weight, I still struggle with my food obsession every day. Plus, being here at the convention center brings back memories of my convention days when some jackass advised me to dress as Jabba the Hutt, instead of Natalie Portman's glamorous Queen Amidala. (A bad costume choice, perhaps, but I was in the throes of my weight-loss regime and had already dropped thirty pounds. I wanted to show off a little.)

"Be right back," Dennis says as he dashes around the corner to find a bathroom. A few minutes later he returns. I have to give myself credit—he looks amazing. Much better than I've ever seen him look before.

"See, you should reconsider your position on the Gap. Their clothes suit you really well."

He grins. "Thanks."

"Jessica is going to love you," I assure him. "Anyway, I'll get going now so you can meet her."

"Stay!" he says, a little too quickly. "I don't want to wait by myself. I'll look like a loser."

"Dennis, I've seen five guys go by dressed as Jar Jar Binks. Freaking Jar Jar Binks, who isn't even a good character. Trust me, your prediction from earlier was right. You're going to be the coolest guy in the room."

"But remember what you always say about spending Friday and Saturday nights alone," he reminds me. "I'll look cooler if I have someone waiting with me."

I'm not sure it's the best tack for Dennis to wait for his date with another girl, but he looks at me with such desperate, pleading eyes that I can't say no. Besides, it's not like I have anything better to do.

"Okay, I'll stay. But just until she gets here."

We make small talk while we wait. I'm pleased to see how much Dennis's social skills have improved since I first met him. He seems surprisingly at ease around me. He keeps up his half of the conversation, asking me about my weekend and my family (he had read an article about Swank in the paper, and is interested in finding out more about Dad).

"How are things going with Cummingtonite?" I finally ask.

Dennis's ears turn pink. He always reacts this way when I bring up the band. He frequently e-mails me new song lyrics and burns me copies of videos, but it embarrasses him to talk about it in person.

"Fine," he mumbles.

"Any new songs?"

"There is one, yeah."

"Can you tell me about it?"

Dennis shuffles from one foot to the other. "Yeah, okay. It's about a type of rock called gneiss." He pronounces it *nice.* "The song is called 'Gneiss Gneiss Baby.' It's performed to the tune of 'Ice Ice Baby.' "

"Pretty clever," I say.

"It is. Except, uh, there's a flaw with it," he explains. "Ice is actually a type of rock. So I should have left that part of the lyric alone. I could have just rewritten the other parts, and made it a funny song about ice. There was no need to rewrite the title and chorus."

"So why did you?"

"Uh, gneiss is pretty much one of the hardest rocks in the entire world. . . . And so there was a lot to work with there."

"I follow you."

"Plus, I thought if I left it as 'Ice Ice Baby' people might not get it. Most people probably don't realize that ice is a rock." He shakes his head, as if such a mistake were unforgivable. "Most people probably think ice is nothing more than frozen water."

"Isn't it?" I ask.

Dennis closes his eyes and then opens them again. I get the feeling he's counting to ten, trying to let his exasperation die down before he gives me a response. He lets out a deep breath. "Yes. But it's so much more than that."

I decide to change the subject. "I bet Jessica will be here soon!" I say cheerily. "Are you excited about meeting her?"

"I'm mostly nervous."

"What does she look like?" I ask. "You guys have exchanged pictures, right?" Please tell me they have. Otherwise, Dennis might be in for a big shock—or the other way around.

"We have. She's pretty." He doesn't offer a more detailed assessment.

"What did she say when you sent her your picture?" I know it's a bit rude, but I can't help myself.

He beams. "She thinks I look like a real original."

Truer words have never been spoken.

"Well, I don't think you have anything to be worried about. I predict you guys are going to get along fantastically."

"She should be here any minute," Dennis says, glancing down at his digital watch.

But the minutes stretch on and still no Jessica.

"It's ten past nine," I say finally. "Why don't you try her on her cell?"

"She doesn't have a cell phone. She thinks they're annoying. Says they only interrupt movies and cause car crashes."

"She might have something there," I agree, even though I would never, ever give up my cell. You'd have to pry it from my cold, dead hands.

We wait and wait and Jessica never shows. I'm not sure if something came up or if she got cold feet. Perhaps she got to the convention center and bolted when she discovered Dennis's big date involved a night of light sabers and alien impersonators. Maybe she saw Dennis himself and changed her mind. Any way you slice it, he's been stood up.

We wait until almost ten o'clock—watching the stream of Han Solos, Grand Moff Tarkins, and Yodas pour out of the convention center. Finally, when the corn dog vendor has called it a night and the last Queen Amidala has strolled by, we give up.

"I'm sorry she did this," I tell him, as we walk through the cold toward the El station. "It's not your fault."

"It's *all* my fault. This was the worst night of my entire life," he groans, stubbing his foot against a crack in the sidewalk.

"It's not exactly a red-letter day for me either, if that helps."

Dennis scowls. "I guess spending time with me ruins any girl's night."

"Hey," I say softly, "that's not what I meant at all."

"Yeah, right. There are ten million other things someone like you could be doing right now."

Sure there are, I think to myself. *Like huddling under the covers and watching* Becker *and wallowing in self-pity over the fact that Ty Benedict is an asshole.*

"Instead, you're with me," Dennis goes on. "See, this is why I don't like to go out. I'm happier at home with my stupid rocks and my stupid minerals and my stupid DigiCart music mixer."

"Dennis, please don't do this to yourself. Jessica sucks for standing you up. But it's not your fault. You can't let one bad night determine how you live the rest of your life."

"I'm sorry I'm such miserable company." He stops in his tracks and glares at me. "I can walk the rest of the way on my own, thank you very much." He folds his arms across his chest.

"Dennis." I turn and put my hand on his shoulder. "Listen, it has nothing to do with you. The reason I had a bad night was . . . well, personal problems." I figure it's best to gloss over what happened with Ty Benedict. There's no need to let my clients in on those kinds of details. Plus, I'm not eager to recount the story.

"Oh, *please.* You're just saying that because you can't think of anything off the top of your head. You can't even come up with a decent lie. But that's okay. I know I'm a loser!"

I squeeze my eyes shut. "I got stood up, too, okay? This guy made a date with me and then he never showed up."

Dennis stares at me for a long time—so long it starts to feel uncomfortable—and then he reaches into his backpack and pulls out the Darth Vader mask. "Here." He offers it to me.

"Do you want me to hold this?"

"No, I want you to *have* it."

I stare at him, confused.

"I know it seems weird, but I've always thought of him as a good-luck charm." He pats the helmet. "That's why I wanted to give it to Jessica. She's been down on her luck lately, and I thought it might cheer her up."

"That's sweet, but I can't take it."

Dennis shakes his head in frustration. "No, you *have* to!" he insists. A few people turn to stare and he, thankfully, lowers his tone. "It would mean a lot to me. But just the mask, okay," he says, suddenly worried that I'm trying to snag the whole outfit. "I'd really like to hang on to the cape. It doubles for my Darth Maul costume."

"I see." I take the mask from his hands. "In that case, thank you."

We trudge along in silence for a few minutes, and then Dennis says, "So we both got betrayed. Two bad occurrences in one night. Who'd have thought?" He gives me a lopsided smile. "Then again, they say bad things always happen in threes."

"That's an old wives' tale," I say. "You make your own luck."

He looks hurt for a moment. "So you don't want my Darth Vader mask?"

"No, I didn't mean—" I start. "I'd love to have the mask," I say. "I'd be honored."

Dennis smiles, then looks embarrassed. His face starts blushing, a bright crimson red that almost matches his hair.

"Thanks, Ms. Chase. You know, this night wasn't so bad after all."

* * *

Dennis and I part ways at the station and I hike the rest of the way back to my apartment in the Gold Coast. I live in a fairly upscale, yuppieish area. Even so, walking alone at night isn't always the smartest idea, so I make sure to keep my eyes open and my pace quick. I'm actually getting a decent workout, which is good, considering I skipped my belly-dancing class earlier tonight.

As I get closer to my apartment complex I start to smell it—that unmistakable stench of smoke. Something's burning. I can't make out where it's coming from, because the sky is too cloudy. Maybe it will rain soon, I think, and help put out the blaze.

I don't see it until I'm almost there. As I round the corner onto my street I catch sight of it in the distance: a bright, horrifying ball of smoke and flames.

My apartment. Oh please God, don't let it be my apartment! The office building next door, the rare antiques shop on the corner—anything but my apartment.

I break into a run, but the closer I get, the more horrible it is.

Well, I think wryly, for once Dad's stupid astrology chart was right. Bad things are happening to me.

My cell phone starts ringing. Automatically, I bring it to my ear.

"Kylie! We're watching it on the news!" my father blurts out before I can even mutter hello. Maybe he's psychic, too. "Are you okay?"

"I'm fine," I mumble, out of breath and unable to comprehend what's happening. The whole night feels like a weird, lucid dream. I'm going to wake up tomorrow and realize that all of it—Ty and the sci-fi convention and the burning lights—has merely been a figment of my imagination.

Dad's questions are coming so fast. "Did you lose all your stuff? Do you need a place to stay? You want me to drive into the city and pick you up?"

"I-I don't know," I stutter. "I can't really talk right now."

My dad has never been one to take a hint. He keeps going, rambling about insurance premiums and fireproofing and the general dangers of apartment living. "Why don't you come stay with us, Kylie? You'll be safer out here in the suburbs."

"Let me just . . . let me find out what's happened." I can barely get the words out. "I-I'll call you back when I know the extent of the damage."

But even from here, more than a hundred feet away, I can tell it's *bad*—twenty-nine years of my life up in smoke bad. I spy Genevieve and her husband off in the distance, but I don't feel like seeing anyone. I turn and move the other way, jogging briskly down the path until I'm safely out of view, until the fire is just a small blip of light in the distance.

Then I sit down on the curb—cell phone in one hand, Darth Vader mask in the other—and start to cry.

7

Cool Rule #7:

No ifs, ands, or buts about it: living with your parents after you've reached age twenty-six is horribly uncool (twenty-four if you're a guy).

Whoever coined the phrase "bad things come in threes" didn't know what they were talking about.

Bad things also come in fours, fives, sixes, sevens, eights, and nines. I'm living proof.

Bad Thing Number One: My apartment is *gone.* I have lost everything. Clothes. Books. Movies. Photographs. You name it, I no longer have it. (Maybe losing the photographs isn't so bad. At least all evidence of my fat years has now been destroyed.)

Bad Thing Number Two: I am a complete moron who opted not to renew her renter's insurance when the policy expired last fall. In other words, I have absolutely no way to replace all the things I've lost.

Bad Thing Number Three: I have nowhere to live. Despite my father's assumption, I am obviously not going to be moving back into my parents' house—for reasons too numerous to list here.

Bad Thing Number Four: Ruby has offered to let me crash at her place, but that's not really an option.

Ruby's condo is where frat boys go to die.

I'm serious; it's a hellhole. She has three roommates, but from the look of the place you'd think a dozen people lived there. Her driveway—which can squeeze in three cars—is always full, and there are usually two or more vehicles parked out on the street. Her living room is constantly overflowing with an assortment of frat-guy trash: empty beer bottles, fast-food containers, cigarette cartons, crumpled magazines, and dirty clothes.

Ruby's three roommates—Marty (a girl), Kelly (a guy), and Selby (also a guy)—are all Greek expatriates. Greek as in "Greek Life" and "Go Greek!"—not as in the Mediterranean country. There's also an assortment of regular visitors. You know the type. Those leeches who hang out at an apartment so often they might as well live there.

I have never understood why Ruby doesn't just move out and get her own place. She could certainly afford it. Her modeling work brings in plenty of money.

"I'm never there, so what does it matter," said Ruby when I asked her about it several months ago.

It was true. When she and her boyfriend, Davey, were in an "on" phase, Ruby spent all of her time at his place.

"Why don't you stay with Davey until I get back?" she suggested when I turned down her offer to stay in her condo. "I know he wouldn't mind."

It was a generous offer, but Davey lived in a studio apartment. While stylish, it afforded virtually no privacy. And I'm not sure I want to get that up close and personal with Davey, who is a Buddha-loving, clothes-hating, acoustic-guitar-playing "artiste." Much as I appreciated Ruby's offer, the idea of waking up to Davey's naked guitar strumming was not my idea of fun. Plus, I knew there was a fairly decent chance they'd be broken up again by the end of next week. I didn't want to be in the middle of that.

Bad Thing Number Five: All of my art supplies—and my entire collection of work—got destroyed. My sole possession is a Darth Vader mask.

Bad Thing Number Six: Courtney tracked the BIG ONE license plates down. They belong to a cheeky seismologist from the University of Chicago. But he's in Michigan for the next six weeks, and we won't be able to swap license plates until he gets back.

Bad Thing Number Seven: Ruby is in Koh Samui, Thailand, on that photo shoot. I know this is ultimately a good thing. I'm really happy for Ruby that she got this great assignment. But I can't help feeling bummed. I'm going through some tough crap right now and I could use her support. I got to talk to her briefly this morning (she called after getting my e-mail about the fire).

Bad Thing Number Eight: Dennis still doesn't know why Jessica stood him up. She never answered her phone, and she hasn't returned any of his messages.

Bad Thing Number Nine: I still don't know why Ty Benedict stood me up. He never answered his phone, and he hasn't returned any of my messages.

Bad Thing Number Ten: Dennis Moop has enrolled in a Magic for Beginners class to cheer himself up. In other words, he's just undone months of hard work in one fell swoop.

* * *

I opt not to stay at my parents' house and get a hotel room instead. Naturally, there's a huge advertising convention in town, so I wind up paying $220 for one night in a crappy, freezing-cold room on the outskirts of town. I toss and turn all night long, shivering beneath the flimsy blankets.

Every time I start to drift off, my cell phone rings. It's always the same person—my father—calling to check and see how I'm doing and to beg me to come stay at their house. Around five a.m. I finally shut my phone off. But I don't stop thinking about his offer.

Maybe I could just pop by my mom and dad's house for a shower and a fresh change of clothes? Actually, that's not a bad idea. I have a couple of boxes of clothes stored in my parents' attic. Most of them are old "fat clothes," which aren't of much use to me right now (thank God). But I did put a box of summer clothes over there a few months ago.

My mood perks up when I remember that. At least I haven't lost everything. I rack my brain, trying to remember what's there. As best I can recall, I have a few L.A.M.B. tops, some Joie outfits, a Miss Sixty skirt, and two pairs of Dolce & Gabbana jeans. A pretty nice collection, indeed.

So that settles it. I'll go out to my parents' house, have a shower, pick up my clothes, and then be on my way.

* * *

My parents live in Oak Park, Illinois. It's about a twenty-minute train ride from downtown Chicago or, in my case, a thirty-minute car trip. Not a terribly long commute. Unless you consider the fact that I'm still cruising around with license plates that read BIG ONE.

Fortunately, I make it out to Oak Park without incident.

Oak Park is best known as being the home of the largest collection of Frank Lloyd Wright houses in the world. More than twenty-five buildings in Oak Park were designed by

Frank Lloyd Wright. Some of the houses are still being lived in; others have been turned into show homes. All of them are worth millions.

My parents do not own one of the Frank Lloyd Wright houses. Although I wish they did. That would be infinitely cool.

Instead, my parents live in a nice, yet modest, two-story detached house with a good-sized backyard and an indoor hot tub. They had the hot tub installed when I was fourteen years old, although I can honestly say I've never so much as stuck a pinky toe in it. And for once this has nothing to do with my weight (although I do cringe whenever putting on a bathing suit—even now).

I caught my parents having sex in the hot tub the night after it was put in. It was a horrifying, nauseating moment for all of us. And I have never been able to look at hot tubs in the same way since.

As I turn off the expressway toward Oak Park, all I can think is, *I am not supposed to be here. I am Not Thirty years old. I cannot do this.*

When I pull into their driveway, a thought occurs to me. I hadn't bothered to call and let them know I was coming. I hope they won't mind. I park my car and get out.

I am only staying for a few days. I am only staying for a few days. I am only staying for a few days.

It plays over and over again in my mind as I stroll up the driveway. I reach the front door just as my dad is pulling it open.

"Kylie!" He runs forward and gives me a hug. Despite the fact that he is a professional chef, surrounded by scrumptious food all day, my father has never had a serious weight problem—he's only pleasantly plump. And my mother can easily fit into a size two. As a matter of fact, I'm the only one in our family who has ever struggled with weight.

"I thought you might wind up here." Dad doesn't seem surprised in the least, just happy. "Come on, let's go inside."

"Hi, Kylie," Mom says, greeting me as I come into the living room.

"I've got something for you. Wait right there," Dad instructs me and goes dashing off toward the kitchen.

Wow! In anticipation of my arrival, he must have prepared some food. I can't eat it, though. My diet doesn't allow most of the things Dad cooks. Then again, I've been through a hellacious night. A little treat is in order. I wonder what Dad has cooked up for me? Maybe he's going to bring me some of his delicious ginger crème brûlée. I haven't had that in almost ten years. Or possibly his famous anise and orange-braised scallops. Although, given that it's only ten in the morning, he's probably fixed some type of breakfast food. Like homemade cinnamon rolls with walnuts and dried cranberries. I'm salivating at the thought.

"Here it is!" Dad gasps, holding up a piece of paper. Where's the food? "Didn't I tell you this was going to happen? Didn't I predict it, just yesterday?"

Mom ignores him. "Sweetie, can I get you anything?" she asks, putting her arm around my shoulder. "Something to eat? Drink?"

"You don't understand," Dad rushes on, before I can answer. "Didn't I tell you Kylie was in for a bad spell?"

Oh, God. Here it comes. I lean back against the wall.

"Carl, be quiet," Mom says, shooing him away. "Kylie's been through a lot. She doesn't need to hear about your inane predictions right now."

Dad waves the piece of paper in front of my face. "It's Mars! Mars did this to her."

My mom snickers. "Mars burned down Kylie's apartment building?"

Dad grabs my arm and squeezes it. Hard. "Mars was in the worst possible position on your chart, Kylie. I tried to call you and warn you. You should fire that assistant of yours! If only she'd given you the message," he says, shaking his head. As if this is Courtney's fault. As if by somehow hearing his prediction I could have stopped the apartment complex from burning down. Or Ty from standing me up. Or Jessica from breaking Dennis's heart. Or the BIG ONE license plates. Or any of the other bad things that had happened over the past couple of days.

Although I have to hand it to him. Whether it was caused by Mars or not I can't be sure. For once Dad's astrology prediction has come true. My life is a total wreck at the moment. I guess even the unluckiest gambler hits the jackpot every once in a while.

"Carl, why don't you go fix Kylie some breakfast. And remember what we talked about yesterday . . ." Mom says. She gives my dad a pointed look, and he nods knowingly. Then he retreats out of the room.

What's that about? I wonder. I feel my pulse quicken. Is it something to do with my weight? Oh, God. It has to be. I've been slacking off a teeny bit lately—missing workouts and indulging in carbs after six p.m. I can tell I've put on five pounds or so lately (which, coupled with my Christmas weight, is quite a load). Obviously, my parents have noticed. Mom is probably signaling Dad to let him know to fix something low-fat.

"How are you?" Mom asks, steering me toward the couch.

"You look tired. And your Chanel suit is a wreck." She makes a face. It's true. I've been wearing the Chanel suit ever since I went to meet Ty at the bar. It went with me to the *Star Wars* convention and I slept in it all night. I'm a sweaty, wrinkled mess.

"Why don't you take a shower?" Mom asks. "Then you can wear something from my closet. Just don't touch my Prada skirt. Or my Burberry Argyle sweater. And also if you could leave my Gucci—" Mom stops midsentence and smacks herself on the forehead. "Oh, God, I'm sorry, sweetie. That was incredibly rude of me. You take whatever you want, okay? Anything at all."

I nod, flattered that she even thinks I can fit into her clothes. Mom is considerably thinner than I am.

As I've mentioned, she's also something of a major fashion hound, which is one thing we have in common. The difference is Mom has always loved designer clothes, whereas I've only recently gotten into them. When I was fat, I had absolutely zero interest in labels like Marc Jacobs or Robert Rodriguez. This was more sour grapes than anything. If they weren't going to make clothes that fit me, then I wasn't going to pay attention to any of their lines.

The other difference between Mom and me is that while I have about ten pieces that I build my outfits around, Mom has an entire closet full of designer duds. And she's also paid full price for most of them. (I've been lucky enough to score a few complimentary things.)

"Thanks, Mom," I say, trudging up the stairs. "But I have a box of my summer clothes in your attic, remember? I'll just wear something from that."

"I'll bring it down for you. Just take a nice warm shower

and by the time you get out we'll have your clothes and a nice meal waiting for you," she promises.

Things are getting better by the second. But I have to keep reminding myself that this isn't a long-term solution. Or even a temporary one. In a couple days' time, I'll be out of here, cruising away from Oak Park and back toward Chicago in my Toyota Prius with the BIG ONE license plates.

I'm not quite sure where I'll go. I haven't figured out that part yet. But I know one thing for certain—I can't stay here with my mom and dad.

I can't break my own rule. I can't sink to this level of uncoolness. I have a reputation to uphold.

Then again, I won't be much good to my clients if I'm tired, grumpy, and disorganized. Staying with my parents—just for a few days, maybe a week—may not be such a bad idea. It will certainly help alleviate some of the monumental stress I've been feeling.

Living with your parents is never preferable, but it becomes kind of pathetic once you're past the age of about twenty-five. And seeing how I'm Not Thirty—well, it would be desperately uncool.

* * *

I have a lot of friends who are not my friends. I realize this now. Those seventeen hundred numbers stored in your PDA don't mean jack if none of the people actually give a damn about you.

Oh, it's not that I think they hate me or anything. I just don't think they care. They're fair-weather friends, happy to hang around when things are good, the first ones out the door when they're not.

I have a few cursory *I'm so sorry* e-mails, a few *Heard about the fire, that sucks!* comments on MySpace. But since my apartment building went up in smoke, no one has actually picked up the phone and called. For some reason, this upsets me. It's like they're doing the bare minimum necessary to maintain a friendship.

Or am I overreacting? I'm so emotionally drained right now. Am I taking things too personally?

Maybe everyone thinks I'm busy. In theory, there is probably a lot to do after a fire. Sort through your burned-up possessions, buy new things, find a place to live, meet with the fire inspectors, et cetera, et cetera.

But it's not quite like that in real life. I am too numb to do much of anything—not that there is much of anything to do. I haven't been cleared to go back into the building yet, so I have no idea how much of my stuff is salvageable (although from the preliminary report, I believe the answer is none). The living situation is taken care of (for the time being), and Courtney cleared my schedule for the next couple of days (something she did without asking—but I'm grateful for it). So I am basically sitting here, twiddling my thumbs, waiting for the next step.

Around four-thirty that afternoon it comes. I open my e-mail and—surprise, surprise—I have a message from Ty Benedict.

Kylie,
I am so so so sorry. There are not even enough words in the dictionary to describe how bad I feel. A good friend of mine got into a car accident Friday night and I was at the hospital with her. I lost my cell phone

somewhere on the way and your number was in it. I feel like a real cad.

If you'll give me another chance, I'd love to take you out again. I promise to show up this time. ☺

Also, I need to get started on my interview if you're still interested in letting me do the story (I hope). Could I call you tomorrow night around eight? Let me know if that's okay. And if so, e-mail me your number.

Yours,

Ty Benedict

I think it over for a minute. He really hurt my feelings. Then again, I understood better than anyone how things could blindside you out of nowhere.

I decide to give him another chance.

* * *

The next night I'm sprawled out on my decade-old daybed, in the pale-pink room I grew up in. A poster of the movie *Dazed and Confused* hangs on the wall—one of my many vain attempts to fit in. And a Smashing Pumpkins CD is playing in the background. I feel fat, and depressed, and lonely. And I'm waiting for a guy to call.

In other words, it's like I'm fifteen again.

I boot up my laptop and start playing a game of online Scrabble, which proves to be a wonderful distraction. I waste thirty minutes without even noticing. I've just found a killer move—I can spell out the word SQUEEZE, and get a double bonus—when my parents' landline rings. I glance at the Caller ID. It's Ty Benedict—finally!

I don't want to pick up on the first ring—way too eager—so I let it go for one . . . two . . . three . . . four. Midway through the fourth ring, the phone goes silent and, in a panic, I grab it.

"Hello," I say casually. I hear someone click off the extension—one of my parents likely picked up at the same time I did. Phew. Thank God I got the phone before they had the chance to talk to Ty. I didn't want to give Ty my parents' number, but since my cell phone is dead (my charger got burned up in the fire, and I haven't had a chance to pick up a new one), I didn't have much choice.

"I'm looking for Kylie Chase."

"You've got her."

He laughs good-naturedly. "This is Ty Benedict from *Metro Guy*. I'm so sorry I'm late." He sounds incredibly sexy. His voice is husky and deep, with a slight Southern accent. I never knew people from Nashville sounded so hot!

"That's okay," I tell him, even though I'm a little ticked off.

"My agent's in town from L.A.," he explains. "We were supposed to meet for a quick drink but it wound up turning into a three-hour event. Anyway, didn't mean to keep you waiting. I'm sure you've got a million other things you'd rather do than chat with some journalist." He sounds genuinely apologetic.

"Don't worry about it. I promise it's okay."

"Thanks! You're the best, Kylie. Now, we'd originally discussed an hour-long interview, but since I'm so late I imagine you'll want to wrap this up by nine. I figure you've got somewhere exciting to run off to . . ."

"Nah. No big plans for tonight."

"Really? I find that hard to believe. You seem like a pretty in-demand person. I bet your social schedule is packed."

I'm about to tell him that it's not—that I'm just sitting home playing Scrabble—when common sense gets the best of me. As charming as he might seem, Ty Benedict is a journalist. I have to keep my guard up. I can't let him know how boring my life really is. And I certainly can't give away the fact that I've moved back in with my parents. I can imagine the headline now: "Cool Instructor, or Fool Instructor? Despite appearances, Kylie Chase is little more than a fraud."

"My social calendar is pretty full," I inform him.

"I thought you said you were free tonight."

"Ah, yes, but that's because it's Sunday. I always take Sunday nights off," I ad-lib. "You know, to give myself some time to regroup and relax."

"Why Sunday?" I can hear him typing in the background. "By the way, I'm recording this conversation—I hope that's okay."

"Of course it is. No problem."

"Great! So, anyway, why Sunday nights? Why not Monday or Wednesday or Friday?"

"Sunday is the perfect time to cool down after partying," I say. "You don't want to stay home on the weekends, for obvious reasons. That's one of the first assignments I give my clients. I instruct them to start finding stuff to do on Friday and Saturday nights. Whether it be going to a big party, or an art opening, or even attending a sci-fi convention," I say, thinking of Dennis. "They just need to get out of the house and interact with other people."

"Do you find it's true that a lot of," he pauses, "quote unquote . . . nerds . . . tend to spend a considerable amount of time absorbed with gadgets? You know, computers, video games, et cetera?"

"Oh, yeah. There's a lot of truth to that. People with social insecurities often spend a considerable amount of time sitting around the house—their homes really do become their fortresses."

"Very true," Ty agrees. "That's why I'm rarely ever home."

I laugh. "I'm surprised a big celeb like yourself is kicking back at home tonight."

"It's a rare event," he says. "But it's nice, just sitting in my jammies, talking to you and listening to satellite radio."

"Howard Stern?" I guess.

"Nah, XM." Ty laughs. "Believe me, my brief, *brief* time at *The Howard Stern Show* was enough to burn me out completely."

He's given me the perfect opening, so I go ahead and ask it. "That seems like kind of an odd place for you to have worked. It's sort of the polar opposite of what *Metro Guy* stands for. I know I've heard Stern bash the magazine on the air before."

"I kind of looked at the Howard Stern thing like an experiment," Ty says. "You'd be amazed the kinds of things you learn working there."

"Like how to spot implants? Or the best place to buy midget porn?"

Ty chuckles. "For sure. But that's not what I meant. You know, Howard is a decent guy. He means well, he really does. But the guests are so ridiculous, it's hard to take the whole thing seriously."

"I see what you mean."

"The people we had on there were so sad. They're so desperate for attention that they're willing to do anything, go to any embarrassing length you ask them to, for that small three-minute window of fame."

"Good point."

I normally hate being interviewed, but with Ty it's fun.

"I can't believe you're only twenty-two," I tell him. "You seem so mature for your age. I remember what I was like at twenty-two. I was a mess."

"I'll let you in on a little secret—that's not my real age," he says. "I'm actually twenty-four."

"Really?"

"Mmm-hmm. My manager thought it would be a good idea to amp up my credentials, you know, make me more bankable before my agent sent my script out. So we beefed up my qualifications and shaved a few years off my age."

"But you're already so young!" I exclaim. "What difference does it make if you're twenty-two or twenty-four? It's still impressive."

"Thanks," he says. "But Hollywood is a cutthroat town. There are seventeen-year-old kids inking million-dollar deals every day. I had to think outside the box if I wanted to compete."

Outside the box of reality, I think to myself. Although I have no room to talk, what with my trumped-up bio and all.

"So what's your screenplay about?" I ask. "Or are you not allowed to talk about it?"

"Oh, I can definitely talk about it."

I can tell he's dying to give me all the details.

"It's called *The Bad Old Days*, and it's about a forty-year-old guy who's obsessed with his youth. He still plays with army men and watches cartoons."

Sounds like a few guys I know.

"He's tired of paying bills and going to meetings and having to answer to his wife. More than anything, he wishes he could just be a kid again, back when things were simple."

"So let me guess," I jump in, "he lies about his age and convinces the world that he's only twenty-two!" I mean it as a joke, but Ty doesn't seem to find it too funny.

He clears his throat. "No, actually, what happens is one night he wishes on a shooting star," Ty continues. "He wishes to be transported back in time so he can recapture the glory days of his youth. Then he wakes up the next morning and discovers his wish has come true. He's now twelve years old again, with braces and acne and bad hair. Only nothing goes according to plan. Hence the title, *The Bad Old Days.*" He pauses. "What do you think?"

I have to admit, it doesn't blow me away. It's a cute enough idea, but I don't see what makes it so unusual, so spectacular, that it has netted Ty a six-figure deal. And the whole wishing-on-a-star bit seems pretty contrived. Maybe the writing is truly amazing? "That sounds awesome," I lie. "But where does Reese Witherspoon fit in?" I ask.

"Reese Witherspoon?" He sounds puzzled.

"I heard she's going to be starring in it."

He bursts out laughing. "I don't know where you get your Hollywood info, but you obviously don't have a subscription to *Variety.* There isn't even a female lead in my script."

I feel stupid. "Oh, well," I chuckle, playing it off. "I guess my source was wrong." No female lead? How is that going to work out?

"We're going after Will Ferrell for the main role. He hasn't signed on officially yet, but he loves the script and we're really confident he'll say yes."

"That'll be awesome," I say. "He'd be perfect for the part. The story sounds like it's got great comic potential."

"Oh, wait," Ty cuts me off. "You haven't heard the best part. Are you ready for this?"

I tell him I am.

"When the main character, Jeff, goes back in time, things get really wacky. See, this is the kicker. While the characters in the film see this twelve-year-old kid, the *audience* sees a grown man. So you've got this grown man—Will Ferrell—running around, doing silly stuff like hanging out at a roller-skating rink or playing Little League or going on a Boy Scout camping trip. Only he doesn't really fit in, because he's forty. It's comic genius! Because the line between what the viewer sees and what the characters in the movie see is completely blurred!" he finishes triumphantly.

Huh?

"It sounds kind of like an updated version of *Big*," I offer.

"Not really," he says. "In *Big*, you have Tom Hanks playing a little kid in a grown man's body. And in *The Bad Old Days*, you have something entirely different."

Something entirely different? From the sound of it, what you have is Will Ferrell playing a grown man in a grown man's body. It just doesn't make sense. Then again, I'm not a screenwriter. What do I know? Paramount obviously wouldn't pay so much money for a script that doesn't work.

"I see," I say.

"This is crazy," Ty laughs. "*I'm* the one who's supposed to be interviewing *you*."

"Right, you are."

"Hang on a sec." I can hear him ruffling through a stack of papers in the background. "You've gotten me all flustered. I can't find my notes. Ah . . . here they are. All right. You ready?"

"Definitely!"

He starts off with the obligatory questions: Where was I born? What had prompted me to start How to Be Cool? Who were some of my most interesting clients? He then moves on to asking about my Cool Rules. "I've got the list right here," Ty says. "These are some really interesting suggestions. Which one do you, personally, like best?"

I think it over. "Probably rule number fourteen: *Learn to be cool within your own limits.*"

"Yes." I can hear him typing in the background. "What exactly does that mean?"

"Well, everybody has limitations. Just because you're good at one thing doesn't mean you're going to be good at *everything.* Take professional athletes, for example. Andy Roddick is an excellent tennis player, but he might be an awful swimmer. And Lance Armstrong kicks ass at the Tour de France, but he probably couldn't win an NBA game to save his life."

"In other words, everybody's different."

"Right. And if you try to give yourself a complete and total makeover, if you try to ditch every single aspect of your personality, you'll never succeed. You have to learn how to work with what you've got," I say. "And that's why I also like rule number twenty-two: *You don't have to give up everything you love in order to be cool. But there are certain things you might want to rein in.*"

"So if some Trekkie comes to you for cool lessons—"

"And I get a few of those," I interject.

"I'll bet," he jokes. "But let me get this straight. Trekkies don't have to give up *Star Trek* in order to shed their nerdy image?"

"Correct."

"How can that be?"

"The trick is balance. The main thing they have to do is learn how to dial their fixation back a little, learn how to love something without obsessing about it. That's probably the most universal quality of nerds. They tend to have this very single-minded focus," I explain. "They find something they love—be it baseball or Everquest or just computers in general—and then they focus on it twenty-four-seven. They meet new people and they have to talk about their online role-playing game, even though no one else in the room has any interest in it whatsoever. They don't know how to check their obsessions at the door, so to speak."

"Yeah, but let me play devil's advocate for a minute here," Ty says. "I understand your argument, but I don't really know if I buy it."

"Why not?"

"Lots of people fixate on things. I'm sure Kobe Bryant eats, breathes, and sleeps basketball. He probably talks about it constantly, droning on and on to anyone who'll listen. Yet, no one on this earth would classify Kobe Bryant as a nerd. I don't think it's the obsession itself that's the problem. It's the object that the person's obsessed *with.* If you like sci-fi, for example, that's nerdy. It doesn't matter if you like it a little bit or if you like it a lot. You're still a nerd. There are some hobbies that, no matter how much you scale them back, are still going to be geeky."

An excellent point. But I have a good counterargument ready. "It's true that certain hobbies are, as I like to call it, 'nerdy by nature.' But just because you like them doesn't automatically make you a nerd."

"I'm listening. . . ."

"Okay, take *Star Wars,* for example. Those films earned billions of dollars worldwide. Hundreds of millions of people have seen them."

"True," he admits.

"A regular person like you might call up a couple of your friends and go see *Star Wars* on opening weekend. You like the series, but it's not your life. A nerd, on the other hand, spends all year talking about the films nonstop. He stakes out Skywalker Ranch. He spends hours reading *Star Wars* message boards and visiting chat rooms. And then he puts on his Han Solo costume and camps outside the theater for a month awaiting opening night," I conclude. "His life revolves around *Star Wars.* Yours does not."

I don't mention that at one point my life also revolved around *Star Wars.* Noel and I stood in line for nearly two days when *The Phantom Menace* opened. Fortunately, I had kicked my *Star Wars* hysteria by the time *Attack of the Clones* and *Revenge of the Sith* rolled around.

"You see what I'm getting at?" I ask him. "Millions of people read Harry Potter. But most of them don't sit around playing Quidditch for ten hours a day. And millions of people watched *Star Trek.* But when the show ended, they left it in the TV. Nerds can't make that distinction. They're not the least bit passive with things they love. It's almost as if they jump into a fantasy world—usually something sci-fi related—because they have more success there. They're more comfortable, less awkward, in these make-believe places than in the real world." I flop back on the bed, making myself comfortable. "That's a big part of my job. I try to coax them out of the fantasy and into reality."

He lets out a low whistle. "That's pretty screwed up. But I've gotta hand it to you. You really do know your stuff."

I blush at the unexpected compliment. Fortunately, he can't see me over the phone. "Thanks."

"Thank you for clearing it up. But I do still have one question," says Ty.

"Sure, ask me anything."

"How come when I called earlier your mother answered the phone? You don't live with your parents, do you?"

Anything but that.

8

Cool Rule #8:

There is such a thing as selective honesty.
You don't always have to tell the truth,
the whole truth, and nothing but the truth.

If I've learned one thing from being interviewed over the years, it's that you don't always have to answer the exact question you've been asked. If you give a good enough sound bite, and if you cover up smoothly enough, most people won't even realize that you've ignored what they've asked.

"I feel like being around one's parents—reconnecting with your youth and your family—is a very important aspect of coolness," I say, dodging the specific question. "So I invite my mom over once a week."

Ty is quiet for a minute, and I'm worried he's going to call me out. But he doesn't.

"Well, thank you, Kylie," he says. "I think I've got all the info I need. Now there's only one thing left to do."

"There is?"

"Yeah. We've got to meet."

"Definitely!" I'm looking forward to this. "I can't wait."

"How about tonight? I'm free."

"Me, too," I blurt out, without thinking.

"Great! So give me directions to your place and I'll be right over."

"My place?" I squeak.

"Yeah. I really need to get a sense of where you live. I want to include it in the article."

"Oh. I don't know how I feel about that. . . ."

"It's kind of crucial to the story. Whenever we're doing a profile piece, it has to encompass the whole person—where they work, live. What they like to do for fun. Your house is just one more piece of the story."

"Ah, I see." But I really don't. If Ty's the managing editor, then doesn't that mean he takes orders from himself? Couldn't he skip this step if he wanted to? I'm positive I've read profiles before that don't talk about the people's homes.

"So what do you say? Can I swing by tonight?"

"Tonight would be good. But, uh, I'm not in the city."

"I thought you just said you were at home?"

"I, uh . . ." I gulp. "I don't actually live in Chicago. I have a, um, house in the suburbs. Oak Park, to be exact."

"Really?" Ty says, sounding excited. "What a fresh angle! So, moving to the suburbs . . . that must be the new cool thing, right? Otherwise you wouldn't have bought a house there."

I'm stuck. "Yeah, it is. Big trend."

"I'll have to drive out there and see it. What day is good for you?"

"Well, um . . . I'll have to check with my assistant and get back to you."

He laughs. "You have to ask your assistant before you invite people over to your house?"

"No, no . . . of course not. It's just . . . my schedule is so busy this time of year. And I accidentally left my day planner at the office. How about if I check tomorrow and get back to you?"

"Perfect," Ty says. "But make sure you give me a call tomorrow. We need to get the ball rolling on this. This was originally envisioned as a long-lead piece, but with all the changes at the magazine—and with me coming on board so late in the game—I'm afraid I've got a fairly tight deadline. So it looks like you and I will be seeing quite a bit of each other over the next couple of weeks. I hope that's not a problem."

A problem? Is he kidding? At least I'll have something exciting to look forward to, something to take my mind off the fire.

"No, it sounds great."

"Good. Because I was kind of hoping I could shadow you, get a real sense for how you spend your days. I'll want to meet with some of your clients—former and present. That way I can get a real feel for how the program works. I want to give *Metro Guy*'s readers a kind of 'before and after' picture. I bet you've got some really interesting clients."

"Yeah, I can't wait for you to meet them." I'm about to launch into a story about Dennis Moop—I checked with him the other day, and he's already agreed to be a part of the article—when I hear my dad yelling up the stairs.

"Dinner's ready!"

Good God, I never realized how loud my father's voice is.

"So I was thinking—" Ty begins, but I rush to cut him off.

"Tomorrow," I say, as my dad calls out again. "I'll call you tomorrow and then we'll go over everything." I've got to get him off the phone, ASAP. If past behavior is any indication, then my dad will probably pick up the extension in about two seconds. That's what he used to do when I was in high school. Anytime he wanted to get in touch with me, he'd yell up the stairs. And if I didn't answer right away, he'd grab the extension and talk to me that way.

"I was hoping . . ." Ty begins.

"Gotta go!" I say. "I'll call tomorrow." And then I hang up the phone and head downstairs for dinner.

* * *

"What I really need to do is have sex with someone famous. And then I can 'leak' the video on YouTube."

"You don't want to do that."

"Oh, yes I do," Charity St. James says. "Maybe I'll fly out to L.A. this weekend, hit the pool at Chateau Marmont." She snaps her fingers. "Better yet, I'll go to Vegas. Yes, Vegas is perfect! I'll fuck some A-list star or another this weekend, upload the video Sunday night, and by Monday morning everyone in America will know my name!"

We were sitting in my office, having a civilized conversation while sipping Fiji water, when Charity came up with her plan.

And she looks pretty pleased with herself, too. "What is this, Wednesday?"

I nod.

"Only four more days of being a total nobody." She raises her bottle toward me in a mock toast.

I don't return the gesture.

"Why so sour?" Charity asks.

"I'm not sour. I just . . . I thought you wanted to take the whole brainy socialite approach."

"Wasn't working."

"Give it some more time. Fame doesn't happen overnight."

"It does if you play your cards right. And a crazy sex romp with some huge actor? That's the perfect way to incite a media frenzy!"

I consider this. "You'll start a frenzy, I suppose." *If you can pull it off,* I add silently. Although I don't think she'll have a problem. She's certainly good-looking enough to merit a one-night stand. "But it will be the wrong kind of frenzy. People will view you as an opportunist, a gold digger."

"But I'm rich!"

"They'll say it anyway."

"But won't the negative publicity help? You know, scandal sells and all that?"

"It won't be *your* scandal," I point out. "Sleeping with an actor doesn't guarantee you much of anything. My God, imagine how many struggling actresses have done that hoping to get ahead."

"That's because no one knows about their sexcapades. If I make sure to get the whole thing on tape . . ."

"You still won't become a household name."

She sighs, exasperated. "Yes. I. Will."

I mull it over. "You know Colin Farrell had a sex tape scandal, right?"

Charity brightens. "Of course. See, that's exactly what I'm talking about. I remember how it was when that tape came out—it was all over the blogosphere, and every entertainment news program and magazine in the country ran a story about it."

"They did," I agree.

She folds her arms across her chest. "Which kind of goes against your point."

"What was the name of the girl in the video?"

She doesn't answer.

"Was it even one girl? Or did he have a threesome?"

"I don't know. Who cares?" She sees where I'm going, it's pretty obvious, so she tries to undercut it. "Those girls—girl, whatever—were total nobodies. They had no breakout potential. Besides," she smirks, "I bet they had awful bodies. Once people see me naked . . . well, how can they resist?"

"Easily." I play with the pale-blue Fiji bottle. "This is America. People exploit themselves all the time. Think about all the girls who've stripped down for *Girls Gone Wild* hoping to catch a big break."

"That's different. Those girls aren't looking for fame—a lot of them aren't even thinking clearly. They're totally wasted."

"Most of them, yeah. But you'd be surprised how many girls think they're going to parlay thirty seconds of skin into an actual career." I think back to what Ty said about working on *The Howard Stern Show.* How people were willing to do anything for the chance—the teeny, tiny, slim little chance—that people would pay attention to them. "It's just not worth it," I continue. "Putting your sex life out there for all the world to see—you risk winding up a laughingstock, like Monica Lewinsky or Daisy Wright."

"Who?"

"That nanny who slept with Jude Law." This is the kind of useless information I know. I know the name of the nanny who Jude Law cheated on Sienna Miller with. Sometimes I worry that in my quest to become an expert on all things popular, I have turned into a walking, talking issue of *Us Weekly.* Or *InStyle.* Not that there's anything wrong with those magazines . . . but why can't I be *Vanity Fair*? Or, better yet, *The Paris Review.* I would really like to be *The Paris Review.*

"So you think sex is the wrong way to go?" she asks, finally getting it.

"Yes. Definitely. I'm not saying that we're not going to court the media, that you shouldn't do things strictly for attention. But you've got to aim higher. A sex tape will get you fifteen seconds of fame—let's at least shoot for fifteen minutes."

"So instead of sleeping with a star I should maybe try to date one?"

"That would definitely help." And now I feel bad, because I'm basically advising Charity to whore herself out. "Even then, there's no guarantee."

She rolls her eyes. "Yeah, right. If I started dating George Clooney, I'd become a huge star, trust me."

"Not necessarily." She starts to object, but I don't let her. "Clooney used to date that Celine Balitran girl, and she's not exactly famous. And he also dated Krista Allen for a long time. . . ."

"I know who Krista Allen is," she says. "That TV actress. She's such a bombshell. But I see what you're saying. She isn't that well known. I only remember her from *Days of Our Lives.*"

We sit there in silence for a minute, and then Charity says, "So famous people are out. Sex tapes are out. Going to A-list places and A-list parties—which is what I've been doing for two years now with no luck—is out."

We're dancing around the real problem here.

"So what am I supposed to do?"

Might as well be honest. "I wish your family were more . . . noteworthy," I tell her. "This would be so much easier if your dad were someone like Donald Trump or Tommy Hilfiger or Paul McCartney." I don't want to insult her, but I figure it won't so I add, "Or Hugh Hefner. Then we could pitch a reality show and be done with it."

"Tell me about it." She hangs her head.

"Or if we could build something out of the company . . . you know, if you were the heir to De Beers or Smirnoff. Then we could make up a fun name for you, like the Vodka Princess or the Diamond Debutante. It sounds stupid, but you'd be surprised how well that kind of branding works."

Even if she were the heir to, say, T-Mobile, we'd be in a better position than we're in now. Charity's family made its money from a frozen food empire. Which, for an heiress, is about as low-rent and unglamorous as you can get.

The other problem is that Charity doesn't seem to want to do anything. If she wanted to sing or act or write books, there'd be more to go on. Oh, sure, she sometimes talks of becoming a designer, but I've yet to see her do anything about it.

"My fate sucks," she says.

Can't you just be happy with the money? I want to say. *Most people would be.*

"Why can't I be Louis Vuitton's daughter?"

"Because Louis Vuitton died in the eighteen hundreds."

"Whatever. That's impossible."

A male voice calls out, "No, it's true." For a second I think it's Kevin—this is exactly the kind of conversation he'd jump right into. Or even Josh. Although it doesn't sound like either one of them. And it's not.

It's Ty Benedict, in the flesh.

"You're paying for a dead guy's name," he continues. "Louis Vuitton, the actual designer, died more than a hundred years ago."

"Who are you?" Charity flashes her biggest smile, showing off both her upper and lower teeth. "You look familiar. Do we hang out at the same places?"

"It's possible." He extends his hand. "I'm Ty Benedict."

"That name sounds so familiar. Did you go to Arlington Prep?"

I want to laugh. It just shows that fame—like coolness—doesn't stretch to all circles. Unless you reach Tom Cruise or Madonna proportions, there will always be people out there who don't know who you are.

"Nah," Ty says. "I went to school in Nashville."

She looks interested. "Are you a country music star or something? Is that how I know you?"

"Afraid not. I'm just a writer."

It strikes me as a little weird that Charity can't place him. After all, Ty's a pretty regular fixture in the gossip rags. If she reads them all the time, dreams about being in them, then wouldn't she recognize him instantly? He has the exact kind of exposure she's trying to achieve.

"Books?"

"Not yet. I mainly write magazine articles."

"Maybe you can write one about me someday." She winks.

"Maybe. At the moment I'm here to write about Kylie."

They both turn to face me. "Uh, hi," I say. And then I just shut up, which is pretty lame. But I can't help it. I'm still shocked. I can't believe Ty Benedict is here in my office.

"You must be Kylie Chase." I nod. He walks over and shakes my hand. "It's so great to finally meet you."

"Yes, it's nice to meet you, too," I say, recovering my composure.

I don't know how it's possible, but Ty Benedict is even better-looking than I'd expected. His pictures didn't do him justice. In person, he's taller, his smile's brighter, his eyes are bluer.

I can't believe he's here, in the flesh. After our phone call three nights ago, I got an e-mail from Ty suggesting that we meet on Thursday. Yet here he is, a day early.

Charity clears her throat. "You two have never met before? What is he, some guy you found on eHarmony?" She giggles. " 'Cause if that's the case, then I think I'll get an account right now."

Ty laughs good-naturedly. "I'm a writer for *Metro Guy*. I'm here to do a story on How to Be Cool."

"I figured that was just a cover," Charity says. "Are you sure you're a journalist? Because you don't really look like one. And I mean that as a compliment."

"Yep, I'm the real deal." He turns to face me. "I know I probably should have called first, but I had an unexpected opening in my schedule. I was hoping we could get started today . . . if you're not too busy."

"I'd love to, but I'm right in the middle of a client meeting," I explain.

"That sounds perfect," Ty says. "Maybe I could sit in the corner and watch if you wouldn't mind. I'd love to start off by observing what you do. And I'd love to interview some of your clients for the story." He turns to face Charity. "Would that be all right with you?"

"Actually, I have to get going," she says, standing up. "I've got a really busy day."

Ty fishes a business card out of his wallet. "Give me a call," he tells her. "Whenever you're ready to do that interview."

"Um, no offense, but I think I'll take a pass." She hands Ty's business card back to him. "Hiring a 'cool instructor' . . . it's a little avant-garde, and I'm not sure how my friends and family would feel if the news got out."

"Ah, come on," Ty urges gently. "Don't tell me you're embarrassed."

"A tiny bit," she says. "Think about it! If people found out I was worried about my 'coolness,' so to speak . . . who wants to advertise that? If I were an obvious nerd, that would be one thing, but I'm not."

"Which is exactly why I'd like to talk to you," he says. "You're the polar opposite of how I pictured Kylie's clients. And that's intriguing, the exact kind of thing my readers would love to hear about."

Charity shakes her head. "I really don't think so."

Ty presses on, reselling his pitch, refusing to give in. It's a little off-putting, but what are you going to do? Journalists aren't known for being pushovers. "At least take my card. Think it over."

"All right," she finally agrees.

"And is there a number where I can reach you?" Ty asks.

"As a matter of fact . . ." Charity reaches over and grabs a Post-it note off my desk. "I was just going to suggest *you* call *me.*" She scrawls down her number, throws me a quick wink, and then hands the note to Ty.

It's the blow-off line, of course.

"Thanks," Ty says, placing the Post-it in his wallet. "I'll give you a call in a couple of days."

I almost feel bad for the guy; he's got no clue he's being set up.

I used to think Charity's blow-off number was a passive-aggressive way of avoiding confrontation, letting people down easy. But I've come to see it as something else—a twisted way of stringing people along, having the upper hand, getting the last laugh. She passes that number out right and left, often giving it to guys who would never have the nerve to ask for it. (She nearly slipped Dennis Moop her blow-off line when she bumped into him at my office a few weeks ago. Fortunately, I intercepted just in time.)

"Later," Charity says, waving at me and blowing Ty a quick kiss before she heads out the door.

"So I'm sorry for the sneak attack," Ty says, plopping down in the chair closest to my desk. "I hope I didn't put too much of a chink in your schedule by dropping by."

"No, it's fine," I say, even though I'm kind of flustered. I wish I'd known he was coming. I would have dressed up—or at least normally. I'm wearing a pair of jeans and a wool sweater. This wouldn't be a problem—Kevin doesn't mind if we wear jeans to work—except my entire outfit came from the Gap.

We're supposed to wear designer clothes to work every day, and it gets a bit tiresome. When I first started this job, I loved how label-crazy everyone was. It made me feel like part of some big, sophisticated world, a million miles away from the Kylie Chase of my high school days. But after a while I grew sick of being forced to shell out so much money for clothes. It all gets a bit absurd at a point. And, honestly, as much as I love Dolce & Gabbana and Michael Kors, some days I find myself wishing I could just pick up a nice $30 outfit at Target.

Because Target really does have some cute clothes. And it's not a major tragedy if you spill ketchup on a $15 shirt. (I would never, ever say this out loud, lest I lose my reputation, my boss's respect, and half my client base.)

But wearing the Gap outfit to work had been a major no-no.

Kevin immediately laid into me at the staff meeting this morning. (Yes, I know, wearing an outfit like this to a staff meeting was asking for it. But I completely forgot that we were meeting this morning, or I'd have made sure my Escada suit—one of the few items that didn't get destroyed in the fire—was back from the cleaners. I'm normally more organized than this, but moving back in with my parents has thrown a real wrench into my routine.)

"Jesus, Kylie, could you be any more pedestrian?" Kevin asked, eyeing my outfit. "If you're going to shop in the Gap family, at least have the decency to go to Banana."

Josh, who was standing there at the time, had to throw in his two cents. "Be grateful she didn't slum it down to Old Navy," he cracked, and everyone laughed.

"Sorry," I mumbled. "It's been a little tough with the fire and all."

"Oh, that's right!" Kevin said, smacking his forehead. "I forgot you lost all of your stuff. Poor baby." I couldn't tell if he was being sarcastic. "That must have been painful watching a half mil worth of clothes go up in smoke."

A half mil? Was he joking? My wardrobe wasn't worth anywhere near that amount. I'd had some nice stuff, pre-fire, but most of it was obtained from sample sales or bargain bins. In truth, there was something almost cathartic about watching it go up in smoke.

"After our little pre-interview conversation Sunday night, I was really excited to get started on the article," Ty says, bringing me back to reality.

"Yes, of course." I tug self-consciously at my sweater. "This is good timing," I tell him, "because as it happens my afternoon just freed up. I was supposed to meet with a new client, but he called to reschedule. So my schedule's clear until four-thirty."

"Interesting," Ty says. "Do you get a lot of cancellations?"

It's an innocent question, I suppose, but something in Ty's tone of voice stops me.

"Not really."

"I sorta assumed you'd be booked up for weeks." He pauses. "I figured you'd have a waiting list. You know, one person cancels and you move on to the next name, fill the slot immediately. I'm kinda surprised you've got an entire afternoon free to hang out with me."

"Not the entire afternoon," I remind him. "Just the next four hours."

"That's quite a chunk of time."

Is he trying to imply that business isn't going well, or am I being paranoid? I try to relax. He's just doing his job, poking around, asking questions. But still, I'll keep my guard up. The last thing I want to do is get hosed.

"I guess it's your lucky day," I say, smiling brightly.

"Must be." He grins, flashing his perfectly veneered (or are they naturally that pristine?) smile. "So I was hoping we could hook up with a few of your former clients today. I'd really love to check in and see how they're doing. I think that would give us a great angle on why How to Be Cool is so beneficial."

This is the last thing I feel like doing. At least not while I'm dressed like this. "I think we might have to table that for a few days," I tell him. "My clients are all so busy that I need to give them some advance notice."

"Good answer," Ty says, beaming.

I raise an eyebrow.

"That means you've done your job well. I'd hate to think someone went through How to Be Cool and came out with a terrible social life. Which is why it would be great to drop by and see a few people unannounced. Like, say, Friday night," he continues.

"Friday night?"

"It's one of your golden rules, isn't it? People have to go out on the weekends."

"It is," I agree.

"So we should show up unexpected. You know, find out if they're sticking with the program or if they're hanging around the house eating Chinese takeout in their pajamas."

I have never been a fan of unannounced drop-ins, but I see his point. "We could do that, I suppose. On three conditions."

"Name them."

"The first has to do with confidentiality. I owe that to my clients. If I take you out to someone's house and spring you on them unannounced . . . they might not be so happy."

"Understood."

"If someone doesn't want to be included in your story, then you've got to respect that. That's my first condition."

"Definitely."

"Second, I'd like to arrange a few client meetings, maybe for next week. Drop-ins are good, but people will be caught a bit off guard, and you won't get the whole picture that way." He looks like he wants to object, but he doesn't. "And my third condition—we'll need to be finished early. By, say, nine o'clock at the latest. It's a Friday night, after all—I've got plans."

"Of course you do," he says. "Anything exciting?"

"Absolutely." I don't elaborate, though. By Ty's standards, a night of movies and drinks with a few of my college friends would probably sound dull.

"Now that that's settled, how about we get down to the interview?" Ty asks, pulling out a MiniDisc recorder and setting it on the desk in front of me. "You don't mind if I tape this, do you?"

"No problem."

I get up and close the door. I don't want Kevin walking by and seeing us. If he knew Ty Benedict was in here, he'd probably insist on sitting in and observing the interview. The last thing I need is that kind of pressure.

Ty pulls out his cell phone and switches it off. "This thing is such a nuisance," he says, shoving it back in his pocket. "It rings off the hook."

"I know how you feel," I say, even though I really don't. My phone hardly rings off the hook, but I make a show of pulling out my cell phone and turning it to vibrate. Gotta keep up the image.

"Let's pretend I'm a client," Ty begins. "Tell me how you would fix me."

"Fix you?"

"Right. Let's pretend I walked through the door and said, 'Fix me.' What would you do?"

"That's not really how it works."

"So you're telling me no one's ever walked in here, told you they weren't happy, and asked you to help them fix that?"

"Sometimes . . . maybe."

"But your clients must be unhappy, dissatisfied with some aspect of their lives. No one hires a 'cool instructor' if their life is perfect." He thinks it over. "Or do they? Are your clients desperate, nerdy people who will try anything to change? Or are they bored, overstimulated urbanites who are willing to blow big wads of cash on any little trend that comes their way?"

I shake my head, more in disbelief than disagreement. "Neither. People come for a variety of reasons. You can't put them all in one box."

"Fair enough," he says. "But back to my question. What you're doing here is a tough sell. I know why I need a physician or a dentist or even a dog walker or a personal trainer. But why on earth do I need someone to teach me about being cool? How is this even a legitimate business?"

Wow. He's not pulling any punches. Fortunately I've faced these kinds of questions before, so I'm ready for them.

"I'm like a life coach," I tell him. "Except I help people with their social lives, with their social *skills.*"

"Uh-huh."

"Because being personable doesn't come naturally to everyone. Sometimes you have to learn how to be charming, or how to . . ."

My landline starts ringing. It's Courtney's extension, and I hit the button to send it over to voice mail.

"Do you need to get that?" Ty asks.

"No, it's fine."

I struggle to regain my train of thought, but Courtney's knocking on the door. She cracks it open and sticks her head in. "I'm so sorry to disturb you," she says. "But Austin Dunbar's mom is on line one and she says it's urgent."

"Tell her I'll call her back," I begin. She's probably only calling to cancel our appointment this Friday.

"No, take it," Ty says. "I insist!"

I pick up the phone. "Mrs. Dunbar, hi, this is Kylie Chase."

"Kylie! I'm so glad I caught you."

"I'm afraid I only have a minute. I'm in the middle of a meeting right now."

"Oh." She sounds disappointed. "I was hoping you could come out here today. Austin's in a really great mood—and he's finally agreed to meet with you!"

"I really don't have time to drive all the way out there," I explain. "Today's kind of booked. I'd love to meet with Austin, but it will have to be another time."

"There's no way you could come today? Even for a short visit? Austin's really ready to have the meeting. He really is. We'll still pay you, of course, even if he changes his mind."

"I'm so sorry. But my schedule is packed. Why don't we do it on Friday, like we'd originally planned?"

Ty waves his arms around, trying to catch my attention.

"Mrs. Dunbar, could you hold on a minute?"

"Sure."

I place her on hold.

"Is that a client?" Ty asks.

"Maybe," I tell him. "We're trying to work out the details. I haven't met the actual client yet. So far I'm dealing with his mother."

"And she wants you to meet with him today?" Ty asks.

"Right."

"Let's do it!"

"*Let's?* I don't think they'd be too keen if I showed up with a journalist."

"Ask them. You'd be surprised how many people love being interviewed."

"I don't know. . . ."

"Ask them," he urges. "Just ask them."

So I do. Against my better judgment, I might add. Because as much as I'm eager to let Ty Benedict into my world, as much as I'm grateful he's writing an article about me, I have some nagging doubts. And this whole Austin Dunbar situation is weird enough as it is; the last thing I need is to have Ty there to document the whole thing for posterity.

But Mrs. Dunbar loves the idea. And then she checks with Austin, who also agrees.

We gather up our stuff and head out the door. I'm trying to figure out how to get Ty into my car without him seeing the BIG ONE plates when my phone rings. I don't recognize the number, but it could be Mrs. Dunbar calling, so I answer.

"Could I speak to Kylie?" a voice asks.

"This is she." I usher Ty into the car as I balance the phone against my ear.

"Kylie, hi, this is Dr. Zack Naylor."

I don't say anything. I'm too stunned.

"From high school. Do you remember me?"

It's a stupid question and I'm tempted to say no, just to screw with his head. But I don't. "Yes, of course. How are you?"

"Great!" he says. "I'm so glad I caught you." He starts babbling about the reunion, and how he can't believe it's been twelve years since we graduated. He then asks me to resend my head shot, because his computer "swallowed the other one." The conversation goes by in a blur. My mind is whirling.

Just a few days ago I was down in the dumps, depressed about losing everything in the fire, moving back in (temporarily) with my parents, and my upcoming birthday. But it's amazing how quickly it can all turn around.

I've got Ty Benedict in my car and Zack Naylor on my phone. Things are definitely looking up!

Cool Rule #9:

Never allow yourself to be upstaged.

"I can't wait to meet this kid," Ty says, as I steer the car toward Austin's house.

"Me neither," I say. "Although I wouldn't call him a kid. He's only a couple of years younger than you."

"Yeah, I know. But based on everything you've told me, I keep picturing him much younger."

I know what he means. Austin Dunbar seems like a very young nineteen.

I turn onto the Dunbars' street. I'm still glowing from the Zack Naylor phone call. I can't believe the reunion is only five weeks away. I'm dying—absolutely dying—to see everyone again. My conversation with Zack was brief, but exhilarating.

As if reading my mind, Ty says, "So, did I hear that your high school reunion's coming up? You must be so excited. I can't wait for mine."

I'll bet he can't. If I were a famous playboy/Hollywood screenwriter, I'd be pretty raring to get back to high school, too. "You guys didn't have a five-year?"

"No. They're making us wait until ten."

I'm about to pull into the Dunbars' driveway when my cell rings again. This time it's Mrs. Dunbar.

"I'm so sorry, Kylie," she says, "but I'm afraid Austin's locked himself in his room and won't come out." *You've got to be kidding me.* "You're not almost out here, are you?"

"We're sitting in your driveway."

"Oh." I see the blinds ruffle as she peeks out to confirm this. "Oh, no."

"Since we're already here, how about if we come in and try to talk to Austin?"

"I don't know . . . he's being pretty insolent."

"Why don't you let me come in and talk to him?"

"I wish Austin's father were here—he'd know what to do." She pauses. "Why don't you come back on Friday? I'm so sorry, Kylie; go ahead and bill me for this session. I don't mind paying it." She hangs up the phone before I can respond.

"The kid's changed his mind? Doesn't want to see us?" Ty guesses.

"Yeah." I rap my fingers against the dashboard, thinking.

"Tough break."

I turn off the ignition, pull the key out. "Come on," I say, opening the car door. "Let's go inside."

"Hey!" Ty says, as we get out of the car. "Nice tag!"

I look where he's pointing. Oh, no. He's spied BIG ONE. "Ugh, that old thing?" I groan.

"So, I guess penis size is pretty important to you, huh?" he asks, laughing.

"Oh, yeah, you know it!" I say sarcastically. He laughs. "DMV made a mistake," I add, but Ty's already bounding up the driveway.

"What are you going to do?"

"Austin's locked himself in his room," I say. "I'm going to try to get him to come out. And if he won't, I'll talk to him through the door."

"This should be fun," Ty says. "I get to watch the master at work."

The master? Hardly. I jog up the stairs and ring the doorbell. A second later, Mrs. Dunbar answers.

"Kylie," she says, "I didn't realize you were still here."

I fill her in on my plan. "I don't know," she says. "He's pretty stubborn."

"So am I."

"Well . . ."

It takes a little prodding, but I persuade Mrs. Dunbar to let me have a shot.

We trail Austin's mother up the stairs and to his bedroom. She raps lightly on the door.

"There's someone here to see you . . . Kylie Chase, that lady from How to Be Cool."

Lady. I cringe at the term. I know she's trying to be polite, but it makes me sound so old.

At what point did I cross the line from *girl* to *lady*? From *Kylie* to *Ms. Chase*? With my thirtieth birthday fast approaching, I've become increasingly sensitive about my age. Although Not Thirty hasn't been a walk in the park. In a lot of ways, twenty-eight is your last "safe year." From there on out, it's full steam ahead toward thirty.

"I told you, I don't want to see anyone."

"Kylie and—what was your name again?"

"Ty Benedict."

"Kylie and Ty Benedict drove all the way out here. The least you can do is open the door and say hi."

Silence.

"Austin. I'm really worried about you." She leans against the wood paneling, lowers her voice. "Your father and I have given you a lot of wiggle room, but this isn't funny anymore.

Why can't you be open-minded, give this a shot the way you promised you would?"

More silence.

"Austin, honey, if this keeps up, I'm afraid we're going to have to take Dr. Keebler up on his suggestion."

That does it.

Austin swings open the door. He looks about how I expected. Tall and slim with pale skin, frizzy brown hair, and glasses. His complexion isn't great, nor is his fashion sense. He's wearing a white turtleneck with a Hawaiian shirt buttoned over it. His corduroy pants are too short. His tennis shoes look like something created for a moon mission.

"Hi, come on in," Austin says, stepping aside to let us through.

I blink in surprise. Based on the way things ended the other day, and the way he's been acting this afternoon, I had expected some sort of protest. I'd expected him to throw a temper tantrum, to refuse to come out until we left.

But he's smiling brightly, welcoming us into his bedroom. Er, welcoming *me*, at least. We're halfway through the door when Austin holds up a hand to stop us. "Not him," he says, pointing toward Ty. "I don't want to talk to him."

"Austin," his mother says, "this is the journalist I was telling you about, the one you agreed to meet with."

"That was before I looked him up online." Austin makes a face. "I don't want to be a part of any story written by Ty Benedict. No offense, but I find you kind of repugnant."

"AUSTIN!" his mother shrieks.

"Sorry, that's the way it's gotta be," Austin says. "I read your stuff, your articles about women and sex and partying." He looks at Ty, shakes his head. "No way I'm letting you write about me."

Ty interjects, "It's okay. I understand."

"Honestly, Austin, I just don't understand what's happened to your manners," Mrs. Dunbar says.

"Not everyone likes being interviewed." Ty's voice is low, soothing. "I can wait out in the car."

"Nonsense, you can sit downstairs with me," Mrs. Dunbar says, ushering him. "But really, Austin, I hope your attitude improves in the near future. Otherwise, Dr. Keebler's going to hear about it."

I wonder who this Dr. Keebler is, why he strikes the fear of God into Austin. A psychiatrist, probably.

Mrs. Dunbar and Ty leave, and Austin and I get to work.

* * *

"Make yourself comfortable." He gestures toward the love seat in the corner of his bedroom.

"Thanks for giving this another shot," I say, perching on the edge of the love seat.

"I'm sorry I was unpleasant the other day. I shouldn't have refused to see you."

"That's okay."

Austin sits down in front of his computer. "I've done a lot of research on you, and this seems like something that might work for me. One of the things that appeals to me about How to Be Cool is that it has the potential to break people out of their routines."

"That's one thing we work on," I say, "getting you out of your comfort zone." *And out of your bedroom.*

"I'll be straight with you today," Austin begins. "I'm tired of messing around. Let me just cut to the chase. I'm depressed."

I nod. "I kind of figured."

"And the medicine my doctor has given me. . . . I guess it's working. But I need something else. I feel like something's missing from my life."

"Go on."

"I'm not dense. I know I'm a nerd." He takes a deep breath. "And I want to change," he says, looking shaky. "But I just don't know how. I'm drowning here. I have to figure out how to fit in. And I think that involves becoming someone completely different."

I wonder, though, if this is really true, if he's really ready to give up his old personality in favor of a new one. Most people talk a big game when it comes to change. They bemoan their sad fates and think of all the great things that would happen *if only* life were different.

But when you dig a little bit, you'll often find that's not true. Most people reject change; they fear it, avoid it. I guess it's the whole devil-you-know-versus-the-devil-you-don't argument.

"Can you help me change?" he asks.

"I can try."

He stands up, starts pacing. "I don't want to be myself anymore. I want to throw it all away and start over. Can you help me do that?"

"A complete personality overhaul?" I ask.

"Personality. Appearance. All of it." He stands up, starts pacing the room. "I don't want to be myself anymore."

His insecurity makes me sad. He's got so much going for him; why can't he see that? Is this just what we do? Hate ourselves for no good reason?

"We'll start small," I tell him. "Make some minor changes. See how it goes."

"Okay." He flops down on his bed and stares up at the ceiling. "I'm relatively burned out by life. And I don't think that's normal. I'm only nineteen, but it feels like I've already experienced everything there is to experience." He pauses, blushing. "And the things that I haven't yet experienced . . . well, you reach a certain point where you figure they're not going to happen for you. They're just not."

I start to reply, but he cuts me off.

"Sorry, let's change the subject. I'd rather not go there right now."

I oblige. "Nice," I say, pointing toward a poster of Gwen Stefani that is hanging over his bed.

Austin rolls his eyes. "My dad bought me that. He thought I would like her."

"You don't?" I ask, remembering that he used his iPod to store computer files.

"No." He shrugs. "I don't really like music."

"Really? No music at all?"

"None."

How is that possible? I have to admit this is a new one for me. I've met plenty of dorks who have *bad* taste in music, who adore people like Barry Manilow and Celine Dion. But having *no* taste in music is something else altogether.

"I guess classical music is somewhat decent. I can appreciate the artistry of it," Austin concedes. "But modern stuff doesn't interest me in the least."

"I can understand that," I say. "If all you've ever been exposed to is what MTV plays . . ." I stop, realizing how stupid that statement is. I should know better. I seriously doubt a guy like Austin is sitting around watching *TRL*.

"Since we're on the topic," Austin pauses, looking unsure of himself, "that's one thing I'd kind of like you to help me with. I'd like to have a music collection. Just to be social."

"This will be easy. We can download some stuff to your iPod. Maybe a sampling of a few tracks. And you should start listening to the radio—that way, you can figure out what you like."

"No, no . . . that's not what I meant at all. I don't care about what *I* like—I just want a CD collection that's *cool.* I want something that will impress other people. It doesn't matter if I like listening to it or not."

"We could go that route, but—"

"That's what I want," he cuts me off. "A cool music collection." He reaches into his wallet and pulls out a credit card. Then he starts waving it around in the air. "Take me to the store and help me figure out what CDs to buy—I'd like to get at least two hundred."

"Two *hundred* CDs?" I repeat.

"Maybe that's overdoing it. Maybe a hundred would be better."

"You realize this is going to cost a ton of money. You're looking at a thousand dollars, minimum."

"I thought we could get some used CDs."

"Even then, it's going to be expensive."

"All right, a basic fifty, then. My parents will pay for whatever I ask them to, just so you know. They're always urging me to buy stuff, like it will make me happy."

Great. Maybe he should team up with Charity St. James. The two of them could become shopping buddies.

"I don't care what genre of music, either. And I don't care if I like it or not. It just has to be cool. You can do that, can't you?"

"I can. But are you sure you don't want to find out what you like before you start buying?"

"I couldn't care less about what I like. I like *none* of it, so what does it matter?"

I scratch my head. "So you want to buy an entire CD collection just to fit in?" Actually, it's not that strange. A lot of my clients buy things to be cool—clothes, music, DVDs, books. But fifty CDs? That seems a bit extreme. Why not start with five? Or even ten? Or what about downloading some tunes instead?

"Whenever I meet a new person, one of the first things they ask is what kind of music I like," Austin begins. "And I never have a good answer—or any answer at all. Back in college I *hated* having people in my dorm room. Because they'd come in, see the stereo my parents bought me, and then inevitably say, 'Let's listen to some music.' Or, 'Who's your favorite band?' And then I'd have to explain that the crate of CDs in my room was full of computer files. And that the stereo was only there for decoration—another one of my dad's lame attempts to help me be normal. It got so bad at one point I actually went out and bought some music . . ."

Uh-oh. This can't be leading anywhere good.

"I researched it online and I tried to get what I thought was popular. I bought the whole Britney Spears backlist. I got the first Jessica Simpson CD, because she was on the cover of all the magazines at the time. I even ordered some collection called *Smooth and Easy: Seduction Songs of the '70s* off TV. But considering I wasn't even born until nineteen eighty-six, and considering there were never any girls around for me to seduce . . ." He blushes. "Well, it ended up being a big waste of time and money."

"I see."

"That's why I need your help. I'd like to at least have one area of my life that's set. One area where I don't have to feel like a giant loser all the time. And since my parents are so desperate to help me out, I can guarantee they'll spring for a music collection."

I agree to take him shopping the following week.

We talk for a while, discussing Austin's goals and brainstorming on how to get him from point A (complete and total nervous-breakdown mode) to point B (comfortable with himself and able to chill out around others). Austin promises to make up a list of all the activities that cause him anxiety, as well as a list of the goals he wants to accomplish. Then we make plans to meet early next week to get to work.

"For now, I've got a homework assignment for you. Watch two hours of TV every night for the rest of the week."

"Okay. I can do that."

"But *not* educational stuff."

He starts to protest.

"Or, if you want to watch those, fine. But they don't count for your two hours. I want you to check out primetime TV. Reality shows. *Desperate Housewives*, whatever."

"I am *not* watching a show called *Desperate Housewives*!" he explodes.

"All right, all right . . . it was just a suggestion. Maybe try *The Office* or *Family Guy* or *Scrubs*. Also, *Lost* might be a good bet."

He starts taking notes, frantically writing it all down.

"Although anything you want to watch is fine. Just so long as it's not a documentary or a nature program or something on the History Channel. The idea is to clear your head, so whatever you watch should be relatively mindless."

"Clear my head?" he repeats. "Rot my frontal lobe is more like it."

"You only have to do it for a week. It won't rot your brain, I promise."

"By the time this week is over, I won't even remember what $E = mc^2$ stands for."

"I don't think there's much risk of that happening."

He cracks a smile. "I bet *you* don't know what it stands for."

I wave my hand dismissively. "Mass, energy . . . something like that. It's Einstein's theory of relativity, right?"

"How about I give *you* a homework assignment? For every hour of TV I watch a night, you have to learn one new thing—like what's the biggest river in Venezuela or how many astronomical units is it from the earth to the sun." He winks at me. "I'll give you a hint—that last one is a trick question."

"Ah." I laugh. "I could do that, if you want."

"Great," he says.

"But we'll need to check in with each other," I say. "You've got my business card. E-mail me every day and let me know what shows you're watching."

"And I'll throw in a few questions for you, too," he says, really getting into it. "And you can look up the answers and write me back."

"It's a deal." We shake on it.

I leave Austin to his TV and head downstairs to find Ty. He's sitting at the kitchen table, tape recorder out, talking to Mrs. Dunbar. *Interviewing* Mrs. Dunbar.

I clear my throat.

"You finished already?" Ty asks, looking up. "You've only been up there twenty minutes."

Mrs. Dunbar looks suspicious. "Did Austin clam up?"

"No, no, we had a great talk," I tell her. "I gave Austin a

few assignments . . . I think we're really starting to make some progress."

"Great," she says, brightening. "When will you be back?"

"Next week. We're going shopping for CDs."

Ty's jotting this all down in his notebook. "I think I got everything I need, too. Thanks, Angela," he says, shaking her hand.

Angela? Wow, they're on a first-name basis? She's always introduced herself to me as Mrs. Dunbar, and I've followed suit.

"I'll be in touch if I need anything else," Ty promises as we head out to the car.

"You interviewed Mrs. Dunbar?" I ask, as I put the key in the ignition.

"It was pretty informal," he says. "We just chatted for a few minutes. I think her viewpoint will make a nice addition to the story."

I want to ask him what her viewpoint is, what she's said about me, but I don't.

"Wow, it's almost three o'clock," Ty says, sounding surprised. "I'd better get back to *Metro Guy*, if that's okay. I've got a ton of work to do before my date tonight."

"Date?" I ask.

"Yeah, I'm going out with some model. I don't even know her name. She's in town on an assignment." He pulls out his cell phone and switches it back on. "My agent set the whole thing up." Ty's phone starts ringing. "You don't mind dropping me at my office, do you?"

"I don't mind at all," I say. But Ty's no longer listening. He's already moved on to another conversation.

* * *

For as long as I can remember, we've had a tradition in my house. On nights when my dad's not working at the restaurant, the three of us sit down at nine o'clock for a formal multicourse dinner complete with our best table settings, wine, and jazz music.

As a teenager, I used to love this. It made me feel mature, special. While my classmates ate pizza and frozen dinners in front of a TV, I enjoyed gourmet food and delicious wine. My dad would whip up exotic menus and my mother would fix me a glass of wine. She never believed in the "American drinking age," which was "absurdly high—the Europeans have it right."

Now that I'm living back home, these dinners have become a regular thing.

But although these meals used to be fun, they aren't anymore. Now I spend most of the time ducking my mother's questions and pacing myself so I don't overindulge on my father's fattening foods.

It's not an easy task.

Tonight he's fixed artichoke risotto and braised lamb shanks, with a black-tea-infused crème brûlée for dessert. He brings out a cheese course, with honeycomb and sweetened radish slices.

"This girl came into the boutique today," Mom says, spearing a piece of Camembert with her fork. "You would have loved her, Kylie. Really spunky and fun. But, poor thing, she was looking for a size fourteen Vera Wang and, of course, we don't carry anything even close to that."

"*I* would have loved her?" I ask. "Why, because she was fat?"

"No, of course that's not what I meant," Mom says.

I wait for her to explain what she does mean, but she's

silent. I have always felt sorry for the bigger-sized girls who come into Mom's boutique. Mom rarely has any dresses in stock above a size ten. And even on the off chance that she does . . . well, wedding dresses aren't exactly forgiving. Even if you're a size six, it's easy to wind up looking like a great white whale.

"You ought to let her do it," Mom says, and I stare at her in confusion. I've tuned out of the conversation, and I'm not sure what she's talking about.

"Let who do what?"

"My friend Brenda's son just moved back to town, and she suggested the two of you get together."

"Miller?" I ask.

"Right. Brenda and I were thinking the two of you might really hit it off."

Oh, God, a fix-up.

"I don't know. I'm not really into blind dates," I explain.

"This isn't a blind date," Mom says. "You and Miller used to be classmates, remember?"

"In kindergarten! The last time I saw him he was still eating paste."

"Well, I saw Miller last spring at his cousin's wedding and, trust me, his paste-eating days are long gone. He's quite the catch now, I must say."

I'm curious, but I know better. I don't trust setups. It's a golden rule, one I always tell my clients.

"Thanks, but I think I'll pass."

"I already told him he could stop by the house sometime," Mom says.

"Then *untell* him," I say.

Dad, who has been listening quietly all this time, suddenly

pipes up. "Let it go, Lu," he urges. I think he's about to say something about how I'm an adult and I can make my own decisions, but instead he says, "The sun is in Aquarius right now, and that's the worst possible time for Kylie to start a new relationship. She's a Taurus, Lu! A Taurus can't start a relationship with the sun in this position."

Wow. I should've seen that coming.

It's a crazy notion, but I grab on to it. "Dad's right," I say.

"Oh, give me a break." Mom looks annoyed. "Since when do you care about your father's horoscope predictions?"

"Since my apartment burned down."

"I tried to warn her," Dad says sadly. He leans over and pats me on the hand. "What did I tell you, honey? Mars was really moving in for the kill."

"Oh, good grief!" Mom explodes. "You've made a thousand predictions over the years and one—*one*—finally comes true. What about all those times you were wrong?"

"The stars don't always spell things out for us. They merely provide hints, clues. It's up to us to figure out the rest."

She rolls her eyes. "I really think you should meet Miller."

"Sun in Aquarius," Dad mumbles, taking a sip of coffee. "It's a bad sign."

Mom looks at me and I shrug. "The man's got a point."

Mom throws her arms up. "How can I argue with that logic? I mean, Kylie could meet, excuse me, remeet Brenda Diller's son. But hey, since the sun's in Aquarius, I'd better call the whole thing off."

Her sarcasm is lost on Dad. "Yes, you'd better."

Dad's astrobabble theory is annoying, but at least it does the trick.

Mom lets it drop for now. Hopefully for good.

"You'll thank me later," Dad says. "The sun in Aquarius doesn't bode well for your love life."

I laugh it off—I don't really buy into any of this. Although there's a nagging doubt in the back of my mind. Dad was right last time, about Mars bringing destruction. What if he's right on this, too? And, if so, what does that mean about Ty Benedict and Dr. Zack Naylor?

* * *

I'm supposed to meet Ty on Friday night so we can go visit my former clients. But I get a message from him on Thursday. He's been called up to New York on a job assignment, so he needs to reschedule. Since he's got plans the following weekend, we wind up rescheduling for two weeks from Friday. It seems like a long time to wait. I thought he was on such a tight deadline, but he doesn't seem fazed, merely tells me he's still got plenty of time to get the article worked out.

I take it easy over the weekend—lounging around the house, watching TV, and reading magazines. I don't hit the gym once. My entire routine has been thrown off-kilter ever since I moved back in with my parents, and my workout schedule is no exception. It's been nice relaxing, but the truth is I'm a little worried. I've never slipped like this before. When it comes to taking care of my body, I'm usually like a well-oiled machine: focused, driven, without emotion. I eat the things I'm supposed to eat, exercise as much as I should. In the past five years I haven't deviated for any length of time. Fortunately, though, it doesn't seem to be having too much of an effect. My pants are a little bit tight, but the scale has largely remained the same. True, I'm about eleven pounds higher than I like to be, but when you've lost seventy-five pounds, eleven is nothing. I'll be able to take that off in no time.

Other than answering a few e-mails from Austin Dunbar, I don't do much work. True to his word, Austin has been writing me every day, sending me random questions: *What's the capital of Botswana? When did the Concorde first take flight? Who's the only U.S. president who was never married? True or false: chewing gum while chopping onions keeps you from crying?*

I Google the answers—*Gaborone, 1969, James Buchanan, true*—and then write him back. It takes all of five minutes to track them down. It feels like I'm cheating, but this is what Austin wanted me to do.

Sunday night we're in the middle of our family dinner—beef tenderloin with Stilton and a mushroom tart—when the phone rings. I try to get up to answer it, but Dad stops me.

"You know the rules," he says.

I do. No phone, no reading, no interruptions.

"But this could be important," I protest. "I'm still waiting to hear back from the fire marshal. They haven't determined the cause yet."

"The fire marshal's not going to call on a Sunday night," Mom points out.

"You don't know that." The truth is, I'm waiting to hear from Ty. He promised to call when he got back in town Sunday night. And seeing how he's one of the few people who has my parents' number (I stopped giving it out as soon as I got a new charger for my cell), there's a decent chance it's him.

"You will not get up. Your father has spent a long time preparing this meal and his food is a work of art," she says.

My father, the "artist," is less eloquent. "Our house, our rules," he says, and with that the discussion is finished.

Amazing.

(The call turns out to be for my mother. But even so, it's annoying that I couldn't answer.)

Lately I've been longing to go back in time, to relive my teenage years. And for what? So I can live with my parents full-time, have no say in things, sit around and wait for guys who probably won't call?

Why did I want to be sixteen again? Now that I'm thinking about it, twenty-nine, er, Not Thirty, sounds so much better.

10

Cool Rule #10:

Don't waste time trying to figure out other people's motives.

Monday afternoon I meet Dennis Moop at a trendy café across the street from my office. We have coffee. Well, I do. Dennis orders chamomile infusion with "a splash of lemon, because I'm nursing a sore throat."

It comes in a dainty cup, with an accompanying teapot. With his Hulk-esque body, he looks ridiculous drinking from it. I suppose I should say something. That's my job, isn't it? To point out when he's not being cool, to urge him to order a "manly" drink like black coffee. But it seems mean, unnecessary. *Let the poor guy enjoy his tea,* I scold myself.

After all, things have been going pretty awful for Dennis lately. Ever since Jessica no-showed, he's been down in the dumps.

"Have you been feeling any better?" I ask. "Did you go to that seminar I suggested?" Dennis's lifelong dream is to get into the music industry—hence his "rock" band—and a big music producer from Interscope was recently in town hosting a workshop.

Dennis shakes his head. "It's next weekend, but I forgot to sign up. And now the deadline has passed."

"That's too bad." I think it over. "You should call them

anyway. Be assertive, see if they'll make an exception and let you in the class. You'd be surprised how often things like that work."

"I don't feel like being assertive."

"We can go over some techniques." I sip my coffee. "Would that help?" Dennis and I have spent a lot of time role-playing. It's not as kinky as it sounds. Actually, it's not kinky at all. The thing is, Dennis has a ton of trouble talking to people, standing up for himself. I've tried to help him with that, tried to put him at ease.

"I don't want to. Ever since Jessica dumped me . . ."

I wasn't going to bring her up, but now that he's done it, I say, "But you don't really know that she dumped you. It's still possible she might have gotten cold feet or that something came up."

He doesn't answer, just tosses a piece of paper across the table at me. I pick it up. It's an e-mail from Jessica.

Dennis,
No matter what you might believe, I am not avoiding you. I'm just busy. And I'm afraid I'm going to be busy . . . for a while. Sorry. I didn't realize this when we first started talking. But my schedule has changed. I just don't have time for any kind of a relationship right now.
Good luck and best wishes,
Jess

Ouch. No time for a relationship? Please. There's no one in the world who can't make time for some lovin' if they really want to. She's letting him down easy. Which, despite what most people believe, is so much worse than cold, hard rejection.

"What does it mean?" he demands, then stops himself. "No, don't say it. I think I already know."

"You already know," I agree.

"Why did she do this? I just keep going over that in my head. Why? Why? Why?"

"There're a million reasons. You'll probably never know the truth."

We talk for a little while. He tells me how depressed he is, how much he's not coping with things these days.

"It will get better," I assure him. "The period right after a . . ." I want to use the word *breakup*, but I'm not sure that fits, ". . . change is always tough."

Dennis sighs. "Sometimes it feels like I'm living my life a decade behind everyone else."

"What do you mean?"

He crumples the e-mail in his hands. Balls it up, then smooths it out again. "By seventh grade most of the guys in my class had already kissed a girl. By twelfth grade all of them—I mean *all of them*—had gotten laid. By sophomore year of college everyone I know had already gotten drunk, smoked pot, partied all night. You know, normal stuff you do when you're young." He wrinkles his brow. "But I missed out on all of that. I've never smoked pot. And not because I've got some moral objection to it or something. I've never smoked pot because no one's ever offered me any. I've never stayed out all night partying. My God, I've never even gotten so drunk I've puked!"

"Trust me, you're not missing much," I blurt out, and Dennis glares at me. I'm off my game today, because this is the worst possible thing I could have said. I know that better than anyone—never tell somebody they're "not missing much." It's a slap in the face. Like when a rich person insists they'd rather be poor because money only causes problems. Or when a gorgeous girl tells an ugly one, "Trust me. You don't really want to be pretty. People never believe me, but being beautiful is such a burden."

"I'm sorry," I tell Dennis.

He presses on. "Ms. Chase, I didn't even have my first kiss until the end of my sophomore year of college. Do you know how old you are at the end of your sophomore year? Twenty." He spits the number out before I have time to answer. "Twenty. And that wasn't even a French kiss," he says. "I was almost twenty-two before I got one of those." He crumples Jessica's e-mail back up, tossing it into the trash this time. "I bet you've never heard anything so pathetic in your entire life. I bet I'm the biggest loser you've ever met!"

I ignore Dennis's last comment. I've told him to stop taking potshots at himself—and I don't want to acknowledge it, encourage it in any way. I choose my words carefully. "The thing you have to remember is that everything people tell you isn't necessarily true."

"Huh?"

"Think about this for a second. A big part of why you feel bad for yourself is because you feel like other people are having all of these great experiences and you're missing out. Right?"

"In a way, yeah."

"You feel bad because these other guys were making out with girls in seventh grade and you weren't. You feel bad because senior year everyone was getting laid except you. In college everyone was partying and getting high, and you weren't." I pause. "But the thing is, how do you know this stuff for sure? These people could have very easily been lying. Lots of people blow things up, make their lives sound bigger and better than they are." He doesn't say anything, so I continue. "I very seriously doubt all the guys in your senior class were having sex. In fact, I wouldn't be surprised if half of them were virgins."

"Yeah, right, like anyone would have admitted it."

"Exactly!" I say, snapping my fingers. "Who's going to shout that from the rooftops?"

"Well, nobody."

"Complete strangers aren't going to tell you the bad stuff . . . that's why their lives always seem so perfect."

"You have a small point, but that doesn't help me personally." Dennis shakes his head. "No matter what schedule other people are on—no matter how much I rush, no matter how much I try to catch up—I'm still stuck ten years behind them."

We talk for a while and, as much as I wish I could, I'm not able to make him feel any better.

At the end of our conversation, he says, "Oh, by the way. I referred a client to you the other day. I told one of my friends about the cool lessons I was taking, and she got a real kick out of it."

"Thanks." I blink in surprise. Dennis doesn't have a lot of friends, especially friends that are girls. This is a positive sign. "What's her name?"

"Pamela."

"How'd you guys meet?"

"She runs this really awesome blog. It's huge, they get like seven hundred thousand unique visitors a month."

"That's pretty impressive," I say.

"I know it is. Pamela sent me an e-mail after watching some of my rock videos online. She wanted to write a feature about me for the blog. One thing led to another, and we wound up clicking."

"That's awesome, Dennis. And she lives here in Chicago?"

He nods.

"Is her blog feature on you out yet?"

"No. I think Pamela's holding it hostage. She says she won't run it until she meets me."

"Whoa. You guys haven't met face to face?"

"Uh, no."

"And she lives here in Chicago?"

Dennis sighs. "Yeah. I know I should meet her, but I'm too nervous."

"How long have you been talking?"

"Five months."

Five months? Five months in the same city and they hadn't met face-to-face?

Dennis must be able to read my mind, because he says, "I told you, Ms. Chase. I'm ten years behind everyone else."

* * *

The rest of the day flies by, and as soon as work's out I head to Saks to shop for a reunion outfit. This has become a routine of mine. Nearly every day since I found out about the reunion, I've been hitting various boutiques and department stores, scouring their collections for the perfect dress.

Despite all the preparation it requires, my reunion revenge plan is simple. I'll stroll into the Hilton ballroom—sashaying confidently like a Miss J.–coached contestant on *America's Next Top Model.* My body will be perfect—toned, bronzed (courtesy of a spray-on tan), waxed, and manicured. I'll be decked out in designer duds from head to toe. And I'll have spent half a day in the salon, getting blond highlights that cost more than my monthly car note.

It's a lot to go through, but it will be totally worth it.

I have to be stunning. So stunning that Zack Naylor will fall to his knees, throw his hands in the air, and shout, "Why, God, *why*?! How could I let her get away?"

Oh, yes. It's going to work. I can feel it. Now all I need is the perfect dress. . . .

You're probably wondering why I care so much about my high school reunion, why I've wasted this much time, energy, and money getting ready for it. You already know about Joanie and Hayley and Zack. But even that doesn't give you the full picture of the absolute horror that was my high school career.

As much as I wish I could forget, as much as I wish I could let go of the past and simply move on, I can't.

I remember all of it.

I remember sitting home alone night after night. I remember being picked on, called names, ignored. I remember hiding out in the girls' bathroom during lunchtime because I was too embarrassed to eat in the cafeteria alone. And then, when they installed a pay phone in the main corridor, I remember spending my lunch break waiting in line to use it. I didn't have anyone to call, but it beat the hell out of hiding in a smelly, stuffy bathroom.

At least then I looked like I was fitting in. You see, the popular girls all had older boyfriends—boyfriends away at college, boyfriends with full-time jobs. And they would use their lunch hour to call their significant others.

This was in the early '90s, before the days of compulsory cell phones, and it wasn't uncommon to waste your entire lunch period waiting in line only to have the bell ring before you'd reached the front. Most of the girls hated this, but I loved it. Unlike them, I didn't actually *want* to reach the front of the line. There was no one for me to call once I got there. Sometimes I let people skip in front of me; other times I used my quarter to call the local movie hotline. They had a lengthy automated message that listed all the times of films showing around Chicago. And while the computerized voice droned on about showtimes for *Benny & Joon* or *Tombstone* or *What's Eating Gilbert Grape*, I'd fake a one-sided conversation with Brad, the imaginary boyfriend I'd invented solely for that purpose. Saying things like, "I miss you, too." And, "I know, baby, it sucks that you're going to college all the way in Indiana. But playing football for Notre Dame has always been a dream of yours." And, "At least you'll get to come home this weekend. I can't wait to see you. I'm going to smother you in kisses."

To my ear, these phony conversations sounded ridiculous, and not even remotely believable. But no one ever questioned me. In fact, more than once I caught a couple of the older girls eyeing me with newfound respect.

I kept up the Brad lie for the majority of my senior year. And it served me well. Whenever anyone made a crack about me being single or friendless, I'd merely smile with false confidence as I regaled them with tales of my awesome long-distance boyfriend. And when the prom rolled around and I didn't have a date, I just shrugged it off, telling my classmates that Brad was far too busy studying for finals to drive home and escort me to some "silly little high school dance."

The weird thing was, the longer I kept up the Brad lie the more real it became, until a part of me almost felt like he truly existed.

It's kind of depressing, if you stop and think about it. So I try not to.

I'm not expecting to find a dress today. My luck hasn't been as great as I've hoped for. But then I spy it—a gorgeous, soft-orange gown that falls in sheer chiffon layers.

It's bold and striking and will show off my (soon-to-be-bronzed) skin perfectly. I can't wait to show it off to Zack Naylor and Joanie Brixton and Hayley Hill and the countless other high school minions who never gave me the time of day.

I hug the dress against my body, and I feel dizzy with anticipation.

* * *

"You'll be very proud of me. I've been watching *Survivor*," Austin says the following afternoon. It's day one of his cool training and we're getting ready to enter Tower Records and purchase Austin's new CD collection. We've had a good afternoon. Prior to coming to Tower, we stopped by Starbucks and had a quick round of drinks.

"Ah, plugging into the mainstream. I like it. So what do you think?" I ask as I stroll along the aisles, dropping things into our basket. I grab four Beatles CDs, being careful to steer clear of their greatest hits album, which would be a dead giveaway that he's a casual fan.

"It's not the worst thing I've ever watched. But that host is annoying."

"Jeff Probst?" I pick up a copy of *Blood on the Tracks* by Bob Dylan. Then I backtrack to A and grab the latest release from Ryan Adams.

"No, the British guy. Simon something."

"Simon Cowell?"

"That's it!" He snaps his fingers, nearly dropping the basket in the process.

"Okay, you've been watching *American Idol.* Not *Survivor.* *American Idol* is the singing competition. *Survivor*'s the stranded-on-a-desert-island show."

"I thought that was *Lost.*"

"*Lost* is also on a desert island. It takes place outdoors, too, except when they're having a flashback. Or when the characters go into the hatch—which is not to be confused with *Richard* Hatch, the tax-evading winner of *Survivor.*" I pause. I'm rambling—badly. Sometimes I think I'm a talkaholic. I've always got something to say. And I never know when, or how, to shut up. It's one of the things I've had to rein in over the years.

Austin stares at me in confusion. "So which one takes place on an island?"

"They both do. But *Lost* is a scripted drama. *Survivor*'s a reality show."

Austin glances down at the Ani DiFranco CD I've placed in the basket. Right next to it is the White Stripes.

"*Survivor* is a reality show," he repeats, as if trying to memorize it. "And *American Idol* is a reality show—but with *singing*?"

"Correct." Has he been living under a rock these past few years? "How is it possible for you not to know all of this?"

"How is it possible for you not to know what $E=mc^2$ stands for?" he teases. "In the grand scheme of things I'd say that's a lot more important than reality TV."

"Good point."

"So have you enjoyed the questions I've been sending you?"

"Sure," I say. "Although you know I'm cheating on them, right?"

"What do you mean?"

"I look up the answers on Google. It doesn't even take ten minutes."

Austin grins. "I figured as much. But who cares how you learned that stuff? You know the capital of Botswana now. You didn't know that a week ago."

"True," I admit.

"And you'll probably never forget the tip about chewing gum while chopping onions."

He's right. I won't. I smile. "So it looks like we're both getting something cool out of this, huh?"

We spend the next thirty minutes shopping. I pick up CDs from Kings of Leon, Billie Holiday, Pete Yorn, Jeff Buckley. My concentration's good. I'm working faster now, speeding down the aisles, pulling out Prince, Modest Mouse, the Secret Machines, Al Green, My Chemical Romance, the Rolling Stones, Radiohead, Janet Jackson, the Doors, Sheryl Crow, Stevie Wonder, 50 Cent, Harlan T. Bobo, the Dandy Warhols, the Ramones.

It's going to look like a schizophrenic picked out this collection, but that's okay.

"We'll catalog them all, put stickers on them or something so you can remember what's rock, what's R&B, what's pop, what's trendy, what's indie."

His face lights up.

"That way, when you're back at school and someone comes to hang out in your dorm room, all you'll have to do is ask them what kind of music they like and then pick something out." It's good to do this, to keep clients focused on the future. If he starts thinking about college, maybe he'll be more excited to go back.

"Wasn't that journalist supposed to come along today?" Austin asks, changing the subject.

"Ty Benedict?"

"Yeah, him. Jerk."

"I figured you wouldn't come out if I brought him." This is a big step, getting Austin to leave the house, even if it's just to shop for music for an hour.

"Probably not. I appreciate you taking that into consideration."

He's got to stop talking like that. It sounds too formal, reserved. I tell him this. Gently, of course.

"Right-o," Austin says.

I'm looking at the price tags of the CDs. "Let's put some of these back. We can order a lot of this stuff on Amazon, and it will be cheaper." I begin placing the CDs back in their respective spots. Austin helps out, and before long we've narrowed down the collection to four CDs.

"These will get you started," I say. "We'll order the rest of the stuff online."

"If it's cheaper online, why didn't we do it that way to begin with?"

I give him a playful nudge. "I wanted to get you out of the house."

"Hey, you tricked me!" he says.

We get to the front of the line, and the cashier rings up our purchases. "Maybe a little. But your mom said you hadn't left home in weeks." What she actually said is that he hadn't left his room in weeks, but I see no need to make this distinction.

"True."

"And besides, this way we got to make an afternoon out of it."

He shrugs. "But you've kind of proven my point."

"Which is?"

"That everything is better when you stay at home." He points to his receipt. "I could have sat in my room and saved money. There was no reason for me to go out."

"Yes, but if we'd stayed in and ordered these online, you'd never have gotten that strawberry frappuccino."

"Ah," he says, smiling. "You're right."

We walk outside, and the frigid air hits us like a punch. My car's parked a few blocks up, and we move quickly in the cold.

"I keep thinking about school," Austin says as we hoof along the sidewalk.

"Do you miss it?"

"No, not really."

This surprises me.

"College wasn't . . ." His voice trails off. "It wasn't what I'd hoped for."

"How so?" I ask, shivering.

"I thought it would be more like a movie, that's all. Like *Animal House*."

I'm surprised by this, so I ask, "*Animal House*? You've seen *Animal House*?"

"I've watched it at least once a year, every year, since I was eight years old. It's my dad's favorite movie of all time." He snickers. "*To-ga, to-ga*."

"Your dad let you watch *Animal House* when you were eight?" I've never seen the movie, but I'm pretty sure it's not the kind of thing an eight-year-old should watch.

"No, that's just it. My dad *never* let me watch it. He was adamant about it. Whenever he put it on, he'd usher me out of the room. So it became an obsession of mine, at a very young age. I'd sneak downstairs and watch it early in the morning before my parents woke up."

"I see."

"Have you ever been to the MIT campus, Kylie?"

"No."

"It's nothing like *Animal House.* Nothing at all." He lets out a breath, and the condensation pools around his face. "I'm not a fool. I know *Animal House* is an extreme. But I thought college would be at least a *little* bit like that. I thought it would be fun."

"Whose decision was it for you to go to MIT?"

"My parents.' "

"Did you have a lot of input?"

"None. I'd just turned seventeen. I tried to tell my parents I didn't like MIT, didn't like Boston. I told them I wouldn't be happy in New England, but they didn't listen. I wanted to go somewhere with a more temperate climate."

Hmm.

It's an obvious question, but I've got to ask, "Have you thought about transferring to another school? Caltech, maybe?"

We reach my car. I unlock the door and we climb inside.

"That's the first thing my parents suggested." Austin fastens his seat belt. "But I vetoed it. If I go back. *If, if, if.* I want a total change of pace. Like the University of Florida."

"That's a good school," I tell him.

"They have a pretty good engineering program there. It's not on a par with MIT, of course, but what is? And, anyway, I don't care about that. If I went to the University of Florida, I could learn about Gator football. Pledge a fraternity. All that college stuff people always talk about."

Austin Dunbar in a fraternity? It's hard to picture. But you never know. If this is what will make him happy, transferring to UF and going Greek, then why not?

"I was unhappy in high school," Austin confides. "So unhappy. And I thought once I graduated and went away to college my life could really get going."

Oh, boy, do I know *that* feeling.

"And when it didn't . . . when it was the same old thing, I didn't know how to handle it. And the longer I stayed at MIT, the more convinced I became that I had made a huge mistake. I should have fought harder for Florida."

"It's not too late." I steer the car out of the parking garage. "With your grades and abilities, I'm sure you could get into UF. Talk to your parents. See what you can do."

"They'll never go for it," he says, shaking his head vehemently.

"You have to try."

"I tried two years ago, Kylie. Really hard. Ever since I was fifteen I've known I had to get out of the Midwest, had to get away from the cold and the dark nights. I wanted to be near the beach, in the warmth. And when I found out about the University of Florida, I researched it. I showed my parents how it had a high ranking in *U.S. News and World Report*. I showed them articles from the *Princeton Review*. They weren't having any of it." He sighs. "It was MIT or nothing."

I put on my left blinker and prepare to head to his house. "But you were seventeen then. You're an adult now. It's your decision to make."

"Not entirely."

"It can be," I say. "Your parents desperately want you to be happy. They were willing to pay for a thousand dollars' worth of CDs just to cheer you up." I wave the Tower Records bag for emphasis, but since it's so light (I put all but four CDs back, remember), it doesn't make such a great point.

"That's CDs. That's something they don't care about.

My education is the most important thing to them in the world."

"And I bet they'll be thrilled to see you taking an interest in it again."

"They'll veto Florida. I know they will."

"You're legal," I point out. "If they're that dead set against it, you could look into getting a scholarship—and I'm pretty sure you'd qualify for a full ride. And you could go anyway."

"I could," he muses. "You don't think that would make me a terrible person? Defying my parents like that?"

"Talk to them, Austin," I say, hitting the accelerator. "Just talk to them."

* * *

"I'm almost finished with the article," Ty says when he calls later that day.

"What!" I shriek, nearly dropping the phone. "But we were just getting started! We haven't even gone out to visit my ex-clients yet!"

"I know. And I still want to include that in the story. But I've already gotten so much great information from your current clients. I'm not sure how much more I need."

He has? This seems crazy. We spent only one afternoon together. Wasn't this supposed to be an investigative piece? "Who all have you talked to?"

"Dennis Moop. Teri Morris. Angela Dunbar."

Dennis Moop, I get. But Teri Morris? Teri Morris is someone I've only met with once. In truth, I don't even know if she's planning to commission my services. She hasn't called back since her initial consultation. And Angela Dunbar isn't even a client—she's a client's *mother*!

"How did you meet Teri Morris?" I ask.

"I bumped into her outside your office Monday."

"You weren't at my office Monday."

"Yes, I was. I stopped by to see you, but you were in a meeting. Didn't your assistant give you the message?"

"No, she did not." I can't believe Courtney forgot to tell me.

"No worries. I ran into Teri and we started chatting. She had a lot of great info to share, and I think it'll really add to the story."

"Um, okay. But Angela Dunbar isn't even a client," I point out. "Her son is."

"Angela's the one who's paying you. I think that gives her a voice, don't you?"

"I guess so."

"I also talked to Charity St. James."

"You did? How?"

He laughs. "She gave me her number, remember?"

I guess it wasn't the blow-off line, after all.

"So we're on for next Friday," Ty continues. "And after that I'm going to start working on a rough draft. I might need to follow up with you a couple of times, but I'd say by the end of next week, I'll be out of your hair for good."

Out of my hair for good? Just like that, it's over. I feel stupid, ridiculous, for thinking we'd somehow click and become friends. As if that sort of thing happens in the real world.

Once again I've let my fantasies get the best of me.

11

Cool Rule #11:

Drop-ins are for dummies. Call first. Always.

There's a reason I don't do fix-ups.

I'm sane.

Really, you have to be a loony to agree to go out with someone you've never met. Over the years, I've had lots of friends try to set me up.

When I was fat it didn't happen as much. Although when it did, it was really predictable. People only wanted to set me up with big guys.

Fat girls must date fat guys, after all. (But the reverse is not true. Fat guys can date girls of any shape and size. An annoying double standard.)

Once I got skinny, the fix-up requests became more frequent. But the quality of guys didn't improve as much as you might think. I always thought once I lost weight I'd have hot men beating down my door.

Uh, no.

Double, triple no.

But that's a different topic, one I could easily spend an hour debating, and I need to get back on track.

Where were we? Oh, yeah, fix-ups.

See, the other problem with having your friends set you

up with someone is this: if the guy was so great, then wouldn't they want him for themselves? You could argue that this is only a problem with single friends, but I'll argue back that a lot of people, especially women, hate to see someone else come out ahead of them. If your friend is married to a guy, even if he's a pretty cool guy, would she really like to see you with someone better? Probably not.

My mother is the one who first told me this. Which is why it makes no sense that she wanted to arrange a blind date for me with her friend Brenda's son, whose name, honest to God, is Miller Diller. (Diller is pronounced like "dialer," as in telephone dialer. But still. Who names their son Miller Diller?)

You don't have to be a cool instructor to veto that one.

I thought I made myself pretty clear that I had zero interest in meeting (or remeeting) Miller Diller. So imagine my surprise when I return home from work one evening to find Brenda—and a guy I can only assume is Miller Diller—sitting in my parents' living room.

She's gone and done it. I can't believe it. She's set me up, even though I asked her not to.

And there's my father, beaming proudly, looking as though he doesn't have an astrological care in the world.

"Kylie," Mom says, standing to greet me. "You remember my friend Brenda Diller."

"Yes, of course," I say. "Great to see you again."

"And this is Brenda's son."

"Miller," I say, sizing him up. He's cute, in a quirky, offbeat sort of way. His hair is a thick, curly mop that's hanging around his face.

"Actually, I go by Patrick now. It's my middle name. I haven't been called Miller since fifth grade."

He looks like a Patrick. In fact, he kind of looks like Patrick Dempsey. Which is a positive association, if there ever was one.

"Oh, okay. *Patrick*," I say.

"Brenda and Patrick are going to be staying for dinner," Mom says.

Dad snaps his fingers. "I'd better go check on everything. We're having quail," he says, sounding excited.

I trail him into the kitchen.

"I thought we couldn't do this, because of the sun being in Aquarius and all," I hiss, as Dad takes a saucepan out of the cabinet.

"It's moved into Pisces, so everything's okay now."

Great. I can't believe Mom's done this. I mean, Patrick's cute and all, but I'm sticking to my rule. No fix-ups. Now I've got to sit through dinner with the guy in front of both our parents. Talk about awkward!

"I can't believe you did this!" I say as Mom enters the kitchen.

She motions for me to keep my voice down. "Relax, you're not being set up. Patrick's already vetoed it."

"Oh," I say. "Well, that's good."

But secretly I feel a little stung. Did he get one look at me and call the whole thing off? It's a little disconcerting.

"So no need to worry," Mom says, uncorking a fresh bottle of wine. "You can unwind and enjoy dinner."

Ah, yes, I can think of few things that are more relaxing than having dinner with a complete stranger who has rejected you. *Even though you never wanted to go out with him in the first place.*

But the meal winds up being okay after all. Mom talks a lot, monopolizing the conversation. She runs through all the latest goings-on at the boutique and then turns the conversation to Brenda. Mom and Brenda have known each other for years. They met when Miller, oops Patrick, and I were in Mrs. Sills's kindergarten class in Chicago. They bonded over the fact that they were both former models and party girls who were now embracing the domestic lifestyle.

They've kept in touch over the years, even though Brenda moved to Miami when I was in the third grade.

I listen as they reminisce about the good old days. Then, during coffee, I excuse myself to go upstairs. I'm meeting with Ty tomorrow evening to go visit former How to Be Cool clients, and I want to make sure I'm well prepared. This means going over all my previous case files (I need to make sure I'm versed in my clients' histories). Considering this will probably be the last time I'll ever see him, I want to make the best impression possible. We're going to see four people: Adam Millsap, Grant Lowell, Samantha McGreevy, and Jill Sussman. I spend hours reading through my notes until I've practically got them memorized.

Once I'm finished with that, I pick out something to wear. I've got a big night tomorrow, and I want to dress to impress!

* * *

The sign on the mailbox reads Lowell Grant. This is not lost on Ty.

"I thought his name was Grant Lowell?" he asks, studying his notes.

"It is. Was. Is," I babble.

Ty raises an eyebrow.

"We changed his name," I explain, pressing the buzzer. No response.

"We? Who's 'we'?"

It's seven o'clock Friday night and we're just getting started on the visits to my ex-clients. I'd wanted to take him to see Jill Sussman first, but Ty pointed out that from a geographical standpoint it made more sense to visit Grant first. Jill hired me five months ago, and we've maintained contact even after her cool lessons ended. I know for a fact that Jill is still doing great, that the things I've taught her have really helped. Grant Lowell I'm not as sure of. I try to keep in touch with all of my past clients, but Grant has largely avoided my calls and e-mails. I have no idea what we'll find when—if—he answers the door.

"Grant and me," I explain. "He was born Lowell Steverson Grant the third."

"Pretty sophisticated," Ty says. "But not exactly cool."

"Right."

"I take it he's rich?"

"His family is. Grant had a big falling-out with his father years ago. That's part of the reason for the name change. He wanted to distance himself from the family as much as possible."

Ty's cell starts going off, for what must be the tenth time in as many minutes. "Sorry," he says, switching it off. "My friend Tal just wanted to firm up our plans for tonight."

"Anything exciting?" I ask, trying to sound casual.

"We're going to this new club, 7 of Seven. Have you heard of it?"

I have indeed. 7 of Seven is one of the trendiest nightspots in Chicago, the kind of place that attracts AAA-list stars. My own night, which entails drinks with Ruby, sounds boring in comparison. "That sounds fun."

"Should be."

I ring the buzzer again, and this time someone answers. "Can I help you?"

"I'm looking for Grant Lowell."

"Who's this?"

"Kylie Chase, from How to Be Cool."

"Who?"

I repeat myself.

"Um, hold on. I'll be right down."

A minute later Grant comes to the door and lets us into the foyer of his building. I'm pleased to see that, appearance-wise at least, Grant still looks cool. We did a lot of work together, dressing *down* his wardrobe (Grant was used to wearing blazers, vests, and ties all the time). I took him to Barney's and Banana Republic. Then we spent an entire day scouring the racks of thrift stores, finding deconstructed T-shirts and jeans. After that, it was off to a colorist to have his preppy 'do reshaped into a stylish, spiky coif with blond tips. The end result was a younger, cooler-looking Grant.

And, from the looks of it, the makeover stuck. Tonight Grant's wearing black-and-white Converse tennis shoes and a ratty yellow T-shirt with a hole in the collar. This would all be a bit too junky, if not for the fact that he's sporting a pair of $300 True Religion jeans. It's a perfect blend of cheap and expensive, the kind of thing I taught him to do last year. (Full disclosure: I learned most of what I know about fashion from my co-worker Josh.)

"Hey, Grant, how are you doing?" I ask.

"Good." He seems uncomfortable, nervous.

"I'm sorry to surprise you like this." I introduce Ty and explain what we're doing. "You don't mind being interviewed, do you?"

"I guess not. Come on up," he says, leading us to the stairs. We follow him to his apartment on the second floor. "The place is a wreck," Grant says, as he lets us in through the front door. A few magazines are strewn around the living room, but other than that, it's pretty immaculate.

Ty and I sit down on the love seat, our knees touching. Grant doesn't sit, just stands, pacing nervously, the way he used to do when he first came into my office. This makes me worried. Grant's biggest problem has always been anxiety. He has terrible social skills. He has a lot of trouble talking to people—he doesn't do well making small talk. He once confessed, "It's like, when I meet somebody for the first time, I go through all the possible topics of conversation. What do you do for a living? Where are you from? How about this weather? And then I'm tapped out. Once we get past the basics, I have nothing else to say to them, and I'm incapable of faking it. So I stand there, awkwardly, with my mouth hanging open. Or, worse still, I panic and I start repeating the same topics we've already covered." We spent a lot of time together, working on how to improve this. I taught him how to sustain a conversation, how to use those little icebreakers as a springboard to another topic. I taught him how to talk about himself without overdoing it, how to listen (he was often so nervous when first meeting people that he'd barely pay attention to what they said), and how to respond appropriately. I taught him about body language, how to hold himself properly, how to smile and nod and seem relaxed even when he wasn't.

He seems to have forgotten all of those things.

"What can I do for you?" Grant asks, chewing on his index finger, tugging the nail tip off into his mouth. He's twenty-eight years old. It's heartbreaking to see him pulling up these kinds of bad habits.

"If you don't mind, Kylie, I'd like to ask Grant a few questions."

"Oh," Grant says, moving on to bite his thumbnail. "It's Lowell. I go by Lowell now."

I raise my eyebrows. "You do? I thought you really liked being called Grant."

He exhales loudly. "I did. But it was too hard to keep up. Nobody could remember to call me that. And all my IDs are under the name Lowell Grant. It was too much trouble."

Ty writes this down. "How do you feel Kylie Chase has helped you out?"

"Oh, she's helped. Yes, she's helped," he says.

"Uh-huh," Ty says. "Do you mind me asking how precisely?"

"I, um, I, you see, before . . . I was kind of a, an, awkward person." His voice is so low I can barely hear him.

"I'm sorry, can you speak up?" Ty asks.

"Uh, yes." He mumbles something.

"What kind of areas did she help you out with?"

"I dress . . . different."

"Better?" Ty prompts.

"Yes, better." He chews on his pinky nail.

"What about your social life?"

"It's better."

"How so?"

"I . . . I go out. Lots. I go out lots."

It's like we've regressed an entire year. If it weren't for Grant, er, Lowell's outfit, you'd never know I'd had any effect at all.

"Are you going out tonight?"

"I don't know."

"It's already seven-fifteen. Shouldn't you know whether or not you have plans?"

"Um. Yes. I guess I don't."

I cringe. He could have come back so much better to that, could have said he was playing it cool, that some friends might stop by. That he had so many options he was just trying to decide which one to pursue. It would be lying, sure, but that's part of what I taught him. Some lies are acceptable. (Which reminds me. I need to straighten Ty out on the bio mix-up, sooner rather than later. That's a lie that is definitely *not* acceptable!)

"So you were going to sit home alone tonight, staring at the TV?" Ty asks. "You weren't going to leave your apartment at all?"

"I might have . . . I might have gone out."

"To . . . ?"

It takes him forever to spit out an answer. "Buy some gum at the corner store. And . . . and I need highlighters . . . to help with a . . . a project . . . for work."

Ty keeps grilling Grant Lowell/Lowell Grant, asking about his love life, how many parties he attends, whether he's happy. The answers are single, not many, and mostly.

By the time we leave, I feel horrible. Poor Grant Lowell paid good money for me to help improve his social life, and he got bubkes! On our way to the door, I pull Grant aside. Ty's on his cell phone, checking his billion messages, so he doesn't notice.

"Call me," I whisper. "Please. I'll work with you again."

"I don't . . . I don't know."

"On the house," I say, in case money is what's holding

him back. I really shouldn't be doing this, but I don't care. I'll meet with him on my own time, I'll help him any way I can. I feel absolutely awful, seeing how little impact I've made.

"If it's okay with you," he says, chewing on his lower lip, "I'd . . . I'd rather not."

"I really want to help."

"It's okay," he says.

"But I feel like I didn't do enough for you."

"You did enough."

"But you don't seem," I lower my voice in case Ty's listening, "you don't seem all that happy now."

"I'm happy," Grant says. "Happy enough." I start to object, but he adds, "I could never keep it up, Kylie. I couldn't ever, uh, I couldn't ever be him."

"Be who?"

"Grant Lowell." He blushes. "Maybe I'm meant . . . maybe I'm meant to be Lowell Grant." He doesn't say anything else, just shows us to the door.

And I feel strange, deflated, as we make our way to Samantha McGreevy's apartment. I don't have my car tonight—I left it at the office—so we take the El to Sam's.

"So this is the baseball nut?" Ty asks as I ring the buzzer.

"*Was* the baseball nut," I correct. "She's spread her interests out more now."

Sam McGreevy is a beautiful attorney who came to me last summer when she realized her love life was stalled and her friends all seemed to be pulling away. It didn't take me long to identify the culprit: baseball. Sam had let her love of the White Sox take over every aspect of her life. She was like Jimmy Fallon's character in *Fever Pitch*, living and breathing baseball to the point where everything else in her life was suffering.

"I don't even like the cool team," she'd said. "I like the fucking White Sox."

"Lots of people like the White Sox," I'd pointed out.

"Not obsessively. Not like I do. If this were the Cubs, people might understand it more. And another thing. I'll never meet a decent guy as long as I'm stuck on the White Sox. Guys are completely turned off by my sports obsession."

It seemed crazy. Didn't men always complain that their girlfriends were uninterested in sports? But, as it turned out, the opposite was also true.

"Men don't want to meet a woman who knows more about sports than they do," Sam had explained. "It's the same way they don't want a girl who will drink them under the table, or outeat them at a buffet. It's too masculine."

I'd urged her to reconsider. I didn't think she should dumb down her baseball knowledge just to land a guy.

"It's for my own good more than anything," she'd said. "I'm tired of being known only as the White Sox girl. I need to be a more well-rounded person. I need other hobbies. But I don't know where to start."

So we'd gone on a hobby blitz.

I'd introduced her to pottery classes. She'd made ugly, misshapen ashtrays and I'd made functionally sound coffee mugs and plates. (I'm not being arrogant; I have more of an artist's background than she does.) I'd gotten her involved in tennis lessons. I'd encouraged her to pick up the piano again; she'd played in high school and had let it die down when she went away to college. We took a flower-arranging class together and went to see art openings.

Before long a few of the hobbies had stuck, and Sam had

stopped needing me to tag along. She began reconnecting with her old friends and found a new guy, and her White Sox love slipped into the background.

Sam answers the door. "Oh, my God! Kylie!" she says, giving me a hug.

Right away I'm alarmed. She's decked out in sweatpants and a White Sox shirt and cap.

She sees my stricken expression and says, "Don't worry about these old things! I was cleaning out my closet tonight and I ran across them. Put them on for old time's sake."

Ty gives me a look as if to say, *She's cleaning her closet on a Friday night?*

"And who is this?" she asks, giving me an approving smile.

"Oh, I'm so sorry. Sam, this is Ty Benedict. Ty Benedict, Samantha McGreevy."

"Ty Benedict!" Sam exclaims. "You're that party boy, aren't you?"

"Guilty as charged." He shakes her hand. "I'm here interviewing Kylie for an article. Do you mind if we talk to you for a few minutes?"

She looks unsure. "Well, I kind of have company. I can't really bring you into my apartment. You understand."

"I thought you were cleaning out your closet," Ty says.

"I am. But he's, uh, helping."

"He? A boyfriend?"

"No. My brother."

Oh, God, no. Samantha's brother, Rob, is equally obsessed with the White Sox. If he's over, there's no telling what's going on.

"There's a game tonight, isn't there?" Ty asks.

"Yes, we're playing the Giants." She shifts her feet, impatiently, like an addict waiting for her next fix. She can't wait to get back upstairs and check on the score.

"Close game?" Ty asks, sensing how anxious she is.

"Extremely!" She paused. "Oh, crap. You guys caught me." Sam slumps her shoulders in mock shame. "I'm watching the game. But just this once."

"That's why you didn't want us to come up, isn't it?"

"Yeah," she admits sheepishly. "Anyway, if you guys don't mind, I've got to get back upstairs. Good seeing you, Kylie. Nice meeting you, Ty." She shakes his hand, hugs me goodbye, and then darts back into her building.

"You're oh for two," Ty says, smiling. I grimace, so he adds, "A little baseball humor. Don't look so stressed out, Kylie. I'm sure the next two visits will go better."

I feel awful. What if the entire thing, my entire career, has been a sham? What if I haven't done my clients any good at all?

I'm feeling less than confident by the time we get to Jill Sussman's brownstone. I halfway expect her to answer the door in a muumuu, with her hair in rollers. I also expect her to be about fifty pounds heavier.

Like me, Jill used to be fat.

When we first met, back in September, she was in the process of losing fifty pounds. Most of the work had been done for me. She had only ten pounds left to lose. I helped her out as best I could—gave her all my weight-loss maintenance tips, introduced her to my personal trainer. We talked about style; she met with Josh a few times to get some wardrobe pointers.

But Jill was insecure. She still felt overweight. The whole "once a fat girl, always a fat girl" thing, I guess. I worked to bring her out of her shell. We practiced walking with confidence, going into bars, flirting with guys.

Even though I've spoken to Jill recently, even though she assures me that her social life is "spectacular," after seeing Grant Lowell and Samantha McGreevy, I have my doubts.

But Jill Sussman doesn't disappoint. We catch her as she's on her way out of her apartment, heading off for a hot night out.

"Maybe I'll see you later," Ty says. "I'm going to 7 of Seven."

"Maybe so," Jill says, giving Ty a flirtatious smile. "I'm so sorry I can't stay and talk," she tells me. "I'm meeting my friends for dinner before we go dancing and I'm so late."

"That's too bad. I would have loved to talk to you," Ty says.

Jill gives him her number. "Call me next week, I'll tell you all about this goddess here and how she revolutionized my life." She blows me a kiss as she rushes off down the street.

I'm feeling better after our brief encounter with Jill. It takes us thirty minutes to get to Adam Millsap's place. Then we spend another five minutes ringing the bell. He never answers.

"He must be out," Ty says approvingly. "That's pretty good. See, your batting average is going up."

"Yeah, I guess it is."

"Tell me about this Adam guy again," Ty asks as we walk back to the train. I fill him in on Adam.

"He's your basic computer geek, à la Dennis Moop."

"It's good that he's out, then. These guys tend to be real homebodies."

"Yeah."

"What did you do to help Adam?"

"I got him to stop playing World of Warcraft so much. He was some sort of elf or dwarf or weapons maker. God, I can't remember. He spent our entire initial consultation telling me about his character and what he'd accomplished. World of Warcraft was, seriously, his entire life."

"So it's good that he's not home. Before you got to him, a typical Friday probably involved playing on the computer all night."

"Pretty much. I helped Adam see that any hobby you want to have is okay, but you need to learn to do it in moderation." I'm not doing a very good job of selling this story. I'm distracted, nervous. I can't stop thinking that, true, Adam's not sitting at home on a Friday night. But isn't it just as likely that he's out at a World of Warcraft gaming convention?

"There's something I need to talk to you about," I say, stopping dead in my tracks.

Ty looks confused. "Is everything okay?"

I take a deep breath and let it out slowly. "It's about my bio." I've been thinking about this all night, trying to figure out a way to explain it. I decide to go with the truth. "You see, my assistant actually sent you the wrong bio. None of the things on it were true."

He raises an eyebrow. "You made up a fake bio for yourself?"

"No, no." Ty looks really disturbed, so I immediately start backpedaling my story, shying away from the truth. "It was a bio on one of my co-workers, and Courtney accidentally stuck my name on it. A simple search-and-replace error."

"Whose bio was it?"

"Just this girl who doesn't work there anymore."

"What's her name?"

"Kim something or another," I say. "I'm not really sure. She worked there before me, so I don't know."

This is a horrible lie, and I'm afraid he's going to call me on it. But, miraculously, he doesn't. "That's too funny."

"Yeah."

"So you never went cliff diving?"

"No."

"Or backpacked through the Australian outback?"

"Afraid not."

"Ha." Ty laughs. "Well, I wish I could have met this Kim girl. She sounds pretty cool."

"Uh-huh. She was."

We reach the train platform, and it's time to go our separate ways, Ty to 7 of Seven and me to Ruby's. I haven't seen much of her since the Thailand trip, and I'm dying to catch up.

"Have a great night," he says, pulling out his El pass. "And, hey, if you want, you should stop by 7 of Seven later on. Say hi."

"Really?"

"Sure. It might be fun."

My heart is racing. "I'll have to check with my friend Ruby," I tell him.

"Call me if you decide you want to go so I can put your name on the list."

We say good-bye and the second I'm on the train I call Ruby to ask if she wants to go to 7 of Seven with Ty.

"Are you kidding me?" she squeals. "Absolutely! Call him back! Get us on the list."

So I do. But Ty's phone goes straight to voice mail. He's been switching it off and on all night, and he must have accidentally left it off. I spend the entire train ride to Ruby's dialing and redialing Ty's number, but it always goes to voice mail. I finally leave a message, telling him I've changed my mind and asking him to put me (plus one) on the list.

"Call me back and let me know when you get this," I say. I don't want to go all the way out to the club and be turned away at the door just because Ty didn't check his messages.

I never hear back from him.

I stop by my office building, pick up my car, and head out to meet Ruby at Davey's apartment. Still no Ty.

Someone on Davey's street must be having a party. All the spaces out front are full, and I wind up parking three blocks away. It's freezing cold out, and we're still waiting to hear from Ty, so we wind up ordering Chinese food and watching DVDs.

Around one a.m. Ruby dozes off and I decide to watch the rest of *Roman Holiday* before going home. I've long since given up on Ty, but at one-fifteen my phone rings.

Much to my amazement, it's him.

"I'm so sorry," Ty says. I can hear the music of the club pulsing in the background. "My phone was off. Do you guys still want to come out?"

I do want to, I'm dying to. But Ruby's sound asleep, and it's late. I don't want to appear desperate, showing up alone and at the last minute. "We already made other plans," I say, as I stare at Ruby's TV.

"That's too bad," Ty says, screaming to be heard over the music. "Another time."

"Another time," I agree. And I get the feeling we both mean it.

I finish *Roman Holiday*, shut off the TV, and then let myself out of Davey's apartment. I'm disappointed that Ty and I didn't connect tonight, but the intention is there. He wants to see me, and I want to see him.

It's going to happen. I know it is.

As I walk back to my car, my mind plays U2's *With or Without You* and *Love Song* by the Cure. And I feel energized, excited by what's to come. And even though it's raining lightly and I didn't think to grab an umbrella, I don't once fantasize that I'm Rachel McAdams. I'm not Audrey Hepburn. I'm not Marilyn Monroe.

I'm not even Alicia Silverstone in the Aerosmith videos.

I'm just me.

12

Cool Rule #12:

It's better to underreact than overreact.

I have an urgent message to call Angela Dunbar. I dial her number and she answers on the second ring. She doesn't say hello, just, "I have some bad news."

"Words I am never fond of hearing."

"Would you like to know what I'm not fond of hearing?"

Uh-oh. "Um, okay. What?"

"I'm not fond of hearing that someone *I am paying* to help my son develop his social skills has been butting in where she does not belong. Let me ask you a question, Kylie Chase. Do you have any experience as a college counselor?"

"No, I—"

"Then why in the hell would you tell my son to transfer to some goddamn party school in Florida?"

I don't know how to address this. "Austin mentioned to me that he was really interested in going to the University of Florida, that he thought he might be happy there."

"So you told him to throw his life away and go to some hellhole college on the other side of the country?"

I cradle the phone against my ear. "It's . . . it's a very good school."

"It's a damn sight away from MIT." It's Mr. Dunbar now. She must have passed the phone over.

"This is something Austin feels very strongly about."

"Austin is a confused nineteen-year-old kid! He doesn't know what he wants. When he wakes up six months from now and realizes he's thrown his life away, that he's passed up his chance to graduate from MIT, he'll hate you for it!"

Maybe they're right. But it should be his decision.

"Austin wasn't happy at MIT." I'm keeping my voice calm, even. I don't want to make them madder.

"He would have been." It's Mrs. Dunbar again. "All he needed was more time to adjust."

"He'd been there for two years," I point out.

"Do you know what Austin's doing right now?" she asks. "He's upstairs filling out his scholarship application for Florida!"

She says this like it's the worst thing in the world. "Mrs. Dunbar," I try again. "Wouldn't you rather have Austin back in school? Even if it's not the school of your choice, it's better than sitting around the house all day. . . ."

"Do not presume to tell me what I want," she huffs. "In fact, consider this your last conversation: with me *and* with Austin. I don't want you getting anywhere near him. You're fired."

Mr. Dunbar grabs the phone again. "And that bill your firm sent last week? Don't hold your breath waiting for a check!"

And with that he hangs up the phone.

I've been fired a few times before, but never in such a dramatic fashion. Usually when clients decide they're finished with How to Be Cool they just stop calling. My conversation with the Dunbars was unnerving, to say the least. But there's a part of me that was expecting it. While I'd hoped they'd jump on board with Austin's decision to go to UF, part of me thought that would be too easy.

Maybe I should have kept my mouth shut. Or maybe I made the right choice, urging him to follow his heart. Only time would tell.

I'm in a weird mood for the rest of the day. Kevin's not going to like that "don't hold your breath waiting for a check" comment. He's a dollars-and-cents man, and he won't be happy to see that one of our clients is stiffing us. I could push the Dunbars, try to force them to pay, but I don't want to take that route. A part of me feels bad for interfering. A part of me is worried I've made a bad situation worse.

I get two comps per quarter. I usually save them for frequent clients like Dennis Moop, but in this case I'll use one on Austin Dunbar.

* * *

Miller Diller is back.

He's sitting on my parents' couch balancing a book on his lap.

"What are you doing here?" I ask.

"Your mom invited me for dinner," he says.

Swell. I'm feeling down over my conversation with Angela Dunbar. The last thing I feel like doing is being social. But I know my mother will get on me if I don't, so I give it a shot.

"What are you reading?" I ask.

"*The Unbearable Lightness of Being*," he says. "It's a heady philosophical novel by Milan Kundera. It's set during the era of the Soviet invasion of Czechoslovakia."

"Right, of course," I say, playing it off as if I know what he's talking about. I've definitely heard of *The Unbearable Lightness of Being* before, but I have no clue what it's about.

"You all ready for your high school reunion?" Patrick asks.

"How'd you know about that?"

"Your mom told me. She said you were really excited."

"I am." I sit down in my dad's recliner.

"It probably won't be that great," he says.

"Why does everyone keep telling me that?" I ask, annoyed.

"Oh, sorry. It's just, I remember how crappy my high school reunion was."

"Really? It was that bad?"

Patrick grimaces. "Painfully boring. I showed up. Drank a beer. Ate some pretzels. Talked to a few people. Came home. That was pretty much the gist of it."

I tuck a few stray hairs behind my ear. "You didn't reconnect with anybody?"

"No. I don't have much interest in those people. I haven't kept in touch with anybody from high school."

"Neither have I," I admit.

"There's probably a good reason for that. Some things are better left in the past," Patrick says.

"Then why'd you go?"

"Why not?" He shrugs. "It seemed like the thing to do. I guess I was curious. I wanted to see what people were up to, find out if it was anything interesting. And then I got there and realized that there's a reason I don't talk to them anymore. And I also realized something—all those popular kids, the ones I used to look up to—they were amazingly boring and plain now." He chuckles. "I guess once you pull back the curtain it turns out that most people lead disappointingly mundane lives."

He has a point.

"I think you'll get to your reunion and discover that all these people you want to get in touch with just aren't worth it anymore."

All of a sudden it's starting to feel less like a friendly conversation and more like a lecture. I'm getting a little annoyed, so I decide to change the subject.

"So the last time I saw you, you were in kindergarten. What have you been up to since then?"

Patrick runs a hand through his hair, fluffing out his McDreamy mop of brown curls. "Hmm . . . let's see. What have I done since *kindergarten*?" He pauses. "Well, I grew up. Went to elementary school, then high school, then college. Got my Ph.D. Got married. Invented TiVo. Made millions. Now I'm retired. I spend most of my time ice fishing up in Alaska. I'm just passing through Oak Park for a few days. How 'bout you?"

"Wha-what? Are you serious?"

He grins. "Of course! I want to know what you're up to."

"No, no . . . not about that part. About the inventing TiVo and the ice fishing and . . . all the rest of it." I don't want to come right out and ask about the millions. Or the marriage.

"Maybe," Patrick says, with a straight face. He bites his lower lip. It looks like he's teetering on the verge of laughter. "Okay, no."

"Not about any of it?"

"The school part was true. I made the rest of it up."

"Oooo*kay.*" He might look like Patrick Dempsey, but that's where the similarities end. McDreamy would never make such a bizarre crack.

"I was just trying to prove my theory about people leading mundane lives. If I told you what I really did, you'd have stopped listening as soon as I got past the college part."

I laugh. "Try me."

"My passion is the stars," he says.

My eyes widen. "Oh, God, you're kidding, right?" Thanks to my father, I've had enough astrology mumbo-jumbo to last a lifetime.

He wrinkles his brow. "No, I love astronomy. I teach it, in fact."

"Phew." I breathe a sigh of relief. "Astronomy. I thought you were talking about astrology."

Patrick looks bemused. "There's quite a difference. But you'd be amazed how many people get confused. When I tell them I'm an astronomy professor, they ask me what it means if Saturn is in retrograde or the sun is in Taurus."

"That's my sign," I throw in.

"Mine, too. Hey, when's your birthday?"

"April twenty-fifth."

"Mine's May eleventh." Patrick sets his book down. "And we'll both be turning thirty this year."

I grimace. "Thanks for reminding me."

"Getting older is fun."

"No, it is *not.*"

Patrick shrugs. "It's better than the alternative."

"Which is?"

"*Not* getting older," he says flatly. "Which means you're dead."

"Thank you for that lovely thought."

"Hey, you asked."

"So, are you going to be hanging around the neighborhood for a while?"

"Yeah, didn't your parents tell you?"

"I don't think so."

"See, in addition to being an astronomy professor, I also work flipping houses in my spare time."

"You do?"

He nods. "Uh-huh. I love it. At the moment it's my full-time job, until I decide what university I want to work for next."

"They're all beating down your door, are they?" I tease.

"Uh, kind of the opposite. I worked for two years teaching at a small college in Pennsylvania. But they lost part of their funding and wound up letting a bunch of the professors go. It's tough, because I have a ton of schooling, but I'm still fairly inexperienced. And there aren't a ton of astronomy positions open, and most of the people who are in them already have tenure. . . ."

"Sounds rough."

"It's okay," he says. "You just gotta roll with the punches."

I'm amazed that he's so casual about this. I don't know what I'd do if I'd spent eight years in college only to get shut out of all the good jobs. I don't understand how people are able to do this and not stress out about the future. It's the same way Ruby stays calm about her modeling career, even though the whole thing is so up in the air.

"So how'd you get into flipping?"

"I've always loved carpentry work. And I like having a big project, being able to see it through from beginning to end. It's nice, too, because it's flexible. I can work when I want, and when a project is finished, I can move on. Like, right now, I'm in Oak Park. But four months from now, who knows?"

"What are you working on now?"

"I just bought the house down the street. Er, actually, my mom bought it. She's financing this project for me. But I'll be living there for the next couple of months, until we can get it fixed up and ready to be sold."

"So it looks like we're both living with our parents," I tease him. "In a roundabout way."

"In a roundabout way," he agrees.

"Well," I say, standing up, "I'd better go. I have some work to do."

"Okay." He picks up his book again. "But one quick thing."

I raise an eyebrow. "What?"

"I wasn't reading *The Unbearable Lightness of Being.*" He flips the book over so I can see the cover. "It's a collection of *Mad* magazine comic strips."

* * *

I've just finished writing my account of what happened with Angela Dunbar when Courtney buzzes me.

"Ty Benedict's on line one," she says, singsongy.

I pick up the phone. "Hey."

"Hey yourself." He sounds excited. "Have I got some news for you!"

I haven't spoken to him since the night we failed to hook up at 7 of Seven. Is he planning to invite me out again? "Good, I hope." I don't feel like listening to more bad news.

"It's awesome." He pauses for effect. "I finished the article. And, if I do say so myself, it's brilliant."

"Oh, great! I can't wait to read it. When will it be on newsstands?"

I'm expecting him to say three months, maybe longer. I've been interviewed for long-lead pieces before. Most magazines begin working on their summer issues around Christmas. Sometimes it's an entire year before an article appears.

"That's the great news," Ty says. "One of our freelance pieces fell apart during fact-checking. They needed a last-minute replacement, so they're plugging in the article I wrote about How to Be Cool. You'll be in the May issue, which hits stands the beginning of April."

"Oh, my God!" I shriek. "You're kidding."

"Nope."

"I've never seen such a quick turnaround." The article will be out right in time for my thirtieth birthday, which is April twenty-fifth.

"Neither have I," Ty admits. "But the editor is really pumped about my story. He couldn't wait for me to make my big splash in *Metro Guy*."

I wish it were coming out a few weeks earlier, so I could take a copy along to my reunion. (Although I'd never actually do that. Way too tacky.)

"There's something else."

"Oh?" I ask coyly. "What's that?" There's a part of me that's hoping he'll ask me out.

"Now, I never do this."

"Uh-huh."

"But would you like me to read you the article?"

"Over the phone?"

"Yes. I thought you might like to hear it."

"Can you fax it to me?" I ask, disappointed that he's not looking for a date.

"Now, now, you know better than to ask that." Ty chuckles. "I can't possibly risk a hard copy of this thing leaking out early. My editor would kill me if he knew I was even reading it to you."

"Oh, no, I understand," I say, feeling stupid for asking. I really do know better.

"Okay, make yourself comfortable," Ty says. He clears his throat, and then starts to read:

> *From Steve Urkel to* Saved by the Bell*'s Screech to the Ashton Kutcher–produced* Beauty and the Geek. *There's no escaping it: nerds are everywhere.*
>
> *Just ask Kylie Chase. As founder of the Chicago-based How to Be Cool (an offshoot of Sloane Image Consultants), Chase has seen it all.*
>
> *Nerds with pocket protectors. Nerds with thick glasses. Nerds addicted to video games. Nerds who, at forty years old, are still virgins.*
>
> *Chase spends her days helping social outcasts make the leap from geek to chic.*

"Whoa," I cut in. "That's a little bit misleading, don't you think? Not everyone who comes to see me is some Screech-like dork. I have a huge variety of clients."

"Don't worry," Ty says, "I'm getting to that." He continues reading. There's more stuff about geeks, a quote from Dennis Moop (identified by his first name only) about how I've helped him learn basic social skills. I'm starting to get nervous, when Ty comes to Charity's piece in the story.

> *But not all of Chase's clients can be easily fit into a mold. Take Charity, for instance, a drop-dead gorgeous party girl who secretly longs to be a brainiac.*

He has a few brief quotes from Charity, in which she talks about how I've been helping her explore the world of fine arts and literature. Then it goes back to me.

> *"There are lots of different definitions of cool," Kylie explains as she drives her car toward the home of Austin Dunbar, a nineteen-year-old prodigy who's looking to break out of his "genius" shell. After exhausting their options last fall, Angela and Wayne Dunbar caught Kylie's appearance on* Good Morning America *and were hooked.*
>
> *"It seemed like what we've been searching for," Angela Dunbar says. "The perfect way to get our son, Austin, to come out of his shell."*

At the mention of Mrs. Dunbar, my face falls. I'm glad Ty's not here to see my reaction. I wonder if I should tell him about what happened. I listen as he reads the rest of the article. The Dunbars are featured heavily in the piece, and that doesn't seem right, given that they're no longer clients.

I decide to bite the bullet. "You sure gave Austin Dunbar's story a lot of space," I say.

"I felt it warranted it."

How? As far as I can tell, he never even interviewed Austin. All of the quotes are from Angela Dunbar.

"Austin's a new client," I say. "I've only met with him twice. I kind of feel like it would make more sense to have the story feature clients like Dennis or Jill Sussman. We spent all that time meeting with my old clients, and you haven't even included that in the story."

"I'm still tweaking things," Ty says, sounding annoyed. "I'll probably add some stuff about Jill Sussman and Grant

Lowell at the end, to kind of show how it's all come full circle. But to be perfectly honest, I didn't read you the article so you could tell me how to rewrite it."

I see where he's coming from. I wouldn't like it if someone told me how to do my job. "I'm sorry," I tell him. "It's just, I kind of felt like the Austin thing was still so new." I struggle for the right words. "At this stage, I'm not even sure if Austin will continue on as a client or not. It's still too early to tell." I know I should come right out and tell him that I've been fired, but I'm afraid to. Ty's been really understanding so far—he was kind enough to laugh off the whole fake bio incident. But I don't want to push him.

"Why, did something happen?" he asks.

Then again, don't I owe it to everyone involved—Austin, the Dunbars, Ty, myself—to tell the truth? I take a deep breath. "As a matter of fact, it did. Mrs. Dunbar called recently and said they'll no longer be needing my services."

"Really?" he perks up. "How come?"

"Well, where to begin?" I know he'll want to call Mrs. Dunbar, get another quote from her. But I want to make sure he knows my side of things, too. So I take a deep breath, and I tell him the truth, the whole truth, and nothing but the truth.

* * *

Charity St. James stops by to see me in the office on Wednesday morning.

"Your plan . . . it's not working out as well as I'd hoped."

"Oh? I thought things were going well with the sculptor."

"Blah." She waves her hand. "I'm bored with him."

"Already?" I ask.

"Already. But I did realize I liked learning about art. It all makes me feel so . . . eloquent. Ethereal. Important."

It's a strange combination of words, not the kind of thing she would usually say. We talk for a few more minutes, going over the next phase of the plan. Charity's dad is close friends with a U.S. senator. She's going to fly out to D.C. and spend a few days working around his office, soaking up a little of the political culture.

"I want my résumé to be stacked with as many weird, conflicting things as possible." She laughs.

I'm reminded of that bogus bio Courtney accidentally sent Ty Benedict, and my mood falls.

"But I tell you what, all of this has made me realize one thing."

"What's that?"

"I need to get back in touch with my fashion work. That's where my real passion lies."

"Nothing's holding you back," I say, and it's true. She doesn't have to worry about money, or the constraints of a nine-to-five job, like most people. She's free to follow her dreams. And that's one advantage that the super-rich have over the rest of us. Oh sure, people like Stella McCartney or Tori Spelling or Andrew Firestone may claim that their wealthy upbringings and famous families had nothing to do with their success. And maybe, to some extent, that's true. But when you're that rich and that well connected, you have freedoms and advantages that can't be measured. Not that she isn't talented, but Stella McCartney wouldn't have become such a big name so soon if it weren't for her father. I instinctively tuck my legs under my chair, feeling guilty—I'm wearing a pair of Stella boots today.

"You're right, nothing is holding me back," Charity says. "Which is why I'm going to start pursuing my true design dream." She pauses for effect. "Wedding gowns!"

Wedding gowns? It feels out of left field. "Huh," I say. "You should talk to my mother."

"Your mother?" She looks bemused. "What, does your mother work for Vera Wang or something?"

"Not exactly." I fill her in on what my mom does, and she seems interested.

"Maybe at some point I should talk to her," she muses. "Does she live in the city?"

"No, Oak Park. But she works in Chicago."

"We'll have to set something up. Although for the moment I think I'm doing fine on my own. Without the help of my father, I've managed to arrange three *very important* meetings next week."

She doesn't elaborate, just gets up to leave. "Good for you."

"Yes," she smiles. "Good for me indeed."

* * *

"If I starve myself, will I look like her?"

It's twenty minutes later and I've just met a new client for breakfast at Bogart's. Her name is Lauren Fuller. She's forty-nine years old and on the verge of a self-described midlife crisis. She's also obsessed with her weight, which appears to be all of a hundred and five pounds. For some reason I find this deeply upsetting. Do women ever reach an age—or a size—where we stop loathing our bodies?

Because the sad part is, even though I love my slimmer frame, I don't *love it* love it. I always thought once my weight clocked in at a certain number, all my insecurities would magically evaporate. I thought I'd become an überconfident, hot-to-trot sex kitten. I thought I'd magically transform into some kind of supergoddess, with Reese Witherspoon's grace, Natalie

Portman's intelligence, and Paris Hilton's in-your-face bravado. (I also wanted Scarlett Johansson's breasts, but you have to be careful how you phrase that, lest people think you're going to pull an Isaac Mizrahi–style Golden Globes fondle.)

Sure, I'm now *officially* skinny (well, I was until I started inching back toward size twelve territory). But what happened to me was not some miracle transformation, some body rebirth. Even if you manage to conquer the beast, so to speak, there are still problem areas. Stretch marks. Loose skin. Disproportionate lumps and bulges.

Lauren points at the stick-skinny waif seated at a nearby table. "Wouldn't you die to look like her?" she asks.

Die. Kill. Maim. Whatever.

"When I was growing up I had a poster that said *A moment on the lips, a lifetime on the hips* taped up on my bedroom wall," Lauren continues. "All the good it did me. I still have a huge butt." She drums her fingertips on the table. "I can't shrink it; it's not possible."

"What do you weigh, like a hundred and two pounds?" I joke.

"Add ten pounds to that, and you're right on target." Lauren looks depressed. "*One hundred twelve pounds,*" she whispers. "I never thought I'd be in triple digits. When I was in college I weighed ninety-eight pounds. Now I'm one hundred and twelve pounds!"

I want to tell her that in my world, one hundred twelve pounds is absolutely nothing, a nonexistent number. I can't imagine stepping on the scale and seeing it register something that low. Lauren would freak if I told her I weigh more than one hundred forty pounds.

"I used to wear a zero. Now I'm a three." Lauren shakes her head in disgust.

"There's nothing wrong with that." She'd die if she knew that, despite claiming to wear an eight, at least half the clothes in my closet are a size ten. And that in a trunk in my parents' attic, I have some eighteens and twenties.

"So, why don't you tell me why you're interested in How to Be Cool?" I ask, changing the subject. *For the love of God, if she tells me she's here because she wants to lose weight, I'm throwing myself out the window.*

"I need to reconnect with my daughter, Lily."

"Reconnect how?" I ask, jotting down notes.

"Lily's twenty-two now, and every year it feels like we grow further apart. She spends all her time with her boyfriend and her sorority sisters and she wants nothing to do with me."

I hate to break it to Lauren, but that's pretty typical. How many twentysomethings like spending time with their parents?

"Before Lily was in college we spent tons of time together. We used to have mother-daughter dinners and lunches. Now Lily hangs out at bars and nightclubs every night. I'm not saying we have to spend every waking moment together. But she's never invited me along, not even once."

"Your daughter's probably going through a lot of changes right now," I say, trying to approach it delicately. "Getting out into the world, finding herself. I remember how I was at that age. Sometimes you just need your freedom. If you give Lily some time, I bet she'll come around."

Lauren shakes her head. "That's only part of my motivation. I don't want to 'get cool' for Lily's sake alone. I also want to do it for revenge."

"Revenge?" I ask.

Lauren scowls. "Yes. I'd like to get back at my husband—my *ex*-husband," she corrects herself. "I'd like to show him what he missed. It's like they say. Living well is the best revenge."

"That's true," I agree.

"My husband just left me," Lauren goes on. "*Bastard.*" She sounds the word out so it sounds like *bass turd.* "He traded me in for some young slut he met on a business trip. Of course, he had the decency to give me the stupid Balenciaga he brought back from China first. Dirty creep."

Balenciaga. What is *that*? I rack my brain. I know I've heard that term before . . . but where? As a cool instructor, I'm supposed to know a little bit about everything popular—vacation destinations, music, movies, fashion, sports, and so on. The fact that I don't immediately recognize Balenciaga is bothering me. "He brought Balenciaga back from China?" I ask, fishing for information.

"Yes." She looks disgusted. "Balenciaga Lariat. From China, for God's sake! Can you believe that? What kind of inhumane jerk does that to his wife? Now I've got to get rid of the thing."

Whoa. Balenciaga Lariat. It has to be an STD. Or, at the very least, some rare tropical disease he picked up in Southeast Asia. I make a mental note to Google it as soon as I get back to the office.

"So what exactly did you have in mind?" I say, changing the subject. "One thing I like to do is have my clients make out a list of goals. What's working in their life, and what's not. What hobbies they have, what hobbies they'd like to cultivate."

Lauren begins rattling off a list of areas she wants to learn about: fashion, Hollywood couples, everything that's trendy and hot with the under-thirty set, popular cocktails, where to meet men.

"I should be able to help you with those things." Even though I'm not a pro at any of them myself, I think. Oh, well, I guess it's like the saying goes: Those who can't do, teach.

"I'm tired of being the odd woman out," Lauren says. "I'm tired of struggling to keep up with certain conversations. I manage a bookstore and all of my co-workers are younger than I am. You would think, working in a bookstore, that it wouldn't be this way. You'd think all the kids would want to talk about Don DeLillo or Jhumpa Lahiri or even Candace Bushnell," she says. "I can talk about Candace Bushnell! I've read *Sex and the City.* I've seen the show. But, no. My co-workers want to talk about TomKat and Lindsay Lohan and *The Real World* five hundred forty-seven."

"Five hundred forty-seven?"

"I don't know." She throws her hands up in the air. "As far as I can tell, that obnoxious little show's been on since the creation of time."

"I think it's closer to fifteen years," I say, laughing. "Although I'll agree with you on the 'obnoxious' part. It's pretty bad." I reach into my notebook and take out a survey. "I also ask my clients to fill out this questionnaire, which helps me assess their needs better." I hand her the paper.

"When do you need this back by?"

"Since we're having our first session on Friday, it would be great if you could e-mail or fax me your answers by Thursday. That way, we'll be ready to go when you get to the office."

"Great!" Lauren says, standing up. "Thanks, Kylie. I really appreciate your taking me on."

"Of course. I'm happy to help. Oh, and good luck with the Balenciaga," I say, as she gets up to leave. "I hope you get that all sorted out. Those tropical bugs can be nasty."

"What?"

"Oh, sorry. The Balenciaga Lariat."

She eyes me with confusion. "Uh, thanks."

The second she's gone, I realize my mistake. I can't believe I've just done this, mistaken one of the biggest designers in the world for a fucking tropical disease.

This is why I need my index cards. This is why I should be prepared at all times.

But in truth, I've never heard the word pronounced before. And *Balenciaga Lariat* isn't spelled exactly how it sounds.

But I'm making excuses. The truth is, I screwed up. And I wouldn't be surprised if Lauren Fuller never calls again. (As it turns out, she doesn't.)

Great, two clients in one week.

13

Cool Rule #13:

Never argue with a compliment.

There's a naked man three feet in front of me.

He's so close that I could lean forward and graze my fingers against him. If, you know, I actually wanted to. Which I don't. In fact, I want to run screaming from the room.

The nude male body is not a work of art. Oh, you may think it is. And you could even hold up an example or two—Brad Pitt, Jude Law, Ty Benedict possibly—to prove me wrong. But let's face it. Most men—most people, in fact—don't look all that spectacular once you undress them and flip on the fluorescent lights.

Which is exactly what we've done today.

I have an unobstructed view of every blotchy patch of skin, every untoned piece of flesh. I have an unobstructed view of, you know, *down there.* And let's just say it's a cold day and leave it at that.

This is what I get for sitting at the front of the class.

Larry (and, really, has there ever been a hot guy named Larry?) has so much body fur, I wonder if he'll be using his nude model wages to get laser hair removal. And then I feel mean. I should be happy that he feels good enough about himself to get up in front of a room naked.

I've always wondered what kind of people have the gusto to be nude models.

Life drawing—in case you didn't know—is just a code word for nudes. Yes, I'm taking a nude drawing class.

This was Ruby's bright idea. She signed us up to take art classes together.

"I've always wanted to try it, and you're practically a natural," she said, when she pitched the idea over the phone last week. "I know how depressed you've been over losing all your artwork in the fire. . . . I thought this would help make up for it. Plus, it'll be a great way for us to see each other more."

"I don't know," I hedged.

"Come on, it'll be fun."

"Maybe. But why do we have to start with life drawing? You know that's nudes, right?"

"Oh. *Oh.*" She sounded surprised. "I kind of thought it was 'life' as in 'still life.' You know, bowls of fruit, vases of flowers, stuff like that. Are you sure that's not what it is?"

"Positive. Ruby, didn't you read the course description before you signed us up?"

"I don't know, I can't remember. I'm sure I skimmed it." I heard her ruffling through papers. A moment later she said, "Whoa. Uh, it looks like you're right." And, "Oh, shit! It says in here 'Not for beginners. Serious art students only.' "

"Right. They probably don't want a bunch of horny guys signing up thinking they'll see a little T and A."

"Uh-oh. Do you think they'll care that I'm not an artist?"

"Maybe. . . ."

"Well, I've already paid for it, so we're going." I'd started to object, but she pressed on, putting a positive spin on the whole thing, reassuring me that a six-week course of drawing naked men would do me good.

It had sounded likc a fun idea at the time. But sitting here now, staring at a hairy naked man, it doesn't seem so hot.

"Why are we doing this again?" I whisper. My face is glowing bright red with embarrassment. I already told you movie sex scenes make me blush. Can you imagine how I feel about in-your-face nudity?

"I didn't think they'd have fully naked guys on the first night," Ruby says, looking shocked. It takes a lot to shock her. "I thought they'd ease us into it. Show us how to draw a naked foot first, then a thigh, then maybe work their way north."

"Nope. We're getting the whole deal."

"Shouldn't the teacher go over some basic techniques first? Like what stroke . . ." she pauses, giggling, "like what stroke to use."

"This isn't a beginner's class, remember? It's also drawing," I say. "Not painting."

"God, I can't look at him," she says, staring at the ground. "How am I ever going to draw this guy if I can't bring myself to look at him?"

"Beats me." I pick up my pencil, turn it over in my hands.

"Why are you nervous?" Ruby asks. "You must have done this kind of thing before. You've taken these kinds of classes before."

"I took art in high school," I remind her. "You don't do nudes until college. For obvious reasons."

"Ah," she says. "Makes sense."

I look around. The instructor has just said something, but we've missed it. Everyone is picking up their utensils, getting started. I follow suit, beginning with his toes. I concentrate on the nails, the calluses, the curves and angles of his feet.

This isn't exactly pleasant. I think of my high school reunion, of the beautiful orange dress I'm going to wear. I took a digital pic of it the other day, and I've been carrying around the printout in my purse. Whenever I feel down, I look at it. I wish I could take the photo out, draw the dress instead.

Poor Ruby is completely lost. Her rendering is sloppy, a few notches above a stick figure. True, she doesn't have a natural ability for this. But she's going too fast, not concentrating enough.

"You don't have to draw all of him tonight," I whisper. "He'll be back again next class."

"Eek." She grimaces. "Now you tell me." She flips to a clean sheet of sketching paper. Then Ruby follows my lead and gets to work on his extreme lower half. We both spend the next hour drawing out the details of his feet.

When the class is over we gather up our things and head out to my car.

"Are you up for a drink?" she asks. "I could really use one."

"Sure, that sounds great." I feel like unwinding myself. Besides, it's not like I have anywhere else to be, or any reason to go to bed early.

As we're walking toward my car I hear a voice call out, "Kylie Fucking Chase! I thought that might be you."

I whirl around. There, standing less than ten feet away, is Charity St. James.

"What's up?" I call out.

"I'm taking an art history class," she announces proudly as she walks over. "This place is kind of a dump. It's certainly a far cry from Yale," she giggles. "Isn't that what you suggested? I take classes at Yale?"

"Something like that."

"You guys going somewhere?" she asks, noticing my car.

"For a drink," Ruby says.

There's this awkward pause, so I add, "You can join us, if you want."

I don't expect her to say yes—why would she? As far as I can tell, Ruby and I aren't exactly up to her speed.

But she does say yes. "Hold on, I'll give my driver the night off." She picks up her cell phone—one of the four, I'm not sure which—and makes a call. A minute later, she's ready to go.

I open my purse to get my keys out and the photo goes flying onto the ground.

"Is this your dress?" Ruby says as she bends down to pick it up.

"Yeah," I say sheepishly, trying to get the photo back. I'm too late. Charity snatches it from her hand.

"D&G," she nods approvingly. "Excellent choice. It's from the spring line, right?"

I have never been able to do this—identify designers at a mere glance. It's the kind of talent I should have, but don't.

"Yes. Orange is the new black," I joke, and she gives me an odd look.

"What's it for?"

"Her high school reunion," Ruby supplies as I unlock the car.

"Yeah, it's next weekend," I tell her.

"But what's it *for*?"

"My high school reunion," I repeat. Is she not paying attention?

"I know that," Charity says. "I mean what *guy* is this for. An ex-boyfriend? A guy you lusted after from afar?"

"There is no guy," I say, putting the key in the ignition, starting it up. I can't believe Charity St. James is sitting here in the backseat of my car, like we're friends or something. "I just want to look good for the actual reunion. For all of my old classmates."

She giggles loudly. "No offense, but you're a terrible liar."

It's true. I am. "Well, there might be someone. . . ."

Charity waves her hand impatiently, urging me to get to the point.

"His name is Zack," I say. "Zack Naylor," I add. I figure I'd better get it right out in the open, in case she knows him or something. The last thing I need is to launch into the Zack Naylor story only to find out, halfway through, that Charity's his next-door neighbor or squash partner. Or fiancée. Charity St. James is exactly the kind of girl I've always pictured Zack ending up with. Then again, there's no ring on her finger, and his dental experts profile says he's single. But a little caution never hurts.

"Zack Naylor." Charity giggles. "Zack *Nail Her.* I bet he did a lot of that in high school, huh?"

It was probably true. I had no doubt that Zack slept around. What teenage boy didn't? (Well, the Dennis Moops of the world didn't. But guys who looked like Zack, guys who could get any girl they wanted, usually took advantage of it.) But that was one of the things I'd always loved about him; he never bragged, never showed off. He never talked about his sex life, never kissed and told. He was respectful in that way.

I give Charity the bare-bones outline of the story, leaving out the part about *Mango.* And about how, despite the fact that Zack and I have had zero contact in nearly twelve years, I still think about him now and again. I still wonder *what if . . . ?*

"Don't feel bad about it," Charity says, cutting to the chase in her usual blunt way. "Every girl has one of those guys."

"That's what I keep telling her!" Ruby says.

They're right about that. But the difference is, I don't have just one. It's more like ten. As I listen to Ruby and Charity talk, listen to them go on about "the proverbial one that got away" and how "it takes a while to get over unrequited love, if you ever get over it at all," I start to feel depressed. I know they're trying to make me feel better, but it's having the opposite effect. All I can think is that, when you get right down to it, most of the guys I've loved, I've loved from afar. A guy doesn't have to do a hell of a lot to keep me interested. He just has to exist. I fall in love at the drop of a hat.

I feel like that Morrissey song, "The More You Ignore Me, the Closer I Get." And now the lyrics pop into my head, so I flip on the car radio to drown them out.

I haven't had a lot of relationships. And the ones I have had weren't overly satisfying. I never make the first move, never take initiative. I just sit back and wait for the guys I like to come to me. And when they don't, I take the next best thing. I settle for the first semidecent guy who asks me out.

I guess my standards are too low. Or are they too high? At what point do you throw in the towel and just accept that your knight in shining armor isn't coming and that you'd better buck up and be happy with what you can get?

"You're too picky," my mother used to tell me. This was back in college and high school, back when I was fat. She quit saying it so much once I lost weight. (I'm not sure what the subtext is here—that thin girls can be choosy, but fat girls have to settle? Maybe that's not what she meant. But I kind of think it is.)

"I bet once you see Zack at the reunion you won't want him anymore," Charity predicts. "I bet he'll be old and fat and bald."

"No, he's still hot," I confirm.

"Google Image," Ruby says. "Kylie checks him out at least once a week, right?"

"No."

Charity bursts out laughing. "You care that much? Isn't that a little obsessive?"

"No," I say again, defensively this time. "I've just been thinking about him a lot more lately because of the reunion." And because of the fire. And because I'm about to turn thirty and I'm living with my parents. And because I seem to be crashing and burning with Ty. (I haven't talked to him in over a week.)

"I see."

It's sad, actually. Some people escape through drugs or alcohol or even shopping or sex. I escape through obsessing. I temporarily fixate on something (or someone) to the point where it takes my mind off all the other things that are wrong in my life.

"So where do you guys want to go?" Charity asks. Then she adds, in a tone that reminds me why I often find her grating, "I can get us in anywhere in the city, just so you know. I'm a definite VIP," she informs us. "Or VVIP, is what I think they're calling it these days. I'm not trying to be a snob, you know."

"Of course not," Ruby says, throwing me a quick look.

"I just think it's important to make the distinction. There's

Very Important. And then there's Very *Very* Important. And I don't want to be confused for one, when I'm so clearly the other."

"Clearly," I say. I guess it's like how a girl who wears a double zero doesn't want to be confused for a size two. Or how someone who drives a Maserati wouldn't be caught dead in a series three BMW.

Charity begins rattling off a list of clubs. I feel my stomach lurch when she mentions going to 7 of Seven, because I know Ty hangs out there. It's stupid, I know, but there's a part of me that's afraid of her stealing him.

"That place is too much of a scene," I say, with all the authority and haughtiness of someone who has actually been there. Which I haven't. It's a trick I learned a long time ago: say something with enough confidence and few people will take the time to question you. Kevin does it all the time, pretending to be on a first-name basis with this designer or that nightclub owner. He feigns personal connections to all sorts of artists, musicians, millionaires, and movie stars.

I think the kids today call that lying.

"But I love that place," Charity pouts. "Everyone worth anything hangs out there."

"Then we'll be trendsetters," I say. "Go somewhere new."

"But . . . there's nowhere that compares."

"What about Bungalow?" Ruby suggests, before this can get out of hand.

Charity has never been to Bungalow, never even heard of it.

Ruby fills her in. "It's snazzy, but low-key enough that we won't have to be 'on game' all night, if you know what I mean. Besides, they have a drink named after me."

Charity's eyes get wide. I can't believe this impresses her, but it does. "Really?"

"Uh-huh," I say. "It's called The Ruby. It's this really great martini with pomegranate juice."

"One of the guys who worked there was absolutely in love with me," she says, "so he named one of their signature drinks after me."

The Bungalow Lounge really does have a drink called The Ruby, but, sadly, it has nothing to do with Ruby Gallagher. Ruby loves telling people otherwise, although we always cut them in on the joke before too long. I don't see any need to do this for Charity.

We get there around nine-thirty and wind up staying through four rounds. I down Bungalow Blonde after Bungalow Blonde before switching to a Dreamsicle martini. All of this has way too much sugar, too many carbs. And my pants are tight, and I should be drinking dry, dry red wine or simple shots of scotch or, better still, sparkling water. That's what I usually do. I have one or two "low-carb, low-sugar" drinks, then switch to nonalcoholic beverages for the rest of the night. But tonight I don't sweat it. Ever since the fire my routine has fallen apart. My gym trips are infrequent, my eating scattered. And there's a part of me that honestly doesn't care.

We talk about movies, travel, guys. Ruby and Charity have more in common than I would have expected; for starters, they've both traveled to practically every exotic locale imaginable.

"Although I've only been to sub-Saharan Africa. My family did a Kenyan safari when I was twelve. And I've been to Cape Town a few times. But I'd love to hit northern Africa," Charity says, taking a sip of her Ruby. Yes, she decided to order The Ruby.

"See, I'm the exact opposite," Ruby says. "I've been to Marrakech and Casablanca, Cairo and Alex. But never farther south than that."

"Well, then, we'll have to go together next time," Charity muses.

"Or you could just switch," I throw in, feeling a tiny pang of jealousy over how easily they're bonding. "Since each of you wants to go where the other has already been."

Charity laughs. "Maybe. But it wouldn't be nearly as much fun. Have you been to Africa, Kylie?"

"No."

"Really? Wow, you're missing out. Trust me."

"She's been to Europe," Ruby pipes up. "A couple of times."

"Europe's old news. Paris, Prague, Budapest, what the fuck ever. If you've seen one European capital you've seen them all. They all have trains, trams. Rivers running through the city centers. I swear to God, I spent five days in Dublin last month and half the time I couldn't even remember whether I was in Ireland or England. I didn't know whether I was looking at the River Liffey or the goddamn Thames." She bursts out laughing, then sloppily clinks her glass against mine, showing that she is both joking and drunk.

"Um, anyway . . ." I say, looking to change the subject. Doesn't work.

"The three of us should go to Africa."

"Yeah, it would be nice," Ruby says. "Maybe one day."

"No, seriously," Charity continues. "I really want to go. How about next month?"

"Well, I—"

"Don't worry about the money," Charity says, cutting Ruby off. "My dad has a private plane. Well, he has a lease on a private plane, which is basically the same thing. He can use it whenever he wants. I'm sure he'd let us take it for a quickie to Morocco if I asked him." Charity hops up and goes to the bathroom before either of us can respond.

Ruby shoots me a glance that says, *Is this girl for real?* and I shrug in response. The truth is, I don't know. Charity St. James certainly does things like this—jaunts halfway around the globe on a whim. But she's also really drunk right now. Who knows if she'd actually come through, once she's sobered up?

After Charity comes back we settle our tab and head out. I'm tired—you can't party the same way at Not Thirty that you did at twenty-one. All I can think of is the warm cozy bed waiting for me back in Oak Park. But I somehow get talked into going over to Gunter Murphy's for an end-of-the-night beer.

"You can crash at my place," Ruby offers. "Er, Davey's place, technically. That way you don't have to drive all the way back."

"Drive back where?" Charity asks.

"Oak Park," Ruby says.

"Where your mom lives?"

How does she know this? "Um, actually, yes. I'm staying with my mom and dad for a little while. Since the fire and all. How'd you know my mom lived out there?" I ask.

"You told me, a couple of weeks ago."

I don't remember doing this, but I must have.

"That sucks," Charity says, "living with your parents."

"It's not so bad, a nice temporary stopover," I say, trying to sound optimistic, like I'm barely bothered by the whole thing.

We settle into a booth near the back by the fireplace and

down our drinks—pilsner for Ruby and Charity (who seems to be copying Ruby's every move tonight) and draft Guinness for me. I should be having Michelob Ultra or even Bud Light. But instead I'm having Guinness, with its powerful one-two punch of carbs and calories. The Irish always joke that Guinness is a meal, not a drink, and there's some truth to that. But I'm throwing caution to the wind tonight; I'm letting go.

We knock our glasses together in a loud cheer, and I take a huge gulp of the thick liquid.

After all, when you start to slip, when you feel yourself failing, isn't it best just to go ahead and rush the inevitable? Isn't there something to be said for failing grandly?

* * *

I am still failing grandly the next morning, because when I wake up I suggest to Ruby that we have breakfast at Orange.

"I'm craving their chai French toast," I say, my mouth watering in anticipation. I've only had Orange's chai tea French toast once in my life—and even then it was only two bites, pinched off my then-boyfriend's plate—but I've always dreamed about going back there.

"You're going to eat French toast?" she asks, looking surprised. "I didn't know you were up for that sort of thing."

"I've relaxed my diet a little," I explain.

Ruby goes over to the coffeemaker and pours two cups. In the corner of the room Davey is snoring, loudly. He's been at it all night. I don't know how she gets any sleep with him around, although she looks well rested and refreshed. "Good for you! I always thought you were too hard on yourself."

But she doesn't know me from before, back when I was too soft on myself. I don't get into this, though. "It's only a temporary thing. But that's why I drank so many cocktails last night."

"I wondered about that," she says, handing me a mug of coffee.

"But I'm going back on my diet tonight," I vow. "By dinnertime I'll be hard core again." Of course, this means I have only a limited number of hours left to eat how I want. I feel panicked, like I need to cram all the food in before my eating free-for-all runs out. "So, Orange?" I ask.

She nods. "Let me grab a quick shower and then we'll go."

Forty-five minutes later we're walking through the door at Orange. It smells amazing, and all of a sudden my mind starts to slip. Maybe I don't want the chai French toast anymore. Maybe I want the Jelly Donut pancakes. Or the grit cakes. And then there's potatoes, a big no-no on my normal diet. Potatoes and rice and pasta are my three mortal enemies. Once I start eating them, I cannot stop. And these carb-fueled foods pack on weight faster than anything else.

I work my way through the menu, debating everything. I want to order it all. I want to taste all of it, even if it's just a bite or two. But I know better than to do this. This isn't an all-you-can-eat buffet. I can't splurge to ridiculous heights.

I stick with the French toast.

And I love it. Every bite. I drink fresh apple juice and pour sugar into my coffee and wish I could eat like this every day. After breakfast, Ruby and I head back to her apartment. We watch a few episodes of *Entourage*, sort through her enormous pile of magazines (Ruby subscribes to everything under the sun), and then head over to the multiplex to catch a showing of a limited-run Spanish film. It was a choice between the Spanish flick, *Hostel*, or a generic-looking Harrison Ford movie called *Firewall.* Neither one of us is in the mood for gore, so the foreign film seems the way to go. But despite the misleading title and poster, it winds up being borderline porn. Erotica, I guess it's called. And now I'm wishing we'd opted for blood and guts.

Once the movie's done we decide to grab lunch back in Ruby's neighborhood. We wind up at Milk and Honey, which is one of my favorite cafés. I usually order a salad with salmon or shrimp. Today I get a turkey sandwich and homemade potato chips. I drink full-calorie soda and top the meal off with two peanut butter chocolate cookies. I halfway expect Ruby to say something about it, but to my relief she doesn't. We spend the rest of the afternoon shopping, chatting, and generally catching up.

It's almost eight o'clock when I pull up in my parents' driveway. I know it's late in the day, and that I shouldn't do this, but all I can think of is a nap. My mother would never approve. So I slip in the front door, call out a quick hello, and then head upstairs and climb into bed.

I wake up a few hours later. My cell phone's going wild. I've got it on ring plus vibrate, so it goes scooting across the nightstand as it buzzes. I'm in a complete fog, and it's a struggle to wake up. Naps are impossible. They always make me feel like I'm emerging from heavy anesthesia.

I manage to reach for my phone. It's a number I don't recognize and, for a brief second, I wonder if it's Ty calling. Pathetic, I know. But a small part of me is hoping he'll call, ask how my weekend was, invite me to 7 of Seven again.

"Hello," I say, trying to sound sexy rather than sleepy.

"Is this Kylie?"

I recognize the voice, but I can't place it. "Yes."

"It's Charity."

"Oh, hi," I say. "I didn't recognize your number."

"I had to get it changed. Some asshole kept calling me."

This makes me laugh. "But don't you have four numbers?"

She sighs loudly. "Yes. And he somehow managed to get hold of three of them and wouldn't leave me alone. He was so annoying."

"I thought you had a brush-off line for people like that?"

She sighs again. "I do. And, ironically enough, that's the only number the jerk didn't have. When I first met him a few months ago I thought he was really cool, so I gave him my regular line. Then we started talking about doing some business together. So, to make things easier, I gave him my business cell, too. How he got my family number is beyond me. But he did, and he's been wearing out his finger dialing all three, day and night. I've been dodging him for weeks, but he would *not* take the hint."

"So, three new numbers?"

"Three new numbers," she confirms.

"Wow." I roll over in bed, stretch.

"Anyway, we're off topic."

I didn't realize we had a topic. "What's on your mind?"

"I was hoping you could introduce me to your mother."

"My mother?"

"The other day you told me your mom sells couture wedding gowns."

"She does, yeah." I suppress a yawn.

"Well, you know I have this budding fashion design business. And I love working with delicate fabrics. Even though I've got a ready-to-wear line in the works, my real passion is wedding couture. I'm kind of hoping to break into that market, become the next Vera Wang," Charity says. "Do you think your mom would mind talking to me, giving me a few pointers about the market?"

"I'm sure she'd be happy to."

My mom lives for this kind of stuff, and I'm sure she'd love to talk shop with someone like Charity St. James. Even if Charity's designs never take off, she's still an extremely well-connected Chicagoan. Not a bad person to have in your Rolodex, so to speak.

"Why don't you come by one day," I offer. It feels strange inviting her out to the suburbs, to see the home that I live in with my parents.

"How about Friday?"

"Friday?" I try to think. I'm still in a nap-induced haze, and I can't remember what day it is. "What date is that?"

"The twenty-fourth."

Oh, God. The reunion. "No, that won't work. I have . . . plans."

"What time are your plans?" she asks, impatiently. "Can I come by before them?"

"My twelve-year high school reunion is that night, remember?"

"Oh, yeah, Zack *Nail Her* and all that. What time do you have to be there?"

"It starts at seven."

"So I'll come by your house about six-thirty."

"It'll have to be earlier. I'm planning to leave at six-thirty."

"Don't forget, you'll want to be fashionably late."

She has a point. "Okay, but not *too* late. I don't want to show up after everyone has gone home."

"I tell you what. I'll come by around four. That way, I can help you get ready," Charity says, and I think, *This is not an entirely bad idea. She has amazing fashion sense.* "And I've got the perfect bag to go with the dress. I'll help you put the whole look together. Then, after we're done, maybe your mom and I can sit down for a quick chat."

"I'll have to make sure my mom's free, but it sounds like a plan."

"Great! Just call me if anything changes."

I give her directions. "See you Friday."

We hang up the phone and I flip on the TV for a few minutes, then head downstairs. I'm in a weird mood. Pensive.

It's pouring rain outside. Ever since I was little, I've loved thunderstorms. I used to sit in my parents' sunroom with the lights out and watch the rain pound on the glass. It's an amazing feeling, being surrounded by a downpour. I go into the sunroom to watch the storm.

I'm surprised to find Miller Diller—Patrick—there.

"What are you doing here?" I ask. "Did you get bored with your flipped house and decide to move in with us?"

"I wish. It's a nightmare living with all that paint and sawdust, but no. I was only here for dinner."

"Again?" It comes out wrong, like I'm annoyed. Which I'm not.

"Again," he says.

I sit down in one of the wicker chairs, facing him. "I love this kind of weather."

"Me, too," he says. "I've been just sitting in here, watching the rain. It's nice, seeing it through all the windows."

"I know."

"Although I'm sure a lot of people would think we're weird, you and I."

I shrug. "What do you mean?"

"Most people sit in a sunroom for the *sun*."

"I suppose you're right."

We sit there for a minute, in silence, listening to the rain.

"Hey, I have a weird question for you."

"Then I have a weird answer," he says.

"I was counting on that." I laugh.

"All right, let me guess: you want to know what I think about Mercury rising, huh?"

"What?"

"And you want to know why scientists always say Venus has a harsh atmosphere, when everyone knows Venus is the planet of love."

Oh, God. "My father got to you."

"Earlier today. He spent forty-five minutes talking to me about the great astronomy-astrology divide."

I hang my head in embarrassment. "I was afraid something like this might happen. I'm so sorry."

"Don't be. He means well."

"You don't find it offensive? I mean, isn't it kind of like someone thinking they know more about surgery than a doctor, just because they've read a few books on it or seen *ER*?"

"A little," Patrick says. "There's absolutely no scientific evidence to back up astrology. And as a scientist, I can't look past that." He runs his fingers through his hair. "But with that said, if people want to have fun charting horoscopes and predicting the future, why not? I don't see any harm in it. And I'll be the first to admit, some of those sun sign descriptions do sound fitting. Like the whole thing about Tauruses being stubborn. God knows that's true of me."

"Me, too." I'd forgotten we had the same sun sign.

"And I also remember hearing that Tauruses love good food, and that definitely fits me. God, eating is practically a hobby of mine."

I've heard people say things like this before, and it always makes me jealous. Especially when they're as lanky as Patrick.

"I love food, too," I admit, "but I try to eat a pretty healthy diet." I don't normally say things like this, because I don't want to remind people that I used to be fat. But since this is the first time Patrick's seen me since kindergarten, and back then I was a tiny kid, there's no reason to be on guard.

People who knew me during high school and college—aka the Fat Years—always want to discuss my weight. They always have a million questions: Have I put any back on since the Big Loss? Is it hard watching what I eat all the time? Did I throw away my fat clothes, or did I keep them "just in case"? This must be killing me, seeing everyone scoff pizza while I'm having salad. Don't I want a teeny, tiny little bite? C'mon, one bite won't make me fat again.

I answer their questions as best I can; I try to be civil. The truth is, it's hard, but it's also easy. I spent a lot of years wrestling with food. One day it was a giant villain, the next my best friend. And then I stopped, looked at it, and realized something. It wasn't that big a deal. It really wasn't. So when people ask these questions, I usually shrug and say, "It's only food."

I usually don't talk about the fat clothes. The truth is, I still have four boxes of them in my parents' attic. I've never been able to throw them away, which is weird. You'd think I'd not be able to stand the sight of them, that I'd want to burn them in some ritualistic celebration of victory. But I don't. In truth, I like keeping them around. They remind me of how far I've come, of what I've accomplished.

I never want to forget the person I used to be—although I never want to go back to her.

"It's not like you have anything to worry about," Patrick says, snapping me back to reality. "You look great now," he says.

Now?

My expression must give it away, because he smacks his forehead and says, "I didn't mean it like that. You looked great before, too. It's just, your dad showed me the pictures of you guys on vacation at the Jersey shore," he says, "from a few years back."

Fat pictures! But they were all destroyed during the fire, weren't they?

Holy shit. My mind flashes back. My family has only been to New Jersey one time, when I was seventeen . . . and more than two hundred pounds. So Patrick has seen the pictures of me, on the beach, in a bathing suit, weighing . . . *oh, God.* When I moved out at eighteen I took all of the fat pics with me—or so I thought. I must have missed a few.

"Why in the world did my dad show you *those*?" I ask, mortified.

"I've been thinking about moving to Cape May when I'm finished here," he explains. "We got to talking, and your dad pulled out the album."

"I can't *believe* he showed you those pictures."

"Why?"

"I hate the way I looked back then. I didn't really want anyone to see them."

"You looked cute in those pictures on the sailboat," he says.

I'm about to protest, but I stop myself. I know which pictures he's talking about; they're actually not half bad. I'd just gotten a nice tan, so I looked thinner that day. Besides, you should never argue with a compliment. It's bad form. "I guess those were okay."

"They're nice," he says, smiling. "You're too hard on yourself."

There's an awkward silence. Then Patrick says, "Anyway, what was this weird question you had for me?"

"Ah," I say. I don't know how to phrase this. "Okay, the thing is, you seem like the kind of guy who follows his dreams."

He cocks an eyebrow.

"You don't have a conventional job, I mean."

"Neither do you, cool instructor," he teases.

"That's the thing. I don't, I just don't know . . ."

He turns to face me, waits for me to go on.

I stare up at the rain, watching it sliding off the glass. "What happens to your dream . . . when it's not your dream anymore?"

Patrick thinks it over for a minute. "Like when you stop doing something for the right reasons?" he asks. "And you only do it because it's what's expected of you?"

"No," I say. "I mean when it comes true, but then you stop wanting it."

"Once you have something, it's never as appealing as when you don't," he points out.

"True, but that's not exactly it. I mean, sometimes a dream comes true, and it's every bit as fantastic as you think it will be. But then something just changes, and it doesn't feel right anymore."

He nods. "Are you talking about your job?"

"Yeah," I admit reluctantly.

"I thought you were happy there? It seems like a cool job. Get it, cool job."

I don't say anything, just stare down at my feet.

"Sorry," he says. "I make bad jokes."

"No, don't apologize. The thing is, I spend all this time teaching people how to fake it."

"Fake what?" he asks.

"Whatever. Take your pick. There's a million ways to go. Everybody's trying to fit into something—or they're trying *not* to fit in. They want to conform to nonconforming."

Patrick laughs. "Yeah, remember how the whole 'freak' thing was big back in high school?"

"God, I hated that. Piercings, purple hair, flannel, combat boots."

"Everyone priding themselves on being different when, really, they were all the same," he says.

We laugh.

"Of course, not to say that I didn't try to do it." I flip down my lip, where I have a tiny scar from getting a piercing there at sixteen. "My cousin's boyfriend pierced that with a safety pin."

"Ouch!"

"The next day the bottom half of my face had swelled up to three times its normal size. Two weeks and a thousand milligrams of penicillin later I was back to normal."

"Is that the craziest thing you ever did to try to fit in?" Patrick asks.

I think it over. "It's hard to say. I did a lot of dumb stuff back in high school. I was obsessed with fitting in, no matter what the cost."

"I was like that, too," he admits. "God, I was such a dork back then."

"Really?"

"Yeah. I was short and scrawny and my name was Miller Diller," he groans.

"I thought you dropped Miller in fifth grade?"

"I did. That doesn't mean all the other kids forgot about it, though. Every couple of months we'd have a sub who'd call me Miller Diller. And then it'd be another couple of weeks of teasing until they'd forget about it again."

"That sucks. I'm sorry."

"Your piercing story's pretty bad."

"I don't know why I did that. It seems so stupid now."

"That's the thing about trends," Patrick says. "They always pass. That's why I try not to get too caught up in any of them. It seems like what's popular changes from year to year."

"That's true," I agree. "What's popular does change from year to year. And from scene to scene." Which is my big problem, I suppose. I exhale slowly. "I feel like I'm teaching people a bunch of useless skills. I feel like they're worse when I get through with them."

"Why do you suddenly think this?"

"There's this journalist who's following me, and the other week we went to visit some of my former clients." I don't mean to tell Patrick everything, but somehow the whole story comes out.

He listens patiently, doesn't interrupt. And when I'm finished, he says, "I can't really give you advice on what to do. It's your decision to make. But don't stress so much about it. There really is no wrong choice here. Even if you make a mistake, it won't be the end of the world. I mean, I know this probably sounds nuts, but I love making mistakes."

"You do?"

"Yeah," he says, "Because that means things are changing. It's very easy to keep doing the same thing, day in and day out. When you do that, when you don't take risks, you don't make a lot of mistakes. Making mistakes . . . it's a sign that you're moving forward, trying something new."

"I never thought of it that way before, but I guess you're right."

He stands up, stretches. "Anyway, I'm sorry I couldn't be more helpful."

But he has been. He really has.

14

Cool Rule #14:

Learn to be cool within your own limits.

Ty calls Wednesday night, around midnight. I'm fast asleep, but I hurriedly grab the phone. I haven't heard from him in weeks. Our promise to get together again never materialized. Could he be calling to reschedule?

"Hello," I answer, trying not to sound groggy.

"I've been thinking," he says, in lieu of hello. "Your high school reunion's this weekend, isn't it?"

"Yes," I tell him. I can't believe he remembers. "Friday night."

"What would you think about me going with you?"

"You want to go to my high school reunion?"

"I thought it might be fun."

Is he talking about a date? *To my high school reunion?*

"Not to mention a great angle for the story," Ty adds.

Oh, right. The story. Of course. "I thought you were finished with that."

"Not completely. Not yet. I went back through it with my editor and we both got the sense that something was missing," he says. "So I wanted to spend a little more time with you, beef it up a bit before we send it to press. I've only got a couple of days, though. The magazine goes to the printer Monday afternoon."

I'm speechless. I've spent countless hours daydreaming about my high school reunion. I've pictured myself strutting in, looking skinny as all get-out in my orange dress. I've pictured Jimi Hendrix's "Foxy Lady" playing in the background. I've pictured Dr. Zack Naylor grabbing onto the bar to steady himself. I've pictured Joanie Brixton and Hayley Hill crumbling to the floor.

I have never once pictured Ty Benedict in any of this.

I honestly don't know what to say.

"We could meet for a drink first, then head over to the reunion," he suggests. "We could put in the obligatory appearance, you could wow your classmates, and then we could go grab dinner. And talk for a while."

This is sounding like a definite date.

"Sure," I say, before I can stop myself. Before I can question whether this is a mistake, whether one of my classmates will spill the beans about my former life as a fatty, whether bringing Ty will ruin my chance to get Zack Naylor.

"Great, I'll see you on Friday, then," Ty says, and we click off the phone.

I should get back to sleep. It's late, and I've got an early meeting with Kevin tomorrow. But I can't. I can't stop thinking, *this is all too perfect, too amazing.*

Wouldn't it be something, I think, if both Zack and Ty wanted me? If we wind up in some sort of love triangle? It's almost too much to wish for.

But I am.

* * *

I meet Ruby for drinks the following night. I'm excited to see her. She's just gotten back from a brief trip to New York. We haven't talked in a couple of days, not since our art class, and it feels like there's so much to catch up on.

"Do you think it's a mistake," I ask, "bringing Ty Benedict to my reunion?"

"Not at all." She tips her head back and downs her martini. "Ty Benedict is asking you for a date. That's what you've been wanting all this time. You'd be crazy to refuse him."

"But what if it screws up my chance to finally get Zack Naylor?"

"Who cares? I'd take Ty over Zack any day."

"You don't even know Zack!"

"I know his type. Those high school crush things never pan out. You're probably going to go back and find out he's got a huge beer gut and a receding hairline."

"No way," I counter. "I've seen him on Google Image, remember."

"But you have no idea how old those pics are." She flags down the waitress and orders a second round of drinks. "Although if Zack really does still look good," she says, "that would be so unfair."

"What do you mean?"

"All the hot guys from high school are supposed to grow up to be ugly. You know, to make up for the fact that we never got to date them."

"Too true." We laugh and clink martini glasses.

"But, anyway. All I'm saying is, I bet you'll be disappointed when you see Zack. I bet he won't live up to what you're expecting."

"And if he does?"

"Then use Ty Benedict to make him jealous. Trust me,

nothing attracts a hot guy like seeing another hot guy." She laughs. "You know what I mean. People, guys especially, love attention. If Zack sees you with Ty, it'll probably make him want you more."

"That's a great point, Ruby." The more I think about this idea, the more I love it.

"Oh! That reminds me. I read something about Ty while I was on the plane coming home."

My pulse quickens. "What was it? A Page Six feature?" Ever since he relocated to Chicago, Ty has been conspicuously absent from the tabloids. Any day now I keep expecting to pick up *Us Weekly* or log on to TMZ and find a picture of him cavorting with Nicole Richie or something.

"No, nothing like that. Just a short blurb in *Entertainment Weekly* about the casting for his movie. What's it called again?"

"*The Bad Old Days.*"

"Do you know the plot?" she asks, raising an eyebrow.

"Ty told me."

"It sounds kind of weird. Stupid, even."

"I'm sure it's really good."

"I have to admit, Ty's writing hasn't impressed me so far."

"What do you mean?"

"Well, I read a few of his articles online the other night and, you know, his writing's only okay. And then to hear the plot of his script . . . it sounds like a stinker."

Suddenly I start feeling defensive. "It has to be good," I say firmly. "Paramount wouldn't pay so much money for a script that doesn't work."

"Oh, *suuuuuure*," Ruby says, sounding unconvinced. "Movie studios never do that. They *never* buy crappy scripts or make bad films. They only release awesome, brilliant masterpieces. That's why *Gigli*, *Battlefield Earth*, and *Batman and Robin* were all green-lit."

"Okay, okay," I concede. "So it doesn't sound like comic genius to me, either. But neither of us has read the script. I'm sure *The Bad Old Days* is a lot funnier once you know the full story."

"Will Ferrell didn't think so," she counters. "He passed on it. That's what the *Entertainment Weekly* piece said."

"Well, I'm sure they'll find somebody else. Jim Carrey, maybe." This is making me uncomfortable, so I change the subject. "So how's work been? You haven't talked about it much lately."

"That's because I'm kind of burned out, to tell you the truth."

"Really?" I ask, surprised. "I thought you loved modeling."

"I do. But you have to put up with so much bullshit when you're on an assignment. Like just this week, for example. I had the most obnoxious conversation with a photographer."

I take a swig of my martini. "What happened?"

"This woman was taking photos for our catalog shoot. She was a total hack. I have no idea why they'd hired her. I mean, she couldn't even figure out how to work the light meter. Crazy, right?" Ruby makes a face. "Anyway, I was the only plus girl there. So after the shoot was finished this bitch came up to me and said, 'You have to know your career is going nowhere.' "

My jaw drops. "She actually said that?"

Ruby waves her hand dismissively. "Oh, I've heard worse. Modeling is hard core. Everyone's only out for themselves, and lots of the girls make vicious comments to each other. The best way to get somebody is if you slam her weight. It's awful. There are size zero girls calling out size two girls for being fat. So you can imagine what they say when they see me."

I have never considered this before. Ruby's modeling career has always seemed so glamorous. I know there's a dark side to the industry, obviously, but I've never paused to consider it.

"That's horrible."

"I haven't even told you the worst part. This photographer woman told me that she could help me salvage my career, if I wanted."

"Yeah, right. Like you'd ask some bitchy stranger for help."

"No kidding. Anyway, you want to hear what her advice was? She told me that if I gained a little weight I could become a BBW fetish model." Ruby makes a face. "It's not that I have anything against BBWs or even fetish modeling. But that's not the path I want to take, you know?"

I nod, still trying to absorb it all.

"I'm always hearing that—gain weight and do fetish pictures or lose weight and become a 'real model.' It sucks," she says, taking a drink of her martini, "that people can't just accept you the way you are."

* * *

I'm so nervous about the reunion that I barely get any sleep Thursday. I wake up at the crack of dawn on Friday and, since I have so much energy to burn, I decide to hit the gym before work.

This is something I haven't done in a while. The gym is so far from my parents' house, and I've been feeling so sluggish, that I've completely slacked off. I leave the house around five-thirty, and make it into the city a short while later. It's nice driving in; the roads are mostly empty and the sun isn't yet up. I feel energized, like I'm getting a proper start to the day.

It's been so long since I worked out that my muscles ache from the exertion. I'm scared I will have lost a lot of ground, but, surprisingly, my body snaps back into its old routine without too much trouble. I'm sweating and panting more than I usually do, but it feels good. I've needed this. I've . . . dare I say . . . *missed* it.

Is it really true, all that stuff they tell you about exercise being addictive? I've never believed it before, but it almost seems possible now.

I shower and change at the gym and then make it in to work around eight-fifteen. I've got an early meeting with Pamela Greco, Dennis Moop's Internet friend. Pamela filled out an application online and I've yet to go over it. This is something I always do before meeting a new client. I print it out and begin reading.

Name: *Pamela Irene Greco*

Uh-oh. Right off the bat Pamela's parents have cursed her. Who gives their kid initials that spell *P.I.G.*? I pray to God that Pamela is thin as a lamppost. Otherwise, you can bet she's had an exceedingly rough life.

Age: *A very young 30*
Occupation: *Lab analyst by day, prolific blogger by night*
Hobbies/Interests: *Pub quizzes, politics, TV, celebrity gossip, music,* Space Ghost: Coast to Coast, Star Trek, *playing the flute (I was in band before it was cool to be a band nerd.* American Pie *changed all that, but too late for me to benefit. If only Alyson Hannigan had stuck a flute*

up her nether regions sooner. I might have gotten more dates!), Superman, *Fibs, They Might Be Giants, travel,* CSI, Arrested Development, *David Lynch, Daniel Day-Lewis.*

There are a few geeky things in there, but her interests are shockingly normal. I was expecting a sci-fi geek.

Tell me something interesting about yourself: *I enjoy herping.*

Herping? What the hell is that? Is herping some weird sex technique I've not yet heard of? It's certainly possible.

I hope it's something a little less freaky—maybe a popular blog or a new band. Whatever it is, it has a horrible name. Anything that close to *herpes* can't be good.

There's one simple way to find out. I pull up my old friend, Google, and type it in. A second later I have my answer. Herping, it turns out, is the pastime of searching for reptiles and amphibians in the wild.

Something I imagine is pretty hard to do living in urban Chicago.

I get back to the application.

Reason for coming to How to Be Cool: *I'll tell you in person.*

Courtney buzzes me. "That seismologist guy brought your license plates back," she tells me.

"Thank God!" I say. No more BIG ONE. No more living in fat fear.

"I'll get them on your car right away. Also, your nine o'clock, Pamela Greco, is here."

I glance at my watch. Pamela is almost twenty-five minutes early. But I don't have anything pressing going on, so I tell Courtney to send Pamela in. A second later she appears in the doorway. I'm instantly relieved to see that Pamela is not overweight.

She's gawky, like a lot of my clients are, and at thirty years old, she still appears remarkably uncomfortable with her body. She has a slim build (thank God my *P.I.G.* fears turned out to be unfounded), a toothy smile, and enough height to play in the WNBA.

Her hair is orange and frizzy, but her haircut is modern. And, of course, she's wearing glasses. I hate to say it, but the stereotype about nerds and glasses really is true. Now, don't get me wrong. I have nothing against glasses. Lots of people wear them—myself included. The difference is that most of us alternate between glasses and contacts. Nerds never do. Are contact lenses against the Nerd Credo or something? And if that's the case, then why don't nerds at least invest in a stylish pair of frames? The majority of them wear the most grandfatherly, outdated styles you've ever seen.

"Hi, Pamela. I'm Kylie. It's great to meet you." I extend my hand. "Why don't you have a seat?"

She plops down in the chair across from my desk.

"Let's go over some of your hobbies and interests, shall we?"

She nods. "Okay."

"You have on here that you like Fibs. Now is there any particular reason you enjoy lying?"

She bursts out laughing. "I don't mean Fibs as in lying. I'm talking about the online activity."

"I'm sorry, but I don't follow."

"Fibs are Fibonacci haikus."

"Excuse me?" This is a new one. "You don't mean . . ."

"They're haikus based on the Fibonacci sequence," she explains.

Now I have heard some nerdy things in my day. I've run up against people with strange, disturbing hobbies the likes of which you could not imagine. But this . . . this Fibs activity. It's beyond even what I'm prepared for. We had reached a new level of nerdiness.

"You're familiar with the Fibonacci sequence, aren't you?"

I nod. "Yes, I am."

It had been one of Austin Dunbar's questions, I remember sadly.

I try to recall exactly how the Fibonacci sequence works. I couldn't remember the specifics, but I knew some centuries-old mathematician had come up with a series of numbers that went something like this 0, 1, 1, 2, 3, 5, 8, 13. . . . You could tell what number would come next by adding the two numbers before it together. So, following 13, you'd have 21, and then 34, then 55, and so on. It was horribly boring, tedious stuff, but apparently it could be used to predict all these things in nature, like the number of petals on a flower or the pattern on a snowflake or even the order in which rabbits mated. But haikus based on it? My five-minute Google hadn't unearthed that.

"This is how it works," Pamela says, eager to educate me on the awesomeness of writing Fibs. "Each line has the number of syllables that corresponds to the Fibonacci sequence. Except you don't go past eight."

"I see."

"It's very popular," she assures me.

Our definitions of *popular* obviously differ.

"I've even gotten Dennis into it."

Oh, no! She's undoing all of my hard work.

"Would you like to read one?"

"Sure, do you have one on you?"

"Yep." She digs into her pocket and pulls out a crumpled piece of paper. "I won a prize for this one," she says proudly, handing it over. She has scrawled out the markings at the top, reminding herself of how many syllables to use in each line: 1, 1, 2, 3, 5, 8.

My
Love
For you
Really rocks
You are Captain Kirk
To my pointy-eared Mister Spock

Oh, my God. This is what people spend their free time doing?

"Um, this is cute," I say. "Where'd you win a prize? Is there some sort of contest for these?"

She nods. "A group of us get together every week to share Fibs. Then we vote on the best one. The winner gets a gift certificate to Amazon.com. Every week we have a different theme. This week we have to do Fibs about wintertime. Last week we had a science-fiction theme. And I took first place."

"That's great."

"I've been trying to get Dennis to come to our group, but he keeps no-showing."

That sounds like Dennis.

"Can I ask you a question?" Pamela says. "Something sort of personal."

"Okay."

"What does Dennis look like? Is he . . . is he ugly?"

I start to answer, but Pamela interjects, "Not that it matters. It's just . . . you talk to a person for this long, you want some idea. And he won't even send me a picture. It's kind of annoying. If I didn't like the guy so much, I'd have ditched him a long time ago." She leans forward. "In fact, that's the only reason I'm here today."

"It is?"

"Yes. I'm here because Dennis asked me to do this. I don't give a crap about cool lessons."

I blink in surprise.

"Sorry, no offense."

"None taken."

"I'm happy the way I am. I don't care if I'm cool or not. I only care about Dennis. I really like him, Kylie. I know how lame that must sound, but I do."

"It doesn't sound lame."

"I just keep hoping he'll come around, agree to meet me. Or at least send me a dang picture!"

I think it over for a minute. I actually have a picture of Dennis on my computer, but it's really not my place to show it to her.

"He's a good guy, he's just nervous," I tell Pamela. "Give me a couple of weeks. I'll work on him, see if I can get him to meet you. At the very least, I'll talk him into sending you a picture."

"Thanks, Kylie," she says. "You don't know how tough this has been. Wanting to see somebody and not being able to . . . it's frustrating, to say the least. I've been starting to wonder if the guy even exists."

"Oh, Dennis exists all right," I tell her. "And with a little luck, I'll have proof of that for you soon."

* * *

The day drags by at a snail's pace. Every five minutes I find myself looking at the clock, willing the time to pass. Finally, after what seems like an eternity, two p.m. gets here. I pack up my things and head home to get ready for the reunion.

* * *

"It doesn't fit."

"What do you mean, it doesn't fit?" Charity asks, staring at me in horror. I'm standing in the doorway to my bedroom, clutching my gorgeous orange dress. A dress, that, five minutes ago, I tried on.

"It just doesn't fit," I wail.

True to her word, Charity showed up at four o'clock this afternoon to help me get ready for the reunion. She spent a half hour painstakingly applying my makeup, and another half hour flat-ironing my hair. The overall result is unbelievable. The final touch was to put on my dress and then head out the door to meet Ty. (We're getting together at six for a pre-reunion cocktail. He'd wanted to meet me at my house, but I'd dodged his request.)

"Let me see it," Charity says, motioning for me to try the dress on again.

I pull myself into it, struggling to get the material to lie smooth against my wide hips.

"Hmm. I see what you mean," Charity says. "Gosh, and it was so gorgeous."

"Thanks, that's a big help," I say sarcastically. I know I'm being a bitch, but I'm in a panic.

When I bought this dress a month ago it was a perfect fit. It was snug, making the most out of every curve, leaving little to the imagination.

Now it won't zip up.

"Didn't you try it on after you bought it?"

"Once or twice . . . but not in a week or two at least."

Is it possible, is it really possible that I've gained so much weight—in one or two weeks—that I can no longer fit into my dress? I stand there like a deer in the headlights, unsure of what to do next.

"How am I going to find something else to wear on such short notice?" I ask, my lower lip trembling.

"Take the dress off."

I oblige. "I just don't see how I'm going to find another outfit."

"Give it to me," Charity says, taking charge. "I'm going to fix this for you."

"How?" I say. I slip back into my robe and sink down on the bed.

"Where's your mother?"

"My mother?"

"Get her for me, please." I stand up, slowly. "Hurry," Charity urges. "We don't have much time. And get me a sewing kit!" she calls over her shoulder.

Ten minutes later they're hard at work. Charity has the dress spread out on my desk and she's studying the fabric. I stand in my underwear—a pretty unhappy pose—as Mom moves a tape measure around my waist, hips, and bust. She calls the numbers out to Charity and I cringe, trying not to hear them.

"You've gained weight, honey," Mom whispers. I ignore her. She's stating the obvious, and I don't have time to get worked up over that right now.

"The top half is fine," Charity says. "But we'll have to let it out a tiny bit around the hips and butt."

Mom passes me my robe.

"This is going to take awhile," Charity informs me. "Don't you have dinner plans with Ty Benedict?"

"Ty Benedict?" Mom says, surprised. "I didn't know you were seeing him! That's so cool, Kylie."

"I'm not seeing him," I tell her. "He's writing an article about me."

Mom and Charity exchange knowing glances. "Then why are you two having dinner tonight?"

"He's going to her reunion, too," Charity chimes in.

"We're not having dinner, just drinks," I say, before the situation can get out of hand. "And Ty's only coming to my reunion because he needs more information for his article."

"Either way, you'd better call him," Charity says. "I'll work as quickly as I can, but it's already five-thirty. It's going to be pushing it to have you fixed up and out the door by seven."

I call Ty's cell. I get his voice mail, so I leave a quick message telling him I'm running late and giving him directions to the Hilton, where the reunion's being held. I tell him I'll meet him outside the banquet room at seven-fifteen, and I apologize for the last-minute change of plans. Then I set to work touching up my hair, which has gotten messed up from pulling the dress off and on over my head so many times.

Charity starts snipping and sewing, trying to work the dress into something wearable.

"Are you sure you know what you're doing?" I ask nervously.

"Yeah, I let clothes out all the time," Charity assures me.

Mom says, "She's doing a great job, Kylie. Really impressive."

As if on cue, Charity's fingers slip, and she slices a small chunk out of the orange chiffon.

"Shit!" she says, rushing to grab the fabric. She looks at Mom. "Sorry."

"For what?"

"You know . . . the S word."

Mom laughs. "Shit, fuck, damn," she says. "You can say them all, I don't care." She doesn't. It's one of the things Mom has never minded. *They're only words,* she used to say. *I'd rather you curse than use drugs.*

"Your mom's so cool," Charity says, turning to me. "No wonder you turned out the way you did. You guys are so much alike."

It's an awkward moment. I don't think anyone's ever told me that before.

"Where did you learn how to sew?" Mom asks.

"I apprenticed with a seamstress."

"You did?" I ask, surprised. It doesn't feel like the sort of thing she would do.

"Yeah. That was back when I was trying to land a spot on *Project Runway.* I figured I'd better learn how to sew before I auditioned."

"You're a fashion designer?" Mom asks.

"A wannabe." Charity winks at me. "I'd love to do couture. Wedding dresses, actually. I was hoping I could talk to you about it later."

"Absolutely," Mom says, watching her handiwork. "But for now, let's get Kylie all fixed up for her reunion." She smiles, and it almost looks sad. "This reminds me of your prom."

"Mom, I never went to prom," I remind her.

"I know that," Mom says wistfully. "But in a way I always wished you had."

There's another awkward silence. Fortunately, Charity breaks it. "Smart move, Kylie. I skipped my prom, too. Who needs that boring shit?" she asks, trying it out again. "Now," she says, before Mom or I can answer, "are you ready to try this on?"

It takes a few more attempts, but before long Charity gets the alterations completed.

I whirl around in front of the mirror. The dress looks amazing, and I'm so grateful for what she's done that I almost want to cry. I don't know why, but I always feel guilty when people do nice things for me. Like I've taken too much, like I don't deserve it. But tonight I push those thoughts out of my head.

"All right, Cinderella," Charity says, giving me a hug. "Your chariot awaits."

15

Cool Rule #15:

Never, ever beg. Anyone. For anything.

Ty Benedict is waiting for me in the parking lot of the Hilton. I get out of the car and make my way over to him.

He lets out a low whistle. "You look hot!" he says. "Hotter than hot!"

This is exactly what I need. A little ego massage to get me in the mood. "Thanks, so do you!" And he does, of course. He's wearing a suit—Armani, I'm guessing. I don't have my index cards, so I don't know. (And I've never been good at placing suits.) His light-brown hair is perfectly coiffed, and his teeth are whiter than ever.

"Shall we go in?" he asks, hooking his arm through mine.

"We shall."

We make our way into the hotel and toward the banquet room. A table is set up outside. Two girls I don't recognize are sitting behind it.

"Kylie Chase, plus one," I tell them, signing in.

I notice Ty fiddling with his cell phone, presumably switching it to silent.

One of the girls hands me a name tag. As I look at it, my mouth drops open in horror. It's a big, obtrusive thing, and it will poke holes in my designer dress, for sure. But that's not what I'm worried about. There, right next to my name, is a giant photocopy of my senior yearbook picture. In full color. With double chin and big fat cheeks gleaming for all the world to see.

"I'm not wearing this," I tell the girl. "It will ruin my dress."

"I'm afraid they're mandatory," she says.

"Can I put it on my purse, then?" I ask. Charity has lent me a gorgeous Gucci bag and I have no intention of piercing it with this idiotic name tag. But I can drape it across the top and then discard it at the first trash can I see.

"I don't know," the girl hedges. "That's not really the rule."

"Well, it is now," I say, not caring if I'm being mean. I've been waiting a long time for this. Walking around with that name tag would be like having a giant *I Used to Be Fat* sticker on my forehead.

I quickly move away from the table before the girl can object. Ty rejoins me, and I stuff the offensive name tag into my purse.

We make our way inside.

"Kylie," Ty says, holding up his cell phone. "I'm so sorry, but my editor called with an emergency. Do you mind if I call him back?"

"No, go ahead."

"Thanks," he says apologetically. "This will only take a minute."

He steps back out into the hallway. I'm tempted to wait for Ty so I can make my grand entrance on his arm. But then I see *him*, and my plans evaporate.

There he is. Zack Naylor, in the flesh.

* * *

It's exactly what I expected. The years have been very, very kind to him. Same incredible build, same thick dark-blond hair, same brilliant smile. He's standing by the bar, sipping a drink and playing with his BlackBerry.

Try as I might, I can't stop staring. Despite the pictures I saw online, part of me had expected Zack to look like an ogre. It only seemed fair. He had lived like a king for so many years; now it was time to step down from the throne. Much in the same way I had lived fifteen years of my life in the shadows, only just emerging into the limelight.

But, no, Zack is still a god.

And, from all appearances, he's here alone. But surely, *surely*, he has a girlfriend. Or, *gulp*, a wife. My heart sinks as I think about it. As I look at him, I know. Zack is married. He has to be. Probably to some equally perfect girl, some Charlize Theron clone who just happens to be a neurosurgeon. Or a pediatrician who worked for Médecins Sans Frontières saving lives in the remotest villages of South America. And what do I do? Take advantage of socially challenged nerds? It's enough to make me want to go home and crawl into bed.

But I decide to go straight up to him.

I've waited twelve years for this moment. No sense in stalling now.

"Hi, Zack!" I say, waving as I make my way to the bar. I do a quick wedding ring check once I'm close enough. His left hand is ring-free! While there might still be a girlfriend lurking somewhere, my fears of a Charlize Theron–esque wife are unfounded.

"Hi, Kylie," Zack says when I approach him.

He looks me up and down. Here it comes, I think. The

"Damn, you look great!" comment. The "I knew you'd lost weight, but your head shot didn't do you justice. And your bio, God, you've accomplished so much." The "Do you know how much I'm kicking myself right now, for missing out?"

Instead, he says, "I'm kind of surprised that there's an open bar. I figured Coverland would be too cheap for that." He polishes off his rum and coke and orders another one.

"I thought you organized this?"

"Nah, I was in charge of reservations. That's it. The actual event was done by Andy Lewiston. You remember him?"

"Yeah, I guess so," I say, nervously. Andy Lewiston is, of course, the goon who pointed out that the *Mango* CD looked like a vagina. "You and Andy used to be best friends, didn't you?"

"Yeah. We don't talk much anymore."

I wait to see if Zack will offer to get me a drink, but he doesn't. I order a vodka gimlet and tip the bartender five bucks.

We stand there for a minute, sipping our drinks in silence. "It's cool seeing everyone again," I say.

"Yeah, it is." He drums his fingers against the bartop absentmindedly.

More silence.

"Have you caught up with many of our classmates?" I ask, keeping the conversation afloat.

"A few of them." He seems bored, disinterested. He picks up his BlackBerry again and begins fiddling with the keys. "Sorry, I gotta check the score really quick. I have a lot of money riding on this game. I get totally crazed betting on this stuff every March."

"Oh," I say, improvising. "Me, too." As soon as the words leave my mouth I want to kick myself. What the hell am I doing? Not only am I totally clueless as to what particular game he's talking about—I don't even know what sport. I rack my brain. It's March. What sports do they play in March? Football ends after the Super Bowl, so it can't be that. Baseball maybe? Or tennis? Zack was the star of Coverland's tennis team and soccer team. Is it possible the Australian Open or something is taking place right now? And then it hits me . . . March Madness. That's basketball, right?

"Basketball is a great sport," I venture. "Don't you just love March Madness?"

"Most of the time," Zack says. "But those fuckers Duke bit it against LSU last night. It's enough to make me swear off The Big Dance for good."

Oh, God. I swallow hard. "The Big Dance kind of sucks sometimes," I improvise. We aren't talking about an *actual* dance, are we? As soon as I get out of here, I will obsessively learn anything and everything I can about sports. It's downright inexcusable for a cool instructor to be this clueless about something so popular.

"Damn it!" Zack studies his BlackBerry for a minute. "The fucking Blue Devils screwed me big-time this year. My bracket's a mess. And tonight's games aren't going any better."

I feign a light laugh. "I know what you mean."

He continues reading through the sports scores. "This is a lost cause," he says, flipping his BlackBerry off. He takes a giant swig of his drink. Jesus. Was the basketball game driving him to drink? I decide to try to lighten the mood.

"Are you having a good time tonight?"

"It's been fun," he says flatly, not really sounding like he means it.

I try desperately to think of something to say. "What do

you do for a living?" I finally ask. *This is good, I think, make it seem like you're uninterested, like you haven't looked him up online, like you don't know he's a dentist.*

Zack takes another drink, then says, "I'm an oral surgeon."

Now there is no reason why a twenty-nine-year-old woman should find this funny. But for some reason when Zack says the word *oral* I nearly explode with laughter, like I'm Beavis and Butthead or something. Am I really that juvenile? Must be nerves. I bite down hard on my lower lip, struggling not to dissolve into a fit of giggles. "That's an interesting career choice," I manage to choke out.

Fortunately, Zack doesn't notice my near meltdown.

"My dad's a dentist, and I grew up working in his office part time," he explains. As if he needs to. I'm willing to bet there's not a girl in the Coverland High Class of 1994 who doesn't know that. Dr. Ron Naylor, D.D.S., had probably treated half the girls in our school, all of them hoping to catch a glimpse of Zack between circular scrubbings and Novocain shots. In a weird way, I guess Zack's dental career began before he even left high school—I know he inspired all of us to keep our twice-yearly dental appointments.

"Going to dental school was a bit of a no-brainer for me," Zack continues. "But in order to become an oral and maxillofacial surgeon you don't just go to dental college and then call it a day. Nope, it requires a lengthy residency. I'm working over at County right now, learning the tricks of the trade." I hang on his every word as he describes how as soon as his four-year internship is up, he'll be qualified to perform everything from wisdom tooth extractions to complicated jaw reconstructions.

It's pretty gruesome stuff—and not particularly interesting. Fortunately, about halfway through a story about tooth decay it occurs to Zack that he's been monopolizing the conversation. "I haven't let you get a word in edgewise," he laughs, flashing his Colgate-perfect smile. "What do you do? Are you working right now?"

"Am I working right now?" I repeat, feeling slightly baffled. How on earth could I afford this dress if I were unemployed? Then it dawns on me. Zack has obviously mistaken me for a trophy wife! I remember Hayley Hill's snide comment in twelfth grade. "The only way Kylie could get a guy to take her to prom is if she paid him!" Now here I am, being mistaken for a rich man's hot-to-trot wife. In a strange way, I'm almost flattered.

"Of course I work. In fact, I've got an awesome job."

"Oh, really?" He chuckles. "I just remember you used to be a *major* slacker back in high school."

Slacker. Was that his euphemism for *fat*? After all, *slacker* is just another word for *lazy.* And I'm well aware that fat people are generally considered the laziest, most slovenly creatures on earth. Actually, make that fat *girls.* Fat guys get to masquerade as tubby, but fit, football players and wrestlers.

"I work pretty hard these days." Didn't he read my bio?

"Doing what?"

"I'm a cool instructor."

He breaks into a wide smile. "A *cool* instructor?"

"I teach a course called How to Be Cool. I make my living transforming the socially inept from geek to chic."

"You know something, Kylie? That's one of the weirdest things I've heard all night." He places his hand on my shoulder and I feel a small rush. "And now can you settle a bet for me?"

"Sure."

I'm expecting this to have something to do with basketball, but he says, "Did you get your stomach stapled after graduation?"

My jaw drops. "No! I lost weight the natural way." I'm horrified.

"Cool! I win fifty bucks," he says, heading over to a crowd of guys.

He doesn't even say good-bye. Suddenly, all of the confidence I'd felt walking in has evaporated.

I guess that's the thing about guys like Zack Naylor. You can spend your whole life waiting for them if you're not careful.

But suddenly Zack comes back—this time with Andy Lewiston in tow. "I need to see your stomach."

"Andy!" Zack gives him a horrified look. Then he turns to me. "He wants proof that you didn't have gastric bypass. He wants to see if you have any scars."

"I am not showing you anything, you jerk!" I say. It's directed at both of them, although I'm staring at Andy.

"Whatever," Andy says, walking off.

"He's just a skeptic," Zack says. He wanders off again. This time he doesn't come back.

Ty resurfaces, startling me. In all the Zack hoopla I'd practically forgotten he was here. "Did you have fun catching up with your friend?" he asks.

"You were watching?" I ask, shaking.

"Yeah."

"You could have come over."

"I didn't want to interrupt. You guys looked engrossed in conversation."

Ha! If only he'd been standing close enough to hear us.

"I didn't mean to desert you."

"You didn't. Besides, I had the chance to talk to a few of your old high school friends."

I look around the room. "Like who?"

"Those girls," he says, pointing.

Oh, fuck! "Joanie Brixton and Hayley Hill?"

"Uh-huh."

"What did they say about me?"

"Nothing, really, just a few funny stories from high school."

I don't want to be here anymore. What was I thinking, bringing Ty? There are too many land mines, too many ways for him to find out the truth about my past.

The soundtrack to my high school reunion is no longer "Foxy Lady." It's more like "Creep," by Radiohead. Because, let's face it, I don't belong here.

"Can we go?" I ask, my voice shaking.

"But we've only been here fifteen minutes."

"I made an appearance," I tell him. "That's all I ever wanted to do."

I look at Hayley and Joanie, watching us, waiting to pounce. I have to get out of here. I don't even care about how much money I spent on the dress, how long I've been looking forward to it. I saw Zack Naylor. That was what I came here to do. And obviously it was a giant waste of time.

"Come on," Ty says, pulling me by the hand. "Let's go get something to eat."

* * *

We end up at a wine bar near my parents' house.

"Well, I've gotta say, that was enough to sour me on high school reunions for a while," Ty says, pouring me a glass of pinot noir. "All those people were so catty, so ready to dredge up the past."

"Definitely," I agree. I sip my wine. Gulp it, actually.

"You want to get a meal?" Ty asks. "Or just tapas?"

"Tapas would be great. I'm not that hungry."

The truth is, I'm starving, but I'm not going to admit this. I can never remember what I'm supposed to do, if I should be a dainty eater or a pig. I always go with dainty eater. But it's annoying, sometimes, when guys talk about how sexy it is to find a girl with a big appetite, a girl who skips salad, who orders dessert. But they don't really mean any of it. They don't want a plus-size girl who does this. They want a Heather Locklear waif who can have her cake and eat it, too, all the while maintaining a perfect size zero figure.

I gulp more wine.

Ty orders olive tapenade and mushrooms and cheeses and a couple of other things, but I don't pay much attention. I fiddle with the cork from the bottle of pinot noir. I need to drown my sorrows. I don't care how drunk I get tonight. I've earned it.

"So do you miss New York?" I ask. "My best friend Ruby was just there."

"The plus-size model? That reminds me." He looks apprehensive. "I know this is probably the worst time ever to bring this up, but I need to talk to you about something."

"Okay, sure."

He sighs. "Wow, I feel horrible about this."

I have no idea what he's about to say.

"I hope this isn't going to sound too rude. But a couple of girls at the reunion told me something about you. My instinct tells me this isn't true. And I wouldn't ask, because I know this is very personal . . . But if someone was saying this stuff about me, I'd want to know."

Oh, my God. Here it comes.

"Did you have gastric bypass surgery?"

Fuck.

My face goes bright red. "I don't know how this rumor got started. But it's absolutely not true."

"So you've heard it before?"

"Yes." I take a deep breath. "I might as well tell you the truth." So I do. Maybe it's the wine talking, but suddenly it doesn't seem so bad. So I was overweight. So what? It's not like it's a sin. It's not even all that unusual.

When I finish with the story, Ty leans over and pats me on the arm. It's a move that by someone else, I might have found patronizing, condescending. But it doesn't come across that way with Ty. With him it seems comforting.

"I'm glad you told me," he says. "It means a lot that you trust me."

"This is probably going to change the whole article," I say nervously. I know he'll want to include it. I'm not naïve enough to think otherwise.

"I don't think it's too relevant," Ty says. He chuckles. "But let's not talk about work now."

"Okay."

It's weird, but now that the cat is out of the bag I feel liberated, free. There's nothing else he can find out about me. Well, except the whole I'm Not Thirty Years Old and I Live with My Parents thing. But even that, in retrospect, seems small.

"You were telling me something about your friend Ruby."

"Oh, yes! I was saying she just got back from New York."

"Did she have a good time?"

"Uh-huh. Ruby loves it up there."

"Is she into the party scene?"

"No, not really," I say. "Not like you, anyway."

"Not like me," he says, pretending to be hurt. "Don't believe everything you read. I'm hardly the party animal people make me out to be."

"Hey, it's not only what I read," I tell him. "There are lots of pictures of you, too. Hanging out with people like Paris Hilton and Jessica Simpson."

Ty laughs. "I've never even met Jessica Simpson. And Paris Hilton," he makes a face, "ugh. That's the whole reason I left New York for Chicago. To get away from people like her. Chicago's a big city, but its party scene is relatively tame compared to Miami or L.A. And that's what I need right now."

"Why the change of heart?"

"I'm growing up," he says. "It's time for me to leave all that behind."

We talk for what feels like hours. I don't know if it's the alcohol, or my renewed self-confidence, or the way Ty's smiling . . . but halfway through our third bottle of wine something changes. He's looking at me more, direct eye contact, and he's sitting closer.

"I can't believe you're single," he says.

"My luck with guys is not what I would like it to be," I say. "I would like to find somebody to settle down with. Who wouldn't? But it hasn't happened yet. Maybe I should shed my inhibitions, act like a nympho or something," I joke. I shouldn't be saying these kinds of things, making myself so vulnerable. But it's the wine talking.

"Wait," he says, as I reach for a piece of olive toast. "Let me." He takes it from my hand, holds it to my lips, and watches me take a bite. It feels awkward. This isn't the kind of food I usually associate with romantic overtones—like strawberries, chocolate sauce—but it still feels strangely intimate.

"I love this, just bein' with you," he says, his Southern accent growing thicker. He takes a sip of his wine. "It's like we've known each other forever."

"I know," I say, feeling my breath catch. This is so surreal, so bizarre. I wish I weren't so drunk, so I could appreciate it more. "I can't believe how comfortable it is being around you. I mean, you're almost like this celebrity dude."

He chuckles, then touches the side of my face with his fingers. "Right back at ya." Suddenly, we're holding hands, and then he's stroking my palm with his fingers, making circular motions. Any second he's going to kiss me, I can feel it. "You know something, I haven't thought about this article all night," he says.

"Me neither."

And I'm spinning in a haze of wine and lust and I just keep thinking, *damn it, why won't he kiss me? Why? Why? Why?*

We keep drinking and then, suddenly, the bottle of wine's empty and Ty's paying our bill and we're standing up to go.

I feel dizzy, so I sit back down. "Can we stay longer?" I ask.

"We're the last ones here," Ty says, prodding me gently. "They closed a half hour ago."

"What!" I exclaim. "It's midnight already?"

Ty nods. "Twelve-thirty."

"We've been here . . ." I struggle to do the math.

"Four hours."

Oh, my God. The night feels like it just got started and then, just like that, it's over.

And then Ty says, "I don't know how I'm gonna drive home." He chuckles. "I hope you've got some strong coffee at your place. I might need to drink a pot or two."

"My place?" I repeat, horrified.

"Oh, don't worry," he says, seeing my startled expression. He puts his arm around my waist, guiding me toward the door. "I know you live around the corner. I need to sober up a little before I head back to Chicago."

Fuck fuck fuck! I don't see a way around it.

"Well, there's a coffee shop down the road. I think they're open twenty-four hours," I fumble. "I'm sure we could go there."

Ty looks hurt. "Is there some reason you don't want me to see where you live?" He rubs his fingers down my back. "Jealous boyfriend?"

"Oh, no no no, nothing like that. I mean, I live alone."

"Ah."

"And I'm single. No boyfriend," I add. *So you can kiss me.*

Ty walks me to my car. "Let's just go back for a bit. I'll have a few dozen cups of coffee," he jokes.

"I don't know . . ."

"Come on, Kylie. I don't bite." He winks at me.

"It's just . . . my house is super messy."

"Hey, at least you own a house," he says, smiling. "I'm still in an apartment. Besides, a little mess never scared me."

"Mmm. I guess not," I mumble, fishing in my purse for my keys. I yank them out and they go flying from my hands, landing on the ground.

Ty leans down and scoops them up. "Maybe you'd better let me drive," he says, suddenly appearing much more sober than before. "Hey, Kylie." He touches my arm. "Don't worry so much. I get this feeling you're nervous, but you shouldn't be. Tonight's been great. Don't stress about the article. We've still got plenty of time to work on it. Just because we didn't start tonight . . . what I'm saying is, my deadline's flexible."

"Sure," I say, trying to calm my nerves. He's right. I am stressed. But not for any of the reasons he thinks.

I climb into the passenger seat, and Ty gets behind the wheel. He spends a minute adjusting the settings, moving the seat back so his legs aren't cramped. Then, leaving his car in the parking lot, we head out onto the street and toward my house.

It's happening, I think, as he drives. In less than five minutes my cover will be blown. My head is swirling. Maybe this won't be so bad. *Maybe Ty won't care. Maybe he won't make a big deal of it, won't print it in the article. Oh, God, he can't put it in the article. I'll beg. I'll plead. Anything to stop him.*

He follows my directions, and a few minutes later we're pulling into the driveway. "Do you park in the garage?" he asks.

"No, uh, I use it for storage." And my parents' cars.

Ty turns the ignition off and pulls out the key. "Whew." He lets out a low whistle. "This is one hell of a house, Kylie. Damn." A second later he's out of the car and, in true gentleman fashion, he opens the door for me.

"Thanks," I mumble. I stand in the driveway, taking deep breaths. Then Ty and I head up to the front porch. I put the key in the lock and pause for a silent prayer. *Please, God, don't let my parents be awake. Please, please, please let them be fast asleep.* I slowly open the door, trying to be as quiet as possible.

"Here it is," I say, stepping aside to let him through.

"Quick tour?" he asks.

"Uh, okay." I grab him by the arm, hurriedly pulling him

through the downstairs rooms—the kitchen, the study, the living room, dining room, den. I'm careful to steer clear of the master suite—my parents' bedroom—which is in the back of the house. The tour lasts all of sixty seconds. "Anyway, that's it," I say, tugging him into the kitchen.

"Your house is *amazing*, Kylie," Ty says, taking it all in.

I can understand his awe. My mother's interior decorator did an incredible job.

As if reading my mind, he asks, "Did you do this yourself or did you hire a decorator?"

"I hired someone. Jessie Julian."

"From New York, right?"

I nod, silently praying that Jessie Julian is not his cousin or something.

"I saw a piece on her in the *Times* recently. She's a huge deal. How did you get her down here to do this job?"

"Oh, I just, you know, asked."

"I heard she doesn't do much work outside New York. That's odd that she'd fly out to rural Illinois to do your house. Did you know her personally or something?"

Good grief. He never quits. I write it off to journalistic curiosity. It's just his nature to be nosy. "My mom did," I admit. "They were sorority sisters." This is actually true. But just mentioning my mother has made me anxious again. "So, you want that cup of coffee?" I ask. "I can make you a triple espresso or something," I say, gesturing toward the machine.

"Maybe in a minute." He pauses. "I was thinking . . . I don't have to be anywhere until tomorrow afternoon."

Is he saying what I think he's saying? And suddenly I don't care that we're in my parents' house. "You wanna sleep over?" I ask, instantly mortified at the childish way I've phrased it. *Sleep over?* What are we, twelve?

"That sounds nice." He pauses, looking me in the eyes. "But, just so you know, I'm a Southern boy, Kylie. We're raised different down there. I'm a gentleman. So it doesn't have to be anything you don't want it to be. . . ."

I don't know what to say. His Southern accent is turning me on so much all I can think about is getting him upstairs, into my bedroom. We make our way up the stairs. I feel giddy, exuberant. I can't explain it, but having him here is so exciting. I feel slightly guilty for lying to him and for sneaking him around behind my parents' backs, but I push those thoughts aside. In some ways, the fear of getting caught is what's making this so much fun.

Growing up, I always marveled at the layout of our house, and how easy it would have been to sneak boys over. My parents' bedroom is on the first floor, tucked away behind the den. There are only two rooms upstairs—my bedroom and the guest room. I have my own bathroom, and it's not like anyone ever comes up there to check.

I could have been having orgies every night of the week and my parents wouldn't have noticed. As I trail Ty up the stairs I feel exhilarated. At long last, I'm actually sneaking a boy up to my room. The secrecy, the rush, the fear of being caught. I feel like a teenager again.

"I love this," Ty says. He kicks off his shoes and settles back onto my bed.

He looks insanely sexy lying there, his arms propped behind his head, his long legs stretched out across the comforter. Suddenly I feel nervous again. "Let's put a movie on or something," I say, reaching for a stack of DVDs. "Any requests?"

Ty shrugs. "Whatever's fine."

I have no idea what he likes, so I grab a Russell Crowe film and shove it into the machine.

"We should make it like a movie theater in here. You know, turn out the lights and stuff," I say, lapsing into a schoolgirl giggle.

"Sounds good."

I flip the switch and the room goes nearly dark. The light from the TV screen flickers almost like a candle. It's cheesy, but in some ways this is fulfilling a high school fantasy. I've always wanted to do this. Watch a movie with a boy in this bedroom.

I join Ty on the bed. He's lying on his back and I curl up on my side, resting my head on his chest. I look up at him, and he's looking down at me. And I think, *this is it.* If he won't do it, I will. I hate making the first move, but this feels right somehow. Plus, the alcohol's making me brave.

I prop myself up on my elbow, move so our faces are inches apart.

"Can I . . . ?" I ask.

I don't get the words out, but he knows what I mean.

"Mmm-hmm," Ty mumbles. He moves toward me and I see his eyes flutter closed just a second before mine.

Our lips meet and I can't explain it, the way it feels to kiss him. It's otherworldly almost, nothing like any of the guys I've kissed before. Ty is strong but incredibly gentle. There's nothing aggressive or rushed about the way he kisses. He makes me feel at ease, relaxed, completely in the moment. I can't believe this is the rough-and-tumble party boy. He feels so innocent, so tender.

We part after a moment, and I snuggle down beside him. We're so close, our heads rest on the same pillow. I just watch him, and I can't say anything. He strokes my hair with his fingers and tells me how beautiful I look.

We kiss again, and he eases me onto my back, slides on top of me. I wrap my arms around him, squeezing tight. His body feels so good pressed against mine. It's all so electrifying, so intense . . . My head is spinning, and I feel dizzy. I can't believe how soft his lips are. This is different from any other guy I've kissed before—so sweet, gentle.

Ty moves away for a second, rolling onto the bed beside me. He takes my hand and pulls it to his lips, kissing my palm.

"God," I breathe. "You're such a good kisser. Just . . . *amazing.*"

"Thank you."

"I mean that," I continue, no longer concerned with appearing cool, calm, and collected. "I can't believe how incredible you are. I could kiss you all night."

I lean in to kiss him again, but he moves away. "I want to just enjoy this moment," he says, pulling me closer, "enjoy being with you."

"Yeah, me, too."

We lie there for a minute. "You know what I love about you?"

"What?"

I'm hoping he'll say my eyes, my lips, my body. Instead he says, "We have great conversations." I guess I should be flattered that he hasn't gone for the shallow answer. But all my life I've been getting complimented on my personality. I want it to be something else.

We talk for a little while, discussing work and our families. I tell him about my mother's unstoppable beauty, my father's astrology addiction.

"What do you think he'd say about me?" Ty asks. His head's resting on my stomach now. "I'm a Sagittarius."

I make a mental note to look in one of my dad's books, to see if Taurus and Sagittarius go well together.

"It's so comfortable being with you," he says. "I can't believe how relaxed I feel. That's unusual for me. You might not know this, but I'm nervous all the time."

"So am I," I tell him. We keep talking for a while, asking each other lots of questions, not holding much back. I drift in and out of consciousness as I listen to his voice. The wine is still weighing heavy on me, and the tension of the day has caught up with me. I listen to Ty's voice, mumble answers to the questions he's asking, and then before long I've drifted off to sleep.

I'm not out for long. Twenty, thirty minutes maybe. I wake up and my eyes adjust to the darkness. There's a small light beside me. I look over. It's Ty's cell phone; he's got it flipped open and he's using the LCD to look at something.

I turn to face him, yawn. My eyes adjust and I see. It's my 1994 Coverland High School yearbook!

"What are you doing?" I ask, suppressing a yawn.

"Nothing," he says, snapping it shut.

"Where did you . . . ?"

"I found this," he says, setting it down on the nightstand beside him. "Sorry."

"You found it where?" I ask.

"I don't know." He looks uncomfortable. "It was lying on the floor, I think."

He's lying. I know exactly where my yearbook was, beneath a pile of clothes in the second drawer from the left. He's been snooping, I know he has. I'm not sure whether to call him on it or let it slide.

"Do you mind getting me some coffee?" Ty says, yawning loudly.

"Now?" I ask, startled.

He gives me an apologetic look. "I'm sorry. I really need to sober up. And you rushed me upstairs so quickly earlier, I didn't get to have any."

"I'll get it in a minute. But first I need to know something. Did you go through my stuff while I was asleep?"

"My God, what the hell kind of question is that?"

This isn't really an answer, so I ask again. "Did you go through my stuff?"

"I find it really insulting that you'd accuse me of that," Ty says.

He's still not answering. "It's a simple question," I say, "yes or no?"

"No!" Ty says hotly. "My God, you're paranoid. Just because I won't sleep with you, don't get all psycho on me."

"Wh-what?"

He sighs. "I'm not going to have sex with you. Okay? You wanted it earlier, and I resisted. So please don't try to get back at me by accusing me of rifling through your stuff."

This is insane. "What do you mean I 'wanted it earlier'?"

Ty rolls his eyes. "Come on. I saw the way you were staring at me right before you passed out. The moves you were making, the things you said. You want sex. And I'm just telling you, I'm not interested."

I'm taken aback. Since when is a guy so worried about a girl trying to sleep with him? "Ty, I really don't . . . I mean, that's not what I'm after."

"Yes, you are," he says firmly. "It's pointless of you to try and deny it, Kylie. I'm not an idiot, I can see what you're doing."

"We kiss, what, three times and you think that means I want to sleep with you?" Admittedly, the thought had crossed my mind. But it wasn't a lustful, oh-I-can't-wait-to-fuck-him kind of thing. It was more of a this-is-so-nice-I-really-hope-we-take-it-slow. Of course, I'm attracted to him, I'm turned on. But that doesn't mean I want to jump his bones.

"Like I said, Kylie, I'm sorry. But I'm just not gonna do it. I believe in making love, not casual screwing."

Now I'm getting angry. "I do not want to sleep with you," I say again, "and I don't appreciate you saying that, either. You're just trying to change the subject."

"Wow, this is rich!" He jumps off the bed. "I'm sorry, but I will not. I will not have sex with you, Kylie. It's against everything I believe in." And without another word he storms out the door and down the landing. I trail after him, in shock, halfway expecting him to turn around. But he doesn't.

I follow him outside. "Fine. If you're going to be a baby about this, then go. I'll even drive you to your car."

"That's okay." He starts off down the sidewalk. "It's a nice night. I'll walk."

I stand there on the front porch, watching him jog off into the distance. I've never seen someone react like this. My God, he acts as though I tried to force myself on him and he had to fight me off with a stick. This, after all the touching and kissing. After all the compliments. Sure, I made the first move, but I asked him before I did it. And he seemed into it, for a moment, but then it was like a switch went off and he became a different person.

I remember the article Ty wrote, "PMS: Pissy Man's Syndrome." It talked about this kind of thing. The moodiness, the sudden changes in attitude that guys sometimes experience. It called it the ultimate sign of becoming metro.

Ha!

If this is what it means to date a metrosexual man, then fuck it, I don't want any part of it!

16

Cool Rule #16:

Cool people do not wait by the phone.

Ty Benedict is not going to call me. It doesn't take a genius to figure this out. You probably guessed it from the way things ended last time.

Yet for the past seven days I've been sitting around like an idiot, waiting for the phone to ring. What's that old saying? There's a fine line between optimism and denial? I guess I don't need to tell you which side of that I've fallen on.

I spent a lot of my high school years waiting for the phone to ring. Waiting to be invited to parties, asked out on dates. Something, anything. I never understood the people who complained about having too much to do. Joanie and Hayley used to do this. I remember one point during junior year when Hayley had six guys vying for her. Six! And those were just the ones I knew about. I'm sure there were countless more, behind the scenes, wishing they could go out with her.

I wonder what that's like—that feeling that no one will reject you. Because, let's face it, when you look like Hayley Hill (then and now), there aren't too many ways that your life can go wrong. Oh, sure, winning the genetic lottery doesn't guarantee you a life free from heartache and pain. Tragedy finds everyone. But your social life—at least you've got that sewn up.

I remember overhearing a conversation between Hayley and Joanie during senior year. Hayley was complaining that it had been "a lifetime" since she'd last gotten laid.

A lifetime? I'd wondered. For Hayley Hill that was probably, what, three days?

"Five fucking weeks," Hayley had moaned, running her fingers through her dark-red hair.

Well, that was longer than I'd have thought. Still, as a certified virgin, I wasn't sympathetic.

It wasn't that I wanted to be running around having sex with any guy who looked my way. But it would have been nice to go on a few dates now and then; to make out with someone.

That's the same thing I want now.

A lot of guys think fat girls are sluts. I was always a giant disappointment in this area. I never slept around when I was big. How could I? I couldn't even bring myself to strip down bare in front of the mirror without cringing. How could I ever do it in front of a guy?

When I was fat I hated sex.

Well, that's not exactly true. I enjoyed it in the way that most red-blooded humans enjoy—as Dennis might put it, "getting their rocks off."

But my enjoyment was always clouded by my weight.

Certain things, I wouldn't do. I wouldn't wear sexy underwear. I wouldn't leave the lights on. I wouldn't let a guy unhook my bra with his fingers (lest he see the four huge clasps holding my 40 DD breasts in place). I wouldn't let him go down on me (my thighs were way too fat for that).

And I wouldn't get on top.

My poor ex-boyfriend Noel really suffered over that. It was the one thing he really wanted and I wouldn't give it to him. No matter how many times he tried to talk me into it, no matter how many *Cosmo* articles he showed me that proclaimed woman-on-top to be the "best orgasmic position ever!" I couldn't bring myself to try it.

For one thing, I was afraid of crushing him. Despite being six-foot-two, Noel weighed only one hundred forty pounds. I feared I'd squash his lithe body like a bug. And besides that, I didn't want to give him an unadulterated view of my stomach and breasts flopping about in all their oversized glory.

The stomach thing you understand. As for the breasts? Well, let's just say that at a certain point, gravity and stretch marks outweigh any porn-star-style fantasies of big-breasted goodness. When it came to cleavage, you could definitely have too much. And 40 DD was too much.

I had never understood why so many women agonized over bra size. I'd had big, succulent boobs all my life, and they hadn't done me any favors. They'd never led to awesome sex or helped me land hot guys.

The media had it all wrong. Most men, as far as I could tell, weren't too picky about chest size. What they *were* picky about was body size. And big boobs usually meant big thighs, big ass, big arms, and big stomach. Whereas a small, skinny chest usually meant a small, skinny girl.

And given the choice, they'd usually pick the flat-chested waif over the big-breasted fatty.

Whenever I had sex I would obsess over what the guy was thinking. I would struggle to put myself in his mind, to imagine what was going through his head as he watched me disrobe. Is he looking at my thighs? Oh, God, my big fat thighs. Or is it my stomach? My ass? My love handles?

I thought once I lost weight, life would be one big sexfest. (It's not that I have an out-of-control libido or anything—but I had a lot of time to make up for.)

But the weird thing was, once I got thin, those hang-ups didn't go away.

My dating life, both pre– and post–weight loss, has been a big fat disaster.

My first, and only serious, boyfriend was Noel Klinowski. Noel was an uptight chem major at UCLA. We bonded over our mutual hatred of dormitory cafeterias and pesky resident advisors. It was love at first sight.

When he dumped me three weeks before graduation, I was devastated. He did it at Gillet's Karaoke Bar on Mercer Street. At the time, I couldn't figure out why he brought me there.

In all the time Noel and I had dated, he'd never once taken me anywhere like that. We'd gone to plays, art openings, independent film festivals, even the odd Lakers game—with his uncle's box seats, of course. But a karaoke bar? Noel was a straitlaced chem major whose idea of rocking music was Bach—as in Johann Sebastian, not that guy from Skid Row. It's not like belting out a Mariah Carey song was his idea of a good time. I don't even think Noel sings in the shower.

But if you could get past the stench of fried food and the off-key singing, Gillet's Karaoke Bar wasn't a bad place to get dumped.

There's something delightfully ironic about listening to a group of drunken sorority girls belt out "I Will Survive" while your soon-to-be ex-boyfriend leans across the table and says, "I'm sorry, this just isn't working out."

I was speechless.

"I honestly don't see this relationship going anywhere,"

Noel had said. "I'll be in med school in the fall, and you'll be . . ." He'd let his voice trail off. I got the feeling Noel was trying to be polite, as if finishing the sentence would only embarrass me. After all, where *would* I be in the fall? I'd been rejected from my top six grad school choices; wait-listed by my two "safe" schools (which, in retrospect, were not so safe after all). My dream of a full scholarship to Stanford and a thriving psychology practice had all but flown out the window.

But how was I supposed to respond to something like that? What do you say when your first serious boyfriend—the guy you lost your virginity to when you were an embarrassingly old twenty-one—basically tells you you're not good enough for him? I mumbled something about me being too good to waste any more time on him, and then I staggered out of the karaoke bar and onto the street.

In all honesty, I felt lucky to have him. Landing Noel was the first thing that had ever gone totally right in my life. After many miserable years of disappointments, rejections, and failures, I had finally gotten something I'd wished for. I'd coupled up with Noel Klinowski, sophisticated future doctor and boyfriend extraordinaire. Okay, so he wasn't extraordinary in the traditional sense. His ears were too big and his teeth could use a good bleaching. In truth, he bore a passing resemblance to Bob Saget. And never mind the fact that he stuttered, had sweaty palms, and often rambled on about scientific theory. In my eyes, Noel was a pretty good catch. He was kind, and he was brilliant, and he made me laugh.

He was my first lover. My first real boyfriend, actually. Teenage boys don't exactly line up for a date with the fat girl. In fact, they tend to run the other way.

I wasn't completely inexperienced. In high school I went

out on a date—*a* date, singular—with my cousin's friend Louis. He took me to see *Jurassic Park* the summer after my junior year. I always thought it was a pity date, although he wound up giving me an ill-timed, tooth-grinding kiss—my first—when he dropped me off at home that night.

I didn't try dating again until my freshman year of college. And even then, it was by accident. I fell into an awkward relationship—hooking up briefly, foolishly—with my pimple-faced math professor. I couldn't even do the "Hot for Teacher" thing right. The cool girls, the popular girls, had enough sense to run around with the English lit professors, who served them red wine and recited Byron. Meanwhile, my pseudoboyfriend taught me about quadratic equations and fed me weak coffee from the school cafeteria. We went out a grand total of four times. Then I panicked, dropped his class, and didn't set foot in the math building again for two semesters.

There was also Justin, but more on him later. . . . (Shudder.)

Noel was the first guy where things had actually worked out. But the shelf life was shorter than I'd ever imagined. It always is, when you're in love.

* * *

"Is he crazy?" Ruby asks.

It's a week later and we're sitting at Navy Pier, sipping hot tea and talking about the Ty Benedict fiasco.

"I don't know." I throw my hands up in the air. "Your guess is as good as mine."

"It's like he had a total meltdown or something."

"That was pretty much how I took it. One minute he was normal, the next he got pissed off and stormed out."

"He had no right to act like that."

"Of course not!" I say, trying to keep my voice down. The truth is, I'm angry. I feel like Ty twisted the situation, somehow turned things around and made me the bad guy. "He had no right to do any of it—to go through my stuff, to accuse me of wanting to sleep with him. Have you ever heard anything like that before in your life? I mean, what the hell was that about?"

"Are you sure it wasn't just a diversion?" she asks. "A way to take the focus off the fact that he was going through your stuff?"

"That's what I thought at first. And I'm sure that's part of it. But he just said it with such conviction. He truly seemed convinced that I wanted to sleep with him. Which is so weird."

"You know," Ruby blows on her tea, trying to cool it, "maybe he's so used to being treated like a piece of meat that he overreacts when any woman so much as touches him."

"How do you mean?"

"Well, suppose you're Adriana Lima," Ruby says. Ruby's analogies often start off with "Suppose you're . . ." followed by the name of some model or another. I don't know how she does it, but she manages to relate every situation to Heidi Klum, or Tyra Banks, or Gisele Bündchen. "Adriana Lima is pretty much considered one of the most beautiful models in the entire world."

"Behind you, of course," I say, grinning.

"Shut the fuck up." She bats at me playfully. "Anyway, Adriana is also a devout Catholic and a self-professed virgin. She's really open about it. So can you imagine how many guys probably go nuts for that? I bet every guy she comes into contact with tries to get her into bed. Because (a) she's fucking gorgeous and (b) she's the ultimate challenge."

"But how does this apply to Ty?"

"Think about it! Adriana's probably paranoid as hell, *just like Ty is.* She's probably got so many guys trying to sleep with her that when a nice boy comes along, he gets lumped into the sex-crazed category by default. After a while everyone's motives start to blend together. You get jaded and all people start to seem the same."

"Yeah . . . but do you really think that's what's going on with Ty?"

"Ty Benedict may seem like a normal, down-to-earth guy, but never forget—he's a celebrity," Ruby points out. "And he's a pretty big sex symbol at that. He's probably got women pawing all over him twenty-four-seven. That old stereotype about guys being sex-crazed and girls resisting their advances . . . the opposite is true nowadays. Lots of girls throw themselves at a guy—offer him blow jobs or whatever else they think he's after. For some guys, it's a dream come true. For others, it likely gets real old, real fast."

I think it over. "So what you're saying is, Ty's so used to women trying to sleep with him that he automatically jumps the gun and assumes that's what every girl is after?"

She nods. "Correct."

The more I think about it, the more convinced I am that she's right. "Wow. No wonder he freaked out. God, the way I was going on . . . he probably thought I was about to rip his clothes off right there." But as I say this, it feels false. I still have a nagging feeling that we're missing the bigger picture.

"Have you talked to him since that night?"

"No. You think I should call him?"

"It might not be a bad idea. I wouldn't apologize—I really don't feel you've done anything wrong. But I also wouldn't rake him over the coals too hard. I'd cut him some slack; he probably feels misunderstood."

* * *

And I believe this. I believe it and I take Ruby's advice and I try to get in touch with Ty Benedict. But he never returns my calls or e-mails, never picks up his phone. I'm still confused, but I give him the benefit of the doubt. Being a sex symbol probably has its trappings. Ruby is right; I should cut him some slack.

But it's hard to feel too sorry for Ty. Having lots of women throw themselves at you is a pretty enviable position. Besides, I know my yearbook wasn't just sitting on the floor. I know he opened that drawer and found it. Which wouldn't be such a big deal, if he'd just admitted it. Maybe Ruby's right. Maybe it was just a diversion.

The truth is, I am in a funk. It's not just Ty. Things have been weird at work lately. Kevin's acting strange—I'm starting to think some of that eyelash dye has seeped into his brain. He's coming in early and leaving late in the evening. He doesn't take lunches or even come out of his office for more than five minutes at a stretch.

It got so weird even Josh commented on it.

"What's wrong with him?" he asked me the other day, as we both gathered up our things to head home.

"Who knows? Your guess is as good as mine."

"If there's something wrong with the business, then he really should tell us," Josh complained, slipping into his Zac Posen blazer. "He kind of owes it to us."

"I'm sure everything's fine," I said.

"Maybe. But he's been acting like this ever since Nathan paid him that visit."

I mulled this over. Nathan is the national director. Now that I thought about it, Josh was right. But I'd been so wrapped up in the fire and the Ty situation I'd barely noticed. In fact, Nathan slipped in and out of town and I didn't so much as utter five words to him. Usually, I make it a point to take him out for cocktails or dinner. You know, schmooze him a little. But I've been totally preoccupied. Suddenly this makes me nervous. Falling out of grace with your boss's boss is never a good idea.

"Did you get a chance to talk to Nathan while he was here?" I asked.

"Absolutely. We had dinner at China Grill."

At the mention of China Grill—my original meeting place for the *Metro Guy* article—I felt a little sick. My face must have shown it, because Josh said, "Chin up, sweetie. You'll catch him next time."

* * *

Ruby's in Florida on an assignment, but I call her later when I get home. It will be great to talk to her, to hear her voice. She answers on the fifth ring.

"Hello?" She's out of breath.

"Hey!"

"Kylie, hi!"

"What's up?"

"I'm, uh, kind of in the middle of something."

I glance at my watch. "I thought the shoot would be over by now."

"It is. I'm . . . there's someone here."

"Oh."

"A guy," she clarifies, although it's not necessary.

"Go you!" My enthusiasm is fake. I feel like a bitch, but

it's hard to get too excited for her. Truth is, I'm jealous. I could go for some mindless sex. I've never done the whole one-night-stand thing, and it sounds pretty nice right about now. Ruby and Davey are on the outs again, so I can't blame her for looking for a little action.

"He's reaaaally hot!" she whispers. "I met him at the assignment earlier."

"Oh, no," I groan. "Not another male model," I plead. Last year Ruby hooked up with a vapid male model named Dane. He was a real drama queen, and he spent most of his free time standing in front of the mirror, practicing his poses. Think Zoolander, only gayer. Ruby really liked Dane, but things ended badly when she caught him making out with someone else. Someone else named Brian.

"Relax. He's a magazine editor. I wouldn't date a male model again if you paid me."

"Ugh," I groan. "I wouldn't date a magazine editor again if you paid me."

"That reminds me," Ruby says. "Hang on a sec." I hear her shuffling around on the other end. A door closes. "Okay, I had to get some privacy. Anyway, Brent—that's his name—knows Ty. He gave me some dirt on him."

"Really?" My ears perk up. I shouldn't care, but I do. "Like what?"

"I don't want to get into too many details right now," she whispers, "but let's just say, be glad you're done with Ty Benedict. You got out at the right time, trust me."

My heart's racing. "Oh, my God! Why?"

"He's a jerk, and a male slut, and he's ruthless," Ruby says. "According to Brent, he'll do anything to get a story."

I don't say anything, so Ruby adds, "See, aren't you glad you got out before things got any more involved?"

"Yeah."

"Anyway, I'd better go. Brad's waiting."

"Brad?" I ask. "I thought his name was Brent."

"Ah, yes. It is. But I keep screwing up and calling him Brad. He looks more like a Brad than a Brent." Ruby giggles. "To tell you the truth, he looks like Brad Pitt's younger, slightly less attractive brother."

Brad. I remember my fake boyfriend, Brad, the one who went to Notre Dame. I feel sad.

"Have fun!"

"Thanks. We totally will. Oh, and before I forget. Can you help me with my stuff for art class?"

"Sure," I say, "I'd be happy to."

"Thanks," Ruby says. "Because I don't think the instructor will be too pleased if I turn in that pile of garbage I've been working on. Hey!" she says, giggling. "Do you think she'd notice if, instead of sketching Larry, I drew Brent instead? I'm telling you, he'd make a much nicer model."

"Good night, Ruby," I say, laughing as I hang up the phone.

17

Cool Rule #17:

Cool people are always prepared, rarely surprised.

"Ty Benedict's assistant called," Courtney tells me when I get into the office the following morning. "He wanted to remind you that *Metro Guy* will be on stands this Friday."

As if I could forget. I've been anticipating this day for weeks.

"He's having a bunch of complimentary copies messengered over today."

"Great!" I say. It sounds hokey—and I didn't even know this was possible—but I'm practically tingling with anticipation. Even though Ty read me the rough draft of the article, I'm still kind of scared. The way things ended between us last time has me worried. What if he got pissed off and decided to rewrite the article so he could butcher me? I would hope he wouldn't do a thing like that, but you never know.

Several hours pass and the magazines don't arrive. I'm going a bit stir-crazy waiting for them. When I get back from lunch, I'm pleased to see a package from Ty on my desk.

It's open.

"Courtney!" I yell.

She appears in the doorway. "I'm sorry," she says sheepishly.

"Kevin caught the courier at the door. He ripped into the package before I could stop him."

"Why am I not surprised?"

"You know Kevin," Courtney laughs. "He practically lives and breathes *Metro Guy.* He probably couldn't stand waiting an extra two days to buy it on the newsstands when he knew you had advance copies."

I think Kevin's more excited about the article than I am. He's been raving about it for months. "Have you looked yet?" I ask Courtney.

"No. I wanted to wait for you."

Anxiously, I rip the magazines out of the packaging. Jude Law's smiling face greets me.

"Ooh, you're in the same issue as Jude!" Courtney says. "I *love* him."

I scan the headlines on the front cover. Nothing jumps out at me, so I flip open to the table of contents. Courtney grabs a copy and sits down across from my desk. I hurriedly scan through the listing, looking for my article.

"Where is it?" Courtney asks.

"I don't know." I wrinkle my brow. "I must have missed it." I read over the table of contents again, meticulously looking at each entry. There are articles about celebrities, sex, spa getaways for men. There are features on television shows, fashion, and sports. But nothing on How to Be Cool.

"Is Ty even in this issue?" I ask, turning the pages. "I haven't seen his byline on a single thing."

"Here's something Ty wrote," Courtney says, holding up a page. I look at the title. "Putting the Man in Manicure: A masculine approach to stylish nails."

"I just don't get it."

"Do you think the article got bumped?"

"I don't see how. . . . I'm sure Ty said it was going to run this month. Besides, why would he messenger these copies over if it's not the right issue?"

Neither one of us has the answer. I instruct Courtney to call Ty's assistant and find out what's up. I could call him myself, but I refuse. Ty and I are now acting as though we're strangers. No phone calls, no e-mails. I won't be the one to break first. I still have a small shred of dignity here, and I don't want to lose it.

"I couldn't get in touch with anyone at *Metro Guy*," Courtney says a minute later. "I'll keep trying."

I decide to put the magazine out of my mind, but deep down, I'm angry. There's only one logical explanation. Following our fiasco, Ty decided to kill the piece. It's an assholish thing to do—letting your ego (or whatever) get in the way of your job. We spent a lot of time on this story, and I can't believe he'd do that. But he certainly has the clout. He probably rushed out and wrote the stupid manicure piece on the heels of my reunion, so he'd have something to sub in the article's place.

I call Ruby and tell her my news.

"But why would he send you all those copies?" she asks.

"To rub it in my face."

"Is he really that big of a baby?"

"It looks that way."

"But would his editors really let him do this?" Ruby asks. "I don't know much about journalism or the magazine world, but there's got to be somebody Ty answers to. What excuse would he give them for pulling the piece? 'I'm in a fight with this girl, so I don't want to run it,'" she says, in a singsongy babyish voice.

"I don't know. He's pretty high up on the masthead over there."

"OH SHIT!" I hear Courtney scream.

"Ruby, I'd better go."

"Okay, call me later," she says.

"Everything okay?" I ask.

Courtney doesn't answer. A second later Kevin appears in my doorway. There's a strange expression on his face, one I've never seen before. He just stares at me, his mouth opening and shutting like he wants to say something but isn't sure what.

"Is something wrong?"

I notice there's a copy of *Metro Guy* in his hand. He walks over and flips it open on my desk. He points down at the page.

"What," he says, "in the fuck is this?"

I'm shocked. I haven't heard Kevin talk like this before. He's got a temper, to be sure of it, but he almost never curses. He always says it's vulgar.

I look down to where he's pointing. The headline reads:

SHE LIKES IT ON TOP:
FEMME FATALES EXPOSED
by Ty Benedict

Then I see the subhead, and I'm even more lost.

Our brave writer introduces you to a new crop of women who are using sex to get ahead.

"Is this your idea of a joke?" Kevin demands. "Or are you honestly this shallow?"

"What?" I ask.

Kevin snorts. "Tarnishing the good reputation of this company to get dates."

To get dates? "What are you talking about?"

"Read the goddamn article," he says.

At first I don't get it. But then I see it—my name, my pictures, actually. There are two of them. One close-up shot of me, sitting at my desk. It's side by side with a picture of me I've never seen before. It looks to have been taken around the time I was sixteen. I'm standing outside somewhere, at a park maybe, looking frazzled and unfashionable.

And fat.

When I see the heading under my picture, I nearly throw up:

Kylie Chase
From Junk Food Eater to Maneater

I sit down at my desk, slowly, with shaking hands. My throat goes completely dry and my pulse starts thumping in my ears. I begin to read.

We've all been there before. You want to cuddle. She's not in the mood. You reach to hold her hand, and she takes it as an invitation to dry-hump you.

For years, men have been chastised for being insensitive sex-crazed louts. But now the shoe is on the other foot—and chances are, that foot is decked out in a spiked heel that's being shoved forcibly against your back.

Welcome to the twenty-first century, guys. Because now it's the girls who want to play. There's a new crop of women who are using sex to get ahead.

I scan the article. Four women are featured in the story. A ruthless stockbroker, a manipulative pastry chef, a man-chasing college professor—and me. It's your typical overblown trash, painting the guys as victims and the women as sex-crazed lunatics who chew up men and spit them out to get ahead.

My part in the story is brief, but mortifying.

Kylie Chase makes her living teaching a course called How to Be Cool, a new-agey kind of idea that attempts to transform the socially inept from geek to chic. But Kylie has a secret. As a teenager she was shy, awkward, overweight. She ate lunch alone, turned to food for solace. But now she's traded that in and is using sex to fill the void. She admits that she uses her taut body to get men, and even attempted to seduce this reporter to help further her career. She doesn't even attempt to hide her motives. On the back of Chase's Toyota Prius is a naughty personalized license plate that advertises what she wants in a man—a large penis.

"WHAT!" I scream. "That's insane."

The story gets worse, talking about how I went to my high school reunion dolled up in a "barely there dress" in an attempt to get attention. The article is peppered with references to how I'm using sex as a substitute for food.

"This is ridiculous!"

I continue reading:

By using sex as a substitute for food, Kylie has turned into a self-professed nympho. And she'll do anything to get a guy into bed, even lying pathologically. "I actually made up a fake bio to impress my high school crush," Kylie admits. "I told him I'd gone cliff-diving in Spain and played poker with Ben Affleck." All in the name of seduction.

I gasp.

Kevin is not amused. "If you're going to pull some shit like this, the least you could do is leave our name out of it."

"You think I did this on purpose?"

He doesn't say anything.

"I'm not crazy! I would never do that."

"We cannot have this kind of thing affecting our reputation!" Kevin thunders.

"*Your* reputation?" I ask. "What about *my* reputation? I'm the one who's really been screwed here."

"And for you to sacrifice the chance for How to Be Cool to have an article just so you could make it all about yourself."

"For the billionth time, I had nothing to do with this!"

"Yeah, right." He rolls his eyes. "You lied and told me Ty Benedict was writing about How to Be Cool, when all along you were planning to use the magazine to get dates!"

It escalates into a full-scale argument. I don't mean for it to happen, but I'm so angry that he doesn't seem to believe me, that he seems to think I've done this just to get ahead. He seems to think what Ty has said is true.

"You know what," Kevin says, his eyes blazing, "maybe you ought to take some time off, wait for this whole thing to blow over."

"That sounds like a fine idea," I say, jumping up. I quickly wave good-bye to Courtney and then I storm out the door.

* * *

I spend the next four hours desperately trying to reach Ty. Finally, after numerous calls, his assistant patches me through.

"What the hell did you do to me?"

"Hello to you, too."

"You fucked me!"

"No, you tried to fuck me. And I wrote an article about it." He laughs. "It's ingenious, if you think about it."

"How could you do this?"

"Look, Kylie, the truth of the matter is my boss killed the How to Be Cool piece," he says. "It just wasn't gelling, it wasn't coming together. Once I found out Angela Dunbar fired you, the whole thing started to unravel. It just didn't have enough punch. So I tagged along to your reunion, hoping to salvage it, but no dice."

"You never told me that!"

"I'm telling you now," he says, sounding annoyed, "and, anyway, I thought you'd thank me."

"Thank you?"

"Yeah, for getting your name in the magazine at all. At first I didn't think I could pull it off. But after the way you came on to me, and when your friend Joanie sent me that picture, I saw a way to do it."

So that's where he got the picture.

"I did not come on to you! And all of those quotes—I never said those things!"

"You did," he says. "When we were together. Right before you passed out."

I have a vague memory of this, of talking with him intimately about my body issues, about the way I'd always felt so inadequate before, when I was fat. But he's blown it out of proportion, twisted it into something else.

"How could you do this?" I say again.

"Look, I got you in the magazine. I even got your company a mention."

"I don't want to be in there under those circumstances!"

"Here's a little lesson for you," he says, "there's no such thing as bad PR. And, really, Kylie, I thought you'd know that, being that you have a background in PR. Supposedly."

I don't even know how to respond to that, I'm so mad.

"You know what . . ." I struggle, searching for the right words. "Go to hell you . . . you Ty Benedict Arnold!"

18

Cool Rule #18:

Never go out in public looking like a wreck.
Do, and you're guaranteed to run into at
least five people you know.

I'm not sure what a nervous breakdown feels like, but I'm guessing this is pretty close.

I can't eat, I can't sleep. My body moves as if it's covered with thick molasses: slow, droopy, out of sync.

I still can't figure out why Ty did this. What motive does he have for revenge? If he'd tried to sleep with me and I'd denied him, that would be one thing. His manly pride would have been hurt, and he'd likely want to get me back. But since he was the one pushing me away, it doesn't make sense that he'd be so pissed off.

Unless . . .

What if the whole "I'm not going to have sex with you" thing was some sort of reverse psychology? Ty's probably got a better understanding of the female brain than your average joe. After all, he got his start at women's magazines. And *Metro Guy* prides itself on showcasing the less piggish, more sensitive side of the male gender. Conventional wisdom says guys are always up for meaningless sex, and girls are always pushing them away. But if Ty took the high road—if he played the "girl part," professing to be a fan of "making love, not casual screwing"—he could circumvent the whole men-are-pigs argument.

Ty probably figured I'd be so touched by his sound morals and deep appreciation for sex that when he did finally try to get me into bed, I'd jump at the chance for some sweet, meaningful sex with a true gentleman.

Jerk.

He must have been short one person for the story, and he found a way to fit me into that mold.

* * *

"Kiki?"

No one has called me that in years. Years.

"Wake up! It's the middle of the afternoon."

Where am I? I roll over, hear her voice again, and I know. I've been asleep since eight o'clock last night.

"Kiki?"

My mother. Of course, I'm at my parents' house. *Ty. The article. The canceled clients. Kevin's cryptic words.*

"Kiki, what's wrong?" she persists. I hate it when she calls me this. I'm not a big fan of nicknames in the first place. It's one thing if your name is Jennifer, but you introduce yourself as Jen. Or you were born Christopher, and you prefer being called Chris. That, I get. But most of the time, at least where I'm concerned, it seems like people make up a nickname without bothering to find out if you like it or not. There are not a lot of great options with Kylie. Ky. K. Kyle (the only one I can tolerate).

Kiki is the worst. It sounds like a little dog, a miniature poodle maybe. Or some 1950s sorority princess—a sweetheart of Kappa Pi, whose hair is always in a ponytail, who always wears a pleated skirt to class. I have told my mother this a thousand times, told her that I love being called Kylie, think it's a wonderful name (I do), and since she gave it to me, why not use it?

"You really have to stop wallowing, Kiki."

Throughout high school and college, she continued to call me Kiki. And then, one day, she stopped. Come to think of it, Mom began calling me Kylie after I lost weight. Which I guess just proves that she listens to me more, respects me more, when I am thin. You think I'm joking, but I'm not.

I open my eyes and look at her. "What time is it?"

I'm expecting her to say noon, or three o'clock. This is my new goal, I've decided. To sleep late.

"It's almost ten-thirty," Mom says, and I'm startled.

"Ten-thirty is hardly 'middle of the afternoon.' I thought it would be later."

"It's late enough. If you don't get up now, you'll waste the entire day."

"Maybe I want to waste the day," I retort.

She gives me a look that says, *Since you're obviously going through something right now, I'll let that one slide.*

"I'll get up in a minute." It sounds irresponsible and lame, but for the next few days all I want to do is take up space, accomplish nothing. Since I stormed out on Kevin, I've really dug myself a hole. I'm lucky he didn't fire me on the spot and only suggested I take a two-week leave of absence.

And how do I plan to spend this glorious time off? There are so many options. I could hit a destination spa in Arizona or book one of those Pilates retreats to Costa Rica. I could go to New York and do a little shopping. Or maybe London; the shopping's great there, too. And I have a friend who lives in London, an old college pal who took a job at Sotheby's a while back. I could always ring her up (see, I'm getting the hang of the lingo already) and see if I could come visit.

But I probably won't do any of this. I will probably just stay here. Why, you ask? For starters, there's the money thing. I'm a little on the broke side, and because I've got to replace all of my possessions from the fire, I'm about to get even more broke.

But, mostly, the reason I want to stay here is this: I'm being lazy. I *want* to be lazy. In the five years since I lost weight, I have never once stopped, never slowed down. I've been afraid to. Terrified that if I stopped to relax, I might slack off. I might quit going to the gym six days a week. I might start baking cookies. And eating McDonald's. And hanging around my father's restaurant to see if I could snag a container of pesto sauce—the kind with vodka and pepper. And then I'd go sit in the back, and dunk piece after piece of bread in it, at five hundred calories a pop.

I couldn't have it both ways. I couldn't have my cake and eat it, too. I had to choose, I really did. Pesto or bathing suits. French fries or size ten. I could have the cheesecake, but I'd also have the fat thighs, and the round face, and the weight that clocked in at more than two hundred pounds.

I know my food problems might seem trivial, insignificant in the grand scheme of things. And I'm not trying to make anyone feel sorry for me. I spent a lot of years playing that card, and it gets you nowhere. Once I accepted, truly accepted, that this was the body I had to work with, I felt a lot happier. And so now I make the choice. I stay strict, I stay focused. I follow the kind of vice-free diet that would make a professional athlete proud.

In five years, I have never faltered. Oh, I've slipped, I've stumbled from time to time. I've skipped the gym, I've had the sliver of birthday cake. It's true what they say. You do start to lose your taste for junk food when you stop eating it for a while. If you try to start back, everything's too salty, too oily, too rich. You'd rather just have a few bites of lean chicken breast instead of a Big Mac. But that doesn't last forever, or even all that long. Eat McDonald's a few times in a row and you'll start wanting it every day. (And besides, no matter what they say, you *never* lose your taste for some foods. Chocolate, for one. Pizza, for another.)

"Did you have a bad breakup?" Mom asks. She nods her head knowingly.

"No! I don't even have a boyfriend," I point out.

"You're not hanging around with the gay men again, are you?" she asks suspiciously. This is one of my mother's greatest fears—that I'm going to "start hanging around with the gay men again." It's not that she's homophobic or anything. After all, this is the woman who changed the boutique's insurance plan so it included life partners in addition to spouses.

"Because you know what happens when you start hanging around with those guys. . . ."

Yes, I do. In college, I went through a brief (okay, fourteen-month) spell in which all of my best friends—all of my friends, period—were gay guys. It was great. Lots of fashion advice, tons of affection. All the things you want from straight guys, without the hassle of sex and commitment.

It all went to hell when I decided to date one. He was trying to be straight at the time, so this worked out well. His name was Justin and we went out for about three months.

In some ways, things were perfect. Constant affection—lots of cuddling, hand holding. I let him guide things; let him tentatively take me to first, second, and then third base.

We'd always stop at a certain point, although not as soon as you might expect. Justin never wanted to have sex, of course, but he seemed happy to do everything over the clothes, and a few things under. It was the kind of groping you have when you're a shy teenager, and I was okay with that. I was a size twenty at the time, and the last thing I wanted to do was strip off all my clothes and engage in crazy, passion-fueled sex.

In the end, my heart got broken, as tends to happen when a straight woman gets involved with a gay man.

In my own defense, I didn't know he was gay (okay, yes I did—I totally did, but denial is a beautiful thing, baby). He was a fashion merchandising major. He worshipped Madonna and Anastacia and Cher. He had posters of Ashton Kutcher and 'N Sync in his dorm room. All his friends were gay men; he was an incredible dancer and dressed better than anyone I'd ever known, my mother included.

She was the one who wrecked us, by the way. My mother. I brought Justin home for Thanksgiving and she cornered me in the living room the second he was out of earshot. "This is a joke, right?" she asked, sizing me up.

"What?" My face flamed hot. I knew what she meant, but was playing dumb.

"You said he was your boyfriend, but what you really meant was *best* friend. Or maybe you meant that you were his hag. . . ."

"Mom!"

"You know he's gay, right?"

"He is not!" I said hotly.

"Oh, honey." She put her arm around me. "He went to New York for Fashion Week. He knows more about the fall line than *I* do."

"That doesn't mean anything," I huffed. "Justin's major is fashion merchandising. You're just stereotyping him."

"He's sweet," she said. "I see why you like him. But he's never going to like you back . . . not in the way you want him to."

I tried to bring my dad into it, for backup. But he was clueless, as usual.

"Let me talk to Justin," Mom said. "Just for a minute."

And so she did. And to this day I don't know what she said. All I know is when we got back to school after break, he came out. It was insane, how quickly it happened. Twenty minutes alone with my mother and he was plastering rainbow flag stickers on his notebooks, joining the Gay Student Union, and dating a guy named Adam.

All of this after he dumped me, of course.

I knew it was for the best, but part of me couldn't help resenting my mother for what she did. All I saw was that, in a roundabout way, she had gotten my boyfriend to break up with me. Couldn't she have left well enough alone? Justin would have come out eventually. He was really close; she merely pushed him over the edge.

But I digress. The point is, my mother has this way with people. She's able to talk to them frankly, cut to the chase, make them see what they've been missing all along.

"I'm not in love with a gay guy, Mom," I tell her.

"Then tell me what's wrong," Mom says, matter-of-factly. "I haven't seen you like this since . . ."

Since you were fat. I know what you were going to say, Mom, I really do.

"You must not have heard," I say, my voice flat.

"Heard about what?"

I prop myself up on my elbows, look at her. She's dressed

beautifully, designer label, of course. The whole package is perfect from head to toe. My mother never has a bad hair day, never has bags under her eyes, never chips a nail.

"The article," I tell her.

"Oh, *that.*"

"You know about it?" I ask anxiously.

"You left a copy of it on the floor of your room. I hope it's not too nosy, but I read it."

My pulse quickens. "What did you think?"

"I think," she says carefully, "that it's not the end of the world."

"I never said it was."

"You're acting like it, Kiki. I know this is shitty, what he did. But you have to let it go."

"The article was awful," I begin.

"Yes, it was." She shrugs. "So what? You think you can go through life without ever encountering anything 'awful'? I didn't raise you to be that naïve, did I?"

I flinch. "I'm not naïve."

Mom's face softens. "I'm sorry, I know you're upset. Things have been rough for you lately. But everybody has those times, those days or weeks—sometimes years—where things aren't going well. You've had a spell of bad luck, but you'll recover soon." She smiles. "You excel under pressure, Kiki. You always have."

Mom sits down on the edge of the bed. "What do you want for your birthday?"

I'm taken aback. For starters, my birthday is still a way off. But mainly I'm surprised because my mother never, *ever* asks this question. She picks what she thinks you need and gives it to you. One year I got laser hair removal for my bikini line. The next I got twelve months of eyebrow waxes. And just when I was starting to think my mom had some kind of weird obsession with body hair, she switched gears completely and bought me a Gucci clutch.

"You really want my opinion?" I ask. "You never want my opinion."

"Yes I do."

I lean back on the pillows, which are horribly uncomfortable. I've forgotten how stiff and awkward they are, how tough it is to sleep at my parents' house, in my old bed. "I'll think about it." I make a move to get out of bed. Maybe I'll ask for pillows.

She pats me on the leg, through the blanket, and then leaves. And I watch her go, and I don't think about how considerate she's being, or about how no matter how abrupt she sometimes comes off, she truly does mean well. No, I don't think about that at all.

I think, *Is she calling me Kiki again because I've obviously gained weight?*

I debate stepping on the scale, but talk myself out of it. A part of me isn't ready, just doesn't want to know how bad this is.

19

Cool Rule #19:

Never assume that other people share your interests—
especially if those interests involve
Star Trek, role-playing games, or magic tricks.

"Kylie. Hi, it's Zack."

I am sitting in the living room, watching a rerun of *The King of Queens* (which I actually find kind of annoying—you know, the whole fat guy/skinny wife cliché) and eating a Snickers bar. And then, just like that, Zack Naylor calls.

I grab the remote and mute the TV.

"Hi."

"You left the reunion really early."

He noticed? This surprises me. "Yes, well, I had somewhere to be."

"You should have stuck around."

"Oh," I say.

"We missed you."

Maybe what Ruby said is true. Maybe seeing me with Ty made Zack jealous. Or something. But really, I'm finding it hard to care. After the gastric bypass comment, I kind of lost interest.

"I would have liked to catch up with you more."

I don't know what to say to this. So I ask, "Was the rest of the reunion fun?"

"We had a good time. You missed out on a lot of stuff, like the awards ceremony. That's why I'm calling, actually. You won an award."

"I did?"

"Yes, for Most Improved."

Most Improved. "Why, because I'm thin now?"

"No, not only that. But also because of your bio. When Andy read it out—well, we were all so impressed with the places you've been, the stuff you've done."

"I made some of that up, you know," I tell him. "I've never jumped off a cliff in Spain, never even been to Australia."

"Ha-ha." Zack laughs. He thinks I'm kidding.

"No, it's true."

He ignores this. "You should get more involved. We're thinking about forming an alumni committee, having regular events, once a year or so."

"Maybe."

"One other thing. I wanted to apologize to you," he says. "I was pretty rude to you at the reunion. I shouldn't have made that crack about your stomach. I was kind of drunk, and I was pissed about the Big Dance."

"You kind of hurt my feelings," I admit. "You know, back in high school . . . I kind of had a thing for you."

"I know."

"You know?"

"Uh huh." He pauses. "So when do you want to come pick up your award?"

"Um, can you mail it?" I don't really care about this award. And not because the title, Most Improved, implies that I sucked before. Although that's part of it.

"Okay, what's your address?"

I give it to him.

"Ah, my parents live out there. Maybe we'll bump into each other sometime around the neighborhood."

"Maybe we will," I say, even though I know that if it happens, we will probably both keep on moving, look away, pretend that we're strangers.

* * *

"We're not having this again," Mom says, dragging the covers off me the following morning. "You've been in this bed for almost fourteen hours. It's going to stop. *Now.*"

"Mmm," I mumble, pulling the covers back over my head. "Just five more minutes."

"I don't think so," she says firmly. "I'm leaving in twenty, so if you want to get a shower before we go then you'd better get up now."

We? Go? What is she talking about? "What are you talking about?"

"I've made a decision," she says. Uh-oh. Whatever this is, I'm not going to be able to argue. When my mother takes a stand on something, she never falters.

"You have two choices. You can come to work with me for the day—I could use some extra help around the boutique."

I hate the boutique. I hate wedding gowns. I hate watching rich, size-two brides try on twenty-five dresses, complaining about all of them—"White always makes my hips look so fat!" I hate listening to my mother fawn all over them—"You couldn't look fat if you tried!" I hate watching her kiss ass and schmooze all day long.

"What's my other choice?" I rub the sleep out of my eyes.

"You can go out and find another job."

"What?" I yelp. "I'm not . . . I mean, I'm still doing How to Be Cool."

"I thought you quit."

"No!" I say, bolting upright. "I'm just . . . I'm taking some time off. I'm planning to go back."

She gives me a look that says, *You could've fooled me*.

"I don't need a new job. Honest."

"Boutique it is," Mom says.

"I don't see why I have to go into your work. I'm taking some time off," I remind her.

"And you'll be using it to help me out at the boutique."

"But . . . why?"

"Because you're not going to mope around the house all day, that's why."

My mom has little patience for self-loathing and pity. This is probably a good thing.

"Feeling sorry for yourself accomplishes *nothing*," she is fond of saying. "If you go around acting like a loser, then you can't get mad when people treat you like one."

She's right. And, though I'd never tell her, that's one of the first things I teach people in How to Be Cool. You are exactly who you think you are.

"I need your help anyway. Your dad and I are leaving town tonight, so I need to close up early. You can help me get everything done."

Twenty-five minutes later we're heading out the door.

"You know something, Kiki," my mother says as she puts the car in reverse and backs out down the driveway, "conventional wisdom says . . ." She begins, and I tune her out.

My mother is a big fan of "conventional wisdom," and she

is always giving out unsolicited advice. Personally, I think conventional advice is overrated.

I never realized this until I started losing weight, but most of the diet tips they give you are a complete joke. Like they tell you to never eat mindlessly, to "savor every morsel of food that goes into your mouth."

This would be sage advice if you were eating, say, fine imported chocolates from Belgium. Or thousand-calorie-a-bite crème brûlée. Or a $50 plate of gourmet macaroni and cheese.

But as a dieter, as someone who is trying to lose weight, you are not eating any of these things. No, you're having bland carrot sticks, wood-chip-flavored bowls of Kashi, egg-white omelets with fat-free cheese. And who wants to savor every bite of *that*?

If I sat down with my bowl of steamed spinach topped with flakes of canned tuna fish (which I have several days a week) and actually *concentrated* on what I was eating . . . if I spent hours lingering over a meal of Brussels sprouts and four ounces of chicken—night after night after night—I'd lose my mind.

Another thing that slays me: all the "healthy swap" recipes. You know, the ones that tell you how to take a Boston cream pie and turn it into the caloric equivalent of broccoli. I don't go for any of that stuff. If I'm eating something that looks like a chocolate éclair but tastes like dryer lint, it won't be long before I get so frustrated that I drive down the street to Madeline's Bakery and buy the real thing. I'm better off just pretending things like Boston cream pie and chocolate éclairs don't exist.

I once saw a recipe for how to make a dieter's version of a

Snickers bar. I never tried it out. A quick glance at the ingredients told me all I needed to know: dates, lime juice, and unsalted almonds. You were supposed to somehow fuse those three things together, bake them in the oven, and wind up with something resembling miniature Snickers bites.

Dates, lime juice, and almonds? Were they kidding?

If I followed this kind of advice, I'd still be fat.

"So what do you want me to help out with today?" I ask as she steers the car down Maple.

"As you know, right now is our busiest time of year."

"Right," I say, although as far as I can tell, it is always their busiest time of year. Wedding season typically runs from April to October, with the busiest months being May and June. But, despite what wedding planners and magazines may tell you, every bride is on her own time line. Some of them pick out their dresses eighteen months in advance; some of them do it eight weeks in advance. It all evens out so that no matter what time of year it is, there are always a ton of girls lining up to get a look at the Vera Wangs and Reem Acras.

It's weird, because you keep hearing so much about how weddings are out, how fewer people than ever are getting married, and how those who do are waiting longer. Yet my mom's business hasn't suffered one bit. I guess selling wedding dresses is one of those recession-proof types of jobs. Unlike, say, being an interior decorator or a travel agent. Or a cool instructor . . .

I spend the afternoon in a sea of weddings. I watch girls try on dresses, give them advice, tell them what works and what doesn't. Everyone I see is so excited. Stressed, to be certain, but excited nonetheless.

There's something nice about it, the way they're all so

happy, optimistic, ready to start the next chapter of their lives. I wish I had that kind of rebirth, that kind of change.

When I first lost weight five years ago, my life was turned upside down—in a good way. But I've become complacent since then. I've gone to the same job, done the same things, not broken out of my shell.

Maybe this is what I need, I think, as I watch a bride-to-be twirl in front of the mirror, her Reem Acra gown flowing behind her. *As simple as it sounds, maybe I just need a change.*

* * *

My parents have gone out of town. They left after my mom got off work tonight. They'll be gone until Tuesday, which means I have the house to myself. This is what I've been wanting; this is what I've been dreaming of since the day I moved back in. Yet now that it's here, I feel depressed. Before, the fact that I had no social life was my parents' fault. Now I have no one to blame but myself. With Ruby in Colorado until next weekend, my social life is pretty dead. And here I thought so much had changed since high school. . . .

I need to fill my car up, so I decide to drive to the gas station down the street. I'll pick up a few lotto tickets—why not, my luck has to turn around—and maybe a case of beer.

I'm going to sit home alone and drink beer while I watch the lotto drawing on TV. It's a wee bit pathetic, but I don't care.

When I get to the gas station, I'm bummed to see that the Mega Millions jackpot is only $12 million.

"Wow, it's low this week," I say, making small talk with the cashier.

"Someone won on Tuesday," he says. "The jackpot just got reset."

Hmm. Maybe this is a bad sign—I decide to play the lottery a few days after someone has drained the account. I haven't even filled out a ticket yet, and already my luck's not great.

Once you take the cash payout and subtract taxes, I'd be lucky to pocket $3.5 million. I was hoping for some ridiculously high number, you know, like $280 million.

Then again, $3.5 million has a nice, comfortable ring to it. It's not chump change, but it's not so outrageous that I'd have to spend the rest of my life looking over my shoulder, watching out for death threats or kidnappings.

Plus, it's more money than Ty made for his script, and that's gotta be worth something.

I debate about the numbers for a minute and then check Easy Pick. My luck hasn't been so great lately, so I figure I might as well let the computer do it for me. A minute later, I stare at my card, eager to see what numbers the computer has randomly selected: 01 02 03 05 12, Mega Ball = 04.

What the hell is this? I've been given 1, 2, 3, 4, 5, if you count the Mega Ball. Easy Pick, my ass. Are they joking? There's no way that's going to come up. I grab another card and fill out a selection of numbers, making sure to cover the full range of choices: 06, 14, 29, 38, 50, with the Mega Ball being 41. I feel pretty good about that, like it's got a real chance of hitting.

I hand the cashier my second card, then grab a bag of Fritos off the rack and toss them onto the counter. I know I shouldn't be eating them. But considering I'll be spending Friday night alone in front of the TV, it just doesn't seem to matter.

* * *

Before I go to bed, I flip channels and watch the Mega Millions picks scroll across the screen.

I haven't even matched one number.

* * *

I once read that most suicides occur on the weekends. At the time, I remember thinking that was bizarre. *Who kills themselves on a Saturday?* I wondered. Monday, of course, would be the obvious choice. Nobody likes Monday—it's the crappiest day on the calendar. A Tuesday, a Thursday—anything would make more sense.

But now I get it, the reason why people get so depressed on the weekends. You're sitting at home on a Saturday night and the phone's not ringing and your e-mail in-box is empty because everyone who's anyone is out doing something. All around you are the sights and sounds of people partying, having fun, enjoying life—and you're not a part of it. Saturday is for dates, for sex. Saturday is vodka tonics with your best friends. And if you don't have anywhere to go or anyone to talk to, it's easy to feel like the loneliest person in the world.

I wish Patrick were home. But I saw him leave earlier.

I snuggle under the covers, trying to relax. I can't believe a few weeks ago I was lying in this bed with Ty Benedict.

I push the thought out of my head and pick up the phone. Fuck it. Enough feeling sorry for myself.

If they won't call me, I'll call them! Surely somebody is up for going out tonight. I scroll through my cell phone directory, starting at A. Adam Armstrong, Alan Jankis, Amy Mancini . . . I keep going, but no one jumps out. I move on to B, then C, D, and so on. I want to start making phone calls, start tracking down plans, but I can't. I don't know any of these people—not really. They're clients, acquaintances.

People I met once at a party. Friends of friends of friends. I can't call any of them. It would be awkward, weird. You just don't do that—phone up a distant acquaintance on a Saturday night and beg them to hang out with you.

I never thought I'd say this, but I wish my parents were here. The house feels so empty and alone without them. In high school I didn't have a lot of friends and rarely went out on the weekends. But somehow I never felt too bad about it. I guess that was because back then I truly believed things would get better. I was in the first part of my life, not even a quarter of the way in. I still had so many things to look forward to: getting a car, losing my virginity, four years of college, my first trip to Europe. The possibilities seemed endless, the world full of promise.

And as I lie on the bed, staring up at my ceiling full of faux glow-in-the-dark stars, I can't help but ask, *what now*? I had gone out, lost weight, embraced life, and yet here I was. Right back where I started.

I watch a rerun of *The Office*, but that doesn't help things because I find myself identifying with Steve Carell's character—you know, the pathetic loser who tries too hard and remains clueless to the fact that nobody likes him.

I've just shut off the TV when I see a light flick on down the street. Patrick! I hop up off the bed and run over to the window. Yep, someone's definitely home. I pull on a pair of Dolce & Gabbana jeans and a red wool sweater. The jeans fit like a second skin—and I don't mean that in a good way. They used to be pleasantly snug, but now they barely zip up. The circulation is being cut off in my thighs, but I don't waste time fretting over it. I slip on the nicest shoes I own—brown knee-high Valentino boots—and then run a brush through my hair. I look good, in a casual this-outfit-took-no-planning kind of way.

I run downstairs and start hunting through my parents' DVD collection. It's a weird assortment. My mom has lots of chick flicks—*Moulin Rouge*, *Bridget Jones's Diary*, *Amelie.* My dad's collection is mostly made up of documentaries and TV shows like *Frasier.* I finally locate a copy of *Pulp Fiction.* That's a good, all-around popular movie. It flies with poseurs and pop culture lovers alike. I tuck it under my arm and go.

A minute later I'm standing on Patrick's front porch, ringing the doorbell. I hope his parents haven't come back into town early.

"Just a sec," I hear Patrick call from inside.

I smooth my hair into place. My roots are showing, but I doubt he'll notice. Guys rarely seem to pay attention to that kind of stuff. What he will notice is that I'm home bored on a Saturday night. Granted, Patrick doesn't seem to care about that sort of stuff. But because it does go against everything I tell my clients, I'd better have an excuse ready. I struggle to think of one, but my mind's blank. The door swings open.

"Hey, Kylie!" Patrick seems happy to see me.

"Hey. I saw your light was on."

"What are you doing home? I figured you'd have a hot date tonight," he teases. "The big social calendar and all."

"Believe it or not, I'm free." I hold up *Pulp Fiction.* "I thought maybe we'd watch a movie. Unless, of course, you've got a better offer."

He bites his lower lip. "My, uh . . . I have company."

Wow. Of course. It's Saturday. Everyone's got a date.

"Oh, I see. Sorry I interrupted."

"No, no, it's okay." He pauses. "Look, why don't you come in for a few minutes. Have a drink with us."

"Thanks, but I should probably get going."

"Rain check?"

"Definitely."

We say good-bye and I walk back to the house, alone.

* * *

Ruby calls as I'm getting ready for bed later. She can't talk long. She's got a catalog shoot in the morning and she needs plenty of rest. It's good to hear her voice, though. "I've been worried about you," she says. I'd read her Ty's article over the phone the day the magazine arrived. "We'll sue the bastard!" she'd exclaimed. It had been a thought of mine, too, but I'd taken media law in college and I knew libel was difficult to prove even in the best of circumstances. Ruby and I talk for a while, dreaming up ways to get back at Ty. But deep down I know there's not much I can do.

20

Cool Rule #20:

Cool people know how to ask for what they want—and get it.

I'm not naïve enough to think this is how it happens. You suddenly hit a bad spell and then life stays that way forever. Even after a tragedy people still have good days. It's not like this is a tragedy. In the grand scheme of things, it's pretty small, insignificant.

Ironically enough, it's Dennis Moop who snaps me out of my spell of self-pity. He calls my cell frantically, and on Monday I call him back. One thing leads to another and I wind up inviting him over for coffee—I'm somewhat desperate.

"For once," he says, stepping into my parents' foyer, "I'm glad I'm not you."

"Thanks, Dennis," I say, smiling weakly. "I needed that."

"I'm glad I'm not the one who's getting crapped on. Because I'm usually the one. Always have been, my entire life. That article was brutal, Kylie. And totally unfair."

"Thanks," I say, mustering a half smile.

"Although that doesn't give me much comfort now," he admits. "I used to like feeling better than other people. I don't anymore. Now it just seems like it doesn't matter. Whether I win or not, nothing matters."

"What do you mean?"

"I just . . . I no longer believe I'm going anywhere, no longer believe I'm capable of great things." Dennis sighs. "It's weird. In some ways, I've gotten more confident as I've gotten older. But every year I lose a little more faith in myself. I figure if the things I want haven't come through yet, they probably never will."

"You can't honestly think that way."

"Don't you?"

I think about it. "No. I have, off and on, for years. But I'm tired of it."

"You know what I'm tired of? I'm tired of thinking I'm not as good as other people."

"So don't."

He grunts. "You make it sound so simple."

"It is. Your inferiority complex exists totally in your head. It really does. All you've got to do is believe you're as good as the rest of the world—which you are—and it'll be true."

"Oh, good God. That's the lamest thing I've ever heard."

"It's all in your head, Dennis. Trust me on this."

He heaves a big sigh. "Nothing's that simple."

"This is. You're only making it complex."

"Stop being stupid."

I ignore his tone, chalk it up to a bad mood.

"Think about it. All the people who have things you don't think they should have. Ugly guys with hot girls. Mildly talented people who've reached the top of their field. What do you think that is?"

I'm expecting him to say confidence, but he doesn't.

"Nepotism."

I laugh, a big hearty laugh.

"I made you perk up!" he says, looking pleased with himself. "And I didn't even have to pull a rabbit out of a hat."

Oh, God. His magic classes. I'm about to say something, but I stop. So what if he enjoys magic. It's not like enjoying, say, armed robbery. Dennis isn't hurting anyone.

"Now if you really want to cheer me up, call Pamela Greco and arrange a meeting!"

"This week," he assures me. "This week."

"At least send her a picture," I urge.

"I will. But after the Jessica thing, it's just so hard."

After Dennis leaves I get a phone call from Patrick. I wonder if he's watching my house, the way I watched his the other night. I wonder if he waited until Dennis left to call.

I don't answer. I'm still embarrassed at having stumbled in on his date. He leaves a message. *"I'm sorry about the other night. My ex-girlfriend was in town, and things were a little weird. Call me about that rain check."*

I wait twenty minutes and then call him back.

"How about Friday night?" I ask. I would not normally be this bold—asking him to do something on a date night and all. But today I'm feeling gutsy.

"Friday sounds great," he says. "Why don't you come over around seven? I'll order some food in and we can watch the movie. We can make an evening out of it."

* * *

Wednesday night, Mom stages an intervention of sorts.

"We're going out tonight," she announces, barging in through the door of my bedroom. "I'm tired of watching you mope. We're going out for drinks."

She takes me to a bar in Chicago. It's a trendy place in the Loop that Charity's mentioned before.

It takes us thirty minutes to snag a table. We sip drinks by the bar—rum and Diet Coke for Mom, scotch for me. I normally don't go for such strong stuff, but I'm way too keyed up tonight to drink wine or beer. Besides, at least this way I'm saving on carbs.

Once we finally sit down Mom begins scoping out guys. "What kind of men are you interested in?" she asks, stirring her drink.

I shrug.

"Well, you'd better start looking. I know that's the reason why you're depressed. You need to upgrade from that Ty Benedict loser."

I like the idea that she's called him a loser. I know she's just doing it to be nice. Ty isn't the kind of guy that Mom would ever classify as a loser. Most people wouldn't, I guess.

"I'll drink to that," I say, tipping back my head and chugging my scotch.

"What about him?" She points toward an attractive, preppy guy over by the pool tables. "I could see you with someone like him."

He's cute, I'll give her that. But he's no Ty Benedict. "Ty was better looking."

"Looks aren't everything." She laughs wickedly. "There's also money. Penis size."

I must have a horrified look on my face, because she quickly dials it back. "Kiki, I'm kidding." I guess I don't look convinced, because she adds, "*Obviously,* I don't think those are the important things in life. Your father and I . . ." She trails off. "We're not together for any of the wrong reasons."

She's right about that. She wouldn't have picked my dad if she was after money or looks or . . . oh, God, let's not finish this thought.

"What I'm saying is . . . Kylie, can I be brutally honest

with you?" Mom seems flustered, nervous even. Which is unlike her. I'm intrigued.

"Sure. Of course."

Mom drums her fingers on the tabletop. "I have known a lot of guys like Ty Benedict. *A lot.*"

I wonder if by "known" she means "slept with." I push that thought out of my head and wait for her to finish.

"Guys like Ty always look great from a distance."

"And then you get close and you see how flawed they are," I finish.

"Sometimes. But not always. Every now and then you get close and they're still flawless." She takes a piece of ice out of her drink and chews on it. "That's the real trick. You can look and look and look all day long and you still might not find anything wrong with them. Some people are as great as they seem. It's like the Jen Aniston thing."

Jen, not Jennifer. Like they're best friends or something. "I'm not following. How does this apply to me? I wasn't in love with Ty. It's not like how it was for Jennifer and Brad."

"No, it's not. But that's what I'm showing you. Here's a worst-case scenario and she's lived to tell the tale. It's not about how you get knocked down," Mom says, "it's all about how you come back in the next round."

"I know. You're right."

"Your problem is that you take everything too seriously. You take *life* too seriously. And you spend too much time inside your own head."

"No, I don't."

"Yes, you do, Kiki."

I sigh.

"You also don't stand up for yourself."

"I do stand up for myself."

"You should have called that Ty Benedict jerk, told him where to shove it. You've got to be more assertive, Kiki."

"Okay, then, how about I start right now?"

She nods her head, looks pleased.

"Don't call me Kiki. Ever. Again."

"Really? You don't like that?"

"I hate it," I say. "But you must have known that."

"How would I?" she says. "You've never told me."

I think this over. Is it really possible that in all these years I've never once told her I hate being called Kiki? Maybe she is right. Maybe I do spend too much time inside my head.

"I thought I did."

"Nope, never," she says, smiling. "But I won't call you that anymore, then. All you had to do is ask."

* * *

When I get home I find an e-mail from Austin Dunbar.

Kylie,

I'm sorry about the way things ended. My parents can be so ridiculous sometimes. I just wanted to let you know that, despite what they might have told you, you really did make a difference. I'm going to Florida in the fall, and it's the best decision I've ever made. And I have you to thank, at least partly, for that. You really helped give me the push I needed, and I appreciate that.

Yours,

Austin

P.S. What's the capital of Ecuador?

21

Cool Rule #21:

Cool people are sometimes down, but never out.

"We're starting a business," Charity says. It's Thursday night and Charity has dropped by my parents' house unexpectedly.

"Who?"

"Me and you," she says, grinning.

"Excuse me?"

"I bought a boutique. I'm starting my own fashion line."

Just like that. She snaps her fingers, and it's hers.

"I want to develop an entire line, eventually transitioning into wedding gowns. And I'd love for you to work with me. I'm going to carry a whole range of sizes, too, which was your mom's idea."

"My mother?"

"Yeah, I talked to her the night of your reunion, remember? Anyway, I was asking her what she thought should be done differently, what area she thought wedding designers were missing. And she said sizing. They should carry plus sizes."

I'm dumbstruck. My mother, a size two waif with Michelle Pfeiffer cheekbones, is stumping for the common girl? It seemed crazy, surreal. Almost as surreal as Charity offering me this job.

I stare at her. "Um, I hate to break it to you, but I'm not a fashion designer."

"So?"

"I don't exactly have anything to bring to the business."

Charity puts her hands on her hips. "Don't you dare do that, Kylie Chase."

"Do what?"

"From day one, you've been preaching about self-confidence and taking chances. And here I am, asking you to take a chance and come on board with me—no risk on your part, at least not monetarily—and you're hemming and hawing like I've asked you to dive off the Golden Gate Bridge."

I start to object, but she stops me.

"You could be my partner. You could help me with sketches, PR. That's what your background is, promoting things, right?"

"It is."

"And that's what you've been doing for the past couple of years, making people cool. So why don't you help me make my business cool?" She's grinning from ear to ear.

"This all sounds great." I giggle. I can't help it. "But why would you want to hire me? You came to How to Be Cool wanting to be a star and I kind of, well, I kind of failed you."

"Eh." She shrugs it off. "I was asking for you to do the impossible. Making a virtual nobody over into a huge celebrity was kind of a tall order."

"But I really wanted to help. . . ."

"And anyway, I've figured out what I really want to do, which is design clothes," she says. "The funny part is, this is what I wanted to do all along. I just went in all kinds of circles before I got here."

"I really appreciate the offer," I say. I'm overwhelmed, unsure of what to say.

"Take a few days to think it over," she says. And then she leans over and gives me a hug.

"What was that for?"

"For stopping me from putting a sex video on YouTube." She grins. "Would have been the biggest mistake of my life."

I laugh as I watch her skip off down the driveway and pile into her Maserati. It seems crazy, ridiculous even, but by the time Charity's driver has pulled out onto the road I already know my answer.

* * *

I'm supposed to go over to Patrick's house on Friday, but I can't wait. I want to tell him the good news about Charity and the boutique.

I knock on the door, but he doesn't answer. I know he's home; his car is in the driveway. I'm about to give up, though, when I hear someone call out, "Back here."

I head around the side of the house and into the backyard. Patrick's got an enormous telescope set up, and he's looking up at the stars.

"Kylie!" He seems surprised to see me. "Did I get my days confused? I thought we were meeting tomorrow?"

"We are. I just thought I'd stop by for a minute and say hi."

Patrick grins. "I'm glad you did. I was just thinking about you." *He was?* "I was thinking how great it would be if you were here so I could show you this amazing planetary nebula."

I giggle. "Well, here I am. Fire away."

"Oh, you laugh now," Patrick says, "but wait until you see it."

He changes a few settings on the telescope, then tells me to look through. There's a swirl of colors—bright purples and oranges, all melding into one.

"Wow!" I say, my eyes registering the light. "How cool is this?"

"See, I told you," he says.

"And here I thought telescopes were just for looking at Orion's belt and stuff like that."

"No, you can see that stuff with your naked eye. Here, I'll show you." He motions for me to come closer. Then he gets behind me, takes my hand in his, and starts pointing. "There's Orion's belt," he says. "And there's Ursa Major and Ursa Minor. Or, as you regular folks call them, the Big Dipper and the Little Dipper." He takes me back to the telescope and starts showing me the planets that are visible from this latitude.

"This is really . . ."

"Cool," he guesses.

"I was going to say romantic."

Patrick blushes. "That, too."

I don't know why, but being around him makes me feel relaxed. Relaxed enough to be bold, to say what's on my mind.

"So I was wondering," he says, "if you were thinking . . ." He stares down at his feet, looks shy for a minute. It's so cute, and all it makes me think of is kissing him. I move forward, lean in, brush my lips against his.

We move into each other, kiss for a minute. It feels amazing, standing outside, being with him like this, underneath the stars. It's another one of those moments. Those moments when I don't wish I were anyone else, when I don't have a song in my head. When I'm just here.

And then my cell phone starts buzzing like crazy.

"Crap!" I say, pulling it out. It's Dennis Moop. I don't want to answer it, but tonight's the night he's supposed to meet Pamela, and it could be important. Even though I'm no longer doing How to Be Cool, even though I'm no longer his personal coach, I still want to be there as his friend.

I answer. "Hello."

"Kylie!" Dennis sounds so frantic that for a moment I can't tell if he's happy or distraught. "I met her!" he says. "She was amazing!" He launches into the story, telling me how they went out for dinner. How no one got stood up. How there was no fainting, no awkward moments. It was, in his own words, perfection.

"But wait until I tell you about her idea. It involves you."

"Can you tell me tomorrow?" I ask. Patrick's back at the telescope, messing around with the controls. I have a nightmare flashback of Ty Benedict, who kissed me and then went batty.

The thought fades out of my head. I don't want to think about Ty right now.

"Sure, Pamela will call you tomorrow with all the details," Dennis says. "Thank you, Kylie. Thanks so much."

We hang up and I go to rejoin Patrick.

"Sorry about that," I say. "Now where were we?"

He turns around and smiles at me. "Just getting started."

* * *

Pamela calls me the next day and fills me in on her plan. It seems surprising at first, but I quickly warm to it.

"I'd hate for what Ty did to be the last word," she says. "You should have your say."

She wants me to write an essay about what happened, exposing Ty for the fraud he is (such as lying about his age, or pretending to be into me so he could rifle through my stuff and find old pictures). I immediately tell her yes. Why wouldn't I want to hose Ty the way he's hosed me?

I feel like I have a million things to say, but when I sit down to write, something changes. I don't really want to have a war with him. I don't want to go tit-for-tat, slamming each other on the Internet and in print.

I call Pamela back. "I want to write something for you," I tell her. "But I don't know if the Ty piece is exactly right."

"Okay," she says. "What did you have in mind?"

I explain my idea.

"It's not as scandalous," she says, "but I like it. Do you think you could have the essay to me by tomorrow?"

It's a quick turnaround, but I tell her I can. And then I get to work, the words flowing faster than they ever have before. When I'm finished, I read it over a few times and correct the typos. Then I log in to my e-mail, type in Pamela Greco's address, and hit Send:

I was fifteen years old when I first realized I wasn't cool.

It started with a party—a party I wasn't invited to.

But this one was different. It was thrown by my best friend, Marjorie, and I should have been there. I would *have been there, if she'd told me about it. But, as I would later learn, Marjorie was embarrassed of our friendship, embarrassed to be seen with me. And so she lied.*

"It sucks that I can't do anything for my birthday this year. But you know how strict my parents are," she complained one day in the lunchroom. "No parties until I'm sixteen."

"You can spend the night at my house," I enthused. "We'll order pizza and play Mario Kart—we'll make it a party of two!"

"No . . ." She looked uncomfortable. "I think I'm gonna hang around at home that night. My mom keeps griping that we don't spend enough time together. Maybe this'll settle her down."

It didn't make a lot of sense, but I didn't question her. Truthfully, I'd felt Marjorie pulling away for a while, but I wasn't the suspicious type. I never saw it coming.

That I didn't find out about her secret birthday party until after it was over shows you how unpopular I was. Marjorie had invited more than thirty people, yet no one ever slipped and mentioned it in front of me. I was so far off the social radar, few of them even talked to me. It was Marjorie's own mother who blew her cover.

As she pulled up after school to pick up Marjorie, she rolled down the window and said, "Kylie! Hello!" She was always so happy to see me.

"Hi." I looked around. I didn't see Marjorie anywhere. We used to meet up after school and walk out together so we could gossip while we waited for our rides. But Marjorie had started smoking a few weeks earlier and everything had changed. She was likely around the back of the gym, sneaking a quick cigarette before she came out to greet her mom.

"I'm glad to see you're feeling better."

"Feeling better?" I walked over toward the car.

"Yes, Marjie told me you were sick."

"Sick?" I asked.

"It's too bad you had to miss the party Friday night," Marjorie's mother said. "But mononucleosis is rough. You were right to stay home and rest."

"Oh." It wasn't much of a response, but I was too shocked to speak.

"Well, take care of yourself. And tell your mom hi for me," she said, rolling up the car window.

I mumbled a quick good-bye and then started walking briskly toward the end of the carpool line.

When I confronted Marjorie about it on the phone that night, she seemed annoyed, and not at all apologetic.

"I didn't mean to hurt your feelings," she sighed. "But I had to do what was best for everyone."

"How is that best for everyone? It's certainly not best for me.*"*

"My other friends don't . . . they don't all get along with you."

"They don't know me," I said, my voice shaking. "They might get along with me if they tried."

"I don't think they'd want to try. Do you know what I mean?"

We didn't talk much after that. Despite feeling stung, I still desperately wanted to be her friend. But Marjorie wasn't into it at all. She had moved into the cool world and she couldn't find a place for me in it. In some ways, I couldn't blame her. She was climbing the social ladder while I was rooted firmly at the bottom. I was pimply and awkward. I had a weird body, bad social skills, and a slew of geeky interests. I loved video games and Star Wars*. An "art geek," I spent more time drawing people than I did talking to them. In* *truth, I felt lucky someone as cool as Marjorie had ever wanted to be my friend at all.*

Being a dork does something to you. After four miserable, lonely years of high school, I vowed to change.

While most of the other students were studying English lit and calculus, I took a crash course in popularity. I became obsessed with pop culture and spent much of my free time poring over fashion magazines and learning how to imitate the trendy kids. I went to great lengths to develop a chic, socially confident, "cool" persona.

I still have those tendencies. But I've figured out how to balance them.

I've figured out how to be cool.

Epilogue

There they are. Thirty candles. Thirty candles on top of a cake that says *Happy Birthday Kylie.*

And you know something? I couldn't be happier.

"Make a wish," Mom says, setting the cake down in front of me.

I feel Patrick's hand resting on my back. At the moment I don't want to wish for anything. It's all too perfect, too amazing. I've got my friends, my family, the new business to look forward to.

I'm still sad about the electrical fire that destroyed my apartment (the fire marshal finally determined the cause—although it didn't help my silly, non-insured butt). But in a way it's kind of cathartic watching all those years of my life go up in smoke. No more clinging to the past. I'm only looking forward now.

There's so much to celebrate. Everyone starts singing "Happy Birthday." It's amazing. In two weeks we'll be doing this again for Patrick. And then after that there'll be the opening of the boutique. It's still a ways off, but Charity has already found the perfect space, already signed the lease. And Ruby's agreed to come on board to model for our first print campaign.

I haven't talked to Ty. And when Ruby read in *Variety* that Paramount had put his script in "turnaround" (a sign of impending doom), I felt a brief surge of joy, as if maybe Karma did exist in the end. But then I felt guilty because, despite what he did, I don't hate Ty. I'm not holding a grudge, like I did for so many years with Hayley and Joanie. And Noel. And even, sadly, my mom.

I'm moving forward now, not looking back.

It's funny, because just a few days ago Patrick and I were out going for a walk in the park when he said, "It's amazing how things worked out."

"I know," I told him. "It is. Funny, too."

"What do you mean?"

"If I'd known all along . . ." I said, walking briskly, getting my heart rate up. "I spent all this time worrying about my high school reunion. When I should've been thinking and planning for my kindergarten reunion." I winked.

He burst out laughing.

Now he's standing here behind me, offering me a piece of cake. I usually avoid these kinds of things; I don't want to get off track, don't want to ruin my diet. But these days I'm not so worried about it; these days I'm easing up.

I take a bite.

Readers Guide

1. To steer her clients away from their poor self-images, Kylie tells them that they are exactly who they think they are. If you think you're a nerd, you're a nerd; if you think you're cool, you're cool. How do you think Kylie truly perceived herself at the beginning of the book? Did her self-perception change at the end?

2. Kylie can trace most of her insecurities back to a time in her life when she was overweight. Ruby is a plus-size model, yet her self-image is much more positive. Why do you feel that is? What made Ruby's persona so different from Kylie's at the end of the book?

3. Kylie speculates, "Coolness is a complicated issue. For starters, there are a million different kinds of cool: art house, trendy, retro, glamour, laid back, et cetera." Do you agree with her statement? Do you have your own definition of cool? Has it changed since reading the book?

4. When in your life have you felt cool, and why?

5. Discuss Kylie's complex relationship with her mother, the former model and Studio 54 groupie. Do you feel she was supportive of Kylie?

6. Do you think Kylie's personal makeover simplified or complicated her life?

7. When Dennis Moop wants to attend a *Star Wars* convention on a first date, Kylie discourages him. Does being cool sometimes mean temporarily denying your true nature, and if so, is it worth it? What do you think Kylie would say?

8. Were there any hints along the way that made you doubt Ty Benedict's motives? How does Kylie's history with men influence her treatment of Ty Benedict?

9. How do you feel Kylie's father informed her personality?

10. In the end, Patrick helps Kylie come to some conclusions about her career as a cool instructor. She decides that all she's been doing is "helping people fake it." Yet she saved Charity, the Paris Hilton wannabe, from making some big mistakes that would have ruined her dream of opening a boutique. Is Kylie being too hard on herself? Or is the cool instructor gig essentially just teaching people how to fake it?